ISLAND OF
THE INNOCENT

BOOKS BY GILBERT MORRIS

Through a Glass Darkly

THE HOUSE OF WINSLOW SERIES

1. *The Honorable Imposter*
2. *The Captive Bride*
3. *The Indentured Heart*
4. *The Gentle Rebel*
5. *The Saintly Buccaneer*
6. *The Holy Warrior*
7. *The Reluctant Bridegroom*
8. *The Last Confederate*
9. *The Dixie Widow*
10. *The Wounded Yankee*
11. *The Union Belle*
12. *The Final Adversary*
13. *The Crossed Sabres*
14. *The Valiant Gunman*
15. *The Gallant Outlaw*
16. *The Jeweled Spur*
17. *The Yukon Queen*
18. *The Rough Rider*
19. *The Iron Lady*
20. *The Silver Star*
21. *The Shadow Portrait*
22. *The White Hunter*
23. *The Flying Cavalier*
24. *The Glorious Prodigal*

THE LIBERTY BELL

1. *Sound the Trumpet*
2. *Song in a Strange Land*
3. *Tread Upon the Lion*
4. *Arrow of the Almighty*
5. *Wind From the Wilderness*
6. *The Right Hand of God*
7. *Command the Sun*

CHENEY DUVALL, M.D.
(with Lynn Morris)

1. *The Stars for a Light*
2. *Shadow of the Mountains*
3. *A City Not Forsaken*
4. *Toward the Sunrising*
5. *Secret Place of Thunder*
6. *In the Twilight, in the Evening*
7. *Island of the Innocent*
8. *Driven With the Wind*

THE SPIRIT OF APPALACHIA
(with Aaron McCarver)

1. *Over the Misty Mountains*
2. *Beyond the Quiet Hills*
3. *Among the King's Soldiers*
4. *Beneath the Mockingbird's Wings*

TIME NAVIGATORS
(for Young Teens)

1. *Dangerous Voyage*
2. *Vanishing Clues*

Lynn Morris & Gilbert Morris
Island Of The Innocent

BETHANY HOUSE PUBLISHERS
MINNEAPOLIS, MINNESOTA 55438

Published by Bethany House Publishers
A Ministry of Bethany Fellowship International
11400 Hampshire Avenue South
Minneapolis, Minnesota 55438
www.bethanyhouse.com

Printed in the United States of America by
Bethany Press International, Minneapolis, Minnesota 55438

ISBN 1–55661–698–8

I must thank:

My father, who fixes it;
My mother, who makes certain it gets fixed;
My daughter, who suffers through it with grace;
Lawana, who helped me with research,
but mostly with her loyal friendship and patient support;
And I'm especially grateful to Mrs. Marian Sparks,
who knew Shiloh better than I did.

GILBERT MORRIS & LYNN MORRIS are a father/daughter writing team who combine Gilbert's strength of great story plots and adventure with Lynn's research skills and character development. Together they form a powerful duo!

Lynn has also written a solo novel, *The Balcony*, in the PORTRAITS contemporary romance series with Bethany House. She and her daughter live near her parents in Alabama.

When men are cast down,
Then thou shalt say,
There is lifting up;
and he shall save the humble person.
He shall deliver the island of the innocent:
And it is delivered by the
pureness of thine hands.
JOB 22:29–30

CONTENTS

———◆◆◆———

NEAR TOGETHER

❋ P A R T O N E ❋

TO JUDGMENT

Keep silence before me, O islands;
And let the people
renew their strength;
Let them come near;
Then let them speak;
Let us come near
together to judgment.

Isaiah 41:1

1

THE HOUSE OF THE SUN

The House of the Sun loomed up, gigantic in the night, swallowing stars and sky and a timid last-quarter moon. At the blunt prow of the *Petrel*, Cheney Duvall considered the monolith, the dormant volcano Haleakala, the ruler of the east on the island of Maui.

It was midnight at the House of the Sun. At dawn, the sun would slowly rise from its house, floating over the craggy peaks of the three-mile-wide crater, flashing its young brilliance over dashing streams, thick jungle, crashing waterfalls, and long-dead lava that bejeweled the sides of the great mountain. But now, in the hours of darkness, the sun slept in its Hawaiian mansion.

As Cheney watched, considering the frailty and transience of man, thin streams of flame began shooting out from the sides of the sleeping volcano.

"What . . . what is that?" she whispered to herself.

But no, she spoke not only to herself, but also to the young man who hovered behind her, respecting her silence and her reverie. He answered her question. "Papala spears."

Cheney started, turned, then smiled and extended her hand, an invitation for him to step closer and join her at the knighthead, peering over it like two children peeking at a sleeping giant. "Walker, why didn't you let me know you were there? Isn't it breathtaking, even in the night?"

The young doctor's eyes slid up, up, to the unknowable height and nodded. "That's why I didn't speak to you. . . . I was watching it. It's difficult to look away." Dr. Walker Baird was a young man, younger than Cheney, and he was shorter than Cheney. But his frame was trim, athletic, and he exuded boyish energy. His thick ash-blond hair had golden lights and a tendency to curl. With his open, friendly face, ready smile, and dark royal blue eyes, he was a most attractive man.

13

"But look! Those shafts of light, of flame—what did you say they were?" Cheney asked.

"Papala spears," he answered. "From the papala tree. The wood is light and very flammable. The ancient Hawaiians made fire-spears, both to honor the goddess Pele and to frighten their enemies. Now they use them sort of as fireworks. A greeting."

"To us? This humble little bark? I would hardly think the *Petrel* would rate such a welcome."

Baird smiled down at her. She was so vibrant, her features so animated, her eyes bright, always sparkling. No wonder men were attracted to her. Rousing himself as she watched him quizzically, he replied, "Captain Bell told me about the papala spears. They're for the *Petrel*, all right. Because it's a Winslow ship, and you're going into Winslow country, Dr. Duvall. Only the Winslow ships land at Hana, and because almost everyone at Hana works for the Winslows, they are generally careful to give their ships a royal greeting." He shrugged, then turned to lean against the knighthead and watch the showers of flaming spears plunge from high up on the slopes of the mountain, arching gracefully on the trade winds, lightly falling into the sea hundreds of feet below. "It's also a signal, you see. Helps the captain make certain of his course. Although the roadstead at Hana is very deep, there are some tricky reefs and atolls in the channel."

Cheney brooded on this but felt no sense of peril. The *Petrel* was a sturdy, businesslike barkentine. From her three masts virgin-white sails flew joyously, the decks gleamed, the brass fittings shone, the crew was seasoned and dignified. Behind Cheney and Walker, amidships, six men of the watch attended to the task of negotiating an anchorage with quiet words and occasional laughter. Captain Bell stood by the wheel, giving commands to the steersman in a relaxed monotone.

The great Pacific Ocean, tonight as well as during the entire two-week voyage, rocked the ship in a sleepy rhythm, unafflicted with the fits and tempers that seemingly ruled her smaller, fiercer brother, the Atlantic. The breeze seemed to be from a scented fan, gliding lightly over the skin, forming languorous waves in the sails that matched the lazy swells of the water. Cheney inhaled deeply. "That scent . . ."

"Mmm," Walker agreeably hummed.

Her eyes on the signal fires and the slim darts of flame that still rained into the sea, she said softly, "Shiloh told me once that it's not the smell of the sea that people are always talking about . . . it's the

14

smell of the beach, actually. I noticed that when you're at sea, an empty sea, an eternity away from land, the only smell is the dull alkali smell of salt. It's the smell of the land, you see, that sailors actually love. . . ."

"Yes?" he said alertly. "That's very interesting. Of course, it makes sense. That wet loamy smell is of earth, not the sea, of earth soaked with aeons of the fish catch and the brine and the salt rain. . . ."

They fell silent in harmony and a restful compatibility. Cheney was thinking what a fine man Walker Baird was and how agreeable it was to have a friend—and now a self-appointed escort and protector—who had such a curious and active mind, who was interested in anything and everything. She recalled once, at St. Francis de Yerba Buena Hospital where they both worked, seeing Walker sitting by a patient's bedside at two o'clock in the morning. Walker was in full evening dress, having come from the theater, and the patient was elderly Mr. Dibley, the butler, who was recovering from pneumonia. The two were deeply engrossed in a conversation about the particulars of polishing silver, and Walker had been so interested in Mr. Dibley's secrets that he hadn't even looked up when Cheney passed. She smiled a little at the memory.

Walker Baird saw the smile and thought what a fascinating woman Dr. Cheney Duvall was. She was different from any woman he'd ever met—any person he'd ever met. Her persona was as unique and engrossing as her looks. She was, he supposed, what was called a "handsome" woman, since she was not classically beautiful. Her face was square, with a strong jaw and full, firm lips, a small nose that would have been pert on a more frivolous woman, heavy and glossy auburn hair, and great sparkling green eyes. The beauty mark beneath her left eye seemed to be imprinted there for the sole purpose of stressing her unusual looks. He had once thought he was falling in love with her. But though Walker Baird was young, he was not a complete fool, and after he'd known her for a while, he'd realized the difference between deep romantic love for someone and loving to be with someone. He loved to be with Cheney. He didn't want to be in love with her.

"I'm glad you came, Walker," Cheney said lightly, jarring him out of his very private thoughts. He blushed a bit and was glad she couldn't see in the purple-black tropical night. Turning back to watch the island spectacle of looming volcano and fire-spears, she said in a carefully neutral tone, "I wish we could just meet Shiloh, tell him to get on this ship, and sail on back to San Francisco. I wish it would be that easy. I

15

wish . . ." She sighed deeply, and Walker waited. Finally she finished, "I wish things were as they used to be."

He made no comment, for there was nothing to say.

In silence they sailed into the shadow of the House of the Sun.

2

A Matter of Honor

"It's certainly not difficult to see Shiloh," Cheney observed. Even at half past midnight, a crowd of people were at dockside to greet the *Petrel*. From the roadstead one hundred yards out, Cheney could make out individual outlines; most of the people—all men, she thought—were short, with dark hair. Two men were quite tall. One was an enormous man, dark-skinned and massively built, as solid as a column. Standing by him was Shiloh: blond hair shining like a beacon, taller than them all, wide shoulders tapering to a flat stomach and slim hips. He was holding a torch, and he waved it over his head in an enthusiastic greeting.

Six canoes were lined up at the small jetty. As soon as the *Petrel* came to a rolling rest, Shiloh jumped into one of them and paddled out to the ship. Behind him came two more canoes, each rowed by another of the men standing dockside. As they neared, Cheney could see that they were Chinamen.

A wooden ladder with a curved top was hooked onto the starboard side for the passengers to descend to the canoes. Searching around, she saw that Walker was giving instructions to one of the sailors about their luggage, and Nia was already at the ladder waiting for her.

"Miss Cheney, you go first . . . no, what are you thinking? Hand me your reticule and fan . . . you can't scamper down that thing with two hands full and another armload." Cheney's maid's bossiness was jarring when one considered her. Nia Clarkson was tiny, delicate, with great dark liquid eyes and a little girl's hands and voice. Though eighteen, she looked about five years younger. She was, however, fully capable of ruling Miss Cheney Duvall within the confines of her responsibilities. Meekly Cheney handed her things to Nia.

Darkly the maid went on, "Now just a minute, Miss Ma'am. What you think you're going to do with them flapping skirts and . . . and . . ."

Nia looked around suspiciously at the men surrounding them and then whispered, "Your other skirts." Nia would never have uttered the word "petticoats" in public. With barely concealed triumph she knelt at Cheney's side and fiddled with her hem. "I just sewed these loops on here, so you can loop them around your thumb and hold them up. But you mind, Miss Cheney. Ain't no need in ever' man in Haw-aye seein' your . . . your . . ."

"Shoes?" Cheney suggested, stifling a giggle. "Never mind, Nia. I'll be circumspect." With very little trouble Cheney gathered up her skirts enough to free her ankles and nimbly descended the ladder.

"Hey, Doc," Shiloh said. He was holding the canoe steady against the ladder.

"Hello." Cheney studied him.

He looked back up and made a slight adjustment to the boat as it rocked slightly. Walker was descending the ladder. "I'm glad to see you, Doc. Are you glad to see me?"

"Well . . . well . . . of course," she stammered. "I . . . you're . . . I . . ." She was trying to say: *You're the reason I'm here. I had to come, to tell you in person about the Winslows. Then you should come back to San Francisco immediately with me and Walker.*

But the sight of Shiloh Irons had wrecked both her composure and her determination.

He looked wonderful. Cheney had fully been expecting to see a melancholy, thin, hungry ghost of the man who had left San Francisco two months ago. Instead, he looked so vital, so healthy, so strong that he could have been a model for a statue of a Greek athlete. His thick straw-colored hair was sun bleached lighter than gold. His skin was darkened to a glowing bronze, which made his strong teeth seem to glow and his light blue eyes startling. Untanned, the V scar beneath his left eye was a defiant white slash. Through the thin white shirt he wore, his hardened muscles were clearly delineated from the light of the lantern behind him. Cheney stared at him in uncomfortable confusion that was quickly turning into embarrassment. Shiloh Irons radiated strength and vigor.

Cheney told herself with raking sarcasm, *And here I am on a noble quest—to rescue you!*

He looked at her, saw her flustered stare, and grinned. "If you fall in the drink," he said, "I'll have to rescue you."

★　★　★　★

Hana Guest House offered the only accommodations in the small port. A plain frame house with a miniature parlor, a generous dining room, and four spare bedrooms, it offered amenities without luxury, cleanliness without sterility, and careful service from the proprietor, a Chinese woman named Tang Lu.

She stood in the parlor, head bowed subserviently, her hands tucked into the sleeves of her plain gray tunic. Loose pantaloons, white stockings, and soft black slippers completed her humble costume. Perhaps thirty years old, Tang Lu had a work-weathered face and guarded dark eyes.

"I should like for my maid, Nia, to have a room next to mine, if possible, Tang Lu," Cheney said decisively. "Please have all of the luggage put into Nia's room. We'll sort it out later. And I should like something to drink—tea, perhaps? Nothing to eat, though. And take some tea up to Nia too."

Without a word, Tang Lu bowed and left the parlor, taking small hurried steps as Chinese women seemed wont to do.

"I wonder if she understood a word I said," Cheney murmured.

"Sure, Doc," Shiloh told her. "She speaks good English."

"I'm glad. I wasn't even certain she could speak, period." Tang Lu had not spoken to Cheney. The Chinese woman had merely acknowledged Shiloh's introduction with a bow.

"White ladies make them nervous. In fact, white people make them nervous. After all, the Winslows are the only ones here, except for Konrad Zeiss, their overseer."

Cheney looked around the room. It was a typical Victorian parlor, with heavy red draperies and an uncomfortable-looking dark velvet couch, two horsehair armchairs, a heavy round tea table with ball-and-claw feet, too many knickknacks on the sideboard, and two lamps burning some kind of oil that smoked and stank. A small but hot fire burned in the grate.

"It's crowded and stifling in here," she complained. "Could we open the windows?"

Walker hurried to the side window, which had drapes from ceiling to floor, and pulled them aside to reveal a ludicrously small window without glass or shutters. Mosquito netting was hung to one side, he saw gratefully, and he arranged it to cover the opening. The two windows that faced the front of the house, however, were a little larger, and as soon as Shiloh pulled aside the heavy draperies, a nice cross-breeze filled the room and made it seem much less oppressive. A gentle hint of spice floated in the thick breeze, and Cheney inhaled gratefully. Hawaiian ginger was planted in flower beds on the front and sides of the house. Seating herself in one of the armchairs, she fanned herself languidly. "That's much better, thank you."

Walker settled on the couch, while Shiloh crossed to the fire and threw in some chips he took from a small ivory box on the wooden mantel. A sultry incense smoke wafted through the room. Cheney sniffed appreciatively. "Mmm, sandalwood, my favorite scent."

"Keeps the bugs away too," Shiloh commented, settling into the armchair closest to the fire, next to Cheney. "How ya doin', Doc? Make the trip okay?"

Cheney replied, "Oh yes, it was a pleasant trip." But she saw that Shiloh was very intent, which meant that the question was serious, even though the words sounded merely polite. "Oh, I see what you mean. Was I seasick? Of course. But only for three days."

"Really?" His ice-blue eyes brightened.

Though Cheney couldn't understand the import of this conversation, she indulged him. Besides, it gave her a little more time to plan her speech. "Yes, and it didn't seem to be as severe as when I've traveled by ship before. Surprising, isn't it? I would have thought that sailing would be much more taxing on the system than traveling by steamer."

"I don't think so," Shiloh said with animation. "I think sailing is great. Somehow it seems like more of a natural rhythm than steaming, at least when the seas and wind are fine. Steaming, to me, was sorta like chopping wood. It was a rhythm, all right. *Chukka—chukka—chukka—*"

"Don't remind me!" Cheney interrupted with a grimace. "Just the very sound . . . perhaps you're right, Shiloh. It did seem that the noise of the paddles invaded your brain until you were struggling to breathe with it, move with it, talk with it . . . wishing your heartbeat matched it, and the blood rushing in your ears would keep up with it. Maybe that's what actually made me so ill. Being out of time with the paddles."

"But you liked sailing?" he persisted, his sharply sculptured features oddly boyish.

"Why, yes, I enjoyed it once I felt myself again. Of course, we had a very uneventful voyage. I suspect that if we'd been in a storm or something I might not be so courageous."

"Yes, you would," Shiloh said, then turned to Walker Baird. "I was kinda surprised to hear you'd be coming, Walker. But I'm glad you did. I think you'll like it here—or in Hawaii, at least. Are you going on to Honolulu or Lahaina for a vacation?"

"No," he replied, gazing steadily at Shiloh. "I am here for the same reason as Dr. Duvall. I wanted to see you and talk to you."

Shiloh was amused. "That's a good enough excuse for an island holiday, I guess." He saw Walker, who was regarding him gravely, and Cheney, who was looking flustered and severe at the same time. "Wait a minute," Shiloh went on, the light dawning on his face. "You mean that's the truth? The only reason you came to Hawaii was to see me—to talk to me?"

Cheney cried, "No, I want to talk to you, and then I want you to come back to San Francisco."

"Huh?"

"Now. On the *Petrel*. She's going on to Lahaina to drop the other passengers, and then she's coming back here in the morning to see if I'm ready to return. And I will . . . if . . . if . . . you will."

Shiloh looked bewildered and glanced at Walker Baird. He was still somber. Taking a deep breath, Shiloh turned back to Cheney and spoke with slow patience. "Doc, would you mind starting at the beginning instead of somewhere in the middle? Kinda makes it hard to follow your reasoning, if you get me."

"It's simple," Cheney said stubbornly. "You don't need these Winslow people. You aren't a part of their family anyway. You can't be—it's just not possible. So you need to just come back to work, back to San Francisco tomorrow. With . . . with . . . I mean, tomorrow. On the *Petrel*."

Shiloh settled back in his chair, crossed one booted ankle over his knee, and stared at Cheney as if she had suddenly begun speaking in Urdu. Then his face changed and he chuckled. Walker stifled a grin.

Cheney sat even more stiffly in the horrible chair, her cheeks flaming. "I can't imagine what's so amusing," she said acidly. "Men do have such a crude sense of humor."

Neither Shiloh nor Walker could stifle their laughter. Then Shiloh repentantly said, "Sorry, Doc. It's just that women have such strange ways of reasoning things out. Are you saying that you took a two-week sea voyage, across half the Pacific, to come to this little dot of an island,

21

just to say that? 'Come back to San Francisco with me now.' It wouldn't have—"

"I didn't say 'with me,'" Cheney blurted.

"So even if I go back, you're staying?"

"No! Of course not!"

"You staying if I don't go back?"

"Yes! I mean no!"

Shiloh grinned. Cheney's green eyes glinted dangerously, and she pronounced carefully, "If I can persuade you to return to San Francisco tomorrow, then I shall return too. If I cannot persuade you to return tomorrow, then I shall stay for two weeks, until the *Mongoose* comes here on its way to San Francisco, and then go back. But that is all the time I intend to take to try to convince you."

Shiloh's left eyebrow rose sardonically during this speech, but he grew very still. When Cheney finished, he cocked his head slightly to study her. Her lips were pressed tightly together and her hands were unrestful.

As the silence swelled, Cheney grew more uncomfortable, and the hectic color in her cheeks heightened even more in the warm red light.

Finally Shiloh calmly asked, "Doc, what's wrong?"

Dropping her eyes, she picked at the coarse horsehair upholstery. Shiloh waited, watching Walker Baird for some sign, but the doctor merely shrugged.

Tang Lu silently entered, holding a tray with a plain earthenware teapot and three exquisite porcelain cups. Setting the tray down without a single clink, she asked in a musical voice, "Doctah Duvall, you wish me to pour?"

"No thank you, Tang Lu, I'll pour," Cheney replied with relief. She was glad for the interruption and, with economical grace, made three cups of tea. It was China tea, she saw with some disappointment, for she preferred India. And there was no honey or lemon, only sugar and cream. Cheney put so much sugar in hers that she knew it would almost negate the delicate taste of the tea, but she didn't care. It was, at least, hot, and she felt less ragged after a few sips.

Walker Baird, noting Cheney's continued struggle to broach the subject of why she had come to Hawaii, politely commented, "By the way, Shiloh, I'm a little confused about your connection here with the Winslows. All I know is that you thought Bain Winslow might know something about your parents, and he asked you to come to Hawaii

22

with him to see his mother. Would you mind if I asked the particulars?"

"Sure, Walker," Shiloh said easily, with a knowing glance at Cheney. "You remember, I told you I was an orphan? A foundling. Left on the steps of the Behring Orphanage at Charleston, South Carolina."

"Right," Walker murmured. "You found out you'd been left on the beach after a shipwreck. You found out that you'd been on a clipper, called the *Day Dream*, that sank in the storm. And with you, in the box you were found in, was an Oriental tapestry and a compass in the form of a metal fish."

"We—me and the Doc, here, who helped me find all of this stuff out—didn't understand the significance of either," Shiloh continued, "until Reverend Merced looked at them. He told me that the fish was a compass. And he said the tapestry told a story about a white couple who got a young Chinese girl for a servant, and then the couple had a baby."

"You."

"We think so," Shiloh said, nodding. "The tapestry told us about the Chinese girl—I call her Pearl—and the man and woman that she worked for. They sailed in a great ship with sails reaching up to the sky," he said, his voice growing soft, "all over the world. They lived in a place, an island, with tall black mountains that sometimes were capped with red."

"Volcanoes," Walker murmured.

"Yes." Shiloh made a careless gesture. "Which could have been lots of places in the world. But Hawaii seemed logical, since it's in the shipping lane between China and San Francisco. Anyway, then at Mrs. de Lancie's and the Doc's party, I overheard this man talking about a ship he owned that he had almost bet in a poker game. The name of it was *Locke's Day Dream*. He also said something about betting one of his Sandwich Islands."

"Hawaii."

"Right. The man's name was Bain Winslow, and his family owns the clipper *Locke's Day Dream*, and they've lived here for almost thirty years. Bain had an uncle, he said, who died at sea when Bain was just a child. He said that I probably wasn't connected with his family, but if I wanted I could come here with him—he was returning anyway—and talk to his mother."

Shiloh fell silent, and neither Cheney nor Walker spoke. The quiet was heavy, brooding. Shiloh turned to stare neutrally into the fire. The blood-red glow of the lantern on the tea table flickered high, then faded out, thickening the shadows in the room.

Walker cleared his throat uncomfortably. "Well, Shiloh, Dr. Duvall mentioned a couple of things to me from your letters. I don't wish to pry into a man's private affairs, of course, but would you mind telling us what's happened since you left San Francisco?"

Shiloh shrugged, then gave Walker a mischievous glance. "Guess not. Guess you did come all this way to hear it, didn't you?"

Walker's midnight-blue eyes sparkled. "Did, didn't I? On second thought, I do wish to pry into your private affairs. What's going on, Shiloh?"

"I dunno," he answered wryly. "But I'm going to find out." He noticed Cheney was looking peculiar at this exchange, but he went on, "Well, I guess the first thing that happened was that as soon as I got on board *Locke's Day Dream*, all of Bain Winslow's goodwill went south real quick. When we were pulling away from the dock, he introduced me to Captain Manning and told him that I was going to work my way to Hana. Then he disappeared into his cabin, and I didn't see him again until we got to Honolulu."

The inconstant light made Shiloh's light blue eyes glitter. "Captain Manning looked real, real happy that he had a raw landlubber to work on a clipper. But I can scrub decks and polish brass as good as anyone, I guess. And I did get to learn a lot about sailing. Even started learning about navigation. Didn't turn out to be half bad, you know."

His voice had a tinge of longing, and Cheney said irritably, "Do you mean to tell me that Bain Winslow practically shanghaied you— and you enjoyed it?"

"Well, Doc, that was the best revenge I could think of," Shiloh rasped. "I'm a better sailor than Bain Winslow, and that seemed to kinda bother him."

"I'll bet," Walker said gleefully.

Cheney looked disgusted, so they both sobered, and Shiloh obediently went on. "So we go first to Honolulu, on Oahu, because that's where the Winslows bank. Bain had a chest he personally lugged off the ship, and Perkins, the bosun's mate, told me that the Winslows always get paid for their cargo in gold in San Francisco, because they buy their shipments from China in gold. Currency of the world, you know. Anybody takes gold for anything. . . . What's the matter, Doc?"

Cheney had jerked and made a peculiar sound in her throat. "N-nothing. Please go on."

Shiloh's eyes narrowed shrewdly, but he continued. "So the crew—including Mr. Irons, the best deck swabber in the Winslow fleet—went ashore that night to . . . uh . . . sight-see."

"I'll bet you saw some sights," Cheney muttered.

Shiloh went on innocently. "Oh yes, I did see some sights. Lots of 'em. Took all night, as a matter of fact."

"All night," Cheney repeated darkly.

Shiloh nodded, his expression pious, but then his clean features drew into harsh lines. "Anyway, when I got back to the ship, my stuff was gone. My compass and the tapestry. Funny thing too. They were in my seabag, you know. Seems like it would've been easier just to steal the bag. But no, the thief rifled through it and picked out those two things, then stuffed everything back in the bag and put it back under my bunk."

"I never saw them," Walker remarked. "Were they valuable?"

Shiloh, bemused, looked at Cheney.

She answered quietly, "The compass probably isn't, but the tapestry may be. It's very expensive satin and exquisite work. The intrinsic value, however, is the greatest loss."

"What's that mean?" Shiloh asked bluntly.

"It means," Cheney answered sadly, "that they were worth much more than a price in gold to you."

"They *are* worth that much more," he said harshly. "And I'll get them back."

"All right, you left Honolulu," Walker said with precision, "so what happened next?"

"We came to Hana," Shiloh answered, "and Winslow got off the ship and disappeared. I stayed here that first night. Next morning he came and got me and said he'd take me to see his mother. So we went to Winslow Villa, and I met Mrs. Denise Winslow."

He hesitated, and Cheney prompted him, "And what did she say?"

Grimly he answered, "Not much. She let me know in about four seconds that it wasn't possible for me to be connected to their family. I was mistaken. That was all. I was dismissed."

"But did you tell her about everything?" Cheney demanded.

Shiloh's well-shaped mouth twisted. "What's the point? To win the argument?"

This, of course, was the crux of the matter. Cheney's mind began first to grope, then to whirl. *All this time I've been thinking—or hoping?—that Shiloh's not actually connected with Bain Winslow! But Shiloh obviously thinks, or knows, that he is.... And it does seem that it must be true! Why have I been dancing around it? Why don't I want it to be?*

Cheney dropped her head as she frowned fiercely and pleated her skirt between her long, slender fingers. *It's simple—isn't it? I don't want Shiloh to be a part of this family, to be connected by blood to that terrible man. Face it, girl! It's not quite that easy, is it? Just as you told Walker, you want things to be as they were ... you and Shiloh, close, so close, in fact, because you were his best friend. He depended on you, needed you ... and now that's threatened, and you don't like it one little bit, do you!*

Cheney sighed deeply. It was true. But it was also true that she felt a great pity and sorrow for Shiloh. First he'd had nothing and no one. Now he had a family, and they had cruelly rejected him.

But why? Why have they gone to such great lengths to deny him?

"They think I'm just trying to con them out of some money, I guess," Shiloh murmured, breaking the long silence. "It looks like they have money. I do know they have property. They own this town; this house, in fact, belongs to the Winslows. It was their first home. Now, of course, they have Winslow Villa and a town house in Lahaina. They have a fleet of five ships: two fine clippers and three merchant sailers. This plantation is about eighty thousand acres. They grow sugarcane for export, and they're also experimenting with growing pineapples and sandalwood. And Winslow Brothers ships all kinds of goods back and forth between the Orient and here and San Francisco."

This time Cheney almost choked. Her color furiously high, she dropped her eyes and began to fan herself with jerky movements.

Shiloh watched her discomfiture with a knowing half-smile. Turning to Walker, he said, "Look, Walker, you and the Doc didn't come two thousand miles just to listen to me talk. I think you've got somethin' to say, too, right? Like, 'I came here because of so-and-so'?"

Now it was Walker Baird's turn to look uncomfortable. He shifted on the sofa, and the effect, with his boyish looks, was that of a guilty schoolboy squirming in the headmaster's office. "Actually, Dr. Duvall didn't tell me—exactly—why it was so urgent she see you, only that it was important that she speak to you in person. I ... um ... I ... that is, after I heard, Shiloh, that you wrote Dr. Duvall about this fight, you know—"

Cheney, who was much distracted by her own thoughts, still keyed in on this. Sitting bolt upright, she stopped her furious fanning. "Dr. Walker Baird. Do you mean that the only reason you came was because you wanted to see a *fight*?"

"Well, it will probably be the last time The Iron Man fights," Walker defensively answered. "Right, Shiloh?"

Shiloh, who was grinning, nodded. "Yup. In fact, it will probably be the last time The Iron Man walks, or talks, or breathes."

"I don't believe it!" Walker said sturdily. "You're just being modest. You can beat anyone, Shiloh, and you look as if you're in terrific shape."

"Yeah, well, you oughta see the other guy," Shiloh said dryly, stretching out his long legs and lacing his fingers across his flat stomach. "Meholo. Pure Hawaiian. Weighs about four hundred pounds, I guess. 'Bout six five, six six. Looks like a baobab tree."

"Doesn't matter," Walker said spiritedly. "In fact, it's probably to your advantage. You'll dance around him like he's a pretty little Maypole, Shiloh, and you can run in those sneaky snake jabs to the jaw all day and night."

"Huh," Shiloh grunted. "If we were boxing, maybe. But what Winslow's got in mind is *lua*. The ancient Hawaiian art of hand-to-hand combat." At Walker's bewildered look Shiloh went on, "Wrestling, Walker. Grappling. To put it simply, the man walks up to me and wrings my neck." He made a twisting motion and a crackle-gurgle sound in his throat.

"Oh," Walker gulped. "How unpleasant."

"Yeah," Shiloh agreed.

"No!" Cheney rasped. "Of all the stupid—" Jumping out of her chair, she stamped her foot. "Why don't you just go jump off one of these cliffs, Shiloh? Or . . . or . . . hang yourself from one of the . . . the . . . crosspiece things on Winslow's ship! Make him really happy!"

"Yardarm," Shiloh gravely corrected her.

"It's not funny!" Cheney fumed.

"I'm not laughin'," Shiloh replied. "But I'm not cryin' either."

"I'm not either!" Cheney cried. Whirling, she swept to the window and turned her back on the two men.

Shiloh watched her, then sat up alertly. "She's cryin'. Aw, man," he muttered in a low voice.

Walker looked uncomfortable. "Hate it when they cry. Makes you feel like a great big stupid bumpkin."

Shiloh got up and crossed to the window. Placing his hands on Cheney's shoulders, he turned her around to face him. Her head drooped, and he put one gentle finger underneath her chin.

She looked up at him, defiant and tearful and sad. "Shiloh, you just don't understand. . . ."

"So tell me, Cheney," he said calmly. "I can help you. I'll do anything for you."

Unnoticed, Walker Baird slipped out of the room.

Cheney, now breathless, stared up into Shiloh Iron's clear and honest gaze. "No, no. It's I who wants to help you, Shiloh. I thought—I convinced myself that you couldn't possibly be a part of this Winslow family, and so it seemed so simple. I just wanted to come . . . come get you, bring you back to San Francisco, show you that . . . that . . . there are so many people who care about you. . . ."

"Do you?" he whispered. "Do you, Cheney?" He bent closer to her.

Cheney, almost against her will, felt her eyes flutter and close. His firm, warm lips brushed hers, very lightly, and then he put his hands on her cheeks. She looked back up at him.

But she couldn't answer him. It was better, so much better, to leave it unsaid. She must be silent and not even look too deeply into her heart for the answer to Shiloh's question. She could not—must not—speak the truth. Not now. Maybe not ever.

Taking a deep uneven breath, she turned around, grateful for the cool, wet wind on her face. Shiloh easily let her turn away from him and without pressure rested one hand on her waist.

"Shiloh, you must still leave here," she said, her voice low and throaty. "You're in danger. These people—Bain Winslow—they're much worse than you think."

She felt him shift impatiently. "Well, I'm pretty sure that he's a thief and a liar. That's enough to make any man cautious."

Tears flowed down her face now. Cheney realized that what she told Shiloh was going to have exactly the opposite effect of what she had intended—and what she wanted with her whole heart and mind. But she had no choice. After all, it was Shiloh's family.

"He's also a . . . a . . . how absurd. I've been so carefully brought up that I don't know the word for it." Cheney half sobbed, half laughed. "Shiloh, you remember Zhu Xinlan? The fourteen-year-old who died in the fire in August? Well, she was . . . worked . . . in . . . Lillian Fontaine's. That was the . . . brothel that burned that night."

She took another ragged breath. Shiloh's hand had tightened on her waist until it actually was hurting her. Lightly she laid her fingers, cool and calming, across his hand and continued in a flat voice, staring vacantly out the window. "She'd worked in that brothel for two years. Bain Winslow had bought her, Shiloh, when she was twelve years old. And he brought her to San Francisco to work in his brothel."

A sound, a terrible combination of growl and sick choking, seemed forced from Shiloh's throat. His hand jerked away from Cheney's side, and she tried to pull it back, but he was gone, his boot steps hard and harsh as he stalked out of the room.

Her shoulders bent, her head down, Cheney wept.

I'm such a fool! I should have known . . . this, this terrible thing is the one thing that is guaranteed to keep Shiloh here! He's not only got a family that rejects him, but they're despicable, and hateful, and shameful. Now Shiloh, of course, will be obliged to put a stop to it, and to clear his name! His family name! Oh, that's rich! All his life he's been an honorable, honest man, and he's made the name of Irons something to be proud of. And now he's found out he's a Winslow—and that name is contemptible!

Cheney meandered on in this way for a while. But after a few minutes she could hear through the open window the low murmurs of Walker and Shiloh talking on the front verandah. Walker, in spite of his boyishness, was actually a calm and reasonable man. At least he would keep Shiloh from shooting Bain Winslow down, or beating him to death, or challenging him to a duel, or something.

Drying her tears, Cheney almost smiled. *No, that's not quite true. I wouldn't be a bit surprised if Shiloh did try to challenge Bain Winslow to a duel. That would be his chosen way to settle a matter of personal honor . . . as if Winslow, that cad, would fight Shiloh!*

Suddenly Cheney's eyes narrowed. *Of course Winslow wouldn't fight Shiloh. He would get someone else to do it. Someone like that brute of a Hawaiian, who could . . . could . . . kill him? Would that be legal here, in that kind of fighting—what is it? Lua? Or perhaps it would just be a terrible accident . . . an inexperienced fighter, unable to defend himself. . . . Is that possible? Would Winslow really go that far?*

"It doesn't matter," Cheney said, resolutely straightening her shoulders and strengthening her mind. "I'll pray. I'll pray for him, without ceasing, until this is over." Feeling a sudden peace wash over her, she closed her eyes and took long, deep breaths. The scent of ginger, sweet yet tangy, refreshed her, the smell of the ocean, the salty wind, the briny undertaste, the sleepy susurration of gentle waves on still sand lulled her.

But what's that . . . faint smell . . . just a whiff—

Cheney sniffed, her eyes pressed tightly closed.

Just a breath of something . . . gunpowder? No. Shiloh hasn't shot anyone or anything—yet—what—lucifer match? Yes, Shiloh lit the—but no, he didn't. It's coming from outside. . . . What is that smell? I know it!

Yes, Cheney did know that smell. It was carried on the constant trade winds, sweeping down from the ancient craters of the House of the Sun. It was a gas, released under great pressure and tremendous heat, from a mineral that was used in some prescriptives. It was sulphur.

3

WALKER'S PLAN

"Miss Cheney, it's almost eleven o'clock."

Cheney opened her eyes wide and stared up at Nia. "Is this the train?"

With amusement Nia replied, "You're still asleep. Wake up, Miss Cheney." She opened the curtains at the single window, though it was hardly necessary to let in the sunlight. The curtains in the small, spare bedroom were of the thinnest white linen.

Sitting up, Cheney stretched and yawned achingly, her eyes still dull with sleep stupor. "What time is it?"

"Almost eleven."

Cheney blinked.

"Are you awake now?"

"I think so. I thought I was on a train."

"Well, you're not. You're still in bed, and you're wanting to get up and get dressed."

"I am?"

"Yes, ma'am. And you're wanting to wear this yellow muslin. Mr. Shiloh and Mr. Walker are waiting on a late breakfast for you."

"Oh." Cheney got out of bed and looked around helplessly. "What shall I wear?"

Nia rolled her eyes in a great show of patience. "Y'know, Miss Cheney, I b'lieve you just might still be on a train goin' someplace else that's not here. Now, you are in Haw-aye. It's eleven o'clock. Of the morning. Mr. Shiloh and Mr. Walker are waiting on a late breakfast for you. You're wearing this yellow muslin—see? This one I'm standing here holding?"

"Did you say it's eleven, and Shiloh and Walker are waiting breakfast for me? Well, good heavens, I'm sure they're starving! I'll wear that yellow muslin."

"Yes, ma'am."

"And do hurry, Nia. You're dawdling this morning."

Nia sighed. "Yes, ma'am."

In spite of Nia's dawdling, it only took half an hour for Cheney's *toilette*, but this was mainly because Cheney flatly refused to let Nia comb out her hair, which normally took close to an hour itself. Instead she made Nia pull it back and secure it with combs, so that the heavy auburn curls fell in an undisciplined tangle down her back. As Cheney left the bedroom, Nia was heard to say something to the effect that Cheney's hair wasn't done properly; that she did, in fact, look like some Haw-ayean native woman who used a fish skeleton to comb her hair. Cheney chose to ignore this ungracious observation and hurried downstairs to the dining room.

In contrast to the rococo parlor, the dining room was cool and inviting, spartan in its simplicity. The oak flooring was whitewashed, and white shutters framed two immense windows facing out into a tiny garden on the side of the house. The dining table was covered with a worn but clean muslin cloth. At the back of the room by the kitchen door was a modest sideboard, simply made but polished to a high sheen. Plates and platters of jewel-bright fruits were arranged temptingly upon it, with a plain white ceramic coffee service.

As Cheney entered the room, Walker and Shiloh hurried to their feet to greet her. "Mornin', Doc. You sure look pretty," Shiloh said, the appreciation evident in his eyes.

"Thank you, and good morning, gentlemen. How kind of you to wait breakfast for me." Cheney hurried to the sideboard, her mouth already watering at the hot smell of the coffee. "Mmm, thank goodness! Coffee! I do so love coffee in the mornings rather than tea . . . shall we go ahead? Are we waiting for Tang Lu to serve?"

"She's in the back. I'll go get her." Shiloh hurried through the door to the kitchen.

Cheney shook her head, smiling.

Walker said, "He's already told me all about Tang Lu, her children, her husband, her parents, her husband's parents, her grandparents, her aches, her—"

"I know, I know," Cheney interrupted. "He's not just 'between stairs.' He *is* the stairs."

Walker was laughing when Shiloh came back in, followed by Tang Lu. "I'll serve, Dr. Duvall," she said quickly. "Be seated, please."

Shiloh took the head of the table, with Walker and Cheney on either side of him. The rectangular table seated twelve, but Cheney's family had never held with the formality of seating people with ludicrously long expanses between them. Her father, Richard, had always said that if you were breaking bread with someone, you could certainly sit close to them. Cheney and Shiloh, in their years and trials together, had grown into the habit of sitting close even at the most formal settings.

"May I bless?" Walker asked, then bowed his head. "Thank You, Lord, for our safe journey. Thank You for this food and for the hands that prepared it. Let us walk in Your steps today, and always. Amen."

Shiloh rubbed his hands together briskly. "Now, that's what I call a good prayer. Like your father's, Doc. Short and to the point."

"You're terrible."

"I know. But you like me. You always have."

"Not always."

Shiloh looked naïvely surprised, for to him, this banter was fun, but it was always genuine and truthful, no matter how lightly said. "You didn't? But I thought you did. When didn't you like me?"

Cheney mockingly replied, "When I first met you and found out you were to be my nurse, I thought that it was about the worst idea I'd ever heard of. I was horrified. I almost had the vapors."

"No, you didn't. You had plenty of breath, 'cause you talked a lot. Kinda loud too. Besides," he added smugly, "you still liked me."

"Yes," she said placidly, "I did. I still do."

"Told ya."

Tang Lu, her mysterious Far Eastern features expressionless, served coffee, then plates filled with freshly sliced fruits, a rice pudding with macadamia nuts, and slices of hot banana-coconut bread. Unobtrusively she waited by the sideboard as her guests ate hungrily.

"This is coconut, of course—I love it when it's fresh—and this is pineapple. But what's this?" Cheney asked.

"Those are mangoes, those are papayas, and that's guava," Shiloh said, pointing to the fruits. "They all grow here. The Winslows are cultivating mangoes for export. But the papayas and guavas are fairly plentiful in the wild."

"And the pineapples?" Walker asked with interest.

"They're not native to Hawaii," Shiloh answered, popping a juicy yellow chunk in his mouth and sucking on it happily. "But the Winslows are working on cultivating them too. The climate suits them, you see, but the rainfall is tricky. They don't require as much rain as taro or rice, but they require more than coconut or sugarcane. I think the Winslows have found the answer, though. It's drier up on the high pastures, but they still get plenty of rain on the leeward side. These are Winslow pineapples. Good, aren't they?"

"Mmm, delicious, as sweet as if they'd been sugared," Cheney said. She picked all of the pineapple off her plate, and Tang Lu quickly served her more. "And I suppose the sugar is also the Winslows'."

"Yes, that's their main crop," Shiloh answered. "'Bout fifty thousand acres' worth. Another twenty thousand of taro, rice, pineapple, and mango, and they've got another ten or so thousand that's jungle. They're also working on some experimental projects. They're a pretty enterprising family."

Cheney considered him over the rim of her coffee cup. Carefully setting it down, she remarked, "You seem to be in a fairly good mood today, Shiloh. I'm glad you're not too upset about the bad tidings I brought you."

He frowned, but only fleetingly. "Yeah, well, I ain't quite finished with that little item yet."

"We have a plan," Walker said proudly.

"A plan," Cheney cautiously repeated.

"Yes, a plan. And a fairly good one, I must say."

"Walker thought of it," Shiloh added generously. "His plan was better than mine."

"What was your plan?" Cheney asked with interest.

"To go kill Bain Winslow," Shiloh replied cheerfully.

"I thought as much," Cheney sighed. "I do hope that Walker has come up with a slightly better plan than that one. That one, in spite of its elegant simplicity, does have a few drawbacks."

"But you did say mine," Shiloh repeated grandly, "was of elegant simplicity."

"Yes," Cheney agreed.

"But you think it has drawbacks?"

"A few."

"Ah. Well, I guess that's true. One of 'em bein' that Bain Winslow is my boss, and I'd prob'ly hang if I just up and killed him."

"He's your boss? What do you mean?"

"I mean I work for the Winslows. Have for the last month. In one of the high camps. Growing sandalwood."

Cheney sat straight up in her chair. "How could you? How could you consent to be a . . . a . . . paid employee of those people?"

"I was a paid employee of yours for two years," Shiloh said, his eyes a bright mischievous blue.

"But that's different!"

"Why?"

"Because I . . . because you and I . . . b-because we . . ." Cheney stuttered. Finally she finished, almost shouting, "Because I'm nice!"

Shiloh laughed aloud at this, and Walker unsuccessfully tried to hide his chuckles, while Cheney stared at both of them, her eyes narrowed.

"Yeah, Doc, you are nice," Shiloh agreed. "And yeah, I think that's a pretty good reason for working for somebody. But another reason is if you need money, and they offer you a job. Which Bain Winslow did."

"Well, I don't like it much more than Dr. Duvall does," Walker grumbled. "And neither will my father. You're supposed to be working for him at St. Francis, and he won't like you being stolen away."

"Guess not," Shiloh said dryly. " 'Specially since two of his doctors came dashin' off after me."

"I didn't dash off after you," Cheney retorted.

"Sure you did," Shiloh argued, grinning wickedly. "And I'm really glad too."

"You're impudent."

"I know, but you like me anyway."

"I hate to be rude, but I do believe we've already covered that territory," Walker asserted. "Could we talk about my plan?"

"Of course, Walker," Cheney said with relief. "What is your—wait a minute. How can you have a plan? You don't even know what's going on!"

"I didn't, but now I do. After all, I was obliged to stop Shiloh from running all five miles to Winslow Villa last night. He told me, Dr. Duvall. And I must say that I admire you greatly for not telling this story to anyone but Shiloh. Most ladies—no, that's just not true. Most people can't be discreet about stories they hear about other people. It's just not in our nature."

Cheney's eyes dropped. She forked a piece of mango, then a piece of guava, and turned the fork slowly around in circles so it made a sort of a fruit carousel. "It's . . . not wise to spread stories about people when you don't have firsthand knowledge or incontrovertible proof that is true. And even then, I believe we are constrained by the Lord to still be discreet when it's not our direct concern. I wanted to tell you, Walker, and I especially wanted to tell your father, since I had to ask for this sabbatical. But Reverend Merced and I felt that the story should only be told to Shiloh, as it appears to be his . . . his . . ."

"Family," Shiloh said, his voice as coarse and dry as Sahara sand. "My family. Somehow I always thought that I'd feel a little different about saying those words."

None of the three noticed that Tang Lu, forgotten as she stood by the sideboard, jerked a bit at Shiloh's words. Her face blanched, and her fathomless dark eyes widened. But within the space of a few seconds, she was just as she had been before: small, unobtrusive, silent—and listening.

"Anyway," Walker went on a little awkwardly, "my plan is to do exactly what I . . . er . . . planned. You see, Dr. Duvall, I had no idea of this problem with Shiloh and the Winslows. All I knew was that Bain Winslow had offered to help Shiloh and that the Winslows made a generous contribution to the hospital after the fire. So," he shrugged, "when you told us that you needed to see Shiloh, I convinced my father that I needed to come along. Not to escort you, or because you need protection, or anything like that," he added hastily at the rebellious look on Cheney's face. "But just—because we're friends, and we've been congenial traveling companions, haven't we? I've come to give the Winslows a gift and to thank them for their support of the hospital. My father's been invited by Bain Winslow before, but Father's such a lump, he'll never leave San Francisco. So I came instead."

"So you didn't just come to see Shiloh fight," Cheney stated.

"Well, no, I—"

"You just wanted to come to Hawaii for a holiday and to make a cordial social call on the Winslows?"

"Um . . . sure. I even wrote them and told them that I was coming and hoped to wait on them today," Walker said. "I didn't tell them that you were here, Dr. Duvall, but I see no reason why you, my esteemed colleague, shouldn't make a call on them as well."

"Wait a minute," Shiloh said uneasily. "That wasn't in the plan."

Cheney said accusingly, "What's the matter? Are you afraid I'll be rude to them or something?"

"Uh—yeah."

"Shiloh, you were considering doing away with Bain Winslow, and now you're afraid that I might say something unkind to them?" Cheney said indignantly.

"Well . . . I wasn't going to be *rude* to him." His eyes were sparkling.

"Oh! You—You—" Cheney choked.

"Here, Doc, have some water. Good. You okay, Doc?"

"I'm perfectly fine, thank you," she said unsteadily. "And, Shiloh, I think that if you can restrain yourself from murdering Bain Winslow, I can manage to be polite to him and his family."

"Of course you can," Walker said brightly, as if to a naughty child. "Now, isn't that a wonderful plan?"

"What, to go be nice to the Winslows?" Cheney said acidly. "We're going to kill them with kindness?"

"Well, you gotta understand, Doc," Shiloh said, suddenly grave, "that we do have evidence that Bain's a bounder. But his mother, and especially his sister—that's something else, you know. I mean, they're ladies and all."

"But I thought you said his mother treated you unkindly," Cheney argued.

Shiloh grimaced. "She was just . . . short and to the point. And maybe she knows something about me or my parents . . . I'm just not sure. . . . Anyway, she is a lady, Doc. I can't believe that she'd know about Bain's little sideline."

Thoughtfully Cheney nodded. "Yes, you're probably right. And you said Bain has a sister?"

"Yeah. Her name's Brynn."

"What's she like?" Cheney asked curiously.

"Dunno. Haven't met her." Shiloh's gaze grew distant, and he went on in a softer tone, "But I think I saw her. When I went to the Winslows' house. I saw a lady, a young lady, looking out of the second-story window."

"But how do you know it was Bain's sister?" Cheney persisted. "Perhaps it was a maid."

"No, it was his sister," Shiloh said quietly. "Bain never mentioned her. But Keloki—he's the Hawaiian man you saw with me last night while waiting for the *Petrel*—Keloki brought this to me the next day." Slowly Shiloh took his gold pocket watch out of his breeches pocket and popped it open. Cheney had given the watch to him for Christmas two years ago, and it was his most treasured possession. The song was sad, but Shiloh, who had worn the gray of the lost South, still liked it.

When Johnny comes marching home again, hurrah! Hurrah! . . .

He listened to the tinny chimes for a moment, then took out a piece of paper cleverly folded to fit inside the top of the watch. After painstakingly smoothing it out, he handed it to Cheney. In an elegant hand it read:

> *Dear Mr. Irons,*
> *Please wait for my father to come home.*
> *Brynn Annalea Winslow*

★ ★ ★ ★

A preemptory knock sounded, and with a polite bow to her guests, Tang Lu hurried to answer it. Shiloh, Cheney, and Walker couldn't see the front door from the dining room, but they heard a masculine rumble. Within a few moments Tang Lu came back into the dining room and announced, "Mr. Zeiss has brought the buckboard for your convenience, Dr. Baird. Mrs. Winslow hopes that you will be calling on them today."

Cheney, for the first time, realized that Tang Lu's English was excellent, almost unaccented, but with the different tonal ascensions and descensions so innate to Chinese speakers. Tang Lu did, however, have a great deal of difficulty with the word "Winslow." It came out similar to "Rinsol." Still, her English was much better than that of most of the Chinese people Cheney had spoken with in San Francisco. Evidently Tang Lu was well-educated—in English, at any rate.

"That's good," Shiloh said with relief. "It's five miles—uphill—to Winslow Villa."

"It was kind of the Winslows to offer the use of their buckboard, but of course I was prepared to hire a carriage," Cheney sniffed.

"Uh—well, there's a problem with that, Doc," Shiloh said. "There's not a horse or carriage in Hana for hire. Only the Winslows have horses and two carriages and lots of work carts, of course."

"Oh," Cheney said uncertainly. "I didn't think of that."

"Small town, Doc," Shiloh said, rising. "You two ready to go?"

Cheney jumped up in alarm. "Good heavens, Shiloh, you don't think I'm going to wear a morning dress to make a social call, do you?"

"Uh . . . no, 'course not, Doc," Shiloh said, exchanging a quick amused glance with Walker, who had hurried to his feet when Cheney rose.

"Would be scandalous," Walker intoned, crossing his arms. "Shall we leave in, say, an hour?"

Cheney breezed out the door, calling over her shoulder, "That'll be just fine, gentlemen. In one hour I shall be stunning."

Shiloh and Walker looked at each other uncertainly.

"Whaddya think she's gonna change into?" Shiloh wondered. "A Buggy Dress?"

"I don't know," Walker admitted. "I'm still wondering why she's got on a morning dress when it's afternoon."

"Another of the great mysteries," Shiloh muttered.

"Mysteries?" Walker asked.

Shiloh nodded solemnly. "Of women." He gave Walker a sly sidelong glance. "But ain't it fun tryin' to figure them out?"

Walker wryly answered, "Shiloh, after seeing your way with women, I can see why you think it's fun. But for some of the rest of us poor clods, it's work. Hard, time-consuming work."

Shiloh, staring out the door where Cheney had left, shrugged. "The Doc's not too hard to figure out most of the time," he murmured, as if he spoke to himself. "It's not that she's worried about whatever rule there is about ladies' dresses. It's not about how she looks. It's how she feels."

"I don't get it," Walker said, bewildered.

Shiloh looked at him, now grave. "She's had a hard time of it. You know that, Walker. She's a lady, but she's a doctor. Even—no, especially—people in her own class have treated her badly. She knows that probably the Winslows are going to look down on her. Her manners, her . . . her . . . demeanor are her only defense. And when she's dressed well, she feels confident, and she can command respect."

Walker eyed him intently. "She tell you all that?"

" 'Course not," he answered impatiently. "She wouldn't tell anyone any of that. I wouldn't have told you, either, except for one thing."

"What's that?" Walker asked curiously.

Shiloh gave him a hard stare. "Don't let them treat her badly, Walker," he said harshly. "I don't care who they are. I've never been able to . . . to . . . protect her, because I'm just a thug. But you're a gentleman, you're . . . you're in her class. You don't stand for them talking down to her."

"All right, Shiloh," Walker said soothingly.

"I mean it."

"I know."

"Good." Shiloh nodded once, vehemently. " 'Cause I'll put up with those people insulting me—for now, anyway. But they're not going to insult Cheney, not while I'm on this island."

Walker said quietly, "You know, it's funny. Because that, Shiloh, is exactly the way Dr. Duvall feels about you."

★ ★ ★ ★

It was Sunday, and Hana was sleepy. A Hawaiian couple with three children played in the frisky surf. Four Chinese men in a rickety dinghy, their round straw hats like prim umbrellas, fished and dozed. Behind a small wood-and-thatch fishing hut, a tiny doll of a Chinese girl hung clean laundry out on a clothesline that was so low the pantaloon's cuffs dusted the sparkling sand of her backyard.

In the buckboard, Cheney blinked sleepily beneath the dappled shade of her lace parasol. Her hat, a saucy creation of green felt and filmy white net, provided no protection from the fat and jovial tropical sun. It wasn't hot, however. It was cool enough that she was comfortable in the ensemble that had mystified Shiloh and Walker: the Afternoon Costume.

Early in the year, it had been decreed by that mysterious force that rules women's fashions that a distinct class of dress was required for each occasion. Therefore, a well-dressed woman must, in one day, have anywhere from three to five different costumes, including but not limited to: the private morning dress, worn at breakfast and before calls were received; morning wear with a short skirt that allowed the shoes to peep out, called a walking dress, for morning calls, promenades, shopping, or other outings; afternoon wear, floor-length and with a small train, for carriage, flower shows, concerts, and calls; a semiformal dress for dining at home in the evening, or for small, informal dinner parties; evening wear for large dinner parties and going to the opera or theater. Of course, a well-dressed lady must also have special outfits, such as riding habits and bathing costumes. Cheney's famous six trunks were always stuffed full, and she didn't care a whit if Shiloh Irons grumped about lugging them all over the earth.

Her afternoon costume was very fetching, and Shiloh had been absolutely right about Cheney's feelings. The ensemble, while expensive, was more important to Cheney because she felt trim and confident in it. Made of cretonne cloth, it was a rich hue of green called Metternich, which made Cheney's sea-green eyes take on a mysterious aqua cast. She had a short, tight, plain jacket with beaten silver buttons over a fine white muslin canezou, trimmed with Valenciennes lace in a tiny pattern and fine ruched insertions. The skirt was the newest fashion, the double skirt. The overskirt was gathered up at the sides in a modest pannier, fashioned with ornate silver tassels. The underskirt had a short rounded train, and the hem was trimmed with braided silver satin cord fastening a ruffle that was actually hundreds of pencil-thin, meticulously ironed pleats. Cheney always carefully accessorized her ensembles. With this one she had white kid gloves, a parasol with a silver tassel dangling from the bone handle that was identical to the tassels on her skirt, delicate silver drop earrings with dark malachite stones, and green velvet bows on her ankle boots that had been dyed to precisely match the cretonne cotton dress. Cheney's dressmaker in New Orleans, an octoroon named Angelique, had designed and tailored the dress specifically for Cheney. It fit her perfectly, and when she wore the outfit, her eyes sparkled and she smiled often. Right now a sleepy kitten's smile lingered on her lips, because she had seen the appreciative looks Shiloh had been giving her as he drove the buckboard up the road that snaked up the heights of Haleakala.

"Winslow Villa is right up there," he said when he noticed her watching him. "You can't see it, though, because the place is kinda carved out of the jungle. It's on a cliff overlooking the sea. It's really something."

"This entire landscape is, as you say, really something," Cheney said. "It's kind of . . . overwhelming."

"What do you mean?" Shiloh asked curiously.

"Everything is so . . . so . . . lush, lavish, so . . . so . . ." Cheney struggled.

Sitting in the seat behind them, Walker leaned up to put in, "I know exactly what you mean. Everything's huge, everything's bright, everything's on a grand scale. Haleakala is the whole sky. The sun's like a fat butterscotch disk. The breeze smells like heavy perfume. The surf seems alive, laughing and tumbling and crashing. The colors are blinding."

"Exactly," Cheney agreed.

"Huh," Shiloh said, looking around. "Never thought of it that way."

"As observant and sensitive to things as you are?" Cheney asked in surprise. "You haven't noticed that this place just overloads your senses?"

"No," he answered quietly. "I've just thought how pretty it is, and how easy it is to feel relaxed and quiet here."

Cheney thought about that and realized that once one's eyes grew accustomed to the richness of the landscape, the atmosphere did seem to be one of warmth and peace. They passed, close on either side of the narrow road, ferns with leaves so delicate they looked like lace but were eight feet tall and as large as a parlor. Emerald green *ape-ape* plants had rounded leaves as big as beach umbrellas. Shiloh told them of the trees: the slender, graceful *koa*, from which the Hawaiian craftsmen fashioned their nimble canoes; the ancient, many-trunked *ohia* trees, with their frilly pink pompon blooms; the *kukui*, or candlenut tree, whose oil-rich nuts had provided light to Hawaiians for centuries; and the *papala* tree, from which they fashioned their fire-spears. Shiloh knew the plants and flowers too. He laughed when telling them of the broad-leaved *ti* plant, which gave Hawaiians a skull-popping rumlike concoction called *okolehao* that the Winslows had outlawed but in which his friend Keloki had a brisk black-market business going. He pointed out the *ohelo* shrub, with its sacred bright red berries; the delicate *koali*, with its dreamy morning-glory flowers; the *mamaki*, which gave the Hawaiians their useful *tapa* cloth.

"I had no idea you were such a horticulturist," Cheney teased.

"You shouldn't call people names," Shiloh said with mock indignation. "After all, I am trying to quit."

They traveled slowly upward, the team of two sturdy horses pulling steadily. When they were close to a mile above the sea, the road led onto a plateau of the lushest carpet of kelly-green grass that Cheney had ever seen. A wide drive, carpeted with clean-bleached crushed shells, led to a large but plain two-story house with deep-roofed verandahs surrounding both floors. On either side of the drive, arrow-straight royal palms rose to two-story heights. At the base of them were planted hibiscus bushes, which were all in full bloom, in all colors: deep scarlet, hot pink, lemony yellow, golden orange.

"This is actually the back of the house," Shiloh told them. "But they've put a formal entryway back here anyway. Over there, behind the hedges and casuarina trees, are the servants' cottages, the outbuildings, and two pastures."

"My goodness, this is certainly a good-sized shelf," Cheney observed. "This mountain is so enormous, it's difficult to . . . take it in."

"Yep," Shiloh agreed, staring up at the grand heights to the north of them. "It's over ten thousand feet high. Just the crater is eight miles long and three miles wide. Can't imagine how big the base of the mountain is. Miles and miles."

"We're here," Cheney said a bit nervously. Shiloh jumped out of the buckboard and tied the team to the hitching rail in front of the steps leading up to the double doors. Walker hurried down and then helped Cheney out.

"Yes, we're here," Walker said calmly, "and I know the Winslows are looking forward to our visit, Dr. Duvall."

"I'm sure they are," Shiloh said evenly. "But since I'm just the driver, I'll stay out here. You know that, don't you, Doc?"

Cheney sighed. "Yes, Shiloh, I know it. And I'll go along with it. For now, anyway."

Shiloh shrugged.

Cheney went on quietly, "But I'll tell you one thing, Shiloh. You may not be 'received' by the Winslows, but I'll not stand by like a helpless little fluff and let them insult you. Not while I'm on this island. *You* know *that*, don't you?"

Shiloh glanced at Walker, who stood behind Cheney. Walker winked. Shiloh, hiding his smile, answered, "Doc, I couldn't have said it better myself."

4

WINSLOW VILLA

SWIFT TO HEAR, SLOW TO SPEAK, SLOW TO WRATH . . .

Cheney Duvall was an honest and straightforward woman who believed in speaking her mind; she also had a tendency to do so without the parallel virtues of temperance and discretion. Being aware of this, she repeated the passage from the book of James to herself over and over as a Chinese butler admitted her and Walker Baird into the Winslows' drawing room. She determined that she would not be confrontational. She resolved that she would show the utmost in refinement of manners and gracious civility. She also decided that she would observe the Winslows closely and hope that some keen perception would help to advance Shiloh's cause.

The drawing room, she judged, was reassuring. Strong tropical light blazed through long windows, and fine lace curtains daintily danced in the stiff breeze. It was cool in the room. The furniture was patterned with the palest of pinks and peaches and aquamarines. On the floor, instead of a stuffy wool Persian or Aubusson, was an obviously new sisal rug, cleverly woven.

Two women sat at opposite ends of a Venetian sofa. A young man stood at the fireplace, negligently taking a pinch of snuff and leaning casually against a white marble mantelpiece.

"Dr. Cheney Duvall," the elderly butler pronounced carefully. "Dr. Walker Baird." He left, closing the double doors into the hallway behind him.

The two women nodded graciously. The young man dusted his hands, tucked his snuffbox into his pocket, crossed his arms, and raised one well-shaped eyebrow.

Walker took Cheney's arm and led her to the sofa. "May I have the honor of performing the introductions, Mrs. Winslow? Since we have not yet formally met, I am Dr. Walker Baird. I have the pleasure of introducing to you Dr. Cheney Duvall, who is a staff physician at St. Francis and one of my esteemed colleagues."

Denise Clare Worthington Winslow, Cheney saw, was an attractive woman who gave the impression of youthful energy, even though her dark brown hair was liberally shot with gray. She had a small frame, with modest, even features and dark eyes that raked over Cheney in a thorough assessment. Cheney was caught totally off guard when Mrs. Winslow spoke, for she had a rich and cultured British accent. Shiloh hadn't mentioned that she was English.

"Dr. Duvall, it's such a pleasure to meet you. Welcome to Hana, and welcome to Winslow Villa."

"Thank you, ma'am," Cheney replied with a smile. "It's a very great pleasure to visit Hawaii, and I'm honored to meet you. I hope I am not intruding, as you were expecting Dr. Baird but did not know that I was accompanying him."

"Nonsense," Mrs. Winslow said crisply. "The Winslows always know when important passengers travel on our ships. You are most welcome. Please allow me to introduce my daughter, Brynn."

Cheney moved down to incline her head toward the woman—or girl, really—who sat at the opposite end of the sofa. Brynn Winslow was pretty, with features similar to her mother's, but the younger woman appeared much more vivacious. Her brown eyes sparkled, and she had deep dimples that flashed even as she spoke. She was tiny but moved and talked with animation.

"Dr. Duvall, it's a great pleasure to make your acquaintance." She smiled, and it was more like a playful twelve-year-old girl's grin.

"And this is my son, Bain," Mrs. Winslow continued. "I don't believe you made his acquaintance in San Francisco?"

"No, I'm afraid we never chanced to meet," Cheney said, turning to him.

He bowed smartly and spoke in a pleasantly modulated voice. "Dr. Duvall, it is my honor," he recited. "Dr. Baird, we're so glad you've brought your charming fellow traveler to call on us."

His British accent was not as pronounced as his mother's or his sister's. Cheney was surprised. Somehow she had expected him to look coarser, or at the least, more imposing. He was about her height and slender. His dark brown hair was carefully styled, his aristocrat's hands manicured, his plain black suit finely tailored. He had a full, smooth face, a nonchalant expression, a sophisticated and careless demeanor.

Mrs. Winslow then formally introduced Walker and Brynn. Cheney, who was allowing Bain Winslow to hand her into a chair across from the sofa, saw Walker take Brynn Winslow's hand and bow so low over it that his lips almost brushed her skin. Walker was a most gallant young man and often still greeted Cheney in this way. Brynn Winslow looked surprised, then her eyes glowed.

After Walker settled into a chair and Bain returned to his casual stance at the mantel, Walker said, "Mrs. Winslow, thank you for receiving us, and thank you, Mr. Winslow, for your suggestion that we holiday here in Hawaii. My father sends his sincerest regrets, as he was not able to take a sabbatical at this time. But he and I, along with the board members of St. Francis, wish to express our deepest gratitude for your support of the hospital. I have brought a small gift, which I hope you will enjoy with our compliments." Walker had brought in a box and laid it on the sideboard by the doors.

"May I?" Brynn asked, then jumped up and hurried to open the box with the big red bow. "Oh, Mother, look! It's Ghirardelli's chocolates and cocoa! Oh, we love Ghirardelli's, but we don't get them here. Bain brings them to me sometimes, when he remembers, but he often forgets." She looked at her brother reproachfully, and Bain shrugged with a half-smile.

"Thank you so much, Dr. Baird," Brynn said, giving him both dimples full force.

Walker was utterly smitten. "You're very welcome, Miss Winslow. If I had known that you liked them so much, I certainly should have brought an entire shipload."

There was some talk about the journey and how Walker and Cheney had found the *Petrel* as a passenger ship. Cheney watched and listened closely and thought, *These people seem so . . . normal! Just like so many people of my and my parents' acquaintance. Could I be wrong? Could Shiloh be wrong? Could Reverend Merced have gotten it all wrong?*

Mrs. Winslow's intense gaze turned to Cheney. "Dr. Duvall, it is rare to meet a lady physician. How did you happen to decide on such an unusual occupation?"

Uh-oh, here it comes. . . . "My closest friend, Devlin Buchanan, was adopted as a ward by my parents when we were very young. He decided to become a doctor, and he encouraged me. My parents, too, have been very supportive—even inspiring." Cheney, in spite of her best efforts, sounded stiff, and she could feel her neck muscles tensing up as Mrs. Winslow replied.

"I would imagine that it's been very difficult for you. I'm certain that male physicians have not taken such an affront to their field lightly." Denise Winslow spoke with open contempt.

Even in Cheney's confusion, she reflected that the observation was rather rude to Walker. "Well, the disapproval hasn't exactly been limited to male doctors," Cheney said hesitantly. "Many people feel that it is an unladylike and . . . and . . . vulgar occupation for a woman."

Mrs. Winslow made a sharp, impatient gesture. "Ignorance and stupidity. It's even worse if women denounce it. Women are fully capable of doing anything a man can do. This principle I have tried to instill into my daughter ever since she was a child. I, for one, Dr. Duvall, admire your courage and determination."

Now Cheney was truly out of kilter. She stammered, "Why, th-thank you, Mrs. Winslow."

Now with an air of polite inquiry, Mrs. Winslow asked, "And I understand that you are a good friend of Mr. Shiloh Irons?"

"Why . . . why, yes, he . . . we—" With a concentrated effort Cheney curbed her confusion and answered, "A little over two years ago I employed Mr. Irons as my medical assistant. Since that time, yes, we have grown to be very good friends." Furiously Cheney tried to assess Mrs. Winslow's motive in bringing up Shiloh first thing, tried to understand how this had given Mrs. Winslow a definite advantage, and also tried to figure out how to turn the conversation to her—and Shiloh's—advantage. But Cheney, who was highly intelligent but not very agile in such social maneuverings, was unable to marshall herself adequately.

Mrs. Winslow pressed on in a smooth and confident manner. "Such a tragic story that young man has. Bain had hoped that I might be able to shed some light on his past, since the Winslows have lived here for thirty years. Sadly, I know of no couple with an infant that was lost in a shipwreck in November of 1843. As for *Locke's Day Dream*, that's just a coincidence. We didn't commission and name her; my husband bought her, used, from a shipping yard in Scotland, and she was already christened. I don't believe I've ever known of a ship called the *Day Dream*. Of course, I don't know everything about everyone on Maui, much less on all of the islands. And I'm afraid I never quite understood exactly how it was that Mr. Irons believed his parents lived in Hawaii, anyway."

Cheney answered quickly. "Because a tapestry was found with him after the shipwreck, and it appeared to tell the story of Shiloh—Mr. Irons and his parents."

Denise Winslow nodded slowly. "Ah yes, of course. The tapestry. And it was stolen, I believe."

"Yes. Along with a compass," Cheney replied shortly, with a sharp glance at Bain Winslow. He looked uninterested in the conversation, even appeared to be slightly bored.

Mrs. Winslow said with a very slight emphasis, "But it's my understanding that the tapestry was not at all conclusive. About Mr. Irons' parents or about Hawaii."

Reluctantly Cheney said, "Not in the sense that a written text would be. However, we do strongly believe that it tells Mr. Irons' story quite as accurately and truthfully as if it had been a personal journal."

Mrs. Winslow shrugged slightly. "Perhaps. But I suppose it is of no great portent, at any rate, since Mr. Irons is no longer in possession of it."

Cheney's eyes sparked. Next to her, Walker shifted uneasily in his chair. But Cheney's tone, though clipped, was polite enough. "I'm afraid you're mistaken, Mrs. Winslow. The tapestry is still of great importance to Mr. Irons, and he intends to recover it."

"Of course," she carelessly agreed. "And since Mr. Irons is in such a difficult position, I'm glad that we could offer him employment to allow him to stay on the island as he attempts to pick up the threads, as it were."

"So kind of you," Cheney said evenly.

Mrs. Winslow continued, "But now Bain tells me that Mr. Irons intends to engage in some sort of pugilistic exhibition in order to make a sum of money quickly." Her mouth twisted, and her voice took on an overtone of distinct distaste. "Understandable, I suppose, for someone of Mr. Irons' station."

At this comment Cheney looked clearly rebellious, and Walker hurriedly interposed. "Mrs. Winslow, I wanted to thank you for your kind solicitation in sending the buggy for us. I understand that there are no horses or carriages in Hana for hire?"

"No, the Winslows own the only horses in East Maui," Mrs. Winslow answered with a hint of pride. "However, if you are interested in sight-seeing while you're here, Dr. Baird, we'll be happy to loan you a mount. And you, too, Dr. Duvall, if you ride."

"Yes, I do," Cheney said somewhat defiantly. She had the impression that this woman would be somewhat disapproving of female riders, but once again Cheney was wrong about Denise Winslow.

"Excellent," Mrs. Winslow said briskly. "Skilled horsemanship is a most worthy endeavor. My daughter, Brynn, is an expert and, I may say, a most elegant equestrienne."

Brynn Winslow blushed prettily. "My mother taught me," she told Cheney and Walker. "Certainly the pupil does not surpass the teacher."

"Thank you, dearest," Mrs. Winslow said with unmistakable warmth.

Whatever else Denise Winslow was, however sharp her tongue and haughty her manner, it was clear that she loved her daughter. Perhaps more revealing was the fact that Denise Winslow treated Brynn with respect. Many people with impatient, quick mannerisms appeared to treat others—particularly their children—with disdain. But it was obvious that Denise Winslow loved her daughter unselfishly and unstintingly. Her attitude toward her son was less clear, for Mrs. Winslow had barely looked at her son or spoken to him, and Cheney had had no opportunity to observe the air between them. Cheney again felt her confidence waver. Her perceptions of Denise Winslow were so disjointed that it was impossible for her to form a sure judgment of her character.

Though Cheney didn't notice, Walker was vastly relieved that Cheney was momentarily distracted. He went on quickly, "Then, Mrs. Winslow, and Miss Winslow, I have a humble request to make of each of you. Would you be gracious enough, Mrs. Winslow, to provide us with horses so that we might go on a jaunt up to the crater of this magnificent mountain? And would you, Miss Winslow, please be so kind as to accompany us?"

Suddenly Denise Winslow's eyes grew needle sharp. "Who is taking this 'jaunt,' as you call it, Dr. Baird?"

"Why, Dr. Duvall and I have been looking forward to exploring the crater ever since we decided to come to Maui," Walker lied smoothly. "And, of course, as Mr. Irons is our friend, and has already made the trip, we wanted him to come along, both as a guide and for his companionship. You, Miss Winslow, would make it a most pleasant foursome. We'd be honored if you would come with us."

Denise Winslow opened her mouth, and on her face was a solid "No." But without a single glance at her mother, Brynn asserted, "I'd be delighted to accompany you, Dr. Baird, Dr. Duvall. But to reach the crater, explore it, and return takes two days. Were you aware of that?"

"No, I wasn't," Walker said easily, though he was quick enough, again, to preempt Denise Winslow's protests. The woman cast a quick surreptitious glance at her son. Bain merely cocked his eyebrow again in a bored manner.

"Why don't you accompany us, Mr. Winslow?" Cheney asked with a charming smile. "We would be so happy to have you, and you could chaperone your sister."

Bain Winslow opened his mouth, but once again Brynn spoke first. "Oh, he won't go. He's too stuffy. Business, business, all the time. You're leaving tomorrow, aren't you, Bain? See, Dr. Duvall? He's much too staid for such an exciting excursion. No, here is what we shall do. I'll send my horses home with you tonight. Early tomorrow, you—including Mr. Irons, of course—will return here for a dawn breakfast. Keloki and Leilana will be our guides, and, yes, Mother, you know they're perfectly adequate chaperones."

"No, they are not, Brynn," Mrs. Winslow was allowed to say at last. "They are childish and dreamy natives with no common sense, and they have no notion of seemliness."

"But I do, Mother," Brynn said with genuine sweetness. "And Keloki and Leilana were fine to chaperone me the last time we went up to the crater with the Simmonses."

"The Simmonses were those dreary Methodists," Mrs. Winslow pronounced with an air of finality. "Keloki and Leilana were hardly needed to chaperone you with them and their coarse brood."

"I'm a dreary Methodist," Cheney said brightly. "So if I may cast my shadow on Miss Winslow, so to speak, then that must mean that Keloki and Leilana will provide sufficient chaperonage for her."

"Impertinence, even in a courageous and determined woman, is not an attractive quality," Denise Winslow said in a cold voice. She clamped her mouth shut with unnecessary force.

"I apologize, Mrs. Winslow," Cheney said instantly, though without obvious regret.

Denise Winslow frowned.

"Mother, I truly would like to go," Brynn said softly, but with determination. "Keloki and Leilana are excellent guides, and I—and Dr. Duvall—will be admirably chaperoned." Turning to Cheney and Walker, she smiled brilliantly. "Breakfast here at the villa. At dawn.

Please don't be late, for I'm so excited, I wish we could start now!"

"Me too," Walker replied, obviously unaware of what he was saying. He was staring at Brynn Winslow much as a smitten alley cat gazes longingly after a precious Persian lady. "That is—I mean—we're so looking forward to it too. Also. Aren't we, Dr. Duvall?"

"Oh yes," Cheney replied, stifling a wicked grin. "We are. We're excited too. Aren't we, Dr. Baird?"

"Oh yes!" His face was boyishly flushed.

Brynn giggled, her dimples deepening.

But neither Denise Winslow nor Bain Winslow appeared to find the situation at all amusing. They glanced at each other, and in an uncanny resemblance, their dark eyes narrowed to glittering slits. But the moment passed quickly, and Denise Winslow turned back to her guests. "Very well," she said in a normal tone. "I'm afraid I'm not an early enough riser to greet you in the morning, Dr. Duvall, Dr. Baird. But I'm sure we shall meet again soon."

Rising, Cheney said graciously, "I look forward to spending more time with you, Mrs. Winslow. I regret that Mr. Winslow is not in Hana right now. Perhaps I may have the pleasure of meeting him before I leave?"

Denise Winslow's face grew very still and closed. "Mr. Winslow is not due back for some time, Dr. Duvall. I believe you're sailing in two weeks, when the *Mongoose* is on its western route? I'm afraid you will be back in San Francisco before he returns from the Orient."

At this, Cheney noticed two very unusual things. A small, tight smile flitted over Bain Winslow's face, though his head was down as he appeared to study his hands.

And Brynn Winslow cocked her head, her brow furrowed, as she stared at her mother with open disbelief. She opened her mouth as if to speak. Then it seemed that she thought better of it, and when Cheney and Walker left, she said nothing at all.

5

WINSLOW'S PLAN

Brynn, still seated on the sofa, had not taken her accusing gaze from her mother.

Uncomfortably Denise said, "I'm glad they're gone. Really, morning calls should be of a duration of no more than ten minutes, at most—"

"Mother," Brynn interrupted in a soft voice. "Why did you tell them that Father won't be back before they leave?"

Denise's answer was much too hearty. "Because he won't, of course, dearest! I received a letter from him last week, didn't I tell you? He's decided to extend his tour of the Orient. For another month, at least."

Brynn didn't say a word. She just continued staring at her mother, studying her face as if she weren't quite sure she'd ever seen the woman before. Then she rose, and without a word or backward look, she left the drawing room.

"Hoity-toity," Bain Winslow remarked dryly. "This has been such fun."

"Be silent," Denise snapped. "I must think . . . I must think." She rose, went to the double doors leading into the hall, and called out, "Tang Sun! It's no use hiding. I know you've been sneaking about out here listening. Bring some sherry into the parlor! Snap to!"

With calculated lazy movements, Bain took out a gold case with an ornate W engraved on it, flipped it open, and carefully selected a cigarette. "Really, Mother dear, where are your manners? You know I can't abide that grape juice. I'll have bourbon."

"It's too early for you to drink whisky," Denise said absently, rubbing her temples and pacing up and down. "And how many times have I asked you not to smoke in the house?"

"Countless," Bain said, lighting his cigarette with a flick of a match and blowing smoke with relish.

Denise ignored him, pacing up and down in front of the sofa like a caged panther, massaging her temples. Her face was white with strain, and her steps were jerky, without her usual youthful grace.

Denise paced in silence, and Bain smoked in silence, until the butler brought in the sherry and served Denise. She waved him away. As soon as the doors closed, she drained the glass, refilled it from the fine crystal decanter, and seated herself on the sofa again. Arranging her skirts delicately, she licked her dry lips. "It's unfortunate that you brought that man here, Bain. And now look how very complicated this has gotten. What am I to do, I ask you?"

"Before I answer that question, Mother, may I remind you—again—that I certainly wouldn't have brought Irons here if I'd had any idea of what you'd done," Bain retorted.

Denise frowned. "And may I once again remind you, dearest son, of where and what you would be now if I hadn't thought and acted so quickly when Rory died? You would be no one. You would have nothing. You would be just like your father was before I took this matter into my own hands and made the decision. And it was the right decision, the best for all of us, for everyone: for Hana, for Winslow Plantation, for Winslow Shipping, for our family. For you."

Bain shrugged impatiently. "I'm not disputing that, Mother. I'm not criticizing you for your actions and your decisions. And I would appreciate it if you would stop criticizing me. It's pointless anyway. Irons is here. His influential friends are here. We must make a plan to deal with it."

"Your father," she said between gritted teeth, "is going to arrive in Lahaina any day now. And once he sets eyes on Mr. Shiloh Irons, this will all be gone. Do you understand that, Bain? That man will not only have the right to take everything that we have and leave us penniless but also to demand restitution for the last twenty-five years. And your father is weak and stupid enough to agree to it and to work the rest of his life to try to repay that . . . that . . . nobody!"

"Shiloh Irons," Bain said very slowly, as if to an inattentive child, "has no proof of anything. Not a shred. He can't do a thing; he can't demand a thing. My father can't change that."

"Don't be a fool," Denise scoffed. "Your father can, and would, give everything to him."

Bain sighed heavily, as if he were burdened. "Mother, you're the fool. If we stand up to Father and tell him that he'll have to take up the matter with the law and disgrace his own wife and children, he won't do a thing. You know he won't. He can't. It's not in him."

Denise's dark eyes flickered. "You mean he wouldn't disgrace you and Brynn. He certainly wouldn't hesitate to denounce me. It would probably give him particular pleasure if I were arrested." She was trying to sound insouciant, but the timbre of her voice was petulant.

Bain laughed, and it was a sound that made Denise Winslow's gut wrench. "That may be true, Mother. But you and I both know that he wouldn't do a thing to hurt me or Brynn. Especially Brynn. Never, never would he do that."

"But she didn't have anything to do with any of this. In fact, she didn't believe me just now. She didn't believe me, her own mother. I've never, ever lied to her," Denise fretted.

"Well, you have now, and she knows it," Bain taunted her. "Open your eyes. Don't you see that it's for the best? Now that she's going to be so cozy with Irons and his friends, she won't mention the matter again. Because she knows nothing, and, Mother, I can promise you, Brynn doesn't want to know. That way, she won't be able to say anything anyway. But later, in Father's eyes, it will appear that she helped us to cover up this mess."

Weakly Denise blustered, "But . . . but, Bain, your own sister—"

"Yes, she is. And?" he said coldly.

Denise gulped and stared into space. Her fingers tightened so cruelly around the stem of the sherry glass that the blood ran out of them. Finally she took a deep breath, lifted her chin, and focused back on her son's face. "So you mean that since Brynn really doesn't know anything about Mr. Irons, she can't tell them anything. And we will tell Logan that she was helping us to deceive him."

Bain flicked the stub of his cigarette into the fireplace. "You have a mind like a bear trap, Mother."

Denise blinked several times, and slowly her face changed. It hardened back into the familiar lines of aloof *hauteur*.

"Anyway, Mother, forget about Father. As usual, he doesn't figure into this much," Bain continued sarcastically. "I'm going to Lahaina tomorrow and will wait for him. I'll keep him from coming to Hana. He'll never see or hear of Mr. Shiloh Irons. And that will be the best thing for us all, especially for Father."

"How are you going to do that?" Denise asked doubtfully.

"I'll tell him you're very unhappy with him for taking so long to make the Orient route. I'll tell him that you need more money quickly, and you must speak to him immediately. I'll tell him that the plantation has several problems that need to be attended to, and you fully expect him to stay home at least a month to help you," Bain said with ill-concealed malicious pleasure.

"Yes, that will do it," Denise agreed sourly. "He'll almost certainly tuck his tail between his legs and scuttle back to Burma or Bombay or wherever he's been. Even though none of those things are true."

"That's good to know," Bain said briskly. "I'm glad that the plantation is fine and you have no need of money, because I need cash and I need it now. I sustained a loss in San Francisco. I can recover, but I need quick money, and lots of it."

Denise asked warily, "What about your own funds, Bain? I know you have a reserve. You always have, ever since you were a child."

He shook his head vehemently. "It's not enough. I need more, lots more. I've got to make a fast run to Shanghai, and I've got to return to San Francisco for a couple of months."

"All . . . all right," Denise said hesitantly. "I'll draw up a bank draft you can cash when you're in Lahaina. But, Bain, it's my own reserve, you know. We'll be walking a thin line here at the plantation until you can repay me."

"What do you need money for here?" Bain said carelessly. "Anyway, it's only for a month or two, Mother." He smiled. "My investment has very quick returns, all in cash. You'll get your little shopping fund back soon."

"Fine. Meanwhile, what am I supposed to do with that Irons person? And his boring little entourage?"

Now Bain put his hands behind his back and paced slowly up and down. With the understated elegance of his suit and his thoughtful air, he looked like a congressman considering a particularly thorny political question. "He thinks I'm going to Lahaina to set up the lua match with Meholo. But that won't work now. It's a shame, too, because I was certain to make a lot of money on that match. But it's not feasible now . . . not with those busybody doctors here. They could cause serious problems if he's killed."

"Killed?" Denise snapped. "Are you insane?"

He whirled on her, his face white with anger. "I don't know. I'm told I take after my mother. Do me a favor and be quiet so that I can think, can't you?"

"No, I won't be silent, Bain," Denise said through stiff lips. "I won't countenance—I can't be a part of—"

"Murder?" Bain suggested as if he'd asked her if she'd pass the salt. "Oh, come now, Mother. You know and I know that you'd do it in a minute if Shiloh Irons came to take your fine house and your money and your pineapples and your precious, expensive sandalwood and your army of groveling servants and your carriages and horses. Oh yes, madam. You would. But enough! If you'll stop your silly vapors, I'm trying to tell you that that plan won't work anymore, not now."

For a moment Denise's face was haggard with relief. She looked about a hundred years old. Taking a long swallow of sherry, she asked gutterally, "So, what . . . what shall we do, Bain?"

His movements now irritable, he lit a cigarette, inhaled deeply, and narrowed his eyes to slits against the smoke. "When they return from the crater, tell Irons that you feel sorry for him, and you've convinced me to forgive his debt to us. Tell him that you're freeing him to return to San Francisco with his friends. Fire him, in a nice way. He won't have any place to stay. He'll go back with those two. Especially the woman. In fact, she'd give him the money—she's obviously got plenty—to repay us and to pay for a first-class cabin back. Hint that it's a burden on you, but you're willing to let him go. If he's got no place to stay here, no job, no money coming in, maybe letting his piece of fluff pay up will appeal to him."

"But . . . he . . . doesn't he suspect. . . ?"

"No, he doesn't suspect. He knows," Bain said bluntly. "He has no proof, but he knows very well. It doesn't matter. In fact, that's probably better. He'll feel secure about going back to San Francisco; he'll think that he can find out more, perhaps about the *Day Dream* or Winslow Brothers Shipping there."

"And he probably can," Denise said shakily. "Now that he knows more about the family history. About Rory."

"Yes. But it's of no consequence, Mother," Bain said, now calmly. He even reached out and patted her cold hand. "Because I'll just take care of him later. In San Francisco. It'll be easy. And then, Mother dearest, you and I won't ever have to worry about Mr. Shiloh Irons again."

★ ★ ★ ★

That night Cheney dreamed of the train again.

It was a rather boring dream, actually. She was sitting at a window,

57

staring out onto miles and miles of fields and insignificant hills. The sun was high and indifferent. The landscape never varied. She was alone, so no one spoke. There was just the train, flying on perfectly straight rails, seemingly on an endless journey.

Sluggishly Cheney turned over, then pushed herself up on one elbow. Her bedroom was dark and cool, the wind coming through the open window moist and smelling strongly of salt and flowers. The surf was lazy, sloshing back and forth with hardly any crescendo of breakers.

Wonder if that's what's making me dream of a train? Cheney drowsily wondered. *The rhythm of the surf? No, no, the train . . . train sounds are busy, urgent, clacking, insistent. . . .*

"And boring to dream of," Cheney told herself. With a sigh, she cautiously stood up to arrange her bedclothes, which were in a tangle as complicated as a Gordian knot. Shivering slightly when her sleep-warmed feet touched the cool sisal mat, she marveled at how chilly the evenings were, even though October was considered to be late summer in Hawaii.

Finally she got the bedclothes back into a semblance of order, climbed into bed, and curled up tightly on her side. After a few moments she impatiently pushed away the pillow and turned on her stomach. Cheney knew this wasn't a very good position to sleep in—sometimes she woke up with a catch in her neck—but often it was the only way she could sleep. She must have been, in fact, sleeping in that position, because her pillow had tumbled to the floor. Yawning achingly, her eyes fluttered. . . .

Moments later she jolted upright. Then she lay back down, flat and stiff on the bed, her eyes wide open, her ear pressed to the firm mattress.

"What in the world. . . ?" she whispered. She stayed in that position for a long time.

Throwing back the bedcovers impatiently, she fumbled at the small table by her bedside and lit a candle. Then she set it down and stood, watching the basin of water closely. She bent so far over the basin that her nose almost dipped into the water.

Impatiently she muttered, "Can't see well enough . . . or maybe it's not strong enough. . . ."

Throwing herself back on the bed, she carefully laid her head on the top crosspiece of the iron bedstead. With tiny movements she positioned her ear against the metal tube. Her face darkened with impatience as she listened. Then slowly she reached up to touch the piece by laying her fingers—those ultrasensitive physician's fingers—lightly on the metal. She stayed in that position for long moments, but her expression grew more frustrated.

Then her eyes brightened, and Cheney turned her head until her mouth was resting on the cold iron. Baring her teeth, she touched them lightly to the bedstead.

That did it. She could feel an unmistakable buzzing, a tight but distinct vibration. Quickly she pushed her head back to the bed. She could clearly hear the drone, the continual deep hum that had made her dream of the endless din of a train.

But what could make such a deep and omnipresent sound?

And what could produce such a vibration that it made a heavy iron bedstead tremble?

Cheney didn't know. But before she went back to sleep, she asked the Lord for His protection.

And she slept on her back, with two pillows.

6

TRUE DAWN

Riding through the night to Winslow Villa on the island of Maui was like the most ethereal dreams Cheney had ever had. The road from Hana traced the coastline, and even in the dark the sea appeared to have manganese violet depths, with moon sparkles flickering like tiny torches held by fairy fisherfolk. Indolent surf displayed breakers like filigrees of finest lace. Breezes blew, gentle and aromatic, wispy fingertips of air that caressed Cheney's face and barely teased the loose curls that always escaped from even the severest of her coiffures. The uncountable stars were fuzzy, indistinct lights scattered across the navy-blue sky like a child giant's glass marbles.

Shiloh, riding in front, had carried a small lantern, but about halfway to the villa he extinguished it. Their eyes quickly adjusted, and night on this island was not true dark. Even though the moon had long since been swallowed up by Haleakala, the leftover moonlight and star glow lit their way. He turned in the saddle. "You two all right back there? You're awful quiet. You okay, Doc?"

"Oh yes, I'm just . . . overwhelmed. Again. By the . . . the magic of this place," she answered. *That's it. It's like a child's magic world, a perfect dreamworld, where everything is pretty and smells good, and the sun isn't too hot or the night too dark. . . .*

"I'm doing fine," Walker called as he rode behind Cheney. "Lead on, Shiloh."

Though the road was wide enough to accommodate the three riding abreast, the tropical forest grew so close on either side that the shadows cast by the enormous trees were impenetrable. The soft star glow only lit the center of the path. Shiloh, Cheney, and Walker wound up the side of the great mountain without fear but with caution.

The lower floor of Winslow Villa was lit, the upper story was dark. Brynn Winslow sat in one of the bamboo chairs on the verandah waiting for them.

Shiloh dismounted, tipped his wide-brimmed hat respectfully to her, and began tying up the three horses. Cheney hurried to his side as Brynn came slowly down the steps to greet them. "Miss Winslow, I don't believe you've been properly introduced to Mr. Irons? I have the honor of presenting to you Mr. Shiloh Irons, my colleague of the last two and one half years and a close friend of mine and of my family."

Slowly Brynn held out her hand, and Shiloh swept off his hat and took her hand, bowing slightly over it. She was watching him, searching his features with an intensity that Cheney thought was overdone. But in the grayness it was almost impossible to distinguish the finer points of facial expression, so Cheney really couldn't judge Brynn's reaction too accurately.

Quietly Cheney continued the formal introduction as Shiloh dropped Brynn's hand and stepped back respectfully. "Shiloh, may I present to you Miss Brynn Winslow."

"It's my pleasure to meet you, ma'am," Shiloh said.

"And I'm honored to make your acquaintance, Mr. Irons," Brynn responded in a subdued voice. Her face was still upturned, searching his. He met her questioning gaze with a grave smile, which she didn't return. For long moments she studied him, as if she were trying to decipher a difficult mathematical equation.

Finally Shiloh said politely, "If you'll excuse me, Miss Winslow, Doc, I'll take care of the horses and then go see if I can help Keloki." He turned to finish tying up the horses.

Brynn Winslow roused herself and in a more natural tone said, "Oh no, Mr. Irons, today you're one of my guests, and I insist that you join us for breakfast."

Now Shiloh assessed her questioningly, and she met his gaze with a firm nod. "That's very kind of you, ma'am," he murmured. "You must be an uncommonly kind lady. I guess this is as good a time as any to thank you for your note. It was really nice of you to concern yourself with me and my problems."

Brynn made a dismissive gesture that was awkward and jerky, and Cheney thought that she looked distressed.

"I—that's . . . that's difficult to explain, Mr. Irons, and to tell you the truth, I—it's possible that I might have made a mistake. . . ."

He stepped forward so that he was close enough to her to see her face, but not so close as to impose on her. He spoke so quietly, almost whispering. "You didn't make a mistake, ma'am, and you'll never have to explain anything to me."

Brynn grew very still. "Thank you, sir," she breathed. Straightening, she smiled at Cheney and Walker, who were trying very hard to look as if they couldn't hear a word being said and weren't interested in trying to. "Please, everyone follow me. Breakfast is all ready on the front lanai. And this morning, you're going to see a sunrise such as you've never seen before!"

They followed her around the wide verandah to the front of the villa. All along the generous porch were intimate conversational groupings of three or four chairs and a convenient table. Brynn seated herself in a wicker empress chair with fat cushions and motioned for her guests to join her. Shiloh and Cheney sat together on a loveseat, and Walker sat in a wicker rocker. The seats were gathered around a round tea table that was already set with plates and silver and condiments. Two Chinese servants—the older man that was the butler, and an older woman—stood subserviently by another tea table that held plates and platters covered with linen napkins and heavy glass dome covers.

Brynn made a signal to the servants, and they began to serve the diners, offering them fluffy cheese omelets, grilled chops, thick slices of buttered bread, bacon, jacket potatoes, buckwheat cakes, and a fruit compote of mango, guava, and pineapple. "This is such fun for me," Brynn exclaimed. "I do so enjoy dawn breakfasts, especially at the start of an exciting day. Thank you all for joining me."

"Oh no, it's we who are so indebted to you, Miss Winslow," Walker said ardently. "After all, this is our holiday and our outing. We hardly expected such gracious accommodation."

"Oh, but it is rare that I get to go exploring these days," Brynn protested. "It's a holiday for me. And with such congenial companions, it's just that much better."

"Evidently this is going to be quite a physical exertion," Cheney commented. "I had no idea that climbing Mount Haleakala would take two days. But you do enjoy such outings, Miss Winslow?"

"Oh yes, especially exploring the crater," she answered, daintily spearing a tiny bite of omelet. "It's an experience that is unforgettable, and one that could never become routine. I've been up to the crater several times. Aside from the fact that I enjoy such adventures, wandering the heart of this ancient volcano is much more than sight-seeing. It's something of a revelation and something of an emotional experience. I must sound a bit peculiar, but you can't know what I mean until you've done it. Then I think you'll agree with me."

"I've done it," Shiloh said in a low voice, "and I know exactly what you mean, Miss Winslow."

She smiled at him. "Won't it be such pleasure to take friends and share it with them? Isn't it odd how we feel responsible in some way for introducing wondrous things to people, as if we in some way made it possible?" Then she shook her head slightly. "But no, I wouldn't presume to take any credit for Haleakala. That belongs to the goddess Pele, and I wouldn't want to offend her!"

Politely Walker said, "I've heard the name—Pele—but I'm afraid I'm abysmally ignorant of the local superstitions and legends, Miss Winslow. Why don't you tell me—us—the story of Pele?"

"Oh no, if you haven't heard yet, then I must let Keloki or Leilana tell you," she demurred. "They're true, old-blood Hawaiians, a married couple who have worked for us for decades. It would give them such pleasure to tell you the story, or perhaps we might persuade Keloki to give us a *mele*. That's an ancient form of Hawaiian poetic chant, and the Hawaiians regard it as one of the highest forms of art. Keloki's quite a poet, actually. I'll just bet that he has a mele about Pele and her sister, Na-maka."

"He does," Shiloh stated. "It's a fascinating story, and Keloki tells it like he's watching it, even though he gripes about having to tell it in English. So did I understand that Keloki and Leilana are coming with us, Miss Winslow?"

"Actually, they're already at the high cabin making preparations," she replied. "I sent them up yesterday. I'm afraid I'm a bit of a fraud, going on as if I'm some sort of hardy wilderness adventurer. I think you're going to be surprised at the level of comfort we Winslows require on our outings. I just hope it will be a pleasant surprise and not a disappointment."

Cheney smiled. "No, I don't think I'm going to demand that I sleep on a tree root and eat berries and beetles. If Keloki and his wife are making preparations along the lines of a place to sleep and something to eat, then I assure you I won't feel that it detracts from the excitement at all."

The straight line of the horizon to the east began to lighten to a misty blue-gray. Then, very quickly, as if a child was frantically coloring it with wide strokes, indistinct lines of iridescent purple and dark alizarin crimson formed. Soon they lightened into violet and red and orange, and the first blinding fingernail of bright gold peeked over the knife-edged division of earth and sea. The ocean mirror reflected the rising sun so brightly that the four were obliged to stop looking at it directly. But in the few minutes that they had seen the beginning of the day, the majestic spectacle stopped all conversation. It was like a symphony for the eyes.

In a low, caressing tone, Brynn said, "Everyone else on Maui sees the morning sun rising from the House of the Sun, the great Haleakala. Only we here see the true dawn."

The true dawn, Cheney repeated to herself. *So far it seems to me that what we've seen has been a cloak of darkness, shrouding the truth about Shiloh Irons and his mother and father.* Surreptitiously Cheney studied the younger woman. *May we all see the true dawn, Miss Winslow. All of us.*

★ ★ ★ ★

"The road from here to Kipahulu is fairly good," Brynn commented as the travelers left Winslow Villa. "From Kipahulu to Kaupo, which is about five miles, it's not quite as good. In fact, it's not truly a road. I suppose one would call it a trail. But it's no problem on horseback."

Brynn had provided Cheney and Walker with sturdy mares that had short, powerful legs and wide chests. Shiloh's gelding was taller, to accommodate his height, but was still muscular. The pack horses were actually hill ponies, diminutive but so solidly built they looked almost like squares with legs. Cheney's mare was named Pudding, and Cheney found her to be very sweet-tempered and patient, though her fastest gait was an ungainly trot. Of course, these horses were perfect for climbing the airless heights of a two-mile-high mountain.

The road due south from Winslow Villa was a straight but precipitous descent, since it went down to the coast about four thousand feet. Brynn had asked Shiloh to lead. She and Cheney rode together behind him, and Walker followed, leading the two pack horses.

"I must thank you again, Miss Winslow, for providing this wonderful excursion for us," Cheney said gratefully. "It's far more than one would expect from even the most cordial of hosts."

"Not at all. I was quite sincere when I told you that going up to the crater is one of my most favorite adventures," she replied, her dark eyes shining like those of an excited child. "Bain and I went two or three times when we were younger, but now he's far too busy. I'm afraid that whenever we have guests, I bully them into saying that they'd like to go. My mother gets very out of sorts with me."

"I haven't seen much here except Hana," Cheney mused. "Are there other young people here?"

"Only Hawaiian and Chinese on the east end of Maui," Brynn told her. "My family disapproves of me forming any close friendships with them. Not so much because of their race, you understand, but because they are our employees, for the most part."

"Ah, I see. And do you, too, disapprove?" Cheney asked lightly.

Spiritedly she replied, "No, I don't. In fact, I have very close friends here. Keloki and Leilana are like family. A longtime friend is Alena Zeiss, and another is Tang Lu. You've met her, of course. The Chinese lady that runs Winslow Guest House."

"Of course," Cheney echoed faintly. It seemed peculiar to her, the young Winslow girl being close friends with the older, much more reserved Chinese woman. Then it occurred to Cheney that she didn't have any idea how old Brynn Winslow was. In the muted light of the Winslows' parlor, and then in the early predawn, Cheney had thought that she was perhaps seventeen or eighteen. But now, in the brightest of daylights, she thought that Brynn was older, perhaps twenty-one or twenty-two.

"Alena Zeiss is our overseer's wife," Brynn continued. "She's half Hawaiian and half white. We grew up together, and we've always been very close."

"But your family now accepts these friendships?" Cheney asked curiously.

A wry smile twisted Brynn's kittenish mouth. "After I turned down the only two possible suitors in Maui, and after I turned twenty-one, my mother seemed to sort of . . . shift her focus, if you will. If I am not destined to marry, and since I do love Winslow Plantation so, she's steaming full ahead on the notion that I can stay here and run the plantation myself. Under those circumstances, it's almost impossible not to develop close relationships with the people who work the plantation. Actually, once Mother got over the oddity of it, she seems to like the idea very much now."

"Yes, I see. And that certainly explains her unusual support of me and my choice of a career," Cheney commented. "But how do you feel about it?"

Brynn shrugged. "In my mind it was never a climactic decision, like giving up *this* to get *that*. I've always lived here. I've always loved to learn all I could about the plantation. It's not a career choice. To me it's simply my life."

"It does seem that it's worked out very well for your family. You can run the plantation, while it appears that your brother takes care of the shipping, the exports and imports. Much as it is now, is it not? Your mother tends to the plantation, and your father is mostly involved with Winslow Brothers Shipping?" Cheney asked politely.

"Yes, that's right." Brynn was not exactly wary; she merely appeared to be uncomfortable. "We're coming up on Bain's Stream and the lagoon."

Cheney, content to let her change the subject for now, obediently looked ahead and then gasped. "Oh, how lovely! It's your clipper, *Locke's Day Dream*, isn't it? I caught the merest glimpse of it in San Francisco."

"My brother's ship," Brynn said carefully. "*Locke's Day Dream* is his prize possession. In fact, she's his great passion."

They had reached a slight promontory, with a rocky descent to sea level across a flat shallow stream. It dashed cheerily over smoothly rounded black rocks and encircled great boulders. Bain's Stream emptied into a lovely lagoon, a crescent-shaped cutout in the land bordered by a tiny white sand beach rimmed by a tangled jungle of coconut palms. A wooden pier ran out about a hundred feet. In the exact center of the lagoon was anchored the clipper, weightless and solitary, skimming the still aquamarine water, her slender masts bare of sail.

Shiloh had stopped his horse, and Cheney drew alongside of him. He was looking down at the placid lagoon and the majestic clipper with an expression of wistfulness and longing that almost brought tears to Cheney's eyes. *He has some bond here . . . he feels a kinship here . . . he knows something of this place belongs to him. How can he bear it?*

"Shiloh . . ." she said softly.

"Hmm? Oh yeah, Doc. Lookit that. Ever seen anything so pretty?" Brynn had ridden up by Cheney, and Shiloh suddenly was guarded.

"I don't think so," Cheney said slowly. "No, I really don't think I ever have."

"It's very hazardous to negotiate *Locke's Day Dream* into the lagoon," Brynn explained with only a single curious glance at Shiloh's absorbed expression. "On this side, the northern side, the continental shelf juts out almost to the chain of rocks you see at the sea entrance. And the entire lagoon is ringed, both inside and out, by coral reefs. So there's a narrow waterway right there, to our left, with enough depth for *Locke's Day Dream*, as long as she's not heavily loaded. Bain can't bear to berth her in Lahaina. He always docks her here when he's going to be home for a few days."

"What does he do with the crew?" Shiloh asked curiously.

"If he's only here for a night or two, they stay on the ship," Brynn answered. "But if it's for more than that, Bain sends them to Lahaina on one of our merchant ships."

"How many sailors does a clipper ship ... er ... require?" Cheney asked awkwardly. She wasn't very knowledgeable of the language of the sea.

"At least fifty," Brynn answered casually, spurring her horse to start down the path. "*Locke's Day Dream* has fifty-seven. My father's clipper, *Brynn Annalea*, has fifty-two."

Cheney's eyes grew wide, and she stared at Shiloh. "Fifty-seven! Great blue heavens!"

"Yeah, that's what I say," Shiloh dryly agreed. Then with a touch of sadness he added, "That's why you don't see too many clippers, Doc. They can cut 'em down to three-masted barks, you know, and crew 'em with eighteen or twenty." With a last poignant glance at the idyllic scene below them, he followed Brynn.

They ran the horses on the little spit of beach, with Brynn leading, tossing her head and smiling. Walker, galumphing along on his sturdy brown mare and yanking fitfully on the pack ponies' leads, hurried to catch up to her. Behind, Shiloh and Cheney grinned at each other and slowed to allow Walker to catch Brynn so that he might talk to her alone for a few moments.

Cheney remarked, "Walker is so moony-eyed over Miss Winslow that he's incapable of carrying on any intelligent conversation."

"Yeah? Huh. Guess I'm so moony-eyed over you that I didn't notice," Shiloh teased.

"You've never been moony-eyed in your life," Cheney scoffed. "Much less over me."

"Thought I was."

"Well, you're not."

"Yes, I am. See?" He made Cheney look at him, and he crossed his eyes.

Cheney laughed. "You're not moony-eyed over me. You're just loony, as in lunatic, as in lunar, as in moon."

Shiloh grumbled, "Hate smart women. 'Specially when they're smarter 'n me."

"Then it looks like you wouldn't be moony-eyed over one, would you, Shiloh?" she asked with syrupy sweetness.

"Looks like," he said agreeably, "but I can't help it. It's an infirmity, sorta." He crossed his eyes again.

"Stop it!" Cheney cried, then spurred her horse. "I know you must be seeing two of me. Catch us if you can!"

"Miss Doctor Cheney Duvall," he muttered under his breath as he kicked his poor horse's fat sides vehemently, "I'm gonna catch all of you—if I can!"

On the other side of the lagoon was another stream—Brynn's Stream—which also had to be forded. It was not as wide but was much deeper than Bain's Stream. Brynn told them that this was the southern boundary of Winslow land. The trail, which indeed was nowhere near the condition of a road, ran close to the sea, although this end of the island had very few beaches. At this, the easternmost foot of Mount Haleakala, the land ended in great buttresses like giant's toes, and the surf hammered against the smooth glistening black stone. On their right, the jungle hovered over the path like a thick green curtain getting ready to fall. The path itself was of a heavy, rich reddish soil but was littered with black stones and boulders, weather-sanded and time-smoothed hardened lava.

They saw dozens of waterfalls like strings of pearls in the forests above them. They passed the first of the Seven Sacred Pools, which was in a grotto of unearthly loveliness. They rode through Kipahulu quickly, for it was a collection of exactly eight grass huts and twenty-two Hawaiians. Kaupo was even smaller. At this tiny village they turned right, sharply, and began to ascend the Kaupo Trail. It wound this way and that, struggling through the thickest and lushest vegetation imaginable, always going upward at an alarming incline. At times the path was so overgrown with vines and ferns that the horses plowed through greenery up to their knees.

At about two o'clock they stopped for a rest in a little clearing that had a trickle of a brook bubbling up from between some huge boulders. "Just ahead is the entrance to Kaupo Gap," Brynn told them. "It's a great crevice, a canyon really, that runs straight up the mountainside. It's a bit easier going—at least, I think it will be. The plants grow so fast here that it's difficult to keep the trail cleared." She got her canteen, then knelt at the little fountain. "Let me caution you—well, this is odd." Frowning, she stuck her hand all the way into the small pool that formed before the brook trickled on down the mountainside.

"What is it?" Shiloh asked alertly, coming to kneel by her.

Obviously perturbed, she answered, "It's just that this brook is actually an artesian well. Do you know what that is?"

"Sure. It's an underground stream that gets forced upward through crevices in the rock bed."

"Exactly," Brynn replied. "This is the only one we've found. All of the rest of the streams and waterfalls you see originate from rainwater catches."

"Yes," Shiloh said, puzzled. He stuck his hand down in the stream, unconsciously mimicking her, and his face changed. "This is strange."

Cheney and Walker, who were standing behind them, looked at each other in bewilderment. "Would you two mind explaining to us what you're talking about?" Cheney demanded, rather irritably.

Shiloh frowned, while Brynn felt around in the water, placing her hand here, then there. He finally replied, "It's just that artesian wells, like this one, Doc, are usually real, real cold. So cold that you can hardly drink the water until it's warmed up a little. Freezes your gullet, if you'll pardon the expression."

"And?" Cheney said, then impatiently knelt and thrust her hand into the water. "It's not cold. It's tepid."

"Yes," Brynn murmured. Cupping her hands, she brought the water up to her face.

Shiloh, concerned, muttered, "No, don't—"

"It's all right, I think," Brynn said. "It smells sweet. It's just not cold." She tasted it. "No, it's fine. I don't detect any change in the taste."

"Let me," Shiloh said, then smelled and tasted a handful for himself.

"His senses are very keen," Cheney told Brynn and was immediately uncomfortable at how proprietary she sounded.

Though Brynn's eyes flickered with faint amusement, Shiloh seemed not to notice. "Guess it's okay," he muttered. Turning to

Brynn, he asked, "Why—how would an underground spring get heated?"

"I don't know," she admitted. "All I know is that this spring is always icy, unlike the other pools and streams, which are always sun warmed."

Walker volunteered uncertainly, "Couldn't it just be some slight shift of the underlying rock bed? It's my understanding that it doesn't take much exposure to geothermal heat to warm up water. Perhaps some tiny crack has formed, and heat is seeping up to the stream bed?"

"Perhaps," Brynn mused. "It sounds logical. As a matter of fact, back in April, both Mauna Loa and Kilauea erupted, quite spectacularly. Those are the two active volcanoes on the big island, Dr. Baird. Bain said then that it might be possible that we would experience some shifting of the earth, since it appears that all of the islands are sort of chained together at the sea floor."

"Did you have earthquakes?" Cheney demanded.

Shiloh studied her, surprised at her urgency.

"Why, no," Brynn answered. "We didn't feel a thing, didn't notice, except for the clouds, of course. The eruptions formed huge dark clouds, but even they were not thick ash, merely a heavy sort of fog that cleared when it rained. But no earthquakes at all."

"Oh," Cheney said in a small voice. She was thinking of her train dreams and the vibrations that had caused them.

Still looking at her intently, Shiloh said, "Well, I think the water's all right. Probably nothing to worry about."

They watered the thirsty horses, rested for about half an hour, and then went on. "Now you see why I insisted everyone eat such a hearty breakfast!" Brynn declared. "But we'll reach *Pohaku Palaha Hale* at about four o'clock, and I promise you that Keloki and Leilana will have a sumptuous feast prepared for us."

"What was that again?" Walker asked. "Or rather, where is it we're going?"

"*Pohaku Palaha Hale*," Brynn repeated. "Straight up there"—she pointed up to the heights of Haleakala—"is a rock, a pinnacle, actually, that's been called Pohaku Palaha since bygone times. It's the central reference point, the surveyor's mark, from which royal land grants were measured. The Hawaiian kings had a remarkably sensible way to distribute real estate among the chiefs, or *alii*. They granted them land in great triangles, with their apexes on mountaintops, and their broad bases extending far out in the ocean below. The logic is that the necessities of life are to be found at each level: hardwood for weapons and tools, koa trees for canoes, land for dry farming, land for wet farming, birds for eating and birds for ornament, a portion of the sea for fishing and fun."

"How poetic!" Cheney exclaimed. "Is that true, or is that a . . . a . . . mele?"

Brynn smiled. "You're very quick, aren't you, Dr. Duvall? No. That is a truth about the kings and their alii. And the cabin we built is in a direct line from this point, the entrance to Kaupo Gap, straight up to Pohaku Palaha. *Hale* is Hawaiian for house, so it's called *Pohaku Palaha Hale*."

"And did Kamehameha—let's see, he would have been the Third, wouldn't he?—did he grant the Winslows their lands from Pohaku Palaha?" Cheney asked with genuine interest.

Brynn's animated features immediately lost all expression. In a colorless voice she replied, "I don't know, Dr. Duvall. I believe we're ready to continue, are we not?" Hastily she mounted her horse and, without looking backward, began to ascend the mountain again.

Cheney, Shiloh, and Walker exchanged puzzled looks, then mounted and hurried after her. "She certainly doesn't talk much about the family's past," Cheney said to Shiloh in a low voice.

"No, but she's not a liar either," he replied quickly.

Cheney narrowed her eyes. "How do you know?"

He shrugged. "I just do. It's easy, don't you think, to know a liar when you see one? So it's easy to know honest people too."

Cheney sighed. "Easy for you, maybe, Shiloh. But not so easy for some."

"You don't distrust her, do you?" he asked anxiously.

After a few moments of thought, Cheney shook her head. "No, it's not that, exactly . . . it's just that she does give conflicting signals. One minute she seems so open, so straightforward, so plain-speaking. The next she closes a door tight and shuts everyone out."

"Yeah, and you know what that means, don't you," Shiloh remarked.

"Well . . . no. Except that it confuses people like me."

"All it means, Doc," Shiloh said firmly, "is that there are things that she's not supposed to say. So she won't lie, but she can't . . . can't . . . oh, what's that word?"

Cheney's eyes lit up. "Prevaricate?"

"That's the one," Shiloh said, snapping his fingers. "She can't prevaricate either. So she just closes that door, and no gentleman is going to intrude on a lady when she doesn't want to talk about something."

"Shiloh?"

"Yeah?"

"You're really smart."

"Huh. I didn't know that bloomin' word."

"You're still smart. But there is one other thing you don't know."

"What's that?"

Cheney grinned. "I ain't no gentleman."

7

HIGH PLACES

"Aloha! Aloha! E kipa mai, e kipa mai . . ."
"Aloha, nani haole wahine! Aloha, Nani-Koali!"

Keloki and Leilana greeted the riders with delight as they rode into the camp of Pohaku Palaha Hale. When Shiloh and Walker dismounted, Leilana enthusiastically kissed them on both cheeks as if they were her long-lost children and put garlands around their necks. Leilana was, as true-blooded Hawaiians are, tall, about six feet, with a stately grace and dignity that enhanced, rather than parodied, her size. Her hair was down, a straight fall of ebony with not a single strand of gray, and a crimson hibiscus of dinner-plate size was tucked behind one ear. She wore a gray skirt, but her blouse was a sarong of crimson silk, cleverly wrapped and tied over one shoulder. She was barefoot.

Cheney was still watching this spectacle with awe and amusement when she was literally lifted up in the air, then floated down to earth so slowly and gently she might have been a leaf carried on the breeze. Keloki beamed down at her with a dazzling, toothy smile, placed two leis around her neck, and then kissed her soundly on both cheeks. "Aloha, nani haole wahine. E kipa mai."

Stifling a grin, Shiloh translated. "Keloki says, 'Warm greetings, beautiful white lady. Come enjoy hospitality.' "

"Aloha, sir, and I thank you," Cheney replied politely, and though it didn't seem possible, the Hawaiian's smile grew even wider.

Keloki, the giant Cheney had seen with Shiloh on the beach when the *Petrel* arrived, was even bigger than she had first perceived. He was actually only an inch or so shorter than Shiloh, which would have made him six feet three inches tall. He probably weighed four hundred pounds. But no part of him looked at all rich-fat; his girth was pure, solid muscle. He wore canvas breeches that were roomy enough for his bulk but reached only to midshin.

With the same quick grace as his wife, he moved to Brynn's horse and lifted her off bodily, enveloping her in what must have been a stifling hug, kissing her, and wreathing her with three garlands that were so luxuriant Brynn had to lift her chin or the flowers and leaves would have covered her nose. "Aloha, Kaoli," he murmured with great affection. "You're late. Leilana and me, we think maybe you fall in a *puka*, we come sing to you."

"But you wouldn't come get me out, would you? That would be *kapu*, no?" Brynn laughed. "Aloha, Keloki. Aloha, Leilana." Turning to Cheney, she took her hand in an unexpected affectionate gesture. "I think formal introductions would be superfluous, would they not? Dr. Duvall, this is Keloki and Leilana, my very good friends forever. Dr. Baird, this is Keloki; you've already met Leilana, I believe. These are my friends Dr. Cheney Duvall and Dr. Walker Baird."

The men took charge of the horses, and Leilana took charge of the women. "Come now, Koali, your face is dirty! And, Doctor, you must come wash too. Soon *pua'a pau*, we eat, no? Hungry, no?" Leilana asked hopefully.

"Hungry, yes," Brynn asserted. "And pua'a smells heavenly!"

The high cabin was on a level shelf that was generous enough to accommodate the cabin, a small clearing, and a glade that was amply shaded by four enormous ohia-lehua trees. Three of them were upright, hundreds of feet high, but with low branches that were themselves as big as the trunks of young trees. The other was tilted at a fantastic angle by the wind, its enormous roots partially exposed, but it appeared to still be alive, as its branches that were propped upon the ground had hundreds of the scarlet pompon blooms. Walker, Shiloh, and Keloki tied the horses to a branch of the downed tree, then began unsaddling them and unloading the pack ponies. They were at about six thousand feet altitude, and though the humans hadn't noticed any ill effects, the horses had labored hard in the stringent air.

Leilana hustled them into the cabin, fussing at Brynn—whom she called Koali, Hawaiian for "morning glory"—for her disarray in a manner that reminded Cheney much of Nia and her sister Rissy and their mother, Dally. They all treated Cheney much like she was a newborn chicken, and Leilana hovered over Brynn Winslow in much the same way. In fact, she did some clucking over Cheney too.

"Pretty dress, Doctor, but you're going to be cold," she scolded, putting her arms around herself and shivering to stress the point. "I'll get more wood. Haole wahines need hot fires all night. You wash," she commanded sternly, then sailed imperially out of the cabin.

It could actually have been two cabins, for the Winslows had built it to accommodate both male and female guests. A simple rectangular building made of the durable ohia lehua wood, it had two entry doors, for a wall ran down the exact center of the building to divide it. On each side there was a black stone fireplace. Windows, which were merely holes cut in the front and back walls, had tight-fitting shutters but no glass. The dirt floor was covered with a woven straw mat. Along the back wall was a large table, simply built of the dark red, handsomely grained ohia wood. There were no chairs and no beds, but by the table were cotton quilts and wool blankets folded neatly, stacked in two piles. A plank had been mounted along the wall by the door; iron pots, an assortment of earthenware dishes and cups, and utensils and flatware were piled on it. In spite of its roughness, the cabin was clean—no spiderwebs in the corners, no dust on the table, no specks on the floor mat. On the table was a steaming pot of water, perfumed with chips of sandalwood.

Gladly Cheney stripped off her jacket, rolled up her sleeves, and bathed her face and arms in the welcome warmth. "Keloki and Leilana are the first Hawaiians I've met," she told Brynn. "They're very effusive, aren't they?"

Brynn, who was washing up, too, laughed. "Hawaiians are 'very' a lot of things, Dr. Duvall. They can be as solemn and dignified as archbishops, and as playful and carefree as three-year-olds. They can work like a team of oxen, and they can procrastinate with more slyness than a cat. They love all children without stint. They hate waste and spoil. They are artists and dreamers, and they are also shrewd and efficient craftsmen. They can think all day long about how to phrase a line for a mele, but they cannot understand the simplest techniques for striking a good bargain. They're terrible businessmen because they are so generous. If a friend is somehow hurt, they will mourn with you and for you as genuinely as if you are their only family. When Alena Zeiss lost her baby last year, I saw Keloki cry great tears and fall to his knees and throw dust over his head. He was inconsolable for days, because Alena was so sad."

"Because they love children so much?" Cheney asked curiously.

"No, no, at least not just that. It's because Keloki and Leilana love Alena so much. She's not their daughter, but Hawaiians truly seem to easily almost adopt each other's children. Alena has been a part of Keloki and Leilana's family all her life, has been in their household almost as much as their own children. I've never quite understood Alena's parentage, who her mother and father are. Hawaiians are kind of vague about that sort of thing. All I know is that her mother lived in Kipahulu and is a kinswoman of Keloki's. It's interesting, because Hawaiians have a word for 'child'—*keiki*—but they have no words to denote 'son' or 'daughter.' In fact, an eighteen-year-old girl named Malani lives with them now, and she's lived with them as their daughter as long as I can remember. But she's not their daughter." Brynn shrugged. "I don't know who she is, but to Keloki and Leilana, she's just their keiki."

"They seem very attached to you, too, Miss Winslow."

"Oh yes, they are. Keloki has been with the Winslows since he was a child. He was a cabin boy, once, on a Winslow ship. . . ." Her voice trailed off, and her face took on that careful closed expession. "Are you ready, Dr. Duvall? I'm sure that dinner is ready."

"Mmm, yes! I'm positively ravenous." Cheney was truly hungry; she had a vigorous appetite, anyway, and the smell of spicy roasted meat filling the camp had made her conscious of how very hollow her stomach was. The two women went back outside.

Leilana was unrolling another woven mat underneath the ohia trees. The men were on the other side of the great fallen tree, talking. The fragrant smoke was coming from where they were standing.

Brynn was watching Cheney warily, and Cheney finally understood that Brynn still wasn't quite sure how Cheney would receive such rusticity. Cheney smiled and started to say something, but at that moment Shiloh called out, "Hey, Doc! C'mere, you gotta see this!"

"I'd like to see what's going on over there," Cheney said to Brynn, who looked a little surprised at Shiloh's informality and also relieved at Cheney's words. "I'm so interested in everything here—the flora, the fauna, the weather, the history, the legends—but mostly the food! And I believe that delicious aroma is coming from the men's vicinity."

Brynn giggled. "Then by all means let's go hurry them up, shall we?"

They went to where the men stood, which entailed climbing over the half-fallen tree. Both women handled it with athletic grace, which was fortunate, since the men were having such a lively discussion they didn't notice that the ladies might need assistance.

"Keloki and Leilana have done us an *aha'aina*, Doc," Shiloh said, pointing to a smoking hole in the ground, covered with big leaves. "A great feast. I knew you'd wanta know all about this. You wanta know about everything."

"Not everything," Cheney argued, then relented, "well, perhaps most things. What's this?" Unselfconsciously she bent over the pit, then knelt by it. Shiloh went down on one knee close beside her, and Keloki squatted by them.

"*Imu*, Doctor," Keloki said, pointing down in the hole. "For pua'a and sweet potatoes."

"Yesterday Keloki dug this fire pit, and—hey, Keloki, did you get this boar up here?" Shiloh asked.

A shadow crossed Keloki's jolly features. "Yah, over there," he replied, waving vaguely. "But not boar, wahine pua'a."

"So he killed this wild pig yesterday," Shiloh went on explaining to Cheney. "Leilana built a fire in the pit and heated a bunch of rocks. Keloki skinned out and cleaned the sow, and then they stuffed the carcass with a bunch of the hot rocks and put it down in this pit. They had wire baskets of sweet potatoes and put them down in there too. They seal the imu with layers of wet ti and banana leaves and *lu'au*, the tender young leaves of the taro plant. Then they put canvas and earth over it all and let 'em cook all night and today."

"Keloki, it sounds—and smells—absolutely delicious," Cheney told him enthusiastically. "When can we eat?"

Keloki laughed out loud. "Haole wahine doctor eats good, is good," he roared. "Why you *nani*, Doctor, not look like dead *hinalea*, like some wahine."

"Uh . . . he said you're beautiful, Doc," Shiloh said quickly. " 'Nani' means beautiful, lovely."

"How do you say thank you?" Cheney asked, her eyes twinkling.

" '*Mahalo*,' " Shiloh told her.

"Mahalo, Keloki," she said, rising.

He nodded, then got busy shoveling out the dirt from on top of the imu, and Walker and Shiloh pitched in. Cheney turned to Brynn, who was watching her with her arms crossed and a smile playing at her lips.

"You're a very unusual woman, Dr. Duvall," Brynn said, leading her back toward the camp. "Some women who have come on this excursion haven't been nearly as enthusiastic as you appear to be."

"It's not an appearance. I really am enjoying myself immensely," Cheney assured her.

"I'm so glad," she said, then soberly she added, "and I'm so glad you're here. It's wonderful, and very unusual, to be able to share this with another woman who . . . who . . . likes it."

"You must be lonely sometimes," Cheney said softly.

"Sometimes," Brynn agreed. "But not often. Now let's go beg Leilana for some tidbits to keep us from swooning until the men get the main course ready!"

They went back to Leilana, who was spreading enough food on the mat, it seemed to Cheney, for the entire village of Hana. Brynn and Cheney sat on the ground on the edge of the mat and snacked on *opihi*, limpets with an understated salty taste that were a delicacy of the islands. In a few minutes the men came to the spread with great chunks of smoked pork so tender they fell to pieces on the carved wooden platter.

The sweet potatoes had a burnt sugar taste Cheney found utterly delicious; she ate three of them. They also had boiled *muhe'e*, or cuttlefish, and salted salmon sprinkled with onions and kneaded to a soft, crumbly texture by a technique called *lomilomi*. Keloki had prepared a delicate bonefish, called *o'io*, which was marinated in guava and mango juices and then smoked. They had mounds of opihi, an assortment of mangoes, avocados, fresh coconut chunks, candied ginger, macadamia and kukui nuts. Leilana had also brought *poi*, three types of different consistencies. Leilana, Keloki, and Brynn ate enthusiastically, dipping two fingers into small wooden bowls of the purplish substance.

"I want to try some," Cheney announced. "I wouldn't dream of coming to Hawaii and not trying poi."

"It's an acquired taste," Brynn warned her. "I've grown up with it, and I like it even better than potatoes or rice. But it's different from the dishes you're accustomed to."

"Still, I'd like to try," Cheney insisted.

"Me too," Walker joined in. "I've heard that poi is the magical cure-all, the perfect food."

"All right," Brynn said, smiling. "May I suggest you try this, the thickest mix? And I must tell you that Leilana makes the most delicious poi on Maui. Perhaps in the entire islands. This is the best of the best."

Gamely Cheney held the small wooden bowl up close to her mouth, as she had seen Brynn do, dipped two fingers in the paste, and brought it up to her mouth before it dripped. She rolled the substance around in her mouth, concentrating on the taste and texture. It had a delicate, wholesome taste and was about the consistency of thick gravy. She tried another mouthful, and another. "It's such a subtle flavor," she remarked. "Other things overpower it, don't they? I suspect one would appreciate it more just by itself. And I can see that it's such a substantial food, it would make a meal."

"Very astute of you, Dr. Duvall," Brynn said. "Most Hawaiians do enjoy poi alone, much as we sometimes eat only soup. But once you get a taste for it, you can enjoy it as a side dish too. How about you, Dr. Baird? Please help yourself. There's plenty."

"Er . . . interesting food," Walker said, his cheeks coloring. His mouth, obviously against his will, was puckering. Although poi was in no way sour tasting, the starchy consistency did make some people's mouths rebel.

Everyone laughed. "Don't worry, Dr. Baird," Brynn told him. "As I said, most haoles don't care for poi. Not to worry, though. Keloki and Leilana may not comprehend how it is that you can't taste the delights of it, but they would never be offended if you don't like it."

"Thank goodness," Walker muttered, setting his bowl down hard. "I was considering pouring it into my handkerchief when no one was looking."

"Shiloh, do you like it?" Cheney asked him. He had eaten a small bowl of it.

"Yeah, I do. It's just that I like pua'a a lot better."

Keloki pointed to the platter of still steaming meat. "You eat, Keakea! You skinny, like papala spear! Need big, big arms and neck and stomach for lua."

"Little late for that," Shiloh grunted, reclining back on one arm and propping the other on an upraised knee. "Mr. Winslow's gone to Lahaina to arrange that fight for next week, Keloki. No time to get big, big."

"Shiloh, what are you going to do about that?" Cheney demanded.

He shrugged. "Practice ducking, I guess."

"Excuse me, please," Brynn interposed. "Are you saying that my brother is arranging a lua match for you? With whom?"

"Fellow named Meholo," Shiloh answered, watching her.

She frowned. "Are you practiced in the art of lua, Mr. Irons?"

"Nah," he replied carelessly. "But I'm practiced in the art of run-nin'."

"Don't listen to him," Walker said stoutly. "He's a courageous and skilled pugilist, and he's tough. He's called 'The Iron Man.'"

"But that doesn't matter in lua," Brynn argued. "Have you ever even seen a lua match, Mr. Irons?"

"No, ma'am. Keloki was trying to show me some of the holds, but all I ever saw were my feet going up over my head. Then some stars going around in circles." He grinned engagingly.

"Yes, and I'm certain that Keloki was merely playing with you, Mr. Irons," Brynn said, refusing to joke with him. "I would recommend that you don't try lua, no matter how expert a pugilist you are. Particularly not with Meholo. He's not a bad man, but he's rather brutal. He's like ... like ... a big child who plays too roughly with a kitten. And I'm afraid, Mr. Irons, that Meholo would make you look like a kitten. He's truly a giant. And he's been practicing lua ever since he was very young."

"Listen to her, Keakea," Leilana said disdainfully. "You, too, little fish. Meholo throw you back."

Shiloh merely shrugged. "I'm not too crazy about the idea myself. But it's kind of an obligation." He looked up at the sky in a dismissive gesture. "It's going to be dark soon. You ladies want a campfire outside? Or does everyone want to retire?"

No one was quite ready to go to bed, though everyone was as tired as they'd ever been. Still, Cheney and Brynn helped Leilana wrap the leftover food in washed ti leaves and store it in the cabin, while the men gathered stones for a fire pit and firewood. Soon they had a cheerful blaze, and Shiloh threw on showers of sandalwood chips that heavily scented the air.

Dark came suddenly, with no warning, as the sun disappeared behind the great bulk of Haleakala looming high above them. Cheney and Brynn and Leilana wrapped themselves in woolen blankets and sat as close to the fire as they dared. Shiloh sat by Cheney, holding a dried sandalwood branch and peeling chips off it with his Bowie knife. With great care he picked up every single fragment, no matter how small, and stored it in a leather pouch.

Brynn motioned Walker to sit beside her, to his surprise and delight. The two talked together in low tones. Leilana wrapped her arms around her knees and stared into the fire, humming a song to herself softly. A little apart from them, Keloki stood, his great arms crossed across his chest, searching the black depths of the jungle, frowning.

Cheney stared, mesmerized by the heady fragrance of the sandalwood, the silence of the night, the sparks that seemed to be tiny beings of light trying to fly to heaven. It had grown so cold that their breath made steam when they spoke.

"It's so quiet," she whispered. "No sounds of night creatures, no breeze stirring. There are no crickets here, are there?"

"Don't think so," Shiloh answered. "I haven't heard or seen any. There's great big toads, but they don't seem to call at night like they do in the South. I doubt that there are any up this high, though. They'd freeze. We're even up too high for mosquitos."

"I'd noticed that," Cheney murmured, her mind obviously on other things. "But they weren't very bad, even farther down. . . . Shiloh, please don't fight that man!" Now she turned to him, pleading.

He smiled a little, then laid down his knife to reach out and pluck one of her hands loose from the blanket. "Your hands are cold. Here, let me warm them." Obediently she held them out. He brought them to his face, breathed onto them, then enveloped them in his rough fight- and work-scarred hands and rubbed them softly. "Don't worry, Doc. I'm not worried. Couldn't even if I tried."

"But you should be!" She snatched her hands back and pulled the blanket tightly around herself. "It's just . . . just . . . so dangerous and . . . silly!"

"You don't understand," he said with unusual gentleness and soberness. "The reason I'm not worried is 'cause I don't think it'll ever happen."

"What . . . what do you mean?"

He seemed perplexed. "Can't explain it, but I just can't get myself too worked up about it. I just don't think it's going to happen, Doc. In my mind, it's sorta like . . . there's an unreality about it, I guess is the best way I can say it. It's just not going to happen."

"Shiloh, are you seriously saying you think that if you don't concern yourself about it, it'll just go away?" Cheney demanded with disdain. "That's not like you. That's childish."

"No. You still aren't getting me, Doc," he said with exasperation. "I can't say I'm a hundred percent sure, but I just kinda know that I'm not going to have to wrangle with that giant. Something else is going to happen. Something's going to change."

Now Cheney was astonished. "You . . . you mean you have a premonition? And you have such faith in it that you know you won't be fighting Meholo?"

"Kinda like that. No, not exactly like that." Shiloh was growing impatient, not with Cheney, but with his inability to articulate his instincts. She was silent, waiting, as he struggled. Finally he went on with a hint of exasperation, "No, it's not like I'm seeing the future, Doc. Nothing like that. It's just a feeling I've got. And maybe . . . maybe it's something I sense from Bain. I think maybe he's got something else planned for me. But listen, can we talk about something else?" He reached up and adjusted the blanket Cheney was hugging closely. "You warm enough, Doc?"

"Yes, I'm fine, thank you. Isn't Keloki cold? He's not even wearing a shirt, and he's barefoot. And what's he doing? Do we need to keep a watch?"

"No, there aren't any predators, exactly," Shiloh answered. "Nothing like wolves or mountain lions on these islands. The wild pigs are pretty ill tempered, and one of them can make a big mess of you if he gets it in his head to. But they don't just attack people, and especially a camp, for no reason. No, Keloki's just . . . worried."

"About what?"

Shiloh frowned as he glanced at the big man who stood so still, so darkly, at the edge of their camp. "I don't understand all about it, but he told me that he killed that pig, and then was going to skin it out right there, so as not to have the mess in the camp. He was working on it and discovered that he was in a *heiau*. That's like a sacred place, a temple, only the Hawaiians just used to lay big stones to make sort of a walk-on altar, like. There's lots of them around here in the high places, and they've all gotten grown up so much that they're hard to find. So there Keloki was, and he'd killed that wild pig right there in the heiau. Seems like that's a big *kapu*. Taboo, you know."

"We're not . . . on it, or anything, are we?" Cheney asked, glancing around.

"No, it's over there somewhere. I don't know how far. But Keloki, I think he thinks the *po kane*, the Marchers of the Night, might come charging over here and carry him off to the underworld. To punish him for defiling a heiau." Shiloh spoke without a hint of sarcasm or levity.

"That's sad," Cheney said quietly. "I hate to think of such a gentle man living with that kind of fear."

He glanced at her. "You're such a religious person, I kinda thought you might sneer at it. But no, I know you better than that, Doc. You'd never do something ugly like that. You're too good."

She laughed. "You are talking to me, right? I'm not good, Shiloh. Or, if you see good in me, it's just the Lord Jesus Christ, His Spirit in me that you see. Anyway, I am sorry for Keloki. Is there anything we could do to . . . to . . . help him?"

Shiloh smiled at her, then caressed a curl lightly, his eyes on her hair. By the flickering flames it appeared to be made of molten ebony and copper mixed into a thick river that intertwined but never combined. "I'll watch with him, because he's my friend. And I'll watch for him too."

"Then I know," Cheney said softly, her eyes like dark stars, "that no harm will come to him."

He watched her, and his face was intent, brooding. Before he could speak, Cheney went on hurriedly, "I think it's time for me to go to bed. I'm practically talking in my sleep. Good night, Shiloh, dear."

"Good night, Cheney. I'll always watch with you and for you too," he whispered. But she had already risen and was gone.

★　★　★　★

Cheney slept hard, heavily, unmoving, on a pallet in front of a dying fire. Brynn and Leilana, on thick pallets next to her, also slept soundly. The night was completely silent. Though they didn't see, a ghostly gray mist floated in, creeping under the doors, inching through tiny cracks in the shutters, trickling in through chinks in the wall. As it wandered closer to the fire, it dissipated; but still more and more of the thin wraith's-breath crept inside.

Outside, the stars were suddenly blanked, as if a black shade had been pulled over the sky. Far below, there was a rumble, a grumble, but it was so remote that not even Shiloh, who slept as lightly as a cat, stirred.

Like a stalking lion, the faint roar sounded again, closer, higher up the slopes of Mount Haleakala. Cheney's brain didn't begin the complicated process of awakening from a deep sleep, but her mind did start sending warning signals to her in the form of a dream. She thought, once again, of a train . . . then she saw the flat fields and distant hillocks and the weary sun . . . then she heard the train. But now, in this dream, she was standing, not sitting . . . and she wasn't on the train. In the dream Cheney looked down. She was standing on the railroad track, looking stupidly at her feet, which were primly poised on a crosstie.

Train's coming, the dream-Cheney told herself. *Train's near. Train is coming.* But the thought, the concept, the imperative, was murky, fuzzy, as if she were pronouncing words in a foreign language and didn't know what the words actually meant.

She awoke all at once, her eyes wide, her mind clear.

The noise sounded as if the heavens were made of an iron pot filled with steel shot, and God was shaking it. It was continuous, a seamless tumult. It was an earthquake.

Cheney saw Brynn sit up. Leilana jumped up with a ballerina's grace and shouted something, but the din was so high, filling their ears and their minds, that Cheney didn't even know if she'd heard the woman or not. Then Leilana grabbed Brynn as if she were a little china doll, lifted her up in her arms, and ran out the door. Crockery on the narrow shelf jittered, then crashed to the floor, some breaking, some bouncing. Cheney fully intended to get up and run, but the world shuddering made her knees rubbery, and she sat down in an awkward heap, biting her tongue savagely.

Suddenly she was lifted, almost thrown into the air, then gripped hard by arms like vises. Shiloh held her, and Cheney buried her face in his chest and grasped him around the waist. In two great strides he was outside. Gathering her senses, Cheney stiffened in his arms so that he would put her down. "Should we run?" she screamed right next to his ear.

"To where?" he shouted back.

They stood together, staggering, searching desperately around them. The night was so dark, the sky so black, that they could see absolutely nothing. Shiloh had one iron arm around Cheney's waist, and he held her so tightly that she would have bruises on her side the next day. But at that moment, she was aware of nothing except the terrifying clamor and Shiloh's grim face, a blur in the darkness.

And then it was over.

The silence was numbing.

And the mists began creeping back.

8

FRAME OF REFERENCE

Shiloh was the first one to come out of the shock that had paralyzed them all.

"Keloki!" he called harshly. "Go see about the fires in the cabins!" He barely glanced at Cheney, who still clung to him, but asked, "You okay?"

She nodded, not trusting her voice.

"Then go make sure Brynn and Leilana are okay." Gently he disentangled himself from her clasp.

Gradually Cheney's glazed eyes focused. "Yes, of course," she said and went to where the two women stood, holding each other tightly. Walker was already there, anxiously asking questions and hovering over Brynn.

Shiloh hurried into the men's side of the cabin, saw Keloki beating out a few sparks on the mat, and grabbed a lantern. Lighting it, he hurried back outside and ran to the ohia trees, where they'd loosely tethered the horses. When he reached them, he muttered an oath under his breath. His gelding was gone, and both of the pack ponies had gotten loose. He heard crashing and wheezing nearby, but it was so dark he couldn't see a thing outside the circle of harsh lantern light. He hurried back to the cabin.

"Keloki! Walker! Three of the horses are loose!" The men ran to the cabin to get dressed, for none of them had on a shirt or shoes. Shiloh paused in the doorway and looked at the women huddled close together in the clearing. "Get inside and get warm, ladies," he said curtly. "We're going to have to find those horses or they'll break their fool necks." He disappeared inside.

Cheney and Brynn looked at each other blankly, but Leilana was galvanized. "Get in, go on," she scolded. "Haole wahines like *akua* anyway, got blood like spring water!" Grabbing both the women's upper arms, she practically hauled them bodily into the cabin. Both of them were, indeed, freezing, as they had brought along cotton nightdresses to sleep in and were barefoot.

"What's an akua?" Cheney asked Brynn with weak amusement.

Brynn looked at her blankly, her eyes still showing little whites of panic. Then she took a deep breath and tried to smile. "It's . . . ghosts. Spirits. I've never seen an akua personally, but Hawaiians swear we look like them. They must be . . . um . . . pale."

"Look out!" Cheney cried, grabbing both Leilana and Brynn and pulling them back. "The dishes fell. Don't step on the shards." The cabin was grimly shadowed, for the fire had almost gone out, and Cheney was guessing where the broken dishes were rather than seeing them.

"I'll clean," Leilana ordered. "You dress." She went to the table, lit a lantern, and scowled when she saw the sharp litter on the floor. Cheney and Brynn picked their way carefully to the far wall by the fireplace. Leilana had brushed and spot-cleaned their clothes and hung them up on pegs in the wall.

Cheney frantically began pulling on her chemise, her pantaloons, her petticoat. When she tied her petticoat tight at the waist, she snapped one of the ribbons and muttered darkly to herself "*Malediction!* Now what am I going to do?" Fumbling, she hurriedly tied the shortened ribbon into a rude knot. "Now I'll have to cut the stupid thing to get it off . . . Nia's going to scold me. . . ."

"You're in a terrible hurry," Brynn remarked as she fastened her own underskirts with deliberation.

"I'm going with them," Cheney declared. "I've got to hurry."

Brynn regarded her gravely, but Cheney was still fiddling with the fastenings of her petticoat. "Dr. Duvall, I don't think you should," she said quietly.

"Well, I don't think you have much to say about it, do you, Miss Winslow?" Cheney snapped. Then her hands faltered, and slowly she lifted her head. "I'm . . . I'm terribly sorry. Please forgive me. It's just that when I . . . when I . . ."

Brynn's finely shaped eyebrow lifted, and for the first time Cheney saw a resemblance to her brother.

"When you get scared you get rude?" Brynn suggested, but it was with gentle humor.

Cheney stared rebelliously at her for a moment but then smiled weakly. "As a matter of fact, I do. Of course, it's not the only excuse I use for being rude. I have dozens of excuses. Good ones."

Brynn took down her riding skirt and settled it over her head. She missed the opening, burying herself, and Cheney stepped forward to help her.

"Anyway, why shouldn't I go help them look for the horses?" Cheney insisted. "I'm perfectly capable of taking care of myself."

"I noticed," Brynn said breathlessly after her head popped out of the yards of brown velvet. "But you know men, Dr. Duvall. If you're out there blundering about, they'll all be following you around, watching you, instead of looking for my poor horses."

"Ah, so you're really more worried about the horses," Cheney said dryly. "It would inconvenience the hunt if I went."

"Well . . ." Brynn said reluctantly, giving Cheney a mischievous glance from under her lashes. "I do love my horses so. In fact, I'm positively maudlin about animals. But, too, horses are extremely valuable luxuries here, Dr. Duvall. There are no great breeding ranches in Hawaii. Most all of the horses must be imported, and that is a difficult, dangerous, and expensive undertaking. They're very hard to replace. I should have taken better care to see they were tethered properly, but I didn't know . . . I just didn't know . . . we were going to . . . going to . . . have an . . ."

She was staring at Cheney blankly, and Cheney saw her face drain of all color and her eyes go flat and sightless. Cheney caught her underneath her arms just as she melted to the floor.

"Leilana, get me my medical bag," Cheney crisply ordered. "Yes, the black bag on the table. Thank you. Get behind her, hold her up a little . . . that's right." Cheney opened her bag, reached in, without fumbling pulled out a tiny bottle, uncorked it, and thrust it under Brynn's nose.

For a moment Brynn remained motionless, and Leilana whispered, "Auwe . . ."

Then Brynn's eyes fluttered. Weakly she turned her head away and coughed. "I fainted," she said.

"I noticed," Cheney replied. "No, don't get up, just wait a moment." She went to the pile of unused blankets, pulled three of them, and arranged them with pillows to make a sort of chairback, then helped Brynn get situated sitting up on the pallet. "Leilana, get the fire stoked and start some hot water. Do we have coffee or tea? Good. We could all use something hot to drink. Do you know if the men have any whisky?"

"Keloki has okolehao," Leilana answered. She was still anxiously fussing over Brynn, covering her up to the chin with blankets and tucking them in all around her like swaddling clothes.

"Go ahead and stoke the fire, Leilana. Put on some water and go fetch the okolehao," Cheney repeated firmly. "I'm a doctor. I'll take care of her."

"I don't want okolehao," Brynn said wanly. "It's rich and sweet, and it makes you silly."

"Sweet is good," Cheney said with finality. "Doctor's orders. Just enough in coffee to warm you and get your blood flowing again. You look like an akua now, for certain."

"I feel like one . . . how embarrassing."

Cheney shrugged, then went to finish dressing. Though her navy-blue riding habit was really too heavy for what was supposed to be summer wear, she had been very grateful for it on this adventure. The upper reaches of Haleakala were bitter cold.

"You shouldn't be," she told Brynn matter-of-factly. "People react in different ways to great trauma or stress. I'm rude. You faint."

Brynn laughed. It was weak, but it was genuine. "I think a more accurate analysis would be that you, Doctor, stay calm and tightly controlled, while I have the vapors like most weak and silly women."

Cheney sat down on the pallet, close to Brynn, and pulled on her Wellington boots. They were boy's boots, well fitted for her, but, as did most men, Cheney had difficulty pulling them on because of the tight uppers. "I would imagine that I've had more experience in trauma situations than you have, Miss Winslow," she said between small grunts. "But still, I haven't always been quite so calm in a crisis as you think. A lot of it comes with experience, and still it appears that I'm not completely in control, as you say, because then I wouldn't snap at people and be so impatient. That's just one way I have of dealing with stress, and it's a fault that I obviously haven't yet overcome."

"You will," Brynn said mildly. "I'm sure that you haven't always recovered so quickly and realized your mistake, as you did with me just now."

"True," Cheney agreed. "I've learned a lot from Shiloh. He's always calm and level-headed in every situation. And we've been through some difficult times—some frightening, some exhausting, some stressful, even some very dangerous. But I must say, this is the first time I've ever experienced anything like this—an earthquake."

"Me too," Brynn said in a low voice. "I couldn't think, couldn't move. It was just . . . sheer panic. Terror."

"That was the most . . . helpless, most—" Cheney broke off, frustrated, and also because Brynn was looking pale and sickly again. In a businesslike manner she picked up Brynn's limp hand and began to take her pulse. Cheney wasn't wearing a watch, so she couldn't actually time it, but she could feel that it was steady, though weak. As she spoke, she watched Brynn's respirations and saw that she was breathing regularly, but not deeply. "So I assume that earthquakes are not common on Maui. That's kind of comforting to know. This volcano, I thought, was extinct. It seems . . . feels ancient and quiet."

"It is," Brynn said, her voice growing stronger. "It hasn't erupted since 1790. It sleeps. I think the earthquake was just a . . . just a . . . shift, a settling."

"Probably," Cheney agreed thoughtfully. "Though I must say it was terrifying, now that I think about it. It must not have been as bad as some. I believe some earthquakes actually bring down structures and open great rifts in the earth, don't they? If you recall, it was just more of a . . . shivering, instead of great jarring."

"Yes, that's true," Brynn said with relief. "I believe you're right. I've read of earthquakes where people couldn't stand and houses came down. Perhaps this was just a little settling of this old mountain, much as you can hear houses settle in the night . . . creaks and groans. . . ."

"Feeling better?" Cheney asked. Brynn was brightening up in that intangible way healthy people have when recovering from a sudden shock.

"Yes. Yes, much, thank you."

Leilana, who had been hauling in firewood and stoking the fire and watching and listening closely, set a bottle down on the table and nodded to Cheney. "Men's hale is messy. I clean," she announced with disgust. "You need me, Koali?"

"No, no, Leilana. I feel like myself again," Brynn answered. Leilana glided out the door, scowling and muttering.

Cheney rose and went to inspect the supplies Leilana had brought in. "Now, let me see to this coffee, and oh! this smells invigorating," Cheney said, uncorking the dark green bottle that Leilana had set on the table and sniffing it. Picking up the coffeepot, she stared at it helplessly. "Let's see, I guess I'll try . . . um . . . well, maybe a spoonful for each cup? How many cups are in this pot? Does it say somewhere . . . maybe on the bottom . . ." Cheney upended the blue speckled coffee-pot and squinted at the bottom of it.

Brynn giggled, then pulled aside her covers and rose. "No, no, Dr. Duvall. You just put about six small spoonfuls of coffee in here. This makes twelve cups."

"I can do this," Cheney argued. "You go finish getting dressed, if you feel like it. You're not dizzy? No nausea?"

"No, I'm fine now. Just a little weak-kneed, but I'm sure I'll be all right." Brynn went to finish dressing, watching Cheney as she put the coffee in the pot, filled it with hot water from the kettle that hung over the fire, and then set the pot on a rack just above the coals at the front of the grate. "You're a good physician, Dr. Duvall," Brynn said quietly. "It's reassuring to a person, because you seem very competent. And knowledgeable."

Raking more coals underneath the coffeepot rack, Cheney's face glowed from the heat of the hungry flames. She smiled. "Oh yes, I certainly am an expert diagnostician. Every time someone closes their eyes and falls to the floor, I immediately know that they've fainted. It's one of my specialties."

Brynn giggled, and Cheney stole an assessing look at her. She was looking much better, with the normal pink returning to her cheeks and her eyes sparkling.

Brynn continued, "I've never known a physician with a sense of humor. Most of them are dire. Of course, I've only met two doctors in my life."

"Walker's a doctor," Cheney said casually. "And he's a lot of fun."

Brynn blushed and ducked her head but said nothing.

When she finished dressing, Cheney handed her a steaming mug of coffee with just a few drops of the strong rumlike concoction in it. "Here, drink this, Miss Winslow. I know you feel better, but it is cold and dreary and I think you need it."

Obediently Brynn sipped the coffee. "It really is good. I was just being petulant before. People who don't feel well get fussy like that. But I suppose you know that very well."

Cheney didn't answer; she was studying Brynn Winslow in a cal-culating manner. Brynn met her eyes directly—a sort of challenge, or signal, that she knew what was coming.

"You're an honest and straightforward woman, I think," Cheney said evenly. "May I ask you a question?"

"Yes," she replied shortly.

"Do you know anything about Shiloh's family?"

"No."

Cheney and Brynn stared at each other. Brynn didn't waver, didn't drop her eyes, didn't give any telltale signs that she was lying. Cheney tried another approach. "I don't believe he's had an opportunity to tell you his story. It's difficult to believe that we've been completely mistaken about his past. All of the clues we've been able to uncover about him have led us here . . . to Hana. To the Winslows."

Brynn didn't hesitate. "Now may I ask you a series of questions, Dr. Duvall?"

It was only fair. "Yes," Cheney said.

"I recollect that you spoke very highly of your mother and father and of an adopted ward, a man named Buchanan."

"Yes, he's very like a brother to me." Cheney was mystified at the turn the conversation was taking.

Brynn persisted, "But you have no brothers or sisters?"

"No, I'm an only child."

"Your parents, they support you, love you—I believe you said yesterday that they 'inspired' you in your chosen profession?"

"Yes. They are wonderful, admirable people, and we are very close."

Brynn sighed and regarded Cheney with something akin to sympathy. When she spoke, her words were very gentle. "And if a stranger came into your life and implied to you that your parents, and your adopted brother, were involved in something . . . questionable, perhaps even dishonorable . . . how would you react, Dr. Duvall?"

Cheney was stunned for a moment, but as Brynn Winslow had observed, Dr. Cheney Duvall could indeed recover from shocks quickly. She grinned engagingly. "In that situation, Miss Winslow, I would tell this rude stranger to take a flying leap off the top of Haleakala and take his nosy and disrespectful questions and implications with him."

Brynn smiled back at her with something akin to gratitude.

Cheney asked her no more questions.

★ ★ ★ ★

The men returned shortly after dawn with the three horses. Cheney had thought they would be frozen, but instead they were hot from exertion and dirty from fighting their way through dense jungle. All they wanted was water, lots of it.

"They didn't go far," Shiloh said grumpily, "but they all three made sure they got into the thickest underbrush they could find. Thistle—that littlest pack pony—was tangled in *ieie* vines up to his ears. He was eating the flowers and having a really good time."

Keloki held up his dirty machete and regarded it with disgust. "Ieie vines, you cut them, they just grow longer."

"Does seem like it," Walker added, pouring some water in his hands and rubbing his face. "At one time I swore some of those blasted vines were trying to tie me up and kidnap me."

"Mmm, surely not," Brynn scoffed. "Hawaiian plants are gentle and loving. They have no thorns, no poisons, no evil smells." Stepping close to him, she reached up and gently wiped a smudge from his chin. Walker grinned like an idiot schoolboy.

Shiloh looked up at the gray-blue sky, a small patch barely glimpsed through the tree roof overhead. "Guess we better get saddled up and head back to the villa."

"I'm disappointed that we won't get to see the crater," Walker said, still staring at Brynn in a soggily smitten way. "But after what we've been through, I suppose . . ."

"Yes, since Brynn—" Cheney began, but Brynn suddenly shot her a warning glance, and Cheney coughed awkwardly before continuing, "—er . . . is worried about her mother, I suppose we'd better get back. That is, I know Mrs. Winslow will be worried about us. About you, Brynn."

"Yes, she will, but I still want to go up to the crater," Brynn said stubbornly, with a quick sly glance at Walker. "It's such a shame to take an entire day to come this far and not go on up to the summit. It's very close, you know." She turned to Leilana and Keloki. "Why don't you two go on back to the villa and let Mother know that we're fine? You could get there before we could, even if we left now." She told Walker and Cheney, "They know a footpath that leads north, then down to the villa. That's how you came the first time, isn't it, Mr. Irons? And that's how Keloki and Leilana got here. It's a hard walk, but Keloki and Leilana don't seem to mind. Do you?"

Keloki frowned, and Leilana looked troubled. "But, Koali, you—" she began.

"I'm fine," Brynn interrupted quickly. "And you two were going on back this morning anyway, weren't you? You didn't want to go up to the crater, did you? No, of course you didn't. So it's settled."

Shiloh was watching her, listening to everyone, and giving Cheney suspicious looks. "What does the doctor say, Miss Winslow?" he asked softly.

Brynn was startled by his perception and looked at him guiltily, but Shiloh was watching Cheney.

She shrugged. Shiloh's uncanny instincts were no surprise to her anymore. "We all had a bad scare, but I think we're all right. What about the horses?"

"They're fine," Shiloh rasped. "They had a wonderful little adventure. But how about this mountain? Do we think it's fine?"

An awkward silence greeted this sally, until Keloki suddenly grinned and burst out, "Haleakala, he not mad at me no more! No po kane—just little earth-shake! You go up, Keakea. We go down."

All of the haoles looked at one another, gauging one another, and then nodded in a consensus.

"Okay, Keloki," Shiloh relented. "You go down and we go up. Just tell Mrs. Winslow," he sighed theatrically, "that Miss Winslow is fine. And tell her that in spite of what she may think, this earthquake wasn't my fault."

★ ★ ★ ★

I'm afraid, Cheney thought with some analytical compartment in her mind. *Why is that?*

The whole inner top of the ancient mountain was sunken. Three thousand feet below her dusty boots, Cheney saw a landscape that was so strangely eerie she felt she might have somehow been shunted to another planet. A bitter and forbidding planet.

It's not fear, she decided. *I feel a sort of dread, of foreboding. This place ... it's so ... alien. ...*

"Right through the gap, here, is the best path," Brynn said, speaking in a normal tone that somewhat dissipated Cheney's discomfort. "Shall I lead?"

"If you don't mind, Miss Winslow, I think I'd better," Shiloh said quickly, then maneuvered his horse in front before she could protest.

She didn't, and she and Cheney followed him in single file, with Walker behind.

The ground was hard-baked but not cracked. Going down into the crater was not a steep decline, for on the other side of Kaupo Gap, the slope was gentle, leading down to the sunken floor in a series of gentle rises and falls of the reddish earth. It was a thirsty land, the only colors visible of burnt orange and dull ochre and a thousand tints of brown and lifeless gray and black. Cheney saw that the dust kicked up by Brynn's horse hung sullenly in the air and then settled reluctantly back to earth.

They all stopped in a group when they reached the crater floor, looking around in wonder. It was a strangely beautiful landscape, stern and forbidding. The scorched stones, the reddish-brown ash, the gray cinders crunched with every tiny shift the horses made. But there was no other sound at all.

"Why don't we go that way, straight across the floor?" Brynn suggested, pointing to a high cliff across the canyon. "The famous surveyor's rock, Pohaku Palaha, is on that cliff directly north."

"Suits me," Shiloh said, and Cheney and Walker agreed.

They rode close together. They didn't speak. Each one was turning his head this way and that, their eyes darting from one frame to the next, struggling to adjust their eyes and cognition to such foreign surroundings.

In the distance Cheney saw little cones, perfectly formed. As they rode, she kept focusing on them in the distance. But soon she realized that they weren't "little," not at all. As they neared the first one, she gulped. "My goodness," she muttered. "That thing must be—several hundred feet high."

Shiloh nodded. "I know. It's weird, isn't it? You can't properly judge things here. Your eyes fool you. The . . . uh . . . what do you call it? Frame thing?"

"Frame of reference," Cheney said.

"Yeah, that. It's all wrong."

"It certainly is," she agreed. "First you feel like a giant, and then you feel like a dwarf."

"I always wonder if this is what the moon looks like," Brynn said dreamily. "I've always wished I could be here, on Haleakala, on a night of the full moon. It must be . . . like walking, awake, in a dream. . . ."

The division between light and dark was as sharp as if they'd outlined their shadows with razors. Cheney could see their silhouettes clearly, in detail. She saw, with a trace of amusement, that her hair was the only tangled smudge in their dark reflections.

They neared the first cinder cone, one of a bizarre geometrical forest. Here was the first touch of green. Several plants grew on the sides of the cone, clinging precariously to the crumbly black ash. The leaves of the plant were long and narrow, incurving to the shape of a globe, and were a muted green that glinted silvery in the merciless light.

"What are those?" Cheney asked.

"Haleakala silverswords," Shiloh answered. "That one's not blooming. Maybe we'll see one in bloom; they're really spectacular."

Brynn smiled sadly. "We used to dig them up and take them back to transplant at the villa. But they died. The blooming ones, I mean. We planted one once that wasn't blooming, and it lived for a couple of years, and then we were so happy when it bloomed. We thought it had taken good root and would reproduce. But after they bloom, they die."

Walker and Brynn rode on. Cheney stopped and looked back, for Shiloh hadn't moved his horse. He was looking at the top of the cinder cone, towering three stories above them. Shading her eyes, she followed his line of vision, wondering what he was staring at.

They stood motionless for long moments, and then Cheney muttered, "I see it. . . ."

Even though he was several feet away, Shiloh heard her and walked his horse near. "Do you? It's so fine I thought I was imagining it, maybe."

"No. Little wisps of smoke . . . and look—over there? And that one far off? Aren't there faint smudges?"

"Yeah," he said quietly. "Maybe they smoke sometimes."

Sharply she asked, "Were they smoking when you and Keloki came up here?"

"No," he said curtly. "But maybe it doesn't mean anything, Doc. This place is so strange, who knows what's normal?"

They rode on, catching up to Walker and Brynn.

The flat earth began to get crumbly, and then they were in a rubbly field that had broken, spiny blocks of old lava jumbled crazily together. Stunted trees and low, misshapen bushes weakly clung to life in this barren land. Cheney couldn't get over the silence of the place; it was unnatural. She'd never known another place on earth that had no sound of wind, no movement of any living thing, no murmur of life at all. Again the feelings of formless dread, of aversion, swept over her.

"Over there," Brynn said, pointing to their left, "is a black hole about ten feet across. The rim of it is all jagged with lava spatter. The Hawaiians think it is bottomless, that it goes all the way to the end of the world."

"What do you think, Miss Winslow?" Walker asked curiously.

She didn't scoff, as he had thought she would. Shifting uncomfortably in the saddle, she frowned. "Once Bain and I came up here, when we were children, with Keloki and Leilana and their children. We hid from them and then went to the pit, which was strictly forbidden, of course. Bain had brought three papala spears and lucifer matches—which were also strictly forbidden. Anyway, we lit the spears and threw them down into the hole." She fell silent, her eyes focused on the distant dead peaks. "They fell away, and farther, and longer . . . and dimmed and dimmed. . . . We never heard them hit. They just died."

"How unsettling," Walker murmured.

"Yes. I . . . I still have awful nightmares about it," Brynn said uneasily.

Shiloh and Cheney, who had dropped a little behind Brynn and Walker, suddenly exchanged sharp glances and simultaneously pulled their horses to a stop. Shiloh's brow furrowed, and his eyes took on an inward look as he concentrated hard. Cheney lifted her face and breathed deeply, then sniffed, like a wolf scenting prey. Again she and Shiloh looked at each other.

"You smell it?" Cheney asked in a low voice.

"Yes. You hear it?" he answered curtly.

"No, I can't hear anything," Cheney replied, her voice thick. "But I . . . I think I know what you're hearing."

The other two had become aware that Cheney and Shiloh had stopped, and turned around. "Shiloh? Something wrong?" Walker called. They were several feet ahead.

"C'mon, Doc," Shiloh said. They caught up to Walker and Brynn. "Miss Winslow, I'd kinda like to see that pit you were talking about. Would you show it to us?" he asked politely.

Brynn looked from him to Cheney and back to Shiloh. She licked her lips nervously. "All right." She turned her horse and led off.

Hurrying his mount to catch up to her, Walker said lightly, "Why don't you just show us where it is, Miss Winslow? It's just like Dr. Duvall and Shiloh to want to go look down in a hole. They have very odd impulses to enjoy such strange adventures. They both shoot at jars and bottles all the time, and once I caught them practicing swordplay, of all things. They also seem to think it's just great fun to go to the apothecary at the hospital and mix up noxious drugs. But I'm more interested in less exotic things. Like rocks. I like rocks, always have. While Dr. Duvall and Shiloh are staring down into a black hole, perhaps we could collect some of these interesting lava rocks? I'm no geometrist— or is it geodetic? Or—"

"I think what you're looking for here is 'geologist,'" Brynn suggested, her eyes alight. "And thank you."

"For what?" Walker said, taken off guard.

"For . . . for . . . not expecting me to be . . . courageous. Like she is," Brynn said.

Walker knew very well to whom she referred. "Yes, Dr. Duvall is an exceptional woman. And so are you, Miss Winslow. A lady of kind and gentle manner, but adventurous and strong. You, too, are courageous, in a different way. And, if I may speak bluntly, you are certainly exceptionally beautiful."

Brynn blushed fiercely, and her dimples seemed at least an inch deep as she smiled. "But . . . no, I'm not. I'm not any of those things."

"But you are," Walker said with mock severity. "I'm a doctor. We don't allow people to disagree with us. It's just not done, my dear Miss Winslow."

She gave him a shy glance out of the bare corners of her eyes. "Today I am much inclined to bow to a physician's advice, Dr. Baird. Once again the medical profession has triumphed."

Walker smiled reassuringly at her and began his nonsense about being a "geometrist" again. Finally she pulled her horse to a halt and looked behind at Shiloh and Cheney. "It's . . . it's just up there. I'd really prefer not to go any closer, if you don't mind."

"No, 'course not," Shiloh said gently. "It's all right, you know, Miss Winslow. I just wanta see it."

He moved his horse around them, followed by Cheney, but Brynn called out, "No, stop!" her voice shrill and hysterical. Walker lightly touched her arm with concern. She pressed her eyes closed, then said in a more normal tone, "It's . . . just up ahead, Mr. Irons. Don't ride the horses up to the edge of it, please. It sort of . . . gapes open in front of you."

"Oh. Well, don't I feel like a clinker," Shiloh muttered. "Thanks, Miss Winslow. I wanta see it, but I don't wanta ride into it. Would you two mind holding the horses?"

Cheney and Shiloh dismounted, and Walker and Brynn did, too, though they wandered off in the opposite direction, searching the ground. Cheney and Shiloh walked ahead.

"It's a lot stronger now," Cheney said quietly. "Do you think Walker and Miss Winslow can't smell it?"

"I think they're not paying much attention to anything but each other," Shiloh answered. "There, that must be it." Ahead of them was a jagged line of black rocks, like rotten broken teeth.

Silently Cheney and Shiloh walked to the edge of the bottomless pit and looked down.

The stench of sulphur was strong. Cheney's throat grew thick, and she choked slightly. Shiloh's eyes narrowed to slits.

The pit was like a tunnel. Sound traveled through it and was amplified, but only in the direction of the opening. Standing right over the hole, Shiloh and Cheney clearly heard the sound of the infernal drone that had given Cheney nightmares about trains. They felt it in their teeth, which hummed with an unpleasant vibration when they turned their faces down to the blackness.

They straightened, then stared at each other. Cheney looked pale and strained. Shiloh looked grim. Without speaking, they turned their backs on the bottomless pit and walked away.

When they did, Cheney had the most forceful, frightful feeling that she and Shiloh weren't actually moving ahead. They were slipping behind, losing ground, going inexorably back, and with the next step *forward* they would fall *backward* into that ghastly black hole—

She jerked around, her eyes wide and staring, her breath hissing through her teeth.

"Doc—don't—don't," Shiloh murmured, taking her by the shoulders and gently turning her to him. "Don't be afraid. I can't stand it when you're afraid. We'll be all right. We always are, aren't we? I'll protect you. I'll never let anything happen to you—"

She pulled away from him, ashamed. "I know," she said in a dull voice, her head bent, her eyes averted. "Please, Shiloh, I want to leave this terrible place. Now."

He took her hand, and they walked together without looking back.

9

CAVORTING ABOUT

"Irons? Keloki? What do you two think you're doing?"

Konrad Zeiss, the overseer of all the Winslow Plantation holdings, rode into the high sandalwood camp to see his two workers standing at the edge of the grove, side by side, staring up into the sky. At the sound of his voice, Shiloh and Keloki turned around, and Zeiss knew a moment's frustration. Hawaiians never seemed to get intimidated, yet they were never disrespectful. Shiloh Irons was, at first glance, much like that.

But as Zeiss had observed, his new worker—the only white man who had ever worked for the Winslows—had a certain air about him, an easy confidence and sense of self-worth, that normally only came naturally to the wellborn. As far as Zeiss knew, Irons had no social standing, no family, and so his patrician bearing was an even bigger mystery. But Zeiss had learned in his fifty years not to pry into a man's past or into his personal life. He gave a mental shrug. Both Irons and Keloki were good workers, and he had no quarrel with them. Especially Irons, especially today . . . especially now.

His stern countenance softening, he dismounted, tethered his horse and Plato, the gelding Shiloh had ridden the day before up to the crater. Walking to where the two stood watching him with no sign of unease at being caught not working, Zeiss grudgingly admitted to himself that he had no complaints. The sandalwood grove was successful, and Keloki, his son Ulu Nui, and Shiloh Irons had worked very hard to make it a success.

The grove was simply a square of jungle far up on a plateau of Mount Haleakala that had to be hand-cleared, tendril by tenacious tendril, around the young sandalwood seedlings that could be found growing around the two older trees. Irons alone had cleared most of the half acre or so of solid stifling jungle. He treated the delicate seedlings like infant children, always turning and refreshing the dirt around them, handpicking insects off them, testing all the time to make certain they had water, renewing the muddy soil with mulch when the heavy rains impacted the dirt into sticky mud. Zeiss glanced overhead. Irons had also climbed the twenty- and thirty-foot ohia and olapa trees that overhung the grove and had trimmed the larger branches so the sandalwood trees and saplings could get adequate sunlight. Quite a feat with nothing but an ax and handsaw. No, Konrad Zeiss had no quarrel with Shiloh Irons—far from it. He actually admired the man. Suddenly, Zeiss was disgusted with what he was being forced to do.

"Hello, Mr. Zeiss," Shiloh greeted him. "What brings you to the high camp?"

Zeiss was a man who spoke plainly, without embellishment, so he answered, "Bad news. Keloki, I need to speak to Mr. Irons alone."

Shrugging, Keloki went to the other side of the sandalwood grove. The only other place to go was inside the tiny grass hut that housed Shiloh and Keloki and Ulu Nui when they stayed overnight at the camp. Keloki liked outside better. He turned and began to watch the sky on that side of the world.

His distaste making his tone even more curt, Zeiss stated, "I've just come from the villa. Winslow Plantation no longer requires your services, and you are dismissed immediately."

Shiloh listened without a change of expression. He was looking down at Konrad Zeiss, who was six feet tall and unaccustomed to having to look up at anyone. It annoyed him, and without being aware of it, he backed up a step. He was a forbidding man, with iron-gray hair clipped short, grim gray-blue eyes, and a hard-angled jaw. But he wasn't a cruel man; he was just basically austere and strict. He watched Irons and felt a rush of admiration for him. Whatever the circumstances, Irons was handling getting fired—for no good reason that Zeiss was aware of—very well, indeed. Shiloh's blue eyes had iced over for a split second, but then his usual mild expression had settled back in.

"Hey, Keloki! You can come back over here now," he called. To Zeiss he said calmly, "I don't have much, so I'll be able to clear out in about half an hour, Mr. Zeiss."

Zeiss nodded a quick jab of his head. "I brought Plato. You can ride him into Hana and leave him at my stables." Wheeling, he marched back to his horse but hesitated, his back to the two men.

"Hey, Keakea, what did Konrad say to you?" Keloki was asking in a mock whisper.

"It's not Mr. Zeiss," Shiloh answered in a low tone. "It's just business, Keloki. Or no, maybe it's personal. Anyway, I've just been fired from this magnificent job. All our little seedlings are prob'ly gonna die now, with just you and Ulu Nui to take care of them." Shiloh headed into the hut.

"Hey, I grow good *naio*," Keloki protested, trailing after him. "You come live with us now, Keakea. E kipa mai."

Shiloh stopped midstride, turned around, and smiled at the big man. "Thanks, Keloki, but I don't think that would work. You live in the Winslows' cottage, you see, and I don't think Mrs. Winslow would take it too good if I turned up livin' in her backyard, in her cottage."

"But where you gon' go?" Keloki asked, his strong brown face wrinkling with distress.

Shiloh shrugged, then headed back for the cabin.

"Just a minute, Irons," Zeiss called, the frustration evident in his voice. He stalked back to the two men. "I don't normally interfere in a man's business, but this time I'm going to. Not much, though. I've kept my job—and it's a good job—for twenty-odd years now by staying out of the Winslows' personal problems. Do you understand what I'm saying?"

Shiloh watched him, weighing him, for a few moments. Then he nodded and waited.

Zeiss turned to face away from Shiloh and Keloki and crossed his arms, his impatience with himself and the situation clear. "That big cottage where Keloki lives now used to be mine. Did you know that? No, I guess not. Anyway, when I told the Winslows that I was going to marry Alena, Mrs. Winslow fired me. But Mr. Winslow came right along behind her and hired me back. I couldn't live in the cottage, though, so I built that house in town. With my own hands, and it took over a year, but Alena waited." He gave Shiloh a sidelong glance. "Problem is, I lease the land from the Winslows."

Comprehension dawned on Shiloh's face. He realized that Zeiss, in his abrupt way, was explaining why he couldn't ask Shiloh to stay with him. "I understand, Mr. Zeiss. Thanks for explaining it to me."

"Hmph," he said uncomfortably. Shiloh turned to go, but Zeiss growled, "Wait just a minute, Irons. I'm not through yet. Tang Lu was the housekeeper of Winslow Guest House for a year. After that, she went to Mrs. Winslow and told her that she wouldn't kill herself running that guest house unless they let her buy it—both the house and the land. Mrs. Winslow had a fit, but that little Chinese stood up to her. And Mrs. Winslow really didn't have much choice. It was either sell it to Tang Lu or let it stay empty. So Tang Lu's buying Winslow Guest House. It'll probably only take her about one hundred ten years, but she's doing it. And Tang Lu gets the money from boarders."

"So I wouldn't be paying Mrs. Winslow to stay in 'her' house, huh?" Shiloh said, his eyes sparkling.

"Nope. Denise Winslow can't kick you out of the guest house. She might give Tang Lu a hard time, but Tang Lu's heard it all before, for years. And she's smart. If she's got three good-paying boarders, she's not going to give them a minute's problem, not for Mrs. Winslow or anyone else." He eyed Shiloh speculatively. "You got some money, Irons? I know you've been working off a debt, so you haven't collected any pay."

"I'm fine," he said quickly.

"If you aren't, just say so," Zeiss said gruffly. "I'm no bank, but I could loan you enough to put you up at the guest house for a couple of weeks, until the *Mongoose* arrives."

"No, thank you, sir," Shiloh said politely. "I'm in good shape."

"Don't thank me," Zeiss ordered harshly. "Good luck to you."

"Thank you again, Mr. Zeiss," Shiloh said, thrusting out his hand. Zeiss, with obvious guilt, shook it and walked away.

When Zeiss turned and mounted his horse, he almost laughed to see Keloki and Shiloh. They were again standing at the edge of the clearing of sandalwood trees, staring up into the sky. "I can't leave until I know," Zeiss called. "What *are* you two looking at?"

There was a fluttering sound, a rasping hissing of wings, and loud frightened squeaks. Without turning around, Shiloh pointed. "That," he answered. "All morning, all over the mountain, bunches of them have been getting spooked and flushing like that."

"Huh? Are those—" Zeiss stammered, staring in disbelief.

"Yep," Shiloh replied. "Bats."

★ ★ ★ ★

"Good morning, Mrs. Winslow," Cheney said politely, entering the crowded parlor of the guest house. Denise Winslow stood at the small side window, holding back the drapes with one gloved hand. She was wearing a morning dress that was exquisitely made of a heavy, lustrous taffeta that made crisp sounds when she moved. The dress was a cool shade of lavender, trimmed with black velvet piping. Her reticule, fan, gloves, mantelet, and shoes peeping out from the fashionably shortened skirt were all dyed to match, with black velvet ribbon trimmings. Cheney felt underdressed in her morning gown of white piqué, and she also felt uneasy when she saw the forbidding set of Denise Winslow's jaw and the stiffness in her shoulders. Still Cheney continued politely, seating herself in the red velvet armchair, "I hardly expected a return visit so soon. Won't you sit down?"

"No, I prefer to stand." Denise eyed Cheney for long moments, and Cheney now saw the unfriendliness in the older woman's attitude clearly. She waited.

"Dr. Duvall, my daughter is ill."

"She is? Oh, I'm so sorry. May I offer my assistance?"

Denise made a sharp motion, as if she were cutting something with a large knife. "You misunderstand. I certainly don't require you to attend her. It is, in fact, partly due to you and your friends that she is ill."

Cheney made herself be still and calm. "I beg your pardon?"

Denise's mouth turned downward with ire, and the lines between her nose and mouth deepened to crevices. "I had misgivings about allowing Brynn to keep company with you and Mr. Irons and Dr. Baird, and as it turns out, my instincts were correct. My daughter, Dr. Duvall, is of genteel sensibilities. She has been brought up with a certain delicacy, a certain refinement. I understand that you and Dr. Baird are educated people. You, obviously, have some resources. But also obviously, you and Dr. Baird are no more well-bred than that Irons person. It is no surprise to me that Brynn has taken ill after such base and brutish treatment, in a dangerous situation, by companions who have no finer sensibilities."

Cheney endured this speech with admirable control, though she could feel anger forming a hot liquid fire in her chest. But she managed to hold her temper and responded coolly, "Madam, I'm afraid I don't comprehend a thing you are saying. That earthquake was no respecter of persons. It frightened all of us and put all of us in equal danger. If it hadn't been for the protection and care of Dr. Baird and Mr. Irons, we would have been in trouble, indeed."

Denise drew herself upright. "I hardly think that the lot of you cavorting about all night half-naked constitutes conscientious care of a young, innocent girl. In addition, I had thought that you and Dr. Baird were, perhaps, engaged or at least had some understanding. But I come to find out that you and that Irons person are much too familiar with each other to be mere colleagues, and that Dr. Baird is trying to seduce my daughter. Needless to say, Brynn will not be allowed to associate with the lot of you again. I think it best if you leave Hana. Unfortunately, none of our ships will be here until the *Mongoose* stops in on its western run on the thirtieth. But Bain has gone to Lahaina, and he will find the next ship leaving from there en route to San Francisco. He will instruct it to stop in Hana and pick you up. It should be here tomorrow or the next day, at the latest."

Cheney stared at her for long moments, her bright green eyes wide, her eyebrows winging like dark, graceful birds on her brow. Denise met her gaze arrogantly but then wavered, dropped her eyes, and nervously brushed imaginary specks from her skirt.

Suddenly Cheney burst out laughing.

Completely unsettled, Denise went pale, and then her cheeks colored a hot scarlet. "Are . . . are you insane?" she stammered.

"N-no, no, I don't think so," Cheney said, still giggling. "It's just so absurd. I wanted so badly to kick you out of here, out of my sight, to demand that you leave my presence. But it's . . . it's . . . your house!" Again Cheney tittered, and even—unforgivably—pointed at the woman. "I'm sorry, Mrs. Winslow, it's just that this is the most ridiculous, laughable situation I've ever seen. It's like a comic opera. You can't make me go away because your ships aren't here, and I can't kick you out because you own everything!"

"She doesn't own this house," a deep voice said from the doorway. "She can't kick anyone out of this house." Shiloh Irons crossed his arms and leaned against the doorjamb, a negligent and cocky stance, with one booted foot crossed and toe-up on Mrs. Denise Winslow's fine sisal matting.

Denise gathered up her rustling skirt and stalked to the door, her face as stiff as if it would crack if she spoke. Her eyes were like oily black coal.

Shiloh didn't move. He looked down at her with mild curiosity and distaste, as if she were a new species of insect.

"Ex—" Denise gulped convulsively, then almost shouted, "Excuse me!"

Lazily Shiloh moved aside about six inches. Denise was obliged to brush against him as she went through the door, and she actually visibly shuddered as her skirts touched him. "Loutish cur," she muttered.

Dr. Walker Baird, to his regret, had come up behind Shiloh and had stepped slightly to the side to try to see what was going on. Denise rammed into him at full steam.

"Move aside, you grinning idiot!" she almost screamed.

Walker nearly fell down trying to get out of range, as it were, and Denise Clare Worthington Winslow left Winslow Guest House with a door-slamming that was almost as bad as the earthquake had been.

Shiloh sauntered into the parlor and sprawled on the sofa. "Hi, Doc."

"Hi." She smiled at him, looking only slightly bemused.

"I got fired," he said.

"I got evicted," she said.

"I was asleep," Walker mumbled in confusion. His innocent blue eyes were wide, and he kept looking around as if he wasn't sure what horrible place he had awakened in.

"No, Walker, dear, you were evicted too. Come in here and sit down. Tang Lu was supposed to bring coffee, but I expect she decided to hide until the . . . um . . . storm blew over," Cheney said with the remnants of laughter still coloring her voice.

Shiloh, who was watching her with a hint of anxiety, suddenly relaxed. "Hey, you're really not mad, are you?"

"I certainly am," Cheney said, lifting her chin. "But to tell the truth, that woman is so awful I don't really care what she thinks or says."

Shiloh smiled. "Hey, you ready to go, Doc? That's us, on the move at a minute's notice. I think we just got notice."

"Shiloh, I am ready to shake the dust of this place off my feet this instant," Cheney said firmly.

"But I want to see Miss Winslow," Walker said. His expression was still thoroughly muddled.

"Better forget that one, Walker," Shiloh advised him.

"But . . . but she's wonderful!"

"Maybe so, but how about the mother-in-law?"

"Ohhh," Walker said, the light dawning. "She called me a grinning idiot."

"Uh, yeah, she did," Shiloh agreed. "Can't imagine why." Walker's wide smile was the most childlike thing about him. It lit up his face like a thousand candles. And he smiled a lot. "But I don't even know what she called me, Walker," Shiloh said wryly. "What's a lowtishka?"

Cheney giggled with delight. "No, no, Shiloh, you're a loutish cur. In British."

"Oh. I think I'd rather be a grinning idiot."

"True," Walker agreed, still befuddled.

Cheney rolled her eyes, then said with the first small flash of anger, "Neither of you are anything of the kind, and neither am I—well, never mind that. Yes, that's it—never mind anything that woman says, Shiloh. Do you understand me?"

"Yes, ma'am," he said obediently. "Will you not mind, not ever?"

Cheney thought for a moment, frowning blackly, and then her face cleared. "No, I won't. Just the fact that I didn't lose my temper—well, that's miraculous."

"Sure is," Shiloh agreed much too heartily.

Cheney made a face at him, then sobered again. "Yes, thank the Lord—and thanks *to* the Lord—I can never mind Denise Winslow again. I can."

"Okay, Doc. If you can, I can."

"But, Shiloh, what about . . . your—"

"Never mind all that right now," he said easily. "I don't think staying here is going to do me any good anyway. I've learned a few things, and maybe I can find out some more back in San Francisco."

"Good," Cheney said, brightening. "I'll help you."

"I know."

Walker Baird, his midnight-blue eyes suddenly turning an indignant cobalt flash, jumped to his feet. "What I want to know," he demanded of the world in general, "is who that woman thought she was, calling me a grinning idiot!"

Shiloh and Cheney smiled at each other. "Good morning, Walker," she said. "Glad to see you've finally awakened and joined us."

"Huh? Oh. Good morning, Dr. Duvall. Good morning, Shiloh." He looked around, then said plaintively, "Would someone mind telling me what's going on?"

"She got evicted," Shiloh said cheerfully, pointing at Cheney.

"He got fired," Cheney said, equally lightly.

"But I didn't do anything!" Walker complained.

"You cavorted about," Cheney said gravely. "And so did we."

Walker stared at both of them, then said wearily, "I'm going to go take a nap. It was easier when I was asleep." He wandered out of the room.

Cheney and Shiloh looked at each other and burst out laughing.

THE BLAST OF

❋ P·A·R·T   T·W·O ❋

THE TERRIBLE ONES

For thou hast been
a strength to the poor,
A strength to the needy
in his distress,
A refuge from the storm,
A shadow from the heat,
When the blast of the terrible ones
is as a storm against the wall.

Isaiah 25:4

10

INFERNAL BEASTS

"Hey, Nia! You better get out here and do your chaperonin' job, 'cause I'm getting ready to knock on the Doc's door!" Shiloh called out in the upstairs hallway of Winslow Guest House.

Cheney giggled as she heard Nia's door slam down the hall and the sound of her quick, light footsteps come to Cheney's door. She spoke indignantly, and in spite of the childlike tones, Cheney was reminded of Nia's booming Amazon mother, Dally.

"Mr. Irons! Ain't no cause to go telling all of Haw-eye that you're prowling about Miss Cheney's boudoir! Here, you! Stand over there, and I'll see if she's in and receiving callers!"

Nia opened the door, closed it behind her, and leaned up against it as if to keep out an invasion. "Miss Cheney, are you in and receiving callers?"

He knocked again. "Hey, Doc! I know you're in! How 'bout receivin' a caller?"

"I'm gonna box his ears," Nia vowed.

The mental picture was delightful: the tiny little Negro girl, who looked like a prim twelve-year-old, standing on a step stool to box Nordic giant Shiloh Irons' ears. "You'd better let him in, Nia," Cheney declared. "Otherwise he'll just stand out there making a scene all day."

Muttering fiercely, Nia opened the door to admit Shiloh. "She'll receive you now, Mr. Irons. But if you don't behave I'll—"

"I know. I know. Box my ears. I heard you, Nia, and it scared me bad," Shiloh grumbled.

"Hmph!" Nia crossed her arms and tapped her small foot impatiently.

"I just wanted to talk to you a minute, Doc," Shiloh said, leaning against the doorjamb. "You have any plans for today?"

Cheney was standing at the single window, enjoying the fragrant morning breeze and the benevolent sun. "Why, no. Nia and I have been packing, and I thought we were just going to stay here and wait for the prison ship to come pick us criminals up." Her eyes were twinkling, while this comment brought fresh dire utterances from Nia.

"I ain't too crazy 'bout the idea of turnin' myself in that easy," Shiloh scoffed. "Besides, I'm hungry for some opihi. Wanta go get some?"

"Go get some? Where?"

"At the lagoon."

"The Winslows' lagoon?"

"Yeah."

Cheney slowly smiled. "And if we miss the ship?"

He shrugged. "We can leave word with Miss Tang Lu. If somebody comes to arrest us, she can send them to the lagoon. They can just find us, and then wait for us to get ready."

"All right," Cheney agreed, her eyes alight. "Shiloh, I would love to go to the lagoon. We'll take a picnic." She caught sight of Nia's face, and a wistful look stole over it. Quickly Cheney added, "Nia, I'd like for you to come too. If you'd care to, that is. You haven't been out of this house since we got here."

"Yes, Miss Cheney, I'd love to go," Nia said gratefully. "I would like to see something of this place before we leave."

"Oh, but ... Shiloh, it's about five or six miles, isn't it?" Cheney asked hesitantly.

He grinned, and it was as mischievous as a naughty schoolboy's. "Mr. Zeiss left a message with Miss Tang Lu this morning. He said to tell me that he'd talked to Miss Brynn, and she told him that as far as she was concerned, the horses and cart are ours to do with as we please as long as we are in Hana. Her words."

"Good for her," Cheney asserted. "At least *she* has some sense of decency."

"I guess," Shiloh sighed. "Kind of a shame about Walker, though."

From down the hall they heard "What about Walker?" His footsteps sounded, and he stepped in view behind Shiloh, scanning Cheney's room cautiously. "What did I do now?"

"We're goin' to the lagoon to get some opihi," Shiloh answered. "Wanta come?"

"We might miss the ship," Walker said doubtfully.

"Who cares?" Shiloh replied cheerily.

"Mrs. Winslow, that's who," Walker said, still searching around as if she might be lurking in Cheney's room, preparing to pounce.

"We can go swimming," Shiloh prodded him.

Walker and Shiloh were both members of the Olympic Club in San Francisco. Shiloh spent most of his time in lighthearted boxing with sparring partners and in teaching amateur pugilists. But Walker loved to swim and sometimes swam twice or even three times a day at the club's elegant indoor pool. Now his face lit up, and he forgot all threats by angry matrons. "Oh, that would be capital, Shiloh!" He rushed down the hall and called back anxiously, "You won't leave without me, will you?"

"No, Walker, I wouldn't dream of it," Shiloh drawled. "You're the one who's going to have to teach the Doc to swim."

"Yes, I've always wanted—" Cheney began, but she was soundly overborne by Nia's reedy voice.

"Oh no, you don't! Miss Cheney ain't gonna be dunkin' herself in the water like some Haw-eyean woman wearin' nothing but a hankie tied up—well, never you mind where it's tied up!" Nia spluttered. "You better stand back, mister!"

Shiloh was laughing. But luckily, he was very agile and quick on his feet for his size. When Nia slammed the door, it missed his thin aristocratic nose by at least two inches.

★　★　★　★

"What's all that on the beach?" Cheney asked curiously.

"Dunno. Maybe a high tide washed up some stuff," Shiloh said. "It's still so pretty, isn't it?"

"Sure is!" Walker said enthusiastically. "C'mon, let's go! This has got to be the most beautiful place in the world to swim."

The view of the lagoon was breathtaking, even without the graceful clipper floating serenely in it. The blue-green water was placid, with the barest ripples lapping up onto the beach. In the distance they could hear a constant rumble of waves smashing into the barrier reef, and occasional frothy sprays of surf danced up over the glistening black rocks at the sea entrance.

Carefully Shiloh maneuvered the buckboard down the slope, and the two horses unconcernedly splashed through Bain's Stream. Directing the team to the line of coconut palms, he jumped out and helped Cheney and Nia down.

"Let's unhitch 'em, you want to, Walker?" Shiloh asked. "Since we're going to be here for a while."

"Of course. I'll help. You ladies go on down, if you want to."

Cheney and Nia picked up their skirts and ran down to the water's edge. Littering the pure white beach were rocks of a hundred different hues of gray, from the color of charcoal to a dull pewter. "This is odd," Cheney murmured. "I suppose these washed in. No one would bring rocks and put them on a beach." To Nia she said, "It's just that the other day, when we went up to the crater, there wasn't a single rock on this beach."

Nia was standing at the very edge of the lapping surf, staring out. "This water is so clear, you can see way out there. There's lots of those rocks here, Miss Cheney. They're washing in, all right."

"Hmm," Cheney said, losing interest. She moved up to Nia's side and knelt down, burying her fingers in the wet sand. "Feels good. Cold, but not too cold. Let's take off our stockings and wade. Surely that won't be too unseemly."

Nia smiled. "I think that's a real good idea! Here, now, you sit down—not on those rocks, though, they look really rough—and I'll just do this." She spread her wide skirts for Cheney to hide behind. Cheney shook her head with amusement. Shiloh and Walker were hundreds of feet away and busy with the horses. Still, Cheney knew how stubborn the Clarkson women were, so she obediently let Nia shield her while she removed her shoes and stockings, and then obliged Nia by doing the same for her.

They waded back and forth, marveling at the clearness of the water. Cheney pulled her skirts up high and went out until the water lapped at her knees. "Look! This water is so pure that it doesn't even distort reflections a foot deep!"

"I know. It's hard to believe it's salty," Nia said, then bent and thrust two fingers in the water and put them to her mouth. "But it is, o' course. You'd think salty water would be cloudy, wouldn't you?"

They waded and talked, and then Cheney mischievously picked up one of the gray pebbles and threw it at Nia's back. Nia retaliated by tossing a handful of little pebbles back. Cheney splashed her, Nia splashed back. Soon both of them were laughing helplessly and clasping each other so they wouldn't fall down. But Cheney stepped on one of the loose rocks and suddenly sank, bringing Nia with her. Sitting waist-deep in the water, their full skirts floating in wide, ebullient circles around them, they stared at each other in shock. Then Cheney started laughing. Nia looked horrified for a few moments and then dissolved in giggles.

"You . . . you look so . . . surprised! And . . . funny!" Cheney twittered.

"Oh, you look real dignified, Miss Doctor Cheney Duvall," Nia managed to get out. "I'm glad my mama's not here. She'd pinch my head in two!"

"Y'all havin' fun?" Shiloh crossed his arms, watching them from the water's edge. He had taken off his shirt and boots and was wearing a pair of light canvas breeches. Beside him, Walker wore a pair of denim breeches, shortened to his calves. Both were laughing at the two sodden ladies sitting complacently in the surf.

"I think I'll require some assistance, gentlemen," Cheney declared. "A lady's clothes weigh about thirty pounds when they're dry. I'm not sure we'll be able to stand up."

Sunk in the lagoon, her skirt billowing up for a yard around her, Nia still managed to look prim. "Ain't no need in you telling gentlemen such things, Miss Cheney. It's not a proper topic for a lady."

"Sorry," Cheney said guiltily. Looking back at Shiloh and Walker, she said gravely, "Would you be so kind as to assist me to rise, Mr. Irons? It appears that my appurtenances are inconveniencing me slightly."

"And don't think I don't know what that means," Nia warned. "You don't need to be discussin' your appurtenances with him either."

Shiloh and Walker were already gamely wading out toward them when Shiloh's eyes suddenly narrowed and his mouth tightened. Thrusting out his hand with quick strength, he grabbed Walker's arm. "Don't move, Walker. Stay perfectly still."

"What?" Walker mumbled, but he stopped and stared down into the water, searching. Shiloh's eyes were darting back and forth, scanning the water in front of them.

"Doc, Nia, listen to me," he said quietly without looking up. "Don't move. Don't move your feet, don't shift the way you're sitting."

Nia and Cheney exchanged frightened glances, but they remained carefully motionless. "All right, Shiloh," Cheney said in a clear voice. "What is it?"

"Just a minute, and we'll come get you," Shiloh said, ignoring her question.

Cheney swallowed hard but said nothing else.

Shiloh stood, his hand still gripping Walker's arm, his burning gaze fixed on the water in front of him. "Look there. You see? See, Walker?"

"Yes, I see it," Walker replied. "What is it?"

"Rockfish," Shiloh answered. "Right now I see three—no, four of them. Stand still until you can see them."

The fish were ugly, gnarled specimens. The one that had swum clumsily in front of Shiloh and Walker—they lumbered from rock to rock—was about eight inches long. With its mottled black and gray markings and its knobby skin, it looked exactly like a rock—except for the thirteen needle-like protuberances along its spine.

"I see three," Walker told him in a low voice. "Those two over there, by you. This one right in front of us."

"There's one right by your left foot, Walker," Shiloh said.

"Yes," Walker said after a moment.

"Don't let the spines touch you," Shiloh warned.

"That's a bad thing, is it?" Walker asked with an attempt at lightness.

"Yeah," Shiloh said, but he spoke to Cheney. She lifted her chin, her gaze firm. He nodded slightly and went on, "Doc, this is definitely not good. These fish aren't aggressive, but they can hurt you real bad if you even brush up against them."

"I understand. What can we do?" Cheney asked, faltering a bit. She looked around at her skirt and Nia's, which were like three-foot-wide umbrellas. Underneath that, they both had two petticoats. Cheney met Nia's frightened gaze and said softly, "Don't be scared, Nia. We're just so blessed to have Shiloh and Walker to help us."

"I . . . I knew I shouldn't have let you go wading," Nia said, struggling to tease. "My mama really would whip me if she knew I let you go in water with . . . with . . . mean fish."

Cheney smiled, and Nia smiled back shakily.

"Problem is," Shiloh said softly, "if there's any of those things tangled up in your . . . appurtenances."

"Mr. Irons, I may be pruney but I'm not stupid," Nia maintained solidly. "Could me and Miss Cheney slip out of our skirts? Then just step out of them, kinda?"

" 'Pruney'?" Cheney repeated under her breath. Nia ignored her.

Shiloh did too. He stared at them and their floating treacheries. Then he sighed deeply. "No, Nia, that's no good. There would just be too much flailing around, any way you tried it. And you still couldn't see where you're stepping. So here's what we're gonna have to do. Walker and I will wade out to you. Just sit still. We'll pick you up. You ladies can help us if you'll just stay calm. When we get to you, just bring your knees up real smooth, and—" He swallowed hard, then went on, "Sing out real loud if you feel anything sticking you."

"You don't have to worry about that," Nia muttered.

"Okay. You ready?"

Nia and Cheney nodded.

"Walker, you ready?"

He nodded.

"Go slow," Shiloh ordered. "Don't step on a rock. Find the white sandy places."

"Got it."

As if they were moving through molasses instead of the sparkling water, Shiloh and Walker waded toward Cheney and Nia. Cheney's face was pale, her eyes seemingly too big for her face. Nia kept licking her lips and searching fruitlessly around them. They couldn't see anything, of course, except yards of material. Cheney was wearing royal blue, while Nia was wearing gray. Now both of the skirts looked like wavy black maws surrounding them.

Finally Shiloh and Walker reached them. Both of them looked grim as they clasped Nia and Cheney beneath their knees, for they couldn't see if any of the poison fish were lurking there, waiting for them. But sturdily, calmly, they clasped the women and straightened at the same time.

Walker smiled down at Nia, who managed to look deathly frightened and horribly embarrassed at the same time. "Why, you don't weigh as much as a kitten, Miss Nia," he said kindly. "I think I could toss you in the air and catch you floating down."

"I'd much 'preciate it if you wouldn't do that, Dr. Baird," she said stiffly. "But I am grateful to you all the same."

"Nothing to it," he said lightly. Slowly, with painstaking caution, he turned around to face the beach again. "Would you do me a favor? I'm just going to stand here a minute, and you look and see if there's any of those devilfish in front of us."

"I'm looking," Nia said evenly, "but I don't see—no, there's that one, right over there. Ugly things, aren't they?"

"Sure are," Walker grumbled. "You ready?"

"I'm ready if you are, sir," Nia said. Walker began to plod back to the beach.

Shiloh held Cheney and stood motionless for a moment. Her skirts were indeed heavy, and rivers of water ran from his arms, splashing cheerily in the innocent-looking water. He stared down into her eyes, and she looked back up at him, her eyes huge and dark as emeralds.

"Th-thank you," she murmured. "Again you've rescued me. How many times is it now?"

"Doesn't matter," he said in a low caressing voice, "as long as it's not the last."

She couldn't take her eyes off him. The sun made his hair a nimbus of gold, and his eyes were a startling blue. His chest and arms were bronzed and muscular, and she was fully conscious of how easily he lifted her and held her.

"You're not scared now, are you?" he asked.

"Yes. I'm scared to death you'll step on one of those things," she answered tremulously. "Be careful, Shiloh. I don't ever want anything to happen to you."

His gaze grew fiery, but then his mouth tightened, and he turned around in the water, almost carelessly. "Look out for me, then," he instructed her. "See any of 'em?"

"Yes, I see three," she said, squinting. "Don't you see them?"

"Yeah. Just wanted to make sure you were doin' your part," he said with deliberate lightness. "Y'know, Doc, I think your skirts prob'ly weigh twice as much as you do."

"You ought to try wearing them," Cheney grumbled.

Shiloh grinned. "But it's so hard for me to get the right fit," he lisped in an affected manner. "The length, you know, dearie."

As they waded through the dangerous waters, Shiloh and Cheney were laughing. Walker and Nia watched them from the shore. Walker was shaking his head, looking a little sad. Nia rolled her eyes and muttered to herself, "Laughin', those two think they're above it all, playin' jokes on Old Man Death himself. So funny, those two think. Just inviting more trouble, if you ask me."

But though Cheney and Shiloh had been through dangers together and had always managed to stay strong and lighthearted, that was not to be true always. In just a short time, Nia would recall her half-jesting observation, and the thoughtless words would cause her great pain.

Nia had recovered from the scare, and as soon as Shiloh stepped onto the sand she ordered, "Now, you just put her down so I can get her presentable again."

"I'm pretty sodden, Nia," Cheney said, laughing from sheer relief. "And what's this in my hair? A minnow?"

"No tellin'," Nia said darkly. She took Cheney's arm and hustled her toward the wagon, which was parked underneath two soaring coconut palms. Over her shoulder she announced, "We'll thank you two to stay right there for a bit, 'til we can get sorted out."

"We're going out on the pier," Shiloh told them. "When you ladies get ready, come on out and join us."

Cheney and Nia got behind the wagon and stripped off their sodden skirts. Nia rolled their overskirts expertly in one of the blankets they'd brought to picnic on. This blotted the water admirably, and in a short time they put their overskirts back on but hung their petticoats on a palm that was set back from the beach, growing at a low angle as coconut palms often did. "Now, just so no monkeys nor other infernal beasts steal 'em," Nia muttered wrathfully.

Cheney said, "I don't think there are any monkeys in Hawaii, Nia."

Nia scowled. "Well, if they got sneaky poison fish that looks like rocks and rocks that looks like poison fish, they could have any old thing."

There seemed to be no answer to that.

They walked across the beach carefully, though they knew there would certainly be no dangerous spiky fish lurking in the sand. Still, Cheney was jumpy and she knew Nia was too. They kept their eyes down, judging each step and giving a ridiculously wide berth to the innocuous rocks. Finally they reached the pier.

Shiloh and Walker had disappeared. Then Cheney saw them, swimming around the end of the long wooden dock. Shiloh waved and shouted, "Here we are!"

"That's just great," Cheney grumped. "Just like men! Poisonous fish everywhere, but they still have to show off!"

"You, ma'am," Nia enunciated carefully, "are not sticking your little toe in that water."

"Don't worry," Cheney told her. "I've had enough swimming for one day. Though I truly would like to learn to swim." Nia looked so outraged that Cheney went on hastily, "But not here, not today, oh no."

Nia seemed satisfied.

They reached the end of the dock, and Cheney put her hands on her hips. "Hello, Shiloh. By the way, I did bring my medical bag. Good thing, hmm? All you need to do is tell me what to do when one of those horrid fish sticks you, or poisons you, or whatever it is they do."

"Don't worry, Doc," he said, lazily backstroking in circles. "This water's really deep. You don't walk on the bottom. Those fish, they stay on rocks and ledges and in the coral reefs."

Walker noisily swam by, chopping the water expertly, his feet kicking up sprays three feet high. He was a powerful swimmer.

Cheney sat down on the pier and leaned out over the water.

"Miss Cheney—" Nia warned.

"Don't worry, I'm not going to touch it," Cheney said. She really had been frightened. Cheney, as most women, had never been in water, had never seriously considered learning to swim, would never have even thought of wading if they hadn't been in such a secluded and private place.

She stared into the sun-spangled water, narrowing her eyes against the bright reflection. The water was a jewel-like aquamarine, and even out here in the depths, she thought she could see glimpses of the bottom. She saw shadows, gentle grays and muted blues, wavering languidly in the depths. Then she sat up a little straighter and shielded her eyes with her hand, staring hard. She bent over farther, then scrambled up and searched around at the guileless seascape around her.

Nia looked up at her, then got to her feet, muttering, "Now what!"

Shiloh and Walker were swimming for exercise, going out toward the rocks with strong, even strokes, breathing rhythmically as their heads turned. At a signal they had evidently preset, both dove underwater—Cheney saw their feet as they kicked over—turned around, and came back toward the pier with long, hard strokes.

"Hurry," she muttered, her teeth gritted. She knew it would be no use to call to them. Their heads were underwater except for every fourth stroke, and then surely the churning sounds their swimming made deafened them. "Hurry, hurry, hurry . . ." she went on, clasping her hands.

When Cheney judged they were near enough, she called out, shocking herself at how urgent, almost hysterical she sounded. "Shiloh! Walker! Swim in right now, straight up to the dock, and get to it! Now! Hurry! Hurry!"

In tandem, she saw them give her odd looks, but they heard her and began swimming faster.

Cheney felt a lump, hard and heavy, come up in her throat. Behind Shiloh and Walker, cutting the water smoothly, was a gray triangular fin.

"Figures," Nia commented. But she looked frightened.

Shiloh and Walker swam two more strokes. Suddenly, as fast as a thought, a gray triangle sailed three feet in front of their eyes, crossing their path.

"Don't look! Don't stop!" Cheney shrieked. "Swim!"

The water boiled like rapids, sprayed high in the air by the fury of their strokes.

Shiloh reached the dock first. He pulled himself up to a short stop, like an aquatic ballet dancer, twisted in the water, grabbed Walker's shoulders, and practically threw him up onto the dock. He collapsed into a heap, and Nia threw herself down beside him. Before Walker had moved, Shiloh shot up the ladder slats, stepped over him, and sank down to sit on the pier cross-legged. Both of them were gasping, their chests heaving.

"Sharks," Shiloh finally gasped.

Cheney crossed her arms and frowned ominously. "Yes, sharks," she agreed, her voice like a fresh-honed knife. "And don't ever scare me like that again. Or I'll kill you myself."

Shiloh looked woeful. "I was nice when you scared me."

"Don't joke. It's not funny."

"I know," he said patiently, "it never is. But, Doc, that's one thing I've always liked about you. You make sure you laugh when you feel like cryin'."

"Shiloh, dear," she said with finality, "one of the things I've always liked about you is that you're alive. Stay that way, would you?"

"Sure, Doc," he said agreeably.

"Now," she said briskly, sinking down to sit by him, "why don't you tell me more about this wonderful lagoon? Since you left out the fact that it's a deathtrap?"

He looked troubled, and it made Cheney feel uneasy. For long moments he didn't answer as he stared out to sea. "I just don't get it," he finally said, perplexed. "I've been here . . . lemme see, this is the fifth time. Those rocks on the beach, that's part of the coral reef that's died and washed up. It's never happened before. I've never seen so much as a pebble on that beach. Those rockfish. Never seen one here before. The sharks, now . . ." He focused again and rose to his feet, helping Cheney to rise too. "Can you see 'em? Those are reef sharks, and they're here in the lagoon all the time."

"Oh, well, that's just wonderful," Cheney said sarcastically. "You swim with them all the time? Have you named them too? Brought them home for dinner? Oh, that's right, you *are* dinner."

He almost grinned but quickly sobered when he saw that Cheney really was distressed. "Uh, no, Doc, it's not like that. They're not like that. They're usually out there around the rocks and the encircling reef. Normally they're real shy. They take off as soon as they see you. But these . . . these . . ." He looked to their right. They could see four shark fins now, darting this way, then that, as if they were dancing a confusing jig in triple-time. "They're . . . upset or something."

Cheney sighed theatrically. "And how is it, exactly, that you know when a shark is upset, Shiloh?"

He shrugged. "All you have to do is watch them. They don't act like that normally, Doc. They do swim in groups, but I've never seen them this agitated." He gave her a cautious look out of the corner of his eyes. "I think something's wrong here. Something's really wrong."

She stepped in front of him so she could see his face clearly. "What do you mean? What's wrong here?" she asked anxiously.

He started to answer, then seemed to change his mind. Slowly his eyes shadowed secretively, and his drawl deepened. "Aw, how should I know, Doc? Maybe Hawaiian sharks and rockfish get together for a picnic every October fourteenth. I don't know anything."

She wasn't placated, and she wasn't amused. Cheney watched him, her expression worried, for long moments. He met her eyes but gave away nothing. Finally she said seriously, "I hate to tell you this, Shiloh. I really do."

"What?"

"Today," she announced, "is October nineteenth."

"Ah," he said gravely. "So the annual rockfish-shark picnic is on October nineteenth."

"Yes," she said coolly. "But as I said, an invitation to a picnic is not so much fun when you're the main course. Next time, Shiloh, let's just surrender to the authorities, as all good little criminals should, and let them throw us onto the prison ship."

"I'm with you, Doc," he agreed. "As always, I'm right with you."

11

THE PITCH GROWS DEEPER

No ship came to pick up the exiles that day, nor the next. Cheney woke up early Friday morning, her eyes gritty and red, her head feeling too heavy for her neck. As she rose and went through her morning *toilette*, she snapped at Nia twice. Then she broke a glass and cut her finger. She tore her stockings.

Finally Cheney realized she was being careless and rough because her cotton-woolly feeling was developing into a headache. Cheney was unaccustomed to feeling anything less than strong and energetic. As did many extremely healthy people, she viewed any kind of illness, insignificant or grave, as a personal affront and an irritating hindrance to her normal fast pace.

"I'm sorry, Nia," she said quietly as they picked up the shards of the glass Cheney had recklessly set on the edge of the washbasin. It had promptly tumbled off and shattered on the hardwood floor. "I've been rude to you this morning, and I apologize."

"No need," Nia said kindly. "It's the weather, I believe, myself."

"Do you?" Cheney asked thoughtfully. "But it looks like a lovely day." The sun was shining cheerily through Cheney's open window, though there was no freshening breeze.

"Must be going to storm, surely," Nia said, rising carefully with the sharp glass pieces cradled in her apron. "That thunder just keeps on and on. Sounds like it's getting closer."

Cheney went to the window and leaned out to get a wider view of the sky. "Not a cloud," she murmured. "Not a breath of air either."

"Just like before a storm," Nia said with satisfaction. "It'll probably come busting right over that giant mountain any minute. Clear the air, clear your head."

Cheney turned and smiled. Nia's mother, Dally, had said that for years, whether applicable or not for the circumstances.

Nia went on, "Now, Miss Cheney, you quit paddin' around in your bare feet. I still see little glitters of glass on the floor over here. Why don't you just sit down at the dressing table, and I'll go get a broom to sweep up."

"Yes, ma'am," Cheney said meekly.

Nia went to the door, holding her apron carefully folded up into a pocket. Cheney said, "And, Nia—I'm glad you're here. I really am."

Nia nodded, reassuring Cheney in a manner much beyond her years and appearance. Then she slipped out, closing the door softly behind her.

Cheney brushed her hair and decided to apply a little rice powder and rouge to her face. She had a dusting of freckles across her nose from the sun yesterday, yet she was pale. Normally Cheney didn't wear cosmetics in the daytime, but she determined to try to look her best this morning. It would make her feel better.

Nia returned, swept the entire room carefully, and finished helping Cheney dress. Oddly, she didn't reproach Cheney for wearing rouge; she didn't appear to notice. Also, Nia was subdued, almost absentminded. She knelt to help Cheney with her stockings and somehow managed to get the same torn one for Cheney to put on.

"I'm addled this morning, Miss Cheney," she apologized, rummaging through one of Cheney's trunks to find new stockings. "I'm trying to think, but it's like stirrin' cold molasses."

Cheney said soothingly, "It's all right, Nia. After all, we did have a trying day yesterday. You're just recovering. And really, being a little absentminded is hardly a fatigue symptom to apologize for. Look at me. I'm rude. I'm always rude."

Kneeling to help Cheney with a new pair of stockings, Nia replied, "Not always. Just sometimes. When something's serious." She sat back on her heels as Cheney took over pulling on her stockings and regarded Cheney with curiosity. "Are you scared, Miss Cheney?" she asked quietly.

Cheney stopped, sat back, and stared at her with surprise. "I . . . I . . . why, no, Nia, I'm not scared. What's there to be scared of?"

Nia didn't answer for long moments as she searched Cheney's face, noting the wan look, the fierce light in her eyes, the restless hands. Finally she answered cryptically, "I don't know. I thought *you* might, though." Rising, she went on, "It seems like Tang Lu's having some problems this morning, Miss Cheney. If you don't need me anymore,

I think I'd better go down and see if I can help her with breakfast, or it might be late."

"All right, Nia, that will be fine," Cheney said absently. She hadn't moved, although she was unconsciously twisting the top of her stocking into knots. Nia left, and still Cheney stared into space vacantly. *Afraid? Why should I—am I afraid? Of what? I wonder what Nia meant.... Of course I'm not scared. I'm just—it's just my head, this blasted headache ... and the last few days have been so stressful for me and Nia both. We're just tired, that's all.*

This seemed like a reasonable explanation. As Cheney finished dressing, she determined to eat a good breakfast, even though her stomach was queasy and her mild headache was turning into a nasty, noisy intruder in her brain. Wearily she made her way downstairs and heard again the deep vibration of the far-off thunder. Though not constant, it had been regular since the day before. Cheney now dully recalled waking up several times during the night, foggily aware of the ominous basso profundo in the distance.

And she remembered that she had awakened in fear.

★ ★ ★ ★

All of their meals at Winslow Guest House had been carefully prepared and expertly served by Tang Lu. That morning, however, breakfast could only have been called a slapdash affair. It occurred to Cheney how much she took dedicated servants and superior service for granted when she saw the trouble poor Tang Lu was having.

First of all, there were no eggs. The banana bread was cold. Tang Lu didn't have the pineapple prepared and stuck her finger on the sharp outer spikes, getting blood on the guavas. One of the mangoes was brown, and the coffee was weak. Oddest of all, every time Tang Lu opened the door into the kitchen, thumps and muffled cries came from the back of the house, no matter how quickly Tang Lu tried to close the door.

Walker sat brooding, his unusual eyes fixed, glazed, on his plate even when it was empty. When Tang Lu served him the fresh-cut pineapple, he toyed with it with his fork, not taking a single bite. Tang Lu dropped a chunk of the fruit on the floor by him.

"Oh no, so sorry, sir," she almost whispered. He didn't appear to hear her, or see her, as she knelt to clean up, her eyes downcast. Tang Lu's aloof expression remained unchanged, but two spots of color high on her cheeks were, for her, as striking as if she'd stood up and screeched at the top of her lungs.

"What in the world is going on?" Cheney muttered.

Shiloh gave her a hard look, at first thinking she was complaining. Then his face took on a light of sudden comprehension. "Doc, you've got a headache, don't you?"

"No."

"Liar."

"It's getting better."

"It's getting worse."

Cheney blew out an impatient breath. "How do you know these things, Shiloh? It's really quite . . . unsettling sometimes."

"I hate to tell you this, Doc, but it doesn't take a mind reader to know when you don't feel good," Shiloh asserted. "It's the only time your eyes aren't sparkling and your skin doesn't glow."

"Thank you," Cheney said ironically.

"Welcome. After breakfast, let's go into the parlor, and I'll massage your neck, huh? And I've got a potion for you. Clear that nasty little ninnyhammer right up," Shiloh said confidently.

It was a sign of Cheney's lassitude that she nodded, accepting Shiloh's offer without complaint.

He eyed her sharply. The three ate in silence, barely noticing the food.

Tang Lu returned to the dining room again, and as the door swung open, a woeful, high-pitched cry sounded clearly to the diners. They all sat up, alert, and Tang Lu dropped her head.

"Please forgive me, Dr. Duvall, Mr. Irons, Dr. Baird," she said formally but with open shame. "Normally the peace of my house is not disturbed so."

"That's very true," Cheney said quickly. "It's usually quiet and restful here, Tang Lu. What is the problem today?"

Her head still bent, she shook it slightly. "No matter to you, my guests. Please don't concern yourself. I will fix it quick." With silent steps she hurried back into the kitchen without looking up at the diners.

Cheney and Walker both stared at Shiloh accusingly. He was eating unconcernedly.

"Hmm? What?" he asked innocently around a mouthful of pineapple and macadamia nuts.

"You know what's going on, don't you," Cheney stated.

"Yeah, I do," he replied. He took a bite of banana bread. He'd slathered butter on it, and a fleck of it remained on his lip.

Her stern expression intact, Cheney reached out and wiped it off, then demanded, "Well?"

Shiloh chewed meditatively. "I dunno if I ought to tell you. Tang Lu's kind of a private person, you know?"

Walker burst out, "But she's told you her whole life story, even of her ancestors, both hers and her husband's, Shiloh!"

"Yeah, but that's 'cause she knew I wouldn't go tellin' everybody I meet," he retorted.

Cheney and Walker stared at each other in disbelief. Then Walker, his irrepressible good nature rebounding, grinned. Cheney immediately felt cheered. Walker had such a joyous and childlike smile that it was difficult to be grumpy when he was around. And Cheney liked Walker being around, very much, as she was certain that he enjoyed her company too. She smiled back at him, then said mischievously to Shiloh, "Well, sir, I hardly think that Walker and I qualify as suspicious gossipy persons you've just met on the street."

"Maybe," he admitted with a great show of reluctance, "but the tough truth is that you're both known criminals. Cavorters, and all."

"Hmm," Cheney grumbled, her brow wrinkling. "True. Well, Walker, it looks as if I'm going to be obliged to use all of my feminine wiles to get The Iron Man to talk."

"Looks like," Walker agreed happily.

Shiloh straightened eagerly in his chair. "Hey, this sounds like fun! Go ahead, Doc. Do your worst. I mean, your best. But I gotta warn you, I'm a hard case to break. Might take a long time. Days, months ... decades ..."

Cheney blushed furiously, and now both Shiloh and Walker were amused. "Men," she muttered under her breath, then lifted her chin arrogantly. "I've changed my mind. And my tactics."

Shiloh wilted. "Blast it."

Ignoring him, she pronounced sonorously, "I hate to resort to this—no, as a matter of fact, I don't mind at all resorting to this—both Dr. Baird and I, as physicians on staff at St. Francis de Yerba Buena Hospital, are still technically your bosses."

Grouchily Shiloh grumbled, "Seems like I'm always in trouble with the bosses."

"Big trouble," Cheney said gravely. "So talk. What kind of trouble is Tang Lu having today?"

Shiloh rose and helped himself to a fresh cup of coffee. Without asking, he poured for Walker and Cheney both and then sat back down. "It's the kids," he finally said quietly. "They're restless today, the little two-year-old especially. But I already checked 'em. They're not sick."

"Kids? You mean children? Tang Lu has children?" Cheney asked in astonishment.

"Four of 'em. Here with her, I mean. Her husband has three older kids by his first wife. But Tang Lu's got four, ranging from ten to two years old. That was the baby crying."

"I didn't even know she was married," Walker commented.

"But . . . where do they live?" Cheney asked in confusion. "We've got all four guest bedrooms."

Shiloh jerked his thumb back toward the kitchen door and leaned precariously back on two chair legs. "Back there. The kitchen's on this side of the house, and on the other side she's got kind of a partitioned room. She lives there with the kids even when she doesn't have guests. To keep the guest rooms as nice as they are, I guess."

"I can't believe it," Cheney ventured. "No, no, not that she's living back there with all four children. From what I've seen of the Chinese, they are so frugal and seem to be accustomed to little space that it's understandable for Tang Lu to keep the guest house only for paying boarders. What I can't believe is that I haven't seen, or especially heard, a peep from those four little children!"

Shiloh smiled wryly. "You gotta admit, Chinese kids are almost always different from American kids, Doc. Better behaved, quieter, kinda shy, not aggressive. They're real obedient too. They mind Tang Lu like she's the marshal of Dodge City, even the little ones."

Walker and Cheney both laughed at the vision of the tiny and delicate Tang Lu wearing two six-guns and a ten-gallon hat, striding the dusty streets of Dodge City. Walker declared, "Well, she may not be a deadeye gunfighter, but she sure is tough. From what you told me, she's the only person on this island who's had the grit to stand up to Mrs. Winslow." His eyes crinkled as he added, "I sure didn't. Not going to either."

"It's not worth it," Cheney scoffed. "To us, anyway. But then, we don't have to deal with her."

"True," Walker ventured. "We can run away. I'm for it."

"But what about the wonderful Miss Winslow?" Shiloh teased, but his eyes shadowed slightly with worry.

Walker sighed, then looked down at his plate again and toyed with his untouched food. "After Mr. Zeiss gave you a message from her yesterday, Shiloh, I had thought—hoped—that perhaps she might send me one. But she hasn't, of course. I . . . I don't think—"

"Walker, she didn't send me a message, you little simpleton," Shiloh rasped. "She sent us all a message—including you. She generously gave us the use of her horses and buckboard. And they are hers, you know. Not Mrs. Winslow's, or anyone else's. That means she's standing up to her mother at least that much. You know Mrs. Winslow knows where those horses are. And besides, you're the one who should be sending her messages. You're the man, remember?"

"Yeah, I remember," Walker said with comical somberness. "You really think I should send her a note or something?"

" 'Course," Shiloh answered.

"What should I say?" he asked worriedly. "Her mother—"

"Walker, her mother doesn't have anything to do with you and her," Shiloh forcefully maintained. "The woman is twenty-two years old. She—"

"What?" Walker said, sitting up straight in his chair. "Twenty-two? I thought she was younger than that! And I thought Mrs. Winslow might think I was a filthy cradle-robber or something!"

"No, just a habitual cavorter," Cheney teased, "and a grinning idiot, of course. But, Walker, think, poor lamb. I thought Miss Winslow was younger, too, about eighteen. But even at that age, you would hardly qualify as a cradle-robber!" Walker had just turned twenty-two a few months ago.

"I know," he said sheepishly, "but that woman just made me feel so . . . so sneaky."

"Don't know why," Shiloh grunted. "That sunny grin's always hanging right out there for anybody to see. The women fall over it right in front of their mamas and everybody."

Walker blushed as painfully as a young girl. "That's not true, Shiloh, and you know it. You're the one they're always swooning over. After all, I haven't had any of these beautiful Hawaiian girls like Malani fall in love with me, and try to . . . uh . . ." His words trailed off as he caught a glimpse of Cheney's face.

"Malani? Keloki's daughter?" she asked in a tight, high voice.

Walker swallowed hard, cutting his eyes guiltily to Shiloh, who was staring up at the ceiling, a fierce scowl of concentration on his face. Walker uncomfortably hummed, "Uhh . . . um . . ."

"It's not a trick question, Walker," Cheney prodded him.

"Uh . . . yes . . . yes . . . she's Keloki's daughter."

"Please continue."

"Huh-uh, let's don't do that," Shiloh, finally recovered, said hastily. "We're getting away from the topic, anyway."

"What was the topic?" Cheney asked with disarming calmness.

"Uh . . . it was—just give me a minute," Shiloh fumbled.

Walker snapped his fingers and almost shouted with relief, "Tang Lu! How she stood up to Mrs. Winslow! Tell Dr. Duvall that story, Shiloh!"

"Yes, that was the original topic," Cheney said coolly, "but I don't believe we've quite settled your intentions yet, Dr. Baird. Or yours, Shiloh."

"Honorable," he said quickly. "Always."

"Mm-hm," she said suspiciously.

"Simple," Walker put in with a hint of desperation. "I'm going to send a note to Miss Winslow. As soon as I can. How soon can I, Shiloh? How can I, Shiloh?"

With a last cautious glance at Cheney, who was still eyeing him in a decidedly hostile manner, Shiloh answered, "I don't know if Zeiss would take it to her. It might kind of complicate things for him. But Keloki would," he said, brightening. "He's coming into town today, I bet. He usually does every two or three days."

"So that's settled," Walker said, rising so hastily that he almost knocked his chair over. "I'm going to go compose the note right now. If you'll excuse me, Dr. Duvall." With a quick bow, he left the dining room.

Shiloh turned to her. "Are you mad at me, Doc?" he asked, his eyes twinkling.

"Should I be?" she demanded.

He cocked his head and grinned at her. "Naw, you're not mad. You want to be, but you don't fool me. You just want me to rub your neck so your headache will go away."

She stayed stiff for a minute, then relented and smiled. "And your magic potion, too, remember."

"It's okolehao," he said proudly. "Two or three glasses of it, Doc, and I swear you won't feel a thing. And I mean nothing. Like your feet, or hands, or ears . . ."

She giggled. "You are really, really terrible, Shiloh! Anyway, my headache is better already. Isn't that odd? Maybe eating helped. So go on, tell me about Tang Lu and Mrs. Winslow. I'm very curious."

Obediently Shiloh told her about the guest house, and how Tang Lu had forced Mrs. Winslow's hand in allowing her to buy the house and land together. "Tang Lu used to have a really snappy business," he said quietly. "And so did the Zeisses. You know, they have the general store down the street? The only other two-story building in town? Well, upstairs Zeiss put in a big room with hammocks, and when *Locke's Day Dream* or the *Brynn Annalea* docked here, the crew used to stay up there, and the officers here. But Denise Winslow put a stop to that. About six months after Zeiss finished his house and married Alena, Mrs. Winslow decided that the sailors were too rowdy and said they couldn't stay in Hana anymore. Mr. Winslow and Bain had to start carting them back and forth to Lahaina when they were here. And Zeiss lost his extra income." A flash of anger made Shiloh's eyes a freezing blue.

"And Tang Lu too? Then who in the world ever stays here?" Cheney wondered. "This isn't one of the places that Americans often visit in Hawaii."

With relish Shiloh told her, "Well, the two captains of the ships evidently aren't too crazy about Mrs. Winslow. They and their officers stay here almost all the time. When we came in on *Locke's Day Dream*, Captain Starnes, his first mate, his second mate, and the pilot all stayed here for a week before they went on to Lahaina. I think it might have been just to spite Mrs. Winslow. She's never asked them to stay at the villa, and I think she views them as just more dirty sailors, only better dressed."

"Good for them," Cheney asserted. "And I admire Tang Lu just that much more. In fact, I think we should do something for her."

"You do?" Shiloh asked curiously. "What?"

"Give her a day off, and some peace and solitude."

He smiled slowly. "You mean you want to take those four kids off her hands for a whole day? What are you going to do with four children, Doc?"

She smiled sweetly at him. "I haven't the faintest idea. But you know what to do with children, don't you, Shiloh?"

"Me? How should I know?"

"You're so good with them. You just know," Cheney said, fluttering her eyelashes in an exaggerated manner. "Here, let me get you some more coffee."

"Doc, you don't have to mooch me," he sighed. "We don't have much else to do, anyway, except wait for our prison ship. Guess we could go out in one of the canoes, maybe fish a little, let the kids look for pretty shells."

"Of course! What a wonderful idea. See, I told you you'd know what to do with them."

He shook his head. "Doc, they're not like hard geometry problems or a difficult diagnosis. They're just people. Only littler."

"Simple for you to say," Cheney grumbled. "I've never been around children. I never know what to say to them."

"You were around Buchanan all the time you were growing up," Shiloh maintained.

"But he was always like a little man," Cheney argued.

Shiloh grinned. "Like I said, Doc. Kids are just like little, bitty women and little, bitty men. Just remember that. Don't worry, you'll be fine. I'll take care of you and protect you from them."

"Very funny," she grumbled. "Now, I suppose you'd better go tell Tang Lu our wonderful plan. If she's as smart as she appears to be, she wouldn't dare allow me to be in charge of her children. But she trusts you."

He grew serious. "Do you, Doc?"

She smiled, and this time it was genuine. "Yes, Shiloh. I really do. Even with luscious young Hawaiian girls." He started to say something, but she went on, "Never mind that now. Let's go outside and play!"

★　★　★　★

They made a solemn little procession, Tang Lu's children did. Cheney heartily wished that her friend, Victoria de Lancie, had been there to sketch them.

They walked in single file. Though the boy was the second oldest, he led, and the three girls followed behind. All four of them wore gray tunics with long sleeves and mandarin collars and loose white pantaloons with white stockings and soft black slippers. Their glossy black hair was neatly pulled back and braided into pigtails. Cheney noted that the boy's was pulled straight back, but the girls' hair was parted demurely down the middle. The girls neatly tucked their hands into the sleeves of their tunics, while the little boy's arms stayed at his side as he marched. They followed Nia in a straight line, while Cheney and Shiloh walked alongside.

"Aren't they just darling?" Cheney exclaimed. "What are their names?"

"The little boy is Fang Kwan," Shiloh answered. "He's eight. That's Fang Ming, she's ten. Then Fang Wen, who's five, and the little doll is Fang Liu. She just turned two."

"I don't understand the Chinese names," Cheney complained.

"The first name is the family name," Shiloh explained. "The wife keeps her maiden name. But the children have the father's family name. Tang Lu's husband is Fang Shao. He works at one of the sugar-cane camps. He has two sons and a daughter by his first wife, or second wife, or whatever. The girl's name is Fang Jinglan. She's fifteen, works up at the villa as a scullery maid. Pretty little thing, but a little sullen."

"You said Tang Lu is his second wife?"

Shiloh grimaced. "I don't really get their deal about marriage. She keeps telling me she's really 'third wife.' Evidently Fang Shao has a wife, an arranged marriage in China. She's 'first wife.' The other one, the one that died, was 'second wife,' and the older children were actually hers. So Tang Lu is 'third wife.' I get the impression that that doesn't count for much."

Cheney frowned. "What do you mean?"

"I mean, Tang Lu keeps telling me how all of Fang Shao's children belong to 'first wife.' Their loyalty is supposed to be to her. That's what she teaches them. Tang Lu sends money to 'first wife' in China from the children."

Her eyes round with outrage, Cheney said, "You can't be serious! A woman like Tang Lu actually caters to that . . . that . . . slavery?"

"It's their way of life, Doc," he answered. "In China, it's different—really hard, I guess, for women. They don't even really count the girls when they tell you how many children they have. They just tell you the number of sons. And when a woman marries, she only has loyalty to her in-laws. Her parents just kind of give her away and forget about her, because after she marries she only takes care of, and honors, the man's parents. People really want to have sons, you see. So the son can marry, and then the parents will have a daughter-in-law to kick around. It also has to do with their religion. Something about only boy descendants can honor the ancestors."

"Yes, I remember," Cheney said thoughtfully. "When Reverend Merced was telling us about Pearl, you know. How, since she was a girl, her parents were 'hungry ghosts.'"

"That's the idea, I guess," Shiloh said. "You saw the old couple up at the villa? That's Tang Lu's parents, Tang Sun and Chen Guifei. They call 'em 'Sunny' and 'Fay' because Miss Winslow called them that when she was a baby. Anyway, Tang Lu hardly ever sees them. And they don't seem to view the kids as grandchildren. Kind of sad, isn't it?"

He sounded a little dispirited, so Cheney made a determined effort at cheerfulness. "Well, it's a lovely day for boating, isn't it?"

"Is it?" He squinted up at the sky, his manner calculating.

Cheney looked around for the first time since they'd come outside. The air was still, leaden. Again she was conscious of the underlying rumble, now sounding farther in the distance instead of nearer. The sun was shining, and no clouds darkened the sky. But still, the atmosphere seemed oppressive. The air was curiously tepid—not cool, not hot. It had a numbing sort of deadening effect.

They had crossed the wide strip of red sand that passed for the main street of Hana and were now walking on the beach. Cheney straightened alertly, then shaded her eyes. "Goodness, that seems odd," she remarked. "The surf is whitecapping as far out as one can see!"

Shiloh nodded, his sharp eyes searching the infinite distance of the sea. "Choppy and fussy, isn't she? It is weird, since the waves aren't really that big." He stopped, so Cheney stopped, Nia stopped, and the little parade behind her obediently stopped. The children did, however, crane their necks to look out to sea, as the adults were doing.

Shiloh and Cheney went to Nia. "I don't think going out in one of the canoes with the children is such a good idea today," Nia said anxiously. "It looks kind of mean out there."

"I wouldn't do it," Shiloh agreed emphatically. He turned, and his gaze swept up and down the beach, rich with the common red sand of Maui. The Winslows had built the jetty, which was a barrier of great slabs of flat rock, much like the ancient Hawaiians used for the heiaus, set out about a hundred feet from the beach, running for almost two hundred yards. A walkway ran at right angles to it, so that men could walk along it and easily carry cargoes to and from the smaller boats that moored there.

Shiloh squinted, then said casually, "Why don't you all go over and sit under those coconut palms for a few minutes while I take a look at the beach? I'll see if there are any shells as pretty as you ladies are. If they aren't as pretty as you, they won't be worth picking up."

The two older girls giggled, while Liu, the two-year-old, gazed up at the distant heights of Shiloh's face with awe. He went down on one knee so that he was on her level. "Miss Fang Liu, you want to go with me? I'll carry you, so you'll be up in the sky!"

Her black-pebble eyes shone, and she nodded, then stuck one finger in her mouth. Shiloh swept her up and walked out on the road-stead.

Nia said, "Come along, children, let's go over and sit in the shade. Do you like to sing? Oh, I do. How about if I teach you a song, and then you teach me one? Ming, I'll bet you know a song in Chinese. I'd love to learn a Chinese song! And so would Dr. Duvall!"

"I would?" Cheney gulped. As soon as Shiloh had left, she felt at a loss with the three children's fathomless gazes on her.

"Yes, you would," Nia said firmly. "All of you children come along, especially you, the tall one." Obediently Cheney trailed behind Fang Wen, the five-year-old, who was now the last in the precise line.

Shiloh walked along the jetty, holding Liu securely in his arms. Though she said nothing, she seemed to be delighted. As soon as he had picked her up, she had thrown back her head and stared upward, as if she did believe she was flying in the heavens.

Shiloh's eyes, however, were turned downward. *Just like I thought,* he reflected, troubled. *Jellyfish everywhere! Like a plague. At least there aren't any of those man-o'-war. Those things could kill a child Liu's size.* Unconsciously he clutched her a little tighter, but she didn't seem to mind. In fact, she slid one arm around his neck, though she still didn't look down. She seemed enraptured, staring up at the empty blue sky.

Moodily Shiloh kicked one of the dead jellyfish with his boot. They were saucer-shaped, about a half-inch thick. Clear gel with faint reddish markings, they were almost impossible to see until one was right over them. *Or stepping on them. I wonder if there's a plague of rockfish on this beach too?* He picked up a stick and poked several suspicious-looking rocks, but that's all they were, just rocks. *Don't see any of those things, thank goodness, but I sure don't think the kids ought to be playing on the beach right now. I don't even think adults ought to be on the beach right now. . . .*

The foreboding in the thought suddenly struck him, and he stood still. In his arms, Liu kept her one arm tightly about his neck but raised the other one, her stubby fingers grasping as if she could grab a piece of sky and bring it down to her upturned face. In spite of his dark thoughts, he smiled absently.

Jarringly, the thunder began again. A slow undercurrent of sound, it slowly built up and grew louder, while at the same time, the pitch grew deeper. Shiloh jerked, then whirled around to look behind him. For the first time, Liu looked down at him curiously.

"Thunder," she lisped, as if reassuring him.

"I know, baby," he said warmly, patting her back. Liu, in return, patted his broad shoulders.

But the delightful gesture was lost on Shiloh, for he was distracted. Standing out in the empty amphitheater of the sea, he heard the thunder, as it truly was, for the first time. And it wasn't thunder. It wasn't the sound of great air masses colliding many miles away.

It wasn't a sound traveling through the air at all.

The reverberation was rolling over him, assaulting his body from below. Shiloh could *feel* the sound now, clearly, in his sensitive fingertips, in his teeth, even in his blood, and it made his heart beat erratically.

Because the baleful warning sounds were coming from the earth itself.

Shiloh wheeled and ran nimbly over the treacherous rocks of the reef, then cut directly left and sped toward the stand of coconut palms. "Bet you didn't know a big galoot like me could run this fast, huh?" he said to Liu to reassure her.

But the child didn't need reassurance; she giggled. "Big garoot," she repeated. Shiloh was so athletic, so strong, that his pace was as smooth as a panther's. The baby barely joggled.

Nia and Cheney looked up in surprise, and then alarm. Cheney scrambled to her feet and started to say something. Then, with a cautious look at the children, she said lightly, "Is this a race?"

"Something like that," Shiloh answered, barely breathing hard after his fifty-yard sprint. "Here, kids, let's go out there and play . . . uh . . ." He was pointing out to the clear beach. Anxiously his gaze went up to the bunches of fat coconuts suspended from the branches overhead.

Nia followed his gaze, then looked at Shiloh in disbelief. But quickly she stood up and said, "Yes, let's go out there and play ring-around-the-rosy. Do you know how to play that? C'mon, you'll like it!

We'll all get to fall down!" She took the two little girls' hands and started out toward the empty stretch of sand.

"Even the grown-ups?" Kwan, the little boy, asked in astonishment.

"Even me," Cheney said hurriedly. "Even him. And he looks like a great tree when he crashes to the ground. Come along, Kwan, let's hurry." She tried to take his hand, but he nimbly avoided her and ran after his sisters.

"What is it, Shiloh?" she asked anxiously, stepping close to him.

He glanced meaningfully at Liu, who was watching and listening with interest but without comprehension. "Probably nothing," he hesitantly replied. "Mostly I want you to come . . . uh . . . listen to something. And it won't hurt—" Again he glanced up at the heavy fruit suspended far above them and shrugged slightly. "I just wanted to play ring-around-the-rosy," he finished, following behind Nia and the other children.

Cheney, walking beside him, smiled tremulously and started to speak. But she didn't get the opportunity.

The earth started shaking, jarring, crashing. This time, the earthquake was much more powerful than the one they'd experienced in the high camp. Cheney was immediately thrown to the sand, and for long moments she was so disoriented and dizzy and frightened that she couldn't distinguish which was the earth and which was the sky. Then she felt Shiloh's strong hand on her arm, steadying her, but he didn't try to pull her upright. Instead he slid to a sitting position, still holding Liu in his arms. The child had burrowed into his neck, and her shoulders were shaking. Desperately Cheney clung to Shiloh's hand, then pulled herself close to him. He enveloped her in his other arm, and like little Liu, she buried her face on his wide shoulder and wept.

12

AFTERSHOCKS

"You're all right," Shiloh murmured. "It's all right."

Cheney looked up, her face tear streaked, her eyes wild.

"It's over, Doc. We're okay."

"Yes . . . yes . . ." Cheney rubbed her eyes hard, then pulled away from Shiloh's encircling arm and looked around.

Nia and the other three children were sitting about ten feet away on the sand. People were starting to come out of their houses, their heads whipping this way and that as if they were under attack. Cheney looked back at the stand of coconut trees where they had been sitting only moments before. Not only had dozens of the enormous hard-shelled fruits fallen, but two of the trees had toppled, their fragile roots mere spiderwebs in the air. Cheney swallowed hard. They had fallen directly where she and Nia and the children had been sitting, one on top of the other, in a deadly X.

Liu was crying, and suddenly Tang Lu was there. Wordlessly sliding to her knees, she held out her arms for the baby. Her face was as white as rice paper, her eyes rounded in shock, but she was calm. "I will take her, Mr. Irons. Thank you."

Shiloh gave the baby to her, then stood up and helped Cheney to her feet. "I'm going to go check on Walker," he said. "Then I think we ought to check out all the villagers and see if anyone got hurt. I'll get Walker and we'll go down to see about Alena Zeiss."

Cheney followed him. "I'll come with you. I need to get my medical bag."

They were running by the time they reached the verandah of the guest house, but Walker came out to meet them. He was holding all of their medical bags. "I'm fine," he said curtly. "Some glass things were broken, and a couple of pictures fell, that's all. Neither Tang Lu nor I was hurt. The children?"

"We're all okay," Shiloh said. "Here—"

After some fumbling and checking of contents—all three of them had black leather medical bags—they sorted them out. Shiloh and Walker ran toward the Zeisses', while Cheney headed back across the beach. Close to where she and the children had been sitting was a hut, and before the earthquake a Hawaiian woman had been sitting outside in front of a fire, cooking. Cheney hadn't seen her after the earthquake and thought she ought to check on her first.

The hut was right at the edge of the high tide mark, a small one-room structure made of the lovely blond koa wood and thatched with reeds and fresh palm leaves. Cheney hurried over the dunes, calling "Ma'am? Ma'am? Is anyone here?"

She topped the last dune and saw that the woman was lying flat in the sand by the fire pit, which was why Cheney couldn't see her. She ran to her.

She was an elderly woman, with snow-white hair and a face with age etched upon it. Sturdy, heavy, she wore a shapeless shift of a cheerful yellow color that made her Hawaiian skin look almost chocolate. As Cheney knelt beside her, the woman looked up at her and smiled, and Cheney thought how wonderful it was that the Hawaiians, even in old age, had such fine teeth. Her smile was that of a girl's.

Being large, she struggled in the newly loosened sand to sit up. Cheney laid her hands on the woman's shoulders and said quietly, "Ma'am, I'm a doctor, and I can help you. Why don't you just lie here quietly for a moment and let me see if you're hurt."

The woman yielded to Cheney's pressure and lay back down. She pointed to herself and said, "Mama Nomi."

Cheney nodded politely. "I'm Dr. Cheney Duvall." She pulled her stethoscope out of her bag and placed it on the woman's chest.

Before Cheney could stop the woman, she picked up the receiver of the stethoscope and said clearly, "Mama Nomi!"

Cheney yelped, jumped, and yanked the earpieces out of her screeching ears. The woman beamed at her.

Cheney settled back down and even giggled. "I'm very pleased to meet you, Mama Nomi," she finally replied. "And I don't believe you are much hurt. Hurt? Mmm . . . uh . . . injured? Oh, this is silly."

Now the woman sat up and leaned close to Cheney. With a hand as seasoned as an old saddle, she pointed to Cheney. "*Kahuna*?"

"No. Doctor." Cheney pointed to herself.

"Ahh," Mama Nomi breathed and nodded. "Kahuna." Reaching down, she pulled up the skirt of her shift.

Cheney was appalled when she saw the scalds up and down the woman's shin. Cheney noted the overturned kettle and spicy-smelling puddles. The kettle had been jarred off the tripod, and the boiling contents had splashed on Mama Nomi's leg.

"Burns," she sighed. "I had so hoped never to see them again." In San Francisco, Cheney had gone through a traumatic experience with burn victims. "Well, let's see . . . I'll need to wash them out with cold, clear water. . . . Wonder where. . . ?"

"*Wai*," Mama Nomi said gravely and pointed to the hut.

"Wai? That's water? Fresh water?" Cheney mimicked drinking.

Mama Nomi nodded patiently. She pointed to the sea. "*Kai*," she said, pronouncing carefully. "Wai." She repeated the drinking pantomime, then pointed again.

Cheney ran to the hut. Right by the front door was a heavy wooden bucket with a dipper. "I'm an idiot," she snapped to herself. "By the time I've taken care of this poor woman, she's probably going to be healed." She hurried back with the bucket and dipper.

Mama Nomi smiled politely and pointed to her leg.

"Thank you," Cheney said with amusement. "I don't wonder that you think I'm an imbecile . . . that's probably what 'kahuna' means. . . ." She ran two dippers of the cool water on the woman's leg. Then she started rummaging in her medical bag and talking to herself. "Carbolic acid . . . have to. It'll hurt her . . . oh, good, here's some laudanum. Wish I had some aloe vera. . . ."

She gave Mama Nomi the laudanum bottle and watched her tip it up and take a good drink. The woman made a face and spit it out. "Auwe!" she spat. "Pah!" She said a great many more things, Cheney supposed in Hawaiian, and also supposed that it might be a good thing she didn't know the language.

"It is foul, isn't it?" Cheney agreed. "But really, you'll need it, ma'am. Here." She tried to give the woman the small cobalt blue bottle again, but Mama Nomi pushed it away.

"Okolehao?" she asked hopefully.

Cheney couldn't help but smile. "All right, ma'am, I hear that okolehao is a wonderful anesthetic. But I don't—" She looked around helplessly, wondering if the Zeisses had the locally made concoction in the general store.

Mama Nomi beamed. "Okolehao," she said, rising to her feet.

Cheney jumped up. "Oh no, ma'am, I'll get it for you—"

But Mama Nomi was already heading into her hut, holding up her shift so that the skirt wouldn't rub the scalded places. Soon she came back out with a dark green bottle and two cups made of coconut shells. "Okolehao," she beamed. Like a cowpoke in a saloon, she pulled the cork out of the bottle with her teeth and poured a stiff shot of the strong liquor into each of the two coconut shells she held with one hand. Then she tucked the bottle under one massive arm, took one shell, and thrust the other one to Cheney.

Cheney took it automatically, and Mama Nomi downed the liquor, smacking her lips. Cheney said, "Now this one, ma'am. But this is all, I think, until tonight, yes? Later, maybe, for the pain so you can sleep."

Mama Nomi shrugged, then downed the second shot of liquor. Her eyes glazed over a bit, but she still looked alert.

"All right, now, let's take you back—"

Cheney took Mama Nomi's arm and began to lead her back into the hut. Then she stopped abruptly, thinking, *What if there are aftershocks? There usually are, aren't there, after strong earthquakes? Maybe . . . maybe she shouldn't be in that hut. . . .*

But it occurred to Cheney that everyone in the village wasn't going to stay outside all night, that eventually they would have to go back inside their homes. Certainly Mama Nomi needed to lie down. In spite of the woman's vigor, a burn was traumatic to the system and taxed even healthy people enough to need rest.

"Come along, Mama Nomi," she said with finality. "I'm going to get you to bed and put some more medicine on these burns. Then you need to rest awhile. Take a nap if you can."

They went inside her hut. It was one room, with a woven grass mat for a floor and mosquito netting over the two windows. She had a plain wooden table, made of koa wood, and two chairs. Her bed was in one corner, a very large bed to accommodate her size, and it was neatly made up with clean cotton sheets. Along the walls were hung woven grass rugs of all sizes and shapes, even round ones. Mama Nomi also evidently made straw hats; about a dozen of them hung from hooks, from the chair backs. A half-finished hat and a neat stack of dried palm leaves were the only items on the table.

Cheney sat Mama Nomi in the chair and knelt in front of her. "Ma'am, this is going to sting," she told the woman, even though she knew Mama Nomi didn't understand the words. But she did understand Cheney's tone, for she nodded, pressed her lips together firmly, and stared out the window at the restless sea.

Cheney poured carbolic acid down her leg and anxiously looked up. But Mama Nomi merely took a deep breath, then nodded reassuringly at Cheney.

"Hokay," she said painstakingly. "Hokay."

"Good."

Cheney repacked her medical bag, thinking, *I'll come back later and bring her something to eat. Guess that was her luncheon that's spilled out there in the sand. . . .*

"Havin' a friendly drink, Doc?" Shiloh stood in the doorway, smiling a little, and nodded toward the bottle and two native cups Mama Nomi had set on the table. "Everything's okay. No one got hurt. But I didn't know we were having a party."

"Oh, Mama Nomi and I were just taking care of her leg," Cheney told him. "Her lunch turned over on it, I think."

"Keakea," Mama Nomi said with delight, holding up both arms. "*Hona Kaua wikiwiki!*"

Shiloh came to her, bent over, and Mama Nomi planted a big kiss right on Shiloh's mouth. He turned to Cheney and grinned sheepishly. "Hawaiians, they . . . uh . . . it's their way of greeting, you know. Don't you?"

"Oh?" Cheney said with great interest. "That's odd. She didn't kiss me."

"Well, uh . . . you know, it's—I've known her—"

"Of course. And the other Hawaiian ladies? The young Hawaiian ladies?" Cheney asked politely.

"Oh no, huh-uh, they . . . they're like us now. They don't do that."

Cheney crossed her arms and nodded slightly, eyeing Shiloh with her eyebrows raised high. "Whatever do you mean, Keakea? I've known lots of haole wahines who greeted you just like that."

Shiloh looked confused and started to say something, but Mama Nomi pulled on his hand. With obvious relief he looked down at her. She pointed to her leg and said, "Keakea. *Niu?* Niu."

"What does she want?" Cheney asked.

"I don't know," Shiloh said, frowning. "Mama Nomi? Niu? Coconut?"

She nodded vigorously, then made the universal sign for "small"—

a thumb and forefinger held closely together.

"She needs a green coconut," a voice said from the doorway.

Cheney turned. It was the loveliest woman she'd ever seen.

Alena Zeiss was twenty-four years old. Half-white, half-Hawaiian, she had inherited the most striking features from both races. Her skin was like rich cream-colored satin. Her hair reached her waist in a shimmering ebony fall. Her startling turquoise eyes were framed with impossibly thick black lashes and perfect black brows. Her nose was small and straight, her mouth feline, solemn, and sweet all at once. In a cultured British accent she said, "Hello, I'm Alena Zeiss. You must be Dr. Duvall. It's a pleasure to meet you, even though it is under such stressful circumstances." She glided forward like a dancer, and she and Cheney exchanged dignified nods.

Glancing up at Shiloh, she went on, "Mr. Irons, if you would be so good as to go see if you can find a green coconut and open it, I will take care of Mama Nomi."

"Green coconut? To eat?" Shiloh asked in confusion.

"No, no." She smiled up at him, and Cheney couldn't help but watch him closely to see if he was smitten, as surely most men must be, by Alena's great beauty. "When they're green, the meat is like a jelly. It's good for burns."

"Oh, I didn't know that," he said with mild interest. Even to Cheney's sharp gaze, he evidenced nothing more than that for Alena Zeiss. "Okay, one green coconut's on the way."

"It's kind of you to offer your help," Cheney said. "I was going to come back to take care of her, but it is difficult since I don't speak Hawaiian."

Alena looked mildly surprised and pleased. "How nice you are, Dr. Duvall. Most Americans would be impatient because Mama Nomi didn't speak English."

"How rude," Cheney said mildly. "I'm rude sometimes, but I don't think in quite that way. . . . Goodness, what am I blathering on about?"

"Most people do after a great shock, I believe," Alena said gravely. "It seems to jar the brain a bit, doesn't it?"

"I hope that's the reason," Cheney joked. "I do hope to regain some of my senses. Oh, Shiloh, that was quick."

"Found several new coconuts right out there in the downed trees," he said. "This one was already cracked." Expertly he removed the thinner outer husk, then gave the inside corm a sharp rap on the table to open it completely. Instead of the lining of clean white meat as was in ripe coconuts, the inside was filled with a whitish jelly.

"Mahalo, Keakea," Mama Nomi said and briskly began to apply the gel to the scalds on her leg.

"I'll do that," Cheney protested, kneeling quickly before the old woman. Mama Nomi looked surprised and pleased. Standing above her, Alena Zeiss watched her thoughtfully. Then she turned to Shiloh and considered him for long moments. He was watching Cheney, and his expression was clearly one of warmest admiration.

Alena crossed her arms and, with an air of decision, asked, "Mr. Irons, you do know why they call you 'Keakea,' don't you?"

He was surprised. "Well, no. Keloki called me that from the first time we met, and I thought it was just kinda like . . . sounds he liked. He calls me something else with lots of *k*'s—Keakeakickie, or something. He told me once he didn't like words with *s*'s or *z*'s in them. Said they're bad *mana*. But he says lots of things, makes sly jokes. Anyway, I just thought he made up a name for me."

"I had noticed," Cheney said without looking up from tending Mama Nomi's leg, "that the Hawaiian alphabet doesn't have *s*'s or *z*'s in it. It's odd, Keloki saying that. Those letters do make a hissing sound, but there's nothing here that makes that evil noise, is there? Shiloh told me there are no snakes in Hawaii."

"That is true, and that is an interesting observation by Keloki," Alena observed. "But you must admit his manner of thinking is unique. Even for a Hawaiian."

"But his pet name for me, Keakea," Shiloh ventured, "has a meaning? It's not just sounds he likes to make?"

"Oh yes, Mr. Irons, it has a definite meaning," Alena said quietly. " 'Kea' is the Hawaiian word for 'white.' Not white, like white man—as you know, that's 'haole'—but white, like the color white. And Hawaiians often double words for emphasis. For example, the plant that grows up on Haleakala they call *ahinahina*, which means gray-gray. They have no word for silver, you see, because they had no metals."

"But why would they call me 'white-white'?" Shiloh asked, puzzled. "It doesn't make sense. I mean, look at me, my skin's darker than yours, Mrs. Zeiss. Aw, I'm so sorry, I didn't mean to—"

She laid her hand on his arm and smiled up at him sweetly. "No, Mr. Irons, please don't apologize. It's all right, really. I am a unique color because of my mixed race; you are a unique color because of the sun. Neither of us should be offended at that." In her self-possessed manner, she withdrew her hand and stepped back again into her own little circle of privacy.

Cheney, who had finished and stood up again, smiled up at Shiloh. "Well, I understand perfectly why they call you 'white-white.' Have you looked in the mirror lately?"

"Well, yeah, I guess so," Shiloh answered, still bewildered.

Cheney gave a frustrated sigh, then turned to Alena. "He really has no idea, you know. He's not very perceptive about his looks."

Alena cut her eyes toward him, then looked back at Cheney slyly. "He should be. Most men would be."

"He's not," she said. "Shiloh. You have hair that looks like it's spun silver and gold. You have teeth that positively sparkle when you smile. You are so healthy, so vigorous that the whites of your eyes are that rare, glowing blue-white of only the healthiest of people. That's why they call you Keakea."

As she spoke, Shiloh's face changed from perplexity to comprehension to a hint of embarrassment. "Okay," he shrugged uncomfortably.

"See what I mean?" Cheney said aside to Alena.

"Yes, I do," she answered, but she was somber. Assuming her deliberate air, she went on, "But that's not what they call you, you know. What Keloki named you was 'Keakea-keiki.' "

"Wait, I know that word," Cheney ventured. "It's 'child,' isn't it? They call him 'white-white child'?"

Alena nodded, very slowly. "Yes. What's really interesting is that Keloki, when he was seven years old, met a man, a haole, whom he named 'Keakea-kanaka.' 'White-white man.' The name stuck; everyone here called him Keakea all his life." She hesitated, then looked straight in Shiloh's eyes. "That man was Roderick Winslow. Logan Winslow's brother."

Shiloh stared at her. His expression was not so much startled as it was intense. Cheney stared at him. Alena returned his gaze with a peculiar defiance.

Forgotten, Mama Nomi spoke up, startling the three. She spoke softly, something in Hawaiian that Cheney could barely hear.

Alena's expression turned to sadness. "She said she remembers Keakea-kanaka. He was *no ka oi* . . . the best, a man among men."

"I—Mama Nomi, would you mind if I sat down?" Shiloh asked,

then sat without waiting for her answer. Cheney reflected that it was the first time she had ever seen Shiloh seated when ladies present were standing. As if he'd heard her thoughts, he jumped up again and asked Alena in an even voice, "I don't mean to pry, ma'am, but why exactly are you telling me this? Why hasn't someone mentioned it before?"

Alena, far from taking offense at the slight suspicion in his tone, softened even more. "Mr. Irons, I think you have an insight into these people that most haoles never achieve. If you think about it, you'll know that family connections don't have the same significance to them that they do to us—to white people. For example, Keloki knows that you are connected to the Winslows, but he has no earthly idea how, nor would it ever occur to him to try to reason it out. It just makes no sense to them to labor over genealogies."

"That's true," Shiloh admitted. "And the only other white person here, besides the Winslows, is your husband. And I know he came to work for the Winslows in 1845, two years after Roderick Winslow died."

"Yes," she said with equanimity. "I am the only person in Hana that has suspected who you are."

He looked at her, pleading. "And . . . and . . . who am I?"

Cheney found herself holding her breath.

Alena, for the first time, looked troubled. "I'm so sorry, Mr. Irons, I didn't mean to imply that I knew that, exactly. It's just that I knew the significance of the name Keloki gave you. I knew of Roderick Winslow's Hawaiian name. And I think—I believe— that it's very possible that you are a . . . a . . ."

"Bastard?" Shiloh asked evenly. "Please forgive me, ma'am, Doc, but that is the word for it."

To Cheney's and Shiloh's great surprise, Alena's exotic eyes filled with tears. "Oh, you certainly haven't shocked me, Mr. Irons. Because that's exactly what I am, you see, and I've been called that more than once." Her lovely face twisted with pain. "A bastard. A bastard of the House of Winslow."

"What?" Cheney breathed.

But Shiloh merely nodded, his face absorbed. "Logan Winslow is your father?"

Alena swallowed, hard. "Yes, he is. I've never told anyone that. No one, except he and I, knows it, not even my husband. My mother, my real mother, is dead. I . . . didn't come here—now of all times—to speak of this, Mr. Irons, except . . . when I came in here and saw you, and you, Dr. Duvall, taking such good care of an old woman that no one barely pays attention to anymore . . . I suppose I just felt that I could trust you."

"You can," Cheney assured her. "Neither Shiloh nor I would ever break a confidence for any reason."

Alena nodded. "I know. But, Mr. Irons, I don't know anything more about your story. I've wondered—no, that's not true. I do believe that you are either my half brother . . . or my first cousin."

Heavy silence reigned in Mama Nomi's hut for a long, long time. It was shattered by the first aftershock.

13

PLAGUE AND PESTILENCE

Brynn Annalea Winslow lay awake watching the filmy lace curtains at her open window quivering and trembling as if they were frightened spirits. "*Akua*," she whispered to herself. "Perhaps the akua are frightened too."

Sighing heavily, she closed her eyes. But it proved to be more of a strain than a restful thing, so she opened them again. *I'll never, ever sleep tonight after that terrible earthquake. I can't believe Mother just went to bed and went right off to sleep at nine o'clock, just as she always does, as regular as sunsets and sunrises, as sure as the tides.*

Brynn was disturbed about her mother.

As soon as the thought surfaced in her mind, she shoved it away as if it were an offensive photograph or obscene word. She didn't want to think about her mother and the odd things she had said and done lately. She didn't want to wonder about it. She refused to think of it at all.

Father . . . he'll be home soon.

But that, too, proved to be not a refuge but a trap. *Mother said he would be another month . . . could it have been the truth? Would he let her know without writing me? Could she have been just—mistaken?*

Denise Winslow was rarely ever mistaken about such things. She knew the dates and times of the sailings of all five ships. At any given moment she knew which port they were scheduled to be in. She knew exactly how many pineapples were in the east high camp. She knew when it was time to burn the sugarcane in each field.

Of course, Denise Winslow was careless about her husband. His whereabouts, his schedule, his intentions, his plans, his hopes, his dreams. *His love . . . she cares nothing for that anymore . . . and he gave up a long time ago.* In the darkness, Brynn's childlike face took on a fierce expression. *Still, I'm glad they stayed together—if that's what you* call it—for us. For me and Bain. They're both wonderful parents. They're just terrible at being married.

I wonder what happened to them.

I wonder if it was the terrible row they had about Uncle Roderick . . . so bad Mother forbade us ever to speak his name. I wonder if that's what drove them apart.

I wonder what Mr. Irons has to do with us.

With great determination, Brynn pushed the depressing thoughts and questions away from her conscious mind. Again she became sensitive to the utter blackness of the new moon night, of the trembles of air that stirred the curtains, of the occasional subterranean rumbles that still made her skin prickly. "At least the earthquakes are over," she whispered to herself, partly in wishful, desperately hopeful thinking. There had been two mild tremors following the earthquake, then nothing, not even a shiver. And the earth's rumbles, though they had not completely stopped, had become less ominous, less imminent. They sounded like a great animal's growls slowly dying down.

She dozed, restless, her mind barely beneath the surface of sleep.

She didn't know how much later the screams began.

Brynn leaped out of bed, shoved open her double doors, and ran out onto the verandah. "What is it?" she shouted. "Somebody—what's going on?" Loud cries, hoarse calls sounded from the servants' cottages set far back from the house. Occasionally a high-pitched, terrified woman's scream rent the night.

"What is it?" Brynn whispered helplessly.

The darkness was so complete she couldn't see a thing. She was just getting ready to go back into her bedroom and light a candle when she saw a lamp wavering through the gardens from the direction of the servants' quarters. "What is it? Who's there?" she called urgently.

"Wu Pat!" a young man called. He and his brother were the Winslows' stableboys. "Miss Winslow . . . it's . . . it's bad, very bad! It's bugs! Stinging bugs!"

"What?" Brynn said, shocked into a stupor. "Bugs? You're all screaming because of bugs?"

His face, upturned in the uncertain flicker of the lantern, was a round circle, with dark slashes for his slanted eyes and straight mouth. "Miss Winslow! It's a—I don't know the word! Many, many, and they sting! They bite!"

Brynn shook her head. Then she heard a sound that was like a stab to her heart with a hot knife.

She heard a horse scream.

She came alive. "Wu Pat! Go back, get everyone, get the horses! Now! Bring shovels and picks and hoes! Bring all the coal oil and lanterns you can find! Bring wood—anything! Firewood, papala spears, kukui nuts, anything! And dig a trench, a big round trench in a circle right here on the lawn! The men dig, the women and children gather all the supplies, and—water, too, we must have water! Hurry, Hurry!"

He nodded emphatically. "Yes, yes, I know. I understand!" He turned and ran back, shouting in Chinese and English.

"Brynn! What on earth is going on?" Denise demanded, clutching her dressing gown tight at her neck.

Brynn came running back into her bedroom. "Plague. That's what's going on, Mother. A plague."

"What?" Denise looked at her daughter with open disbelief.

Brynn was rummaging through an armoire, trying to find something suitable to wear. "Don't want these stupid big skirts swishing around," she muttered blackly. "Wonderful thing for them to crawl into.... Mother, I told you. Don't you hear the servants and the horses? Wu Pat said it's bugs, stinging bugs, many bugs. It's a plague, I'm telling you."

"But what . . . what shall I do?" Denise gulped, her face draining of all color.

Brynn frowned and viciously rubbed her eyes as if it would give her visions for their salvation. "I don't—Yes, I do. Go fill up the bathtub, Mother, right now! Hurry!"

"Brynn, I don't understand—"

"Just do it, Mother!" she cried. "If you can't help, at least accept help. Go fill up the bathtub. Now."

Without another word Denise turned. A moment later Brynn heard the pump start up in the bathroom connected to her mother's bedroom.

A commotion sounded closer and closer. Brynn ran out on the balcony again. The servants came running into the yard, and she saw with relief that Wu Pat and his brother Wu Yujin were first, with all four horses on leads. The poor horses appeared almost crazed, but she knew that the brothers were like sorcerers with the animals. The boys, whom she called Pat and Will, would calm them, or nothing and no one would. She also saw that everyone, even the smallest child, carried something. The men were already starting the trench on the north side of the lawn.

Hurrying back into her room, Brynn looked at the scattered skirts with disgust, then ran down to Bain's room. She went to his armoire, but it contained only fine tailored suits. She opened one of his trunks and saw dozens of pairs of shoes. At the bottom, however, she spied a sturdy pair of Western boots that Bain had never worn. He had told her he'd won them from a sucker in San Francisco, and the man had left the poker game in boots so old he was holding them together with twine. Bain seemed to think that was funny, though Brynn didn't. She grabbed them, heedless of scattering the neatly arranged shoes in the trunk. They were going to be too big, but they were much better than her satin slippers or soft kid riding boots. With two pairs of thick socks they'd be all right.

Quickly she threw open another trunk at the foot of Bain's bed. In desperate haste she started pulling out old shirts, a worn wool coat, a pair of beat-up Wellington boots—yes, there they were! Two pairs of denim breeches! They'd be too big, of course, but she could cinch them with a belt.

"What's that?" she muttered.

But she already knew what it was. Now with slow movements, she pulled it out and deliberately unfolded the long length.

It was a tapestry, an exquisite tapestry, on crimson satin backing with painstaking needlework. It was Oriental. Wrapped up in it was a most curious fish of Oriental design, its dead eye staring up at her with a pronounced epicanthic fold.

"Brynn!" she heard her mother scream. "This tub's just about full! What am I supposed to do now? Take a bath?"

"I'm coming, Mother," she called dully. "I'm coming." Without bothering to rearrange everything, she simply laid the tapestry and the fish back in Bain's trunk and left it gaping open.

Resolutely emptying her mind of everything but the emergencies at hand, she dressed as quickly as she'd ever done. Mercilessly she tore down the mosquito netting surrounding her bed and ran to her mother's bathroom.

"Get out of the way," she ordered Denise brusquely. Pulling up the Queen Anne chair that held her mother's bath linens, she knocked off the towels and face cloths and stood up on the chair. "Not a nail, not even a splinter," she groaned.

"Are you wearing your brother's boots and clothing, Brynn?" Denise asked in an icy voice.

Ignoring her, Brynn ran downstairs, shouting, "Sunny! Fay! I need a hammer and some nails right now!"

The older couple were calmly setting out all the lanterns, candles, bottles of coal oil, and jars of water in the kitchen. A Chinese woman, one of the gardeners, was running back and forth carrying them to the fire enclosure.

"Here you are, missy," Sunny said calmly. He disappeared into the enormous pantry and came out with a hammer and handful of nails. "You want me to hammer?"

"Mmm—yes," Brynn said with sudden decision. "Go up to my mother's bath, both of you. Put up the mosquito netting over the bathtub and secure it with . . . with—"

"Twine," Sunny suggested.

"Yes! Just under the lip. All of you stand in the tub, you hear? And get—something, fans or something, to knock the bugs off the netting, and something to put them in when they get in the water. I just hope, whatever they are, they can't swim," she added desperately.

"They can't," Sunny murmured. He lowered his lantern to the kitchen floor where there were four dead things. Brynn leaned closer down, revulsion and fear almost overpowering her. "Centipedes," she whispered in a choked voice. "Oh, horrors! Hurry, Sunny! Hurry!" Grabbing a lantern and two bottles of coal oil, she ran outside into the night, to the nightmare.

★　★　★　★

"Centipedes!" Cheney shuddered and with sheer force of will swallowed the fear that almost closed her throat.

"Are . . . do they . . ." Nia stammered, sounding more like a frightened child than she ever had.

"Yes, they . . . th-they bite," Cheney breathed. "They're poisonous."

They huddled like two frightened children underneath the mosquito netting in Cheney's bed. Nia had come running, shouting, and had jumped into bed with her, pulling the mosquito netting tight and securing it tautly by tucking it underneath the mattress. "What . . . what do we do?" Nia asked in a small voice. "Besides pray, I mean?"

"I . . . I . . ." Cheney struggled to get control of herself. "Oh, Lord, help me! Tell me what to do!" she cried, agonized, then buried her face in her hands.

Shiloh came bursting in, fully dressed, with a lantern. He looked as grim as the Passover angel. "Get up," he growled. "Get dressed, right now. Sturdy boots. No bunches of those frou-frou petticoats either. Hurry." He wheeled and ran out.

As if calm were a shawl she had settled on her shoulders, Cheney's mind suddenly cleared. "Well, he sure isn't the Lord, but he had some good advice. Put my Hessian boots on, Nia, right now. Watch while I'm getting dressed. Then I'll come down with you, and we'll get you dressed. You ready? Now!"

Cheney jumped out of bed, flinching, her toes curling up at the touch of her bare feet on the rug. Shiloh had left the lantern, and she couldn't see a single insect—yet. But outside were screams, children calling, men shouting hoarsely, someone hysterically calling an indecipherable Chinese word over and over.

Cheney grabbed her navy-blue riding skirt and a white blouse, then yanked on her boy's Wellington boots. Nia stood perfectly still, her eyes huge and darting from dark corner to dark corner. She was wearing a white cotton nightdress, pulled up above her knees, and Cheney's polished Hessian boots, with a tassel on the uppers. Cheney reflected dryly, *This will be amusing tomorrow . . . if we live. . . .*

They hurried to Nia's room, which was next to the stairs. Cheney gulped when she saw a line, a single file, of centipedes patiently crawling up the stairway. She could see them on the third from the top step, down to four steps below. She couldn't see past that because of the darkness of the stairwell. "Nia," she gulped. "Hurry, Nia. In fact, I think you'd just better pull on a skirt over—"

Nia was already standing outside her room with a gray skirt pulled over her nightdress.

"Stay to the left," Cheney said calmly. "Don't try to kill them. They're marching, or in formation, or something."

"Yes, let's not upset 'em," Nia said in a high, hysterical tone. Cheney glanced at her anxiously. "No, Miss Cheney. I'm scared to death, but I'm not going to have the vapors or go lunatic on you."

"Good," Cheney said. They started toward the stairwell, but Cheney stopped and grabbed Nia's arm in a frantic viselike grip. "Oh no! I have to—" She whirled and ran back toward her room.

Nia shrieked, "Miss Cheney, don't—"

"Go on down!" she called back over her shoulder. "I'll be right there!"

Nia took a deep shuddering breath, leaned against the wall, and began to pray. She didn't close her eyes to address her Lord, however; she wouldn't dare take her eyes off the creeping dark line only three feet in front of her cringing toes. "Dear Lord Jesus, she forgot her medical bag. You know and I know she had to go get it, but, Lord, please give her wings to fly! And I'm sorry. Please forgive me for forgetting it myself. I should've and did know she'd walk on burnin' coals to get it if she thought—"

Cheney came back. Nia shut her mouth with an audible click, and they went down the stairs, creeping like mice, sliding along the left-hand wall with their backs pressed hard up against it. It seemed that it took a long, long time to reach the bottom step. Another column of centipedes was beginning its ascent. At the front door, Cheney could see many of them, here in no comforting single-file formation, beginning to fog through the door. With horror she saw one monster, a black one, that was at least a foot long. *Oh, Lord, save us, help us! That one could actually kill a child!*

"Oh no," she moaned. "Tang Lu—and the children!"

Nia stopped and looked into the darkened dining room. "Oh, Miss Cheney, we have to try—"

"No, you don't!" Shiloh shouted, standing in the doorway, beating about his feet savagely with a broom. "Run! Jump and run, right now!"

And they did.

Together they leaped off the bottom step, landed both feet down, cringed when they heard the dreadful crunching sound under their boots.

"Run! C'mon!" Shiloh ordered harshly.

On her tiptoes, Cheney flew to the door, and Nia was right beside her. Shiloh grabbed their arms and ran off the verandah, hauling them roughly at his pace. Once Nia stumbled, but Shiloh just kept dragging her at a dead run.

Cheney wondered frantically where they were going—where could they go?

"In the boats," Shiloh shouted. "Get in the boats. Row out, but don't untie. Bail all the water out—all of it! Jellyfish!"

People were running, screaming, shouting, crying. As they ran,

Shiloh kept shouting, "To the boats! Everyone! To the boats!" Some heard, turned their faces to him—white ghosts in the night—then veered around to follow him.

Shiloh ran straight to the jetty, jumped up on it, pulling Cheney and Nia up as easily as if they were saddlebags. "Get in that boat right there, Doc. And listen to me! Do not get out of that boat! Do you hear me?"

"Y-yes," Cheney answered, nodding.

He grabbed her face and leaned down so that his face was even with hers. "Please, Cheney," he said in a desperate voice. "Please do as I say."

"I will, Shiloh," she said firmly. "I promise."

He kissed her lips lightly, then handed her and Nia down into one of the outriggers, a small, light canoe with a single rig on one side. Then he helped a young Chinese couple with an infant into the boat. "Row out as far as the rope goes," he instructed, and the Chinese man began to row sturdily. "And don't forget to bail! Be careful of the jellyfish!"

"We'll be fine, Shiloh," Cheney called. "Don't worry! And, Shiloh, I'll be praying for all of us—but especially for you!"

He waved, and then he was gone.

★ ★ ★ ★

Brynn Winslow looked about her, the shock only now beginning to creep over her, a slow but inexorable paralysis of her thoughts and freezing blue water in her veins. Her eyes widened, and she seemed to be blinking very, very slowly. For a fanciful moment she thought she could hear her eyelids, a drawn-out gritty creak . . . moments of darkness when her eyes closed in this eternal blink . . . an impossibly difficult effort to open them again . . . finally a crack of Stygian firelight dawning . . .

"Koali," a warm, deep, comforting voice whispered in her ear. She felt strong hands on her arms. "Koali, sit down. Here, I'll help you." Brynn sagged, but Leilana's sure grip kept her from falling. Helplessly Brynn sank to the ground and collapsed in a loose-limbed cross-legged position. Leilana's arms provided a secure support for her back, which felt as boneless as a homemade rag doll's.

Leilana sat with her in silence, not demanding anything from her, not cajoling her. The Hawaiian woman's mere presence was a fortress to Brynn. Finally Brynn wearily sat up straighter, focused, and assessed her surroundings.

They sat, with about twenty of the Winslows' servants, in the middle of a raging circle of fire. Brynn felt vast relief almost overcome her. In the panic of the last few hours, she had not been able to assimilate that her plan to keep everyone safe from the invading centipedes had actually worked.

In the very center of the fire were her three horses and Bain's mount. Pat and Will had smeared a foul-smelling liniment on Thistle's centipede bites on her off foreleg. The pack mare was a favorite of Brynn's, and she was heartbroken that the gentle little mare had gotten bitten. Still, Thistle and the other horses seemed to be all right, considering the circumstances. They were calm, though they were jumpy. Their skin shivered and jerked at frights that humans could neither see nor hear, and their eyes often rolled so violently they showed half-moons of white. They stamped nervously. But Pat and Will tirelessly moved among them, patting them, speaking to them in singsong Chinese, giving them a comforting stroke here and there with the curry brushes they somehow had the presence of mind to grab and bring along with the other supplies.

To her right was piled a haphazard heap of thin, straight papala sticks, delicate branches of sandalwood, some with leaves still attached, thick chunks of ohia firewood. They still had a generous supply remaining.

All around the circle were the black outlines of men, the great bulk of Keloki standing out oddly among the slim, agile Chinese men. They stoked the encircling fire, sometimes adding a stick here, sometimes throwing on a few drops of coal oil, and then dashing back away from the small explosions. The ring of fire held.

All around Brynn children were sitting or lying in the grass. Some were crying, some were staring blankly into space, some—particularly the youngest ones, like the darling little girl, four-year-old Atu Ki— were almost asleep. Atu Ki's mother, Zhu Ki, held her son obsessively, rocking and wailing. None of them had been stung, but Zhu Ki, one of the kitchen maids, was hysterical and simply refused to be calmed.

Brynn felt sorry for the young mother; her husband worked in the sugarcane fields and wasn't here. Perhaps that was why she was so panicked. Still, there were other women, servants of the villa, whose husbands worked the plantation, and they were alone too. Almost everyone behaved with great courage and determination. Another exception was Fang Jinglan, the young upstairs maid. She had been hopeless, shrieking and crying all night, clinging frantically to first Pat, then Leilana, and then whoever was standing still at the moment. Right now she was sitting near Brynn and Leilana, not quite daring to approach the mistress of the house. She hugged herself, rocking and moaning in broken Chinese.

But all of the other women were helping the men, bringing wood when needed, carefully storing the coal-oil jars and empty lanterns in the center of the circle, giving water to the men, helping soothe the children. Tending the injured.

On the other side of the horses sat four hunched-over, pitiful shapes, emitting desolate muffled cries and sobs.

"Only four," Brynn whispered brokenly. "Only four people . . . only six bites. That's good, isn't it, Leilana? It . . . it . . . could have been much worse, couldn't it?"

Leilana stretched her massive arms around Brynn and hugged her so hard to her generous breasts that Brynn was almost suffocated. "Oh yes, little Koali. Only four hurt in this bad, bad *piliki*. 'Cause of you, little Koali, you save us all. Koali no ka oi."

Brynn burst into tears, sobbing so hard she thought she might have pulled a rib muscle. Leilana patted her, murmured low, soft Hawaiian words, simple words of comfort. Brynn cried and sobbed and wailed for a few moments. Then with a jerk, she pulled herself upright, scrubbed at her face, and then looked at her hands. They were black. Woefully she looked up at Leilana. "I must look a fright. Is my face black?"

Leilana nodded unconcernedly. "Face black, hair black, clothes black. All black."

"My mother's going to—" Brynn convulsively gulped, and her head jerked up to search the balconies of the villa. To her vast relief, the outside walls weren't a fiendish, crawling mass, as they had been the last time she'd looked up there—how long ago was it since she'd thought about her mother? Hours? Minutes? Brynn didn't know.

Leilana followed her gaze and squeezed Brynn in a bone-crackling hug again. "Your mama, she okay. You did good, Koali. You did good."

Brynn felt a spasm of terrible pain, not in her body, but in what could only be her heart. Closing her eyes, she tried to push the hurt away, out of her mind and soul, but she had no strength left for such an exercise.

Mother . . . my brother . . . what have you done? Who are you? How is it that in the last few days you've become complete strangers to me? You lie, you steal—oh yes, yes, I can't help but think it now! Now, when . . . when I needed someone . . . something . . .

Her internal struggle was so violent that Brynn took harsh gasping breaths, dropped her head, and squeezed her eyes closed so forcibly that it made her face hurt. *I needed Someone, all right. Could it be—it couldn't possibly be, could it, that Mother's lied to us about God too? No, no, that can't be! God is God, the ultimate power in Creation, but He cares nothing for us—for people, for my mother and father . . . for me. . . .*

Does He?

"*I do,*" He answered.

Brynn jumped and actually stared around in shock before she realized that the words were in her mind, not in her ears. She sat still, listening.

She no longer heard the cries and moans of the injured. She couldn't hear the lurid cracks and snaps of the surrounding fires. She didn't hear the sounds of the horses stamping and whinnying. She was enveloped in quiet—a blessed, cool quiet. Her eyes fluttered, then peaceably closed.

I care, He said again. *I love you. Yesterday, now, tomorrow, and forever I love you, Brynn Annalea Winslow.*

She wept again. But this time there were no sobs, no frightened wails, no pain at all. Her tears were soft and warm, like the beloved cleansing spring rains.

★ ★ ★ ★

Cheney looked at her hands.

They were strong hands, long-fingered, agile, lissome. She kept her nails short but filed to pleasing ovals and buffed to a high gloss. She'd always been grateful that she'd inherited her mother's trait: clear, ivory-white half-moon cuticles. Cheney considered that one feature to be very ladylike, and it was a rare mark of beauty that women envied. They were steady, sure hands, nimble and quick. She was grateful to the Lord that He had given her such good hands.

A weak and tentative light rested on her hands. Abruptly Cheney realized how well she could see. At that moment the sun threw its floodlight onto the scene, the instantaneous black-to-white sunrise of a flat eastern horizon.

"Ohh," she murmured in revulsion. Several women screamed, men cursed, and children started to cry. Surrounding the forlorn little group of boats were thousands, perhaps millions, of dead centipedes. Even at a cursory glimpse Cheney could see that many, like the monster she'd seen in the guest house the night before, were at least a foot long.

"Calm down, everyone," Shiloh called sturdily from the jetty. "Just calm down. They're dead, and they've just about stopped coming."

Cheney stared at him. He looked unearthly, like the Greeks must have pictured a fire god, like Mercury. The rising sun turned his thick hair to a silvery fire. He stood shirtless, vigorous and unyielding. The clean geometrical planes of his brow and cheekbones and jaw were carved in golden relief in the light of the morning sun. He showed no weariness at all.

Along the flat stones of the jetty, Walker held the reins of Indie, one of the cart horses. Walker looked exhausted, his back bent, his head bowed. Shiloh stood behind him, holding the gelding Plato's reins, petting him and soothing him. Then came sturdy old Sultana. The oldest and calmest of the four, she stood alone, tethered to a docking ring inset into the rock, shifting her weight patiently. And behind Sultana, Konrad Zeiss stroked his horse Kaiser, as he had done off and on all night.

The barrier fire the men had built across the jetty's walk had died down. Cheney was relieved, not only for the fact that the centipede plague appeared to be over, but because the stench of thousands of burning insects had sickened her all night.

She looked around the boats, taking stock again, as she had done hundreds of times during the endless darkness. Mama Nomi dozed in her specially built dinghy, splendidly alone in the boat that was wide in the draft and low in the water. Her boat alone had not needed to be bailed. The rest of them—more because of panicky flailing by the passengers—had taken water. A young Hawaiian man got stung by a jellyfish that landed in his canoe. Tang Lu, in the canoe next to Cheney's with her four children, was bitten twice by centipedes. A Chinese fisherman whom everyone called Dooley was bitten, and his brother Dan was bitten twice while trying to help him. And a stocky little fellow of ten named Nimi had also been bitten.

Cheney sighed. It had been a terrible ordeal—still was. But it could have been worse, so much worse. She eyed little Liu, who wasn't as big as some baby dolls that Cheney had played with when she was young. A sting from one of the large centipedes, or two bites such as Liu's mother had sustained, would have killed the child. "Oh, thank you, thank you, Lord," she whispered. With dull eyes Tang Lu looked up at Cheney, questioning. Cheney said, "I know you're in great pain, Tang Lu. But I will take care of you as soon as we can get back into the house. And your children, thank the merciful Lord, are uninjured."

Tang Lu's mouth worked, but no sound came out. Finally she nodded almost imperceptibly. She had been in great pain all night, shivering with fever and nausea. Twice she had vomited. But she hadn't gone into convulsions, as Cheney had feared she might; and she hadn't gone into shock, which could, in some mysterious way, kill some people, as their hearts just refused to beat anymore.

Tang Lu had been stung on the ankle and on her calf. She'd been carrying Liu, running to the boats, while Shiloh had carried Ming and Wen. Kwan had run like a deer in front of them, his feet barely seeming to touch the crawling ground. When Shiloh put them into the boat, Tang Lu calmly placed Liu in Ming's lap, sat down, and picked off the two centipedes from her skin. They clung to her, their fangs digging into her skin, but she never made a sound.

Shiloh, knowing there were other people in the village who needed him, helplessly said, "Just wash it out with salt water right now, Tang Lu. Over and over again. But be careful, watch for jellyfish."

She nodded, picked up the small bucket in the canoe, and had begun to carefully skim water when Shiloh turned and ran off.

When Cheney settled into the boat, ten-year-old Ming had said in a small voice, "Doctor Cheney? Will you help my mother?"

Cheney then saw that Tang Lu was leaning against the low side of the boat, her face a sickly white that glimmered in the darkness. Cheney swallowed hard and maneuvered the boat over until it was touching Tang Lu's. She hadn't known what to do except to dab iodine on the bites, which were already inflamed, and apply a little bicarbonate plaster to them. Then she insisted that Tang Lu take a double dose of laudanum, for she was in great pain. The only sign, however, of her discomfort was that she gritted her teeth together so hard that Cheney could hear the grinding sounds. Tang Lu didn't speak all night.

George and Lela Han, the young couple in the boat with Cheney, had a ten-month-old baby named Vanda. They were both Chinese but seemed very Americanized. In the long night, while waiting, George told Cheney that they worked at the villa, training as personal servants to Brynn and Bain. They'd brought the baby to Hana to see Alena Zeiss and to buy some goat's milk, for she'd been colicky. Alena had invited them to stay the night. Cheney promised to give the baby a prescriptive she'd used that sometimes helped infants with colic.

"Where is Alena?" Cheney had asked when they first got into the boat.

George Han answered, "She's down at the end in a dinghy by herself. Mr. Zeiss got her out in the boat first thing."

"He takes very good care of her, doesn't he?" Cheney asked idly. "He's much older than she."

George nodded but said nothing more.

Once Shiloh and the men got everyone into the boats, the horses safely onto the jetty, and a roaring fire built, Shiloh pulled the boats up close and ministered to the others. Throughout the night he had held the boy Nimi, who was feverish and in pain. Shiloh was obliged to work all night, tending and calming the frightened horses, seeing to the fires.

Once during the endless night, they had run low on firewood. While the men discussed it, Shiloh simply leapt over the dying flames on the jetty and took off, disappearing into the darkness before the men decided what to do. In just a few moments he came skimming back, holding an impossibly bulky armload of wood. Cheney then realized that she'd been holding her breath the entire time he was gone and was almost fainting. She bent over, putting her head down on her knees, and fussed at herself until she felt better.

Now, staring at Shiloh in the merciless glare of dawn, she saw an angry red lump on his side. With quick strokes she rowed the canoe up to the jetty, almost throwing poor George Han, sitting at the prow of the canoe, overboard.

"You got bitten," she called out harshly.

Shiloh looked down at her and shrugged, making a who-cares face. "Didn't hurt. I was thinking of other things at the time."

"Was it when you got the firewood?"

"Yeah, think so."

Cheney sat up and said with high indignation, "And you haven't even put iodine on it? Shiloh, you know better!"

He grinned, and Cheney could cheerfully have killed him.

He said, "I was waiting for my doctor. The best in the world. Dr. Cheney Duvall."

"You blithering idiot!" she shouted and stood up. The outrigger rocked precariously from side to side. "I want to get up there! Move aside, Mr.—Mr.—sir! Excuse me, ma'am!" Like a charging lioness, Cheney plowed through the small canoe. The Chinese couple cowered and drew up into heaps as small as possible.

Cheney got to the prow of the canoe. Shiloh reached down, took her hand, and lifted her up while her boots scrambled for a foothold. Then he set her down on the jetty, grabbed her around the waist, and hugged her, lifting her up into the air.

"Shiloh! Put me down!" she gasped, kicking futilely.

He held her up and looked into her face. "I'm glad you're okay, Doc. I'm just really glad you're okay."

Cheney surrendered and grew still. Impulsively she leaned down and kissed his cheek. His eyes glowed, but then she pulled back and frowned down at him ferociously. "I am fine, thank you. But you, sir, are not. As your physician, I'm ordering you to put me down and submit to massive swabs of iodine."

He set her down but kept his hands at her waist. "You minded me, Doc, and good. Fair is fair, so now I guess I'll mind you. Swab on!"

14

FIRE OR WATER?

She came ghosting through the mist, a phantom ship of such beauty that true life-blood sailors only dream of. The air was silvery, moist, like translucent gauze wrapped languorously around the clipper's soaring masts. Her figurehead, a Grecian woman swathed in a flowing white robe with a torch upheld, seemed to be lighting the way as inch by inch, moment by moment, the clipper's slender, sleek lines materialized. The sharp prow dipped tempestuously, as if she resented coming to a stop, and she heeled slightly over in the unrestful sea. Voices, oddly flat and lifeless, deadened by the countless thin layers of fog, carried only a few feet. A splash sounded as a small boat was lowered away.

Bain Winslow sat in the prow of the dinghy, his arms crossed, a scowl marring the smooth planes of his face. He sat backward, facing out to sea, as if he were going into Hana against his will—which, in effect, he was. The swarthy sailor who rowed gave him occasional wary glances from beneath heavy black brows, but mostly he kept his eyes trained ahead, straining to see through the mischievous tendrils and sheets of haze that seemed to be veils over his eyes. It was with relief that he saw the jetty, the flat reddish stones raring up suddenly a few feet in front of the blunt prow of the dinghy. The boat thumped gently against the barrier.

"Easy, man!" Bain growled. "Don't break up the stupid boat."

The sailor, whose name was Lott, had to bite his lip to keep his temper. Owners were always a pain, but this one was a royal one. *Locke's Day Dream* was the only large clipper in the Pacific that the owner used as a pleasure yacht—so he was always sailing with them. Still, Bain Winslow paid a good wage, and his crew ruled their tongues when he was around. In private, however, they were contemptuous of him. He was no sailor, no man of the sea. *Locke's Day Dream* was just an expensive show-off toy to Bain Winslow, and the crew was part of the display. Lott suspected, as did most of the sailors, that Bain paid them so well because he thought he was buying their respect. He got it too. At least to his face. They all were mindful of the men in every port who fought to sail on *Locke's Day Dream*, because the wage was good.

At least Bain Winslow was astute enough to take on a good captain—Captain Geoffrey Starnes. A hard man, a tough man, even brutal at times, he loved the sea, and he loved *Locke's Day Dream* with a harsh passion. Though demanding, he would always do whatever was best for the ship, regardless of whatever silliness Bain Winslow dreamed up. He was a fine captain to sail under, even with the piddling owner along on their voyages.

But Lott, who was shrewd but not very agile mentally, wasn't thinking of all this as the dinghy suffered through the choppy sea. He was struggling to back-row so that the prow wouldn't bang the jetty again, while trying to figure out how to tie off. Bain sat brooding, blocking the tie rope. To Lott's relief, he abruptly turned, looped the rope twice through the mooring eye, and scrambled up onto the jetty. Without looking back, he stalked off into the mists.

"Good riddance to bad rubbish is what I says," Lott muttered as he jerked the line free and rowed vigorously back to his ship. "Yer welcome, sir, an' greet yer fambly from all of us, yer ever-lovin' crew."

Of course Bain didn't hear him. After a taxing night of debauchery in Lahaina, his head was throbbing, his back ached, and he felt nauseated. He was in Hana, when it was the last place on earth he wanted to be. He hated Hana, he hated the plantation, he hated Maui; in fact, he hated Hawaii. Striding toward the Zeisses' stables, he cursed under his breath and swore again that by next year he would be living in style in San Francisco, and he'd visit his mother and sister in Hawaii maybe twice a year. Or maybe once a year.

The sea mist that had been so fine and delicate turned into a tepid rain over land. Bain ran the last few feet into the stables and looked around, sniffing. "What the—?" He smelled something harshly acrid.

Looking down, he saw that the entire perimeter of the stables had mounds of white powder in an uneven line tracing the walls. He bent over to take a pinch, groaning as his head whirled sickeningly and his stomach churned. "Quicklime?" he growled. Impatiently he dismissed the mystery from his mind. Some stupid cleaning fancy of Alena

Zeiss's, no doubt. Quickly he saddled Plato and started to leave, but then took Konrad Zeiss's canvas coat and a wide-brimmed white straw hat from hooks on the wall. No sense getting soaked on the ride to the villa.

Outside the stables, he looked down the sandy street to Winslow Guest House, considering. *I should stop in there and tell them that tomorrow I'm booting them back to San Francisco. . . .*

But as Bain hesitated, his horse standing patiently in the rain, an unwelcome moment of clarity imposed upon his consciousness—and his conscience. He deftly tried to bury the thought before it formed; but as will happen to all men who deceive themselves, sometimes holes in their blanket of deception wear through, and they catch a glimpse into the truth.

Bain Winslow tried to tell himself that he simply didn't want to deal with that harridan of a female doctor and that tiresomely wholesome Baird and that hoodlum Shiloh Irons. He had a vicious hangover, and he was tired from the trip from Lahaina. The weather was foul, and he needed to get home and speak to his mother before it got too late.

Spurring Plato soundly, the gelding reared a little, then ran down the main street of Hana at a full gallop, heading for the great mountain Haleakala.

But as Bain Winslow rode, he heard a nagging, insistent voice in the back of his mind. *You're frightened. You're just scared . . . you're actually scared of Shiloh Irons! Not because of who he is and what he could do to you and your family, but because he's the kind of man you wish you were, you want to be, you pretend to be—but never will be. You're weak, and he's tough. Yes, you are. After all, you're actually intimidated by an ignorant, dirt poor thug. . . .* A lopsided smile, cold and humorless, twisted Bain's face. *Perhaps I'm more like my father than I and my mother thought. . . .*

That was about the limit of Bain's inner tolerance, so he gritted his teeth and spurred Plato recklessly. He made the five miles in an hour and fifteen minutes, a deathly dangerous pace. Poor Plato was lathering and panting as he galloped up to the villa. Carelessly Bain threw the reins around the hitching iron, giving the burned lawn and the litter strewn about it only a cursory glance.

He hurried into the villa, but instead of going straight to the parlor, he turned into the kitchen, shedding his hat and coat as he went. Chen

Guifei's wrinkled face looked up at him, startled, as he entered. "Hello, Fay, don't be alarmed, it's just me. I'm afraid I got this coat and hat soaked—and filthy, too, somehow. They're Zeiss's. I took them from his stable. Will you tend to them and see that they're returned to him? Thanks. Is my mother in the drawing room?"

She bowed, taking the hat and dripping coat. "Yes, sir."

"Tell Sunny to bring me some brandy, would you?"

"Yes, sir."

He went into the drawing room. His mother was tending a fire that roared and crackled as she piled small green branches on it. He came up behind her and put his hand on her shoulder. She jumped, whirled, screamed, and struck out at him.

"Good heavens, Mother!" he blustered, rapidly retreating. "What's the matter with you?"

"I'm frightened out of my wits. That's what's the matter with me," she snapped. "What are you doing here?"

"I'm glad to see you too," he said dryly, settling himself comfortably in an overstuffed armchair. Tang Sun came in with his brandy, and Bain pointed for him to set it on the tea table directly in front of him, then motioned him carelessly away. After draining half a glass, he poured another and held it with pleasure, caressing the heavy crystal as if it comforted him. "What in the world is going on here? Did the witches dance in a circle of firelight last night? And ritual fumigant cleansing now?" His nose wrinkled, and he ostentatiously fanned in front of his face.

"It's *pukiawe,* as you well know," Denise said, throwing the last of the green branches on the fire. "It does have a cleansing incense, and certainly"—she shuddered—"insects are repelled by it."

He sipped the brandy, closing his eyes. The warmth coursed through him, and he felt his aching muscles growing lax. Even the throbbing of his head seemed faraway and unimportant. "It's hard for me to believe," he said in a bored tone, "that the one person who owns the most sandalwood in all of Hawaii refuses to put it to good use. Instead you use that foul-smelling weed for incense." He took a long sip, then turned up his glass, finishing off his second generous shot of the heady liquor. Immediately he poured another, then looked up and asked politely, "Brandy, Mother?"

"Yes, I think I will," she said wearily, sinking ungracefully onto the sofa.

A shadow of concern crossed Bain's face, and he quickly poured her a generous drink, then slid to her side. "Here, sip this slowly, Mother. Something really is wrong, is it?"

"Vast understatement," she muttered, carelessly swallowing two gulps. Leaning at an awkward angle against the sofa back—Bain could never recall his mother's back touching the back of a seat—she passed a trembling hand over her eyes, as if unseen spiderwebs dimmed her view.

Bain waited until she calmed and the fiery whisky put two spots of color on her parchment cheeks. Then she seemed to collect herself somewhat, though she still didn't resume her normal erect and ladylike posture.

"First we had earthquakes yesterday, Bain. And then last night, a plague. Of those horrid centipedes."

"A plague? Surely not."

"I'm telling you, millions of them, everywhere. You should see the loathsome pile of the things that the servants swept up and burned," she argued weakly. "It was a plague."

To her surprise, he shrugged carelessly. "In Lahaina, everyone was talking about the news from the big island. Mauna Loa and Kilauea are erupting again. Not as spectacularly as the last time—in fact, I heard that it's just a leaking fissure on Kilauea. But still, that's probably why we're having earthquakes. And the earthquakes are probably why we had the plague of centipedes."

She stared at him with a mixture of disbelief and forlorn hope. "Do . . . do you really think so?"

"Of course. What do you think it is? The end of the world?"

Dropping her eyes, she muttered, "There were a few moments yesterday . . ."

"Oh, Mother, no! Not you! Not the methodically agnostic Winslow!" he scoffed.

"It's easy for you to say. You weren't here." Curiously she asked, "There was nothing in Lahaina? No earthquakes?"

"Not a shiver," he said reassuringly. "I'm telling you, it's just this old mountain shifting in his sleep. By the way, is Brynn all right?" He smiled, a curious upturn of one side of his well-formed lips. "Did she have the vapors?"

"No, she didn't," Denise answered, pulling herself into a less ungainly position and smoothing her skirt. "She acquitted herself admirably, I must say. She was exhausted, as are we all. She's already in bed, and I was going to retire early as well. I'm afraid you'll have to cajole Chen Guifei into preparing your dinner. I have no appetite tonight."

"After you finish that brandy, Mother, you probably won't be able to stay awake, centipedes or no. But before you retire, we must talk," he said, dismissing the uninteresting subjects of earthquakes and plague. "Father is in Lahaina right now," he told her, his voice thickened by the brandy and his ire. "And he's coming here. I don't know when. All I know is that he's coming to the plantation before he leaves again."

Denise stiffened to attention. "What! Why didn't you dissuade him, as we decided?"

"I tried," he surlily retorted. "But we outsmarted ourselves. He merely told me that he'd take care of everything when he arrived. I couldn't fathom why he didn't just leave from Lahaina, as he's done so many times before. It's as if he has a . . . mission or something." He made an impatient gesture with the brandy glass, sloshing the golden brown liquid. "I don't know. He likely just wants to see Brynn. It has been three months."

Savagely Denise crashed the heavy tumbler down to the table, then stood and began her caged-panther pacing. "This is . . . intolerable. This cannot be! It will ruin everything, Bain, everything—"

"Calm down," he curtly ordered. "And sit down."

She sat, or rather collapsed, back onto the sofa.

With rigidly deliberate movements Bain poured her another glass of brandy and thrust it into her lifeless hand. "Please do me the courtesy of listening before you indulge in hysterics again. The only two ships in Lahaina that were bound for San Francisco were unsuited to take our unwelcome guests. So I—"

"Whatever do you mean, unsuited?" Denise demanded indignantly. "What do we care whether they travel in first-class fashion or not? They must leave!"

Angry now, Bain's face contorted, but with a visible effort he calmed himself, though his voice was strained. "Use your common sense, Mother. We can make them leave Hana, but we can't assault and kidnap them. Dr. Baird, and particularly that woman, would never deign to board a filthy Italian brig with a cutthroat crew. The only other ship I found bound for San Francisco was a German one, and they flatly refused to take a woman passenger. So"—he grimaced and took a very small sip of brandy—"I'll pick them up tomorrow morning and take them back on *Locke's Day Dream*."

She stared at him. "You will?"

"I must, it seems. Although it is a colossal inconvenience. I was planning to be halfway to Shanghai by now."

"But . . . won't that be . . . awkward?"

Bain laughed, a grating sound with no amusement in it. "Awkward! Yes, I should say so—for them. I own the ship, Mother. They must quarter where I say, do what I say, eat what and when I say. And I suppose the best part, the only recompense I have for this entire dreary untidiness, is that Irons will be on the ship."

Denise pressed her eyes shut, then asked with a note of dread, "What do you mean by that, Bain?"

He cut his eyes toward her with disdain. "You know very well, Mother. He'll have to work his way. He hasn't even repaid me for his fare from San Francisco. He's an inexperienced sailor. Clippers are the most dangerous ships for any man who's not a seasoned seaman. Accidents happen. So many accidents happen at sea. . . ."

★ ★ ★ ★

Bain roused out of a heavy, dreamless sleep. He didn't move. He merely swam up out of the depths to wakefulness and with an effort half opened his eyes. He lay there, wondering what had awakened him. Then the low rumble of thunder sounded again. Satisfied, he shifted slightly and closed his eyes again.

But was that thunder?

Opening his eyes again, he leaned up on one elbow and listened, his head flaring with pain. Finally, with a muttered oath, he felt his way around to his night table and lit a candle. Blinking hard, he managed to focus his gritty eyes on his watch face. It was after two in the morning.

Bain sat still and watched the small candle flame wavering weakly. He heard it as distant growling, continuous, as it rose in pitch and timbre, sometimes to a crescendo, then falling away to a noisome hum. He smelled something acrid, something foul . . . just a whisper of a smell, winding through the onerous air as cold currents sometimes thread hauntingly through warm water. He whipped around and stared at his open window. The curtains hung listlessly. Outside dull flashes glowed intermittently.

Rising, he slowly walked out onto his balcony and looked up, high up to the heights of Mount Haleakala. As a man in a dream, he returned to his room, his movements slow and deliberate. From his desk drawer he took a captain's glass and went back outside. For long moments he looked upward, the slender glass almost pointed to the sky.

The ink-black cloud obscured all of the wide summit of Mount Haleakala. It roiled and boiled and showed dirty gray billows when the continuous flashes of short lightning bolts lit the underside. It was so dark, so black, that it blotted out all details of the heights and the bright stars directly above. It looked as if it had devoured the night sky.

Slowly Bain collapsed the glass and went back into his room. He sat again on the side of his bed, staring into space. *Mother ... she can take care of herself, but Brynn ... Brynn ...* A spasm of pain knifed through his chest. *I could wake her. ...*

But since Shiloh Irons had come to Hana, Bain had had an odd feeling about Brynn. He sensed somehow that she was watching him, was measuring him, was suspicious of him. He felt that, for whatever reasons, he was suddenly coming up short in her eyes.

"My first obligation is to *Locke's Day Dream*," he muttered harshly. "It's a substantial investment, probably the highest-valued item that we own. And, of course, I have a responsibility to Captain Starnes, to the officers, to the crew."

Again, his carefully woven blanket of lies shrouded his conscience and numbed the icy pain in his heart. With deliberation he began to dress.

★ ★ ★ ★

"Doc? Doc, wake up."

The knocking on her door was quiet, but Shiloh's voice was insistent.

Cheney sat up, shook her head to clear it, and stared around in a stupor. "It's still night," she told herself. "It's dark."

"Doc, you awake? You hear me? I'm comin' in."

"Hmm? No! No, I'm—just a minute, you bully!" Muttering, Cheney hurried out of bed and grabbed her dressing gown. She put it on upside down in the dark and called out, "Wait just a minute, I'm coming, Shiloh."

"Hurry up."

She frowned. Normally he wasn't so curt. And normally he didn't wake her in the middle of the night. Some mornings he had been known to go aggravate Nia until she agreed to awaken Cheney, but he hardly ever woke her himself, especially so brusquely.

"Unless it's an emergency," Cheney whispered, suddenly frightened. Finally she got the robe secured around her, hurriedly lit a candle, and flew to the door.

He stood in the hall, fully dressed in faded Levi's denim breeches and his old knee-high cavalry boots. He was wearing his canvas overcoat, and it was filthy. In his hands he twisted a gray wide-brimmed hat, and it looked grimy and wet. Cheney particularly noted his stance. He was tense, his shoulders thrown back, his jaw muscles prominent.

"Hello," she said, her throat suddenly constricted.

A flash of amusement lit his eyes. "Hi, Doc. Did you know it's after ten o'clock?"

"N-no."

He grew grim, his mouth tightening into a thin line. "What I mean is, Doc, it's after ten o'clock in the morning."

The candle flame jostled back and forth, creating odd shadows on his face. He reached out to steady her hand. "You . . . you mean . . . it's daytime?" she stammered.

He nodded.

"Oh," she said. "I suppose I'd better get dressed."

He nodded again, gravely.

"Just give me . . . a few minutes," she pleaded. Cheney still wasn't quite lucid.

He turned and headed back to the stairwell. Then, though he was only a few feet away, she could barely see him except as a faint glimmer. He stopped and said, "Doc, I think you'd better wear something . . . uh . . . sturdy. Good boots. A wide-brimmed hat. Not too many fooferies."

"No fooferies," she repeated carefully. "Are you going to wake Nia?"

"I already did. She'll be coming to you anytime now."

"All right, I'll be down in a few minutes." She stepped back into her room, and she heard his voice float down the hallway, low and urgent.

"Hurry."

She chose her navy-blue riding habit. She'd just worn it (*Was it only a few days ago we went up to the crater?*), but it was made of a fine broadcloth, thick and sturdy. Though the jacket had gold filigree buttons and long cuffs embroidered in gold braid, she didn't think that was too much foofery (*I don't suppose that really is far-off thunder I'm hearing*). The skirt, in particular, was good for vigorous exercise (*What in the world am I going to be doing?*) and was comfortable, with only a slightly rounded hem in the back for a train and a deep single pleat in front.

As she dressed, her active mind began to work as it should and always had. Instead of wringing her hands and wondering what was wrong and indulging in a little ladylike panic, she made quick decisions. *The hat, it's good, wide-brimmed felt instead of straw . . . leave on the veil, it would take more time to take it off than to just put it back. And my hair—why not the gold netted snood? I've got to do something with this tangle, anyway. This plain cambric blouse, yes, forget the brooch, forget the stock. My Wellington boots—where are my leather gauntlets? I'll need them. . . .*

Nia came in, her eyes wide, but she was calm. Cheney inspected her and saw with satisfaction that she was wearing a gray cotton skirt, only one petticoat, a white muslin blouse, and a light blue shawl draped around her shoulders and tucked into the front of her skirt. "Wear my Hessian boots, Nia," she said without preamble. "You'll need them."

Nia swallowed. "Why?"

Cheney shrugged. "I don't know. But Shiloh said to wear sturdy boots." Cheney tossed the pair of boots lightly to Nia, who deftly caught them and sat on the bed to change footwear.

"I need my medical bag, my gauntlets—you know, the yellow kid ones?—and . . . and . . . this," she finished with satisfaction. From her bedside table she picked up her Bible, an old, comfortably worn one that her father had given her when she was sixteen. She stared down at it, caressed the age-softened leather cover, and felt tears start in her eyes. Briskly she blinked them back and turned to Nia. Her maid had already found her gloves and was holding out her medical bag, its wide mouth opened.

Cheney dropped her Bible in it, then snapped the bag shut, her jaw tightening and mouth set. "You're going to need a hat. Wear my yellow straw with the wide brim."

"All right, Miss Cheney."

"Are you ready?"

"Yes, ma'am."

"Then let's go find Shiloh."

They had to carry the candle, for it looked like dead of night.

He wasn't downstairs in the parlor, or the dining room, or the kitchen. Finally Cheney snuffed the candle, and they went outside. It was dim, but not the black of nighttime. The light was sullen, like a room lit by a single lantern covered by a charcoal-gray cloth. Cheney blinked several times, thinking to clear her vision, but it wasn't her eyes that were smoky. The air was filled with a fog that was not misty air at all; it was the finest, thinnest ash Cheney had ever seen.

Shiloh was standing out in the middle of the sandy street with Walker, looking up beyond the house, to the heights of the mountain.

"Doc, good," he said with relief. "Come take a look at this."

Wordlessly Cheney and Nia went out to stand next to them.

The entire summit of Mount Haleakala was hidden beneath a cloud so dense that it seemed to be made of pitch. Continuous stabs of lightning shot downward, but even these unearthly lights didn't seem to light up the cloud. Instead, it seemed that the cloud enveloped the shards of brightness and then swallowed them up. The thunder was continuous now, a muted but fierce roar. Standing on the loose sand, Cheney could feel a very slight trembling of the earth. A strong smell of sulphur assaulted her sensitive nostrils.

Cheney, Nia, Walker, and Shiloh stood in silence, just watching, for long moments.

Jarringly, Cheney yawned, so quickly and so widely the corners of her mouth stung. The other three stared at her in amazement.

"Well, excuse me," she declared in a sassy tone. "It's just that these crack-of-dawn catastrophes are really starting to annoy me."

The others suddenly began laughing. At least Shiloh and Walker did. Nia smiled, but just a little.

"See! Didn't I tell you she had more grit than a battalion?" Shiloh chortled, punching Walker on the arm so vigorously that he almost fell down.

"Yes, you told me," Walker agreed good-naturedly. "But I already knew it. Everyone does."

Cheney grew somber and said, "So? What do we do?" She was asking Shiloh.

He, too, grew serious again. "I don't know yet, Doc. I'm thinking."

"Think fast, please," Walker said evenly.

The mountain's growls grew louder for a moment, and the ground shook. But it was a mere tremor that did no more than sift some of the fine sand onto their boots.

The four looked at one another. The three looked up at Shiloh. He frowned.

They heard noise, a new noise to their left.

"What's that?" Nia asked tremulously.

"It's a horse," Cheney answered. "Probably the first of the Four Horsemen of the Apocalypse, the way our luck is running."

But it was only Konrad Zeiss, though he was riding his great black horse Kaiser as if the Four Horsemen were pursuing him. He pulled up to a stop by them, however, and was still self-possessed enough to yank on the brim of his hat to Cheney. "What are you people still doing here?" he demanded harshly.

Shiloh answered, "No ship ever came to pick us up."

"Bain—*Locke's Day Dream*—you haven't seen her either?"

"No, sir."

"Figures," he rasped. "I've just come from the villa. It's not good, Irons. Guess you know that."

Slowly Shiloh took Kaiser's headpiece—he was stamping and rearing—and stroked his wet black shoulder. "Guess I do," he answered calmly. "What are you going to do, Mr. Zeiss?"

"I'm taking Alena up the coast, to Nahiku. Wailua, if we can make it that far," he answered. He spoke stiffly, as if defending himself. "We'll ride double on old Kaiser, here." He stroked the horse with rough affection. "He'll get us quite a ways."

Shiloh nodded, obviously concentrating hard. "You have any suggestions for us?" His voice was even, not in any way reproachful.

Zeiss looked relieved at Shiloh's tone and answered, "Well, I gotta tell you, Irons, some of the villagers seem to be more scared of a *tsunami* than of that old mountain waking up after being dead as a rock for seventy years. Mama Nomi told me that in her lifetime she's seen two tsunamis here but not a single flicker of an eruption."

"What's a tsunami?" Shiloh demanded.

"A tidal wave. Big. Mama Nomi said the village has been wiped clean off the beach twice. The last one—she didn't know when it was, you know, she just said it was before she had her last child—the wave crashed all the way up to the third of the Seven Sacred Pools."

"What?" Shiloh said harshly, then with a visible effort calmed himself. "But you must not be too afraid of that. Not if you're going up the coast road."

Zeiss narrowed his eyes and glanced up at the mountain. "I fear fire more than water, Irons. Might be a sorry way to make a decision, but it's the simple truth."

Shiloh nodded, then turned to the others. "Fire or water?" he asked.

Before they could answer, Zeiss shifted uncomfortably in his saddle and bent his head. His wide-brimmed hat shaded his angular face. "The cart and horses are still in the stable, Irons," he said in a muffled voice. "Guess you might as well take 'em."

Shiloh grew very still. His long-fingered, strong hand stopped on Kaiser's withers. "What about the Winslows?" he asked in a voice filled with dread.

Zeiss didn't look up. One shoulder twitched in a small shrug. "I tried," he said quietly. "I tried to get Mrs. Winslow and Brynn to come with me. I would have let them ride Kaiser down here, and I could have walked—or run, I guess. But—"

"Wait a minute. What about their horses? Their carriages?" Shiloh growled.

"Stolen," he said flatly. "I think it was the workers from the northeast sugarcane camp. You know, the one right below and to the east of the high sandalwood camp."

Now Shiloh shifted uneasily, one booted foot digging into the soft sand. "Are you telling me that Mrs. Winslow and Brynn are up at the villa? Without any horses? And they refused to leave?"

"Mrs. Winslow did," Zeiss answered with frustration. "She swore that Bain was coming back to get them. But she also swore that he was coming to Hana in *Locke's Day Dream* to pick up you four. So I didn't really realize, until I saw you . . . or maybe I would have thought to ride over to the lagoon to see if for some reason the ship is there." His mouth twisted. "But I don't think he is. I think Bain sprinted down to the lagoon, got on that blasted clipper, and took off like the little sneaking weasel he's always been."

"But what about Brynn? Miss Winslow, I mean?" Walker asked tensely.

"I couldn't find Brynn. But she wouldn't leave her mother, I know.

And I hate it, but there must be several of the servants still up there at the villa. I know Tang Sun and his wife are there. I saw them. They said Miss Winslow was with Pat and Will, the stableboys . . . and Keloki and his whole family . . ."

"Oh no," Walker murmured with dread.

"And now we have their only horses . . . and the cart." Cheney sounded anguished.

Shiloh turned and stared at her. His face suddenly looked older, careworn. A weary sadness seemed to diminish him a little, softening the ruler square of his shoulders and the carelessly proud stance.

Cheney's eyes softened to warm greenish-gold. "Well, then," she said briskly. "We'd better go get them, don't you think?"

15

THE AIRS OF DECISION

"You're not going." Shiloh propped his hands on his hips and stepped close to Cheney, towering over her.

With obvious defiance Cheney began her reply, but Zeiss interrupted the coming storm.

"Excuse me, everyone, Miss Duvall. I've got to go check on Alena. But I'd just like to say, Irons . . . uh, ma'am . . . uh, Irons . . . whoever. If you decide to leave, Miss Duvall, I'll be glad for you to come with us. You're welcome to ride Kaiser with my wife. We'll make it just fine." Hurriedly he rode toward his house.

Neither Cheney's expression nor focus had changed. She still stared up at Shiloh defiantly and was impatient for Zeiss's speech to end so she could reply to Shiloh. "I'm going with you, Shiloh. That's all."

"No, that's not all," he growled. "You're going with Zeiss."

She cocked her head. "Oh? And what about Nia? She just trots twenty miles alongside the horse?" His stubborn expression wavered, and Cheney went on, "Besides, I'm a grown woman. I make my own decisions, and I take responsibility for myself. You have no right to make a decision such as this for me."

After a long moment, he shook his head in defeat. "Okay, Doc. Walker? You coming with me?"

"Of course," he said, offended. "What did you think I would do? Go for a swim?"

"Might not be a bad idea," Shiloh said dryly. "But I figured you'd want to go see about Miss Winslow."

"Yes, I do," he declared. "I just hope she'll mind me better than Dr. Duvall minds you. Er . . . um . . . that is—what I meant was—"

"Never mind, Walker," Cheney said, amused. Turning to Nia, she said sternly, "You're going with Mr. Zeiss and Alena."

She shook her head violently. "No, ma'am."

"Yes, ma'am," Cheney argued smartly. "You are."

Nia's pointed chin came up, and her eyebrows rose mischievously. "Begging your pardon, Dr. Duvall, but I'm a grown woman. I make my own decisions. I take responsibility for myself." Nia was not impertinent enough to echo the rest of Cheney's little speech to Shiloh, but the mimic was clear.

Cheney looked comically surprised, and then amused. "Well! That's a very impressive speech, Miss Nia. I must remember it and use it sometime." Turning to the men, who were watching but keeping a cautious distance from the ladies' decision-making processes, Cheney said, "All right, we're all four going. I only have one more question. What about the villagers? Should we just leave? With the only cart and horses available? Or—I suppose that the disposition of this cart is not really our decision to make. It's not ours, after all, but I don't—"

Shiloh stepped close to her, laid his hands on her shoulders, and spoke softly. "Doc, don't agonize over it. You can't save the entire world, you know. Besides, even though I hadn't thought much about it—" He turned and squinted, trying to scan the village. Through the grimy ashfall, however, vision was limited to only a few feet. "I haven't seen another soul this morning. Even Tang Lu and the kids were gone when I got up."

He stood for a moment, considering, then turned back with an air of decision. "Okay, here's what we'll do. Walker and I will go hitch up the cart. Doc, you and Nia want to make the rounds, see if anyone's still here? I guess all we can do is tell them we're going up to the villa and they can ride up if they want to." He shrugged. "Guess maybe the Chinese might be glad to get to the high places. Who knows?"

Zeiss materialized again out of the grimy fog. "Alena already had the cart hitched up for you," he said without preamble. "And don't worry about the villagers. You didn't see Mama Nomi yesterday, about dawn? She never even bothered to go back to her hut. After the sun came up, she just paddled that fat little boat of hers on out, caught the current, and sailed around the headland, north. Those three Chinese, Dooley and Dan and Tinker, weren't far behind. And I think all the rest of the villagers have either sailed off or headed for the hills too. At least all the boats are gone."

"What about Tang Lu?" Shiloh asked. "You have any idea where she went?"

"No, sorry. I haven't seen her or talked to her since yesterday after we all came back home," Zeiss answered. "But I figure she headed up to the sugarcane camp. Her husband's up there, you know. He probably told her to come up there and bring the kids in time of trouble."

"You mean she walked?" Cheney demanded. "But she had two centipede bites! She was feverish and weak when I put her to bed yesterday! And those children—climbing halfway up that mountain, on foot? The eldest is only ten years old!"

Zeiss shrugged. "Tang Lu will do whatever Fang Shao tells her. She has to. She has no choice. That's just the way it is with them. Now, ladies and gentlemen, I want to get my wife out of here. What did all of you decide?"

The four looked at one another, and their expressions were determined. Cheney nodded firmly to Shiloh, who spoke for them all. "We're all going up to the villa, Zeiss. Thank you for your help. Good luck to you and Miss Alena." He stuck out his hand.

Zeiss shook it, then turned to leave.

"Go with God." Cheney smiled at him.

He gave her a clumsily grateful nod, then disappeared into the grimy mists.

★   ★   ★   ★

As they ascended the lower ramparts of Mount Haleakala, the mountain's choler seemed to increase.

It grew hotter. Rivulets of sweat ran down their faces, streaking the ash grime that had colored them all, even Nia, a uniform gunmetal shade. They wet their handkerchiefs in the cask of water Alena Zeiss had thoughtfully put into the cart and dabbed at their faces and throats.

The tremors continued. The mountain's trembles did not seem to be increasing in violence, but they did seem to come more often. The horses were spooked each time the earth shifted eerily beneath their feet, and finally Shiloh halted them at each shudder, jumping out to hold the harness and soothe them before continuing.

The air stank. It was thick with the smell of sulphur and other noxious odors certain to be gases of one kind or another. "It's too bad natural gases don't smell like sandalwood or jasmine," Cheney weakly joked when Nia coughed, making a wry face at a particularly strong whiff.

"Guess God knew what He was doing," Nia commented. "If they

smelled good, us fools would sniff 'em till we died, wouldn't we?"

"Good point," Cheney agreed.

As they crawled up the thickly wooded sides of the mountain and crept nearer the summit, they were able to see the dark cloud that cloaked the farthest heights more clearly. It was thick and inky, and the serrated blades of lightning were diabolical fireworks. The bloated underside of the cloud continuously glowed grizzly gray and darkish purple.

"Seems like it's getting a little bit lighter," Nia said doubtfully. "Sorta like going from dirty gray to smoky gray."

"I think you're right," Cheney agreed. "It's not as if the light has increased . . . I think the ashfall is lessening a little."

They could indeed see a little farther ahead. As they continually, nervously scanned the threatening landscape, thin white tendrils of smoke occasionally shot up, only to be swallowed by the murk and cloud.

"What can that be?" Cheney wondered out loud, watching a plume of oyster-white smoke shoot fifty feet into the air before dissipating.

Shiloh said reluctantly, "I'm no expert, but I think it's steam."

"Oh," Cheney said. "I'm no expert, either, but that's not good, hmm?"

One of Shiloh's broad shoulders jerked up in a tense shrug.

They came to the bridge over Muolea Stream. Great clouds, thick and roiling, writhed around the wooden bridge. Shiloh halted the horses. "Man, oh, man," he muttered, then climbed out of the cart for the eighth time. Cheney had counted.

This time the other three followed him, Cheney scrambling down by herself while Nia fussed and waited for Walker to help her. All four stood at the mouth of the bridge, staring down.

The stream was boiling. Like a tumbling cauldron, great bubbles formed, then burst. The heat rising from it chapped their cheeks and made the sensitive skin of their eyelids and mouth burn. Hastily Cheney and Nia recoiled, stepping back and gasping for cooler air. Shiloh and Walker exchanged hard-eyed looks.

"Think we better run the horses over it," Shiloh muttered. "Their eyes and nostrils are pretty sensitive."

"I think you're right," Walker agreed grimly. "I'll cross with Dr. Duvall and Nia."

"We heard you," Cheney said as he turned to her, his face twisted with concern. "We can run fast, can't we, Nia? Don't worry, Walker. We'll probably beat you across."

"Just try it," Walker taunted them. "Ready?"

"Let's go!" With a last reassuring nod to Shiloh, who was obviously worried, Cheney and Nia picked up their skirts and ran lightly, skimming along on their toes. Walker pounded along behind them. Shiloh watched, but they disappeared into the clouds of steam just a few feet ahead.

"We're fine!" Walker shouted, his voice barely carrying over the tumult of the boiling stream and the mountain's bass reverberations. "Bring 'em across, Shiloh!"

Shiloh climbed back into the driver's seat and cautiously backed up, which was a neat trick for two horses, a cart, and a crooked incline. Still, they cooperated with him, shifting and shuffling until they had pulled back far enough from the bridge to get a running start. In all his life Shiloh had never touched the back of a horse with a whip, but this time he snapped both of the horses' flanks smartly and thundered in a commanding voice, "Giddup there! Hup, hup!"

He almost fell off the seat as the horses nervously took off and hit a full stride in about three lengths. As they flew across the bridge, Shiloh barely had time to observe that he wasn't too sure all four wheels were actually touching the wooden slats. The horses had started off so quickly he felt as if the entire cart was airborne.

They hit the dirt road on the other side, still at full gallop. Shiloh had more trouble slowing and stopping them than he did starting them up, but finally they halted, shivering and pawing the air frantically. Walker, Cheney, and Nia ran to catch up and climbed back in the cart.

They resumed their nightmare journey. From the Muolea Bridge, the road to Winslow Villa grew steeper, with more curves. The horses were nervous and fitful, and Shiloh let them have their heads. By the time they reached the villa, they were lathering and grunting for air with each step, but still straining to run.

Panic reaction, Cheney thought clinically. She was aware that her mind was oddly detached, her observations aloof, as if she were merely an observer instead of a participant. But she was grateful, for with her impassivity came a profound certainty that this was a supernatural self-control that the Lord had instilled in her.

They pulled up to the villa and saw not a soul about. The rain of ash was indeed lighter up here, as if the thinner air had also thinned the grit falling from the sky. The black cloud at the summit, however, seemed to be much, much nearer.

The four got out of the cart and stared up at the house. In the gloom they saw no candle, no lantern. They saw no sign of life at all.

"Maybe they've gone already," Shiloh said tentatively. "Maybe Bain really did come back and get them."

The others looked at one another uncertainly.

Finally Shiloh decided. "Well, I'm going in, anyway. Just to see."

"I'm coming with you," Cheney said. "We all might as well come."

Walker said thoughtfully, "I think I'll stay out here on the verandah. Shiloh, you have a reason, and a right, to go into that house. Dr. Duvall, I think it's wise if a lady goes in too. But I think I'll just wait out here."

"I'm staying out here too," Nia decided. "No call for me to go traipsing in there."

Shiloh and Cheney agreed and walked up to the great double doors. Doubtfully Shiloh looked down at Cheney, and she said, "Of course we have to knock, Shiloh dear. They may be in there, you know."

"Yeah, but are they receiving guests today?" he asked dryly. He lifted the heavy brass knocker and banged it loudly three times.

To their surprise, the door cracked open about three inches, then widened a few more. The Chinese butler, Tang Sun, looked first up at Shiloh and then at Cheney. He said nothing, merely looked at them without moving.

Shiloh saw a glimmer of something—could it be hope?—briefly pass over the Chinaman's impassive face. "Hi, Mr. Tang Sun," he said cheerily, as if he were at the servants' entrance asking for a drink of water. "Is Mrs. Winslow here?"

"Ye-es, sir," he finally answered reluctantly. Guiltily he glanced back over his shoulder. "She's . . . not feeling well, Mr. Irons. Not really wanting to receive guests today."

Shiloh's voice was kind. "I understand. But I'd like to come in, Mr. Tang Sun. In fact, I insist. I'm sure you understand."

Now his wrinkled face showed vast relief, and he bowed deeply, throwing the door wide open. "If necessary," he said somberly, "I will tell Mrs. Winslow that you were very insistent."

"Yeah, tell her I overpowered you, Mr. Tang Sun," Shiloh said easily. "Naw, never mind, I'll tell her myself. Is she in the parlor?"

He nodded, and Shiloh and Cheney hurried up the hallway, entering the drawing room without announcing themselves.

Tang Sun silently followed them and went to a corner of the room where his wife, Chen Guifei, and the young maid, Fang Jinglan, huddled. On the sofa was Denise Winslow, sitting bolt upright, her face set and rigid, her pallor pronounced. Brynn sat at the other end of the sofa, slumped and weary. She looked as if she'd been crying.

When Cheney and Shiloh came in, Denise barely glanced at them. Her nostrils flared with distaste, but she resumed her blank stare into space. "What are you people doing here?" she said in a curiously flat voice. "I don't want you here."

Today Shiloh Irons had no time for etiquette and no patience for theatrics. He walked across the room, his bootsteps hard and loud, and stood right in front of Denise Winslow. She stared straight ahead, her eyes defiantly unfocused. With a stiff and jerky movement she lifted a glass of brandy to her mouth and took a deep drink.

"Mrs. Winslow, you need to leave right now," Shiloh said evenly. "Me and my friends have brought your cart and horses. Everyone here is going to come with us. Now."

Without focusing she said disdainfully, "Bain is coming back to get us."

"I'm afraid that's not true," Shiloh said as respectfully as he could manage. "He didn't come to Hana to pick us up. He's not here. He's gone."

She took another drink, and this time her hand trembled. She swallowed as if her throat hurt, then said in the same dead tone, "Then there must not be any danger. We must not be in any danger, or my son would not have left. If he doesn't return for us, then we must not be in any danger."

Shiloh glanced at Brynn, who sighed so deeply it seemed to come from the depths of her soul. "That's all she's been saying," Brynn said in a low tone. "That's all she will say."

Anxiously Shiloh considered the woman. "Mrs. Winslow, please listen to me. You must leave here. If you can't think of yourself, please think of your daughter. And the servants who've stayed here with you. You're placing them in great danger!"

"There must not be any danger," she repeated. "Or Bain will come back."

Cheney stepped up to Shiloh and took his hand in both of hers. "Shiloh, I don't think it's going to do any good trying to reason with her. I think she's unable to reason right now."

"Then what am I supposed to do?" he said harshly. "Knock her on the head, throw her over my shoulder, and carry her out?" His hand gripped Cheney's painfully, but she gave no sign.

"Of course not," she said gently. "I would think that the proper thing to do in this situation is to let her daughter be responsible for her." She turned to Brynn and went on, "Miss Winslow, I don't think that your mother is capable of making sound decisions right now. Is there anything you can do to help us and help your mother?"

Wearily Brynn shook her head. "Nothing I've said, nothing I've done, no threat or pleas have moved her. It's as if she's . . . hiding and won't come out."

"That is a fair assessment of what she is doing," Cheney said worriedly. "But I just don't know . . . it's not our place to . . ." She noticed then that Shiloh was staring hard at Denise Winslow, his eyes narrowed to azure slits, his jaw so tense it looked like stone. She gave no sign that she was aware of it. She just sat, unmoving, except when she raised the glass of brandy to her lips and drank thirstily.

"Mrs. Winslow," Shiloh said, and suddenly his voice was gentle, persuasive, "perhaps you're right. Maybe Bain will come back to get you." Slowly, hesitantly, her eyes raised to Shiloh's face. In them he saw the faintest flicker of acknowledgment. "If he does, he'll bring *Locke's Day Dream* to the lagoon, won't he?" Shiloh waited for her to answer.

Finally, after an eternity of silence, she said in a creaky voice, "Yes, I believe he would. . . ."

"Then he would have to come on foot to the villa," Shiloh said reasonably, "since no one has taken his horse down to meet him. Wouldn't it be much better for us—for you and for Bain—if we went on down to the lagoon?"

Brynn's face suddenly lit with a ragged hope, and Cheney felt admiration for how intuitive Shiloh was, how astute he was at reading people's inner thoughts.

"Why . . . I suppose . . . it would be easier for Bain. . . ." Mrs. Winslow finally said dazedly.

"Yes, it would," Shiloh said smoothly. "Now, why don't you and Miss Winslow go change into . . . er—"

"Carriage costumes?" Cheney said brightly. "Or perhaps a nice promenade dress?"

"Yes, yes. I think my turquoise carriage costume," Denise hummed in a faraway voice.

Brynn eagerly jumped up and took her mother's arm. "Come along, Mother. Fay and I will help you to dress. All right?"

"All right," she said pleasantly.

Clutching her arm tightly, Brynn led her mother out of the drawing room, followed closely by Chen Guifei and Tang Sun. Fang Jinglan scuttled after them. Brynn glanced back over her shoulder to Shiloh with an intensely grateful, "We shall only be a few minutes, Mr. Irons. Thank you so much."

"Welcome," he said gravely.

Cheney collapsed onto the sofa and asserted, "She's stark raving, you know."

Staring after them, Shiloh replied, "I don't think so, Doc."

"What do you mean? Surely you can't believe she was putting on an act!"

"No, it's just that I think she broke down a little, for a while. She just . . . threw a shoe, like. Makes a horse limp, but it doesn't mean he's lame."

Cheney stared up at him incredulously. "Oh, Shiloh, you are incorrigible!"

"What's that mean?" he drawled. His face was filthy from ash and sweat and the smoke-gray mud the combination of the two made. Oddly, the neutral color made the blue of his eyes dazzling, like blue-white diamonds. "Gee, Doc, your face sure is dirty," he teased as she stared at him without answering his question. "But it sure makes those serpent-green eyes flash."

Cheney blinked, then shot up off the couch. "Good heavens, the sight of us is probably what sent that woman into shock!" she clamored, racing to the mirror over the sideboard by the door. When she saw her reflection, she groaned. "Oh, horrors! I've never been so . . . so—"

"Sure you have," Shiloh said cheerfully, his sooty countenance looming up behind her in the mirror. "Remember in Panama? The explosion? The walk through the jungle?"

Cheney sighed and scrubbed at her cheeks. It made them a smeary charcoal instead of a chalky ash. "Oh yes, I remember all too well. And now a volcano. Or a tidal wave. Or both. Such memories we'll have!"

"To tell our children and our—" Before Cheney could react, Shiloh frowned as his eyes darted to their left and his attention was caught by something out in the hallway. "What is that thing? Aw, man, don't tell me—" He rushed out in the hall and stopped to stare at something hung on the wall. Truth to tell, Cheney was still a little breathless from his unfinished sentence. But evidently Shiloh had already forgotten it, for he muttered, "Doc, you better come look at this."

"What now?" she grumbled, then stalked up beside him.

It was a barometer, a fine one of polished teak with brass fittings. The needle was trembling, shivering. As Cheney and Shiloh watched, it jerked to one side—low pressure—then flicked downward. Shaking and jumping, the needle then crawled back up to the right—high pressure—then shivered, and dropped—

"This—can't be—right," Cheney groped. "Perhaps it's just so . . . so finely tuned, it's responding to the tremors."

"Maybe," Shiloh said quietly.

"Hope so," Cheney whispered.

"Yeah."

From outside, at the back of the house, they heard Walker Baird. He shouted, his normally kind voice kindled with anger, "Hey! Hey, you! Stop that right now!" Loud boots thundered on hollow planks across the verandah.

Shrill shouting filtered down the hall; a woman screamed; Nia yelled, "You better stop in your tracks, woman!"

Shiloh and Cheney, as one, ran. Shiloh reached the door first, threw it open, and burst through it, rudely pushing Cheney behind him. But she jerked around so that she stood beside him as he came to a skidding stop at the top of the steps. With such quickness that Cheney barely saw him move, he pushed back his loose coat, grabbed his Colt, and fired into the air. But no one even looked up.

About twenty Chinese, some women, mostly men, were rushing the cart. Some of them were climbing in the back, two were fighting to get onto the steps, one was already in the driver's seat fumbling to untie the reins from the upright.

Walker had waded into them, and as Cheney and Shiloh burst onto the verandah, he hit one of the men solidly across the jaw. The man's eyes rolled up, and his feet actually left the ground as he flew backward and crumpled to the ground. Another man was already down, rubbing his head dazedly. But two men grabbed Walker, agilely pinning his arms behind him, while another hit him in the stomach. Walker kicked like a mule and twisted like a dervish. The two holding him lost their hold. Walker grabbed the man on the cart step, tossed him aside like a bag of refuse, and jumped up onto the driver's seat.

Cheney was stunned, frozen. She could see what was happening but simply couldn't think of anything to do about it. She saw Nia standing close to the cart and a Chinese woman reaching out toward her with hands curved into claws. Nia, her little girl's face dark with fury, suddenly drew herself up and bashed the Chinese woman across the head with Cheney's medical bag. The woman staggered back, dazed. She fell into a man behind her, who shoved her down. Quickly he stepped up, grabbed Nia's shoulders, and roughly threw her to the ground. Then the man jumped up into the cart.

Shiloh shoved his gun into Cheney's hands, ordering, "Use it if you have to." Then he jumped all the way, disdaining the six porch steps. He headed straight for the cart, and the Chinese on the ground scattered, not even trying to stop him; instead, they ran to the now moving cart and scrambled in. Walker had shoved down the man in the driver's seat and was trying to halt the horses. But finally the Chinese man came up with a stout stick and let out a high-pitched, blood-curdling scream. As fast as a snake striking, he hit Walker across the head, right above his ear. Walker flew out of the cart, hitting the ground with a sickening bone crunch that Shiloh could hear from three feet away. The Chinaman grabbed the reins, and another man laid onto the horses with the whip. They dashed recklessly off, around the path that led past the servants' quarters.

A Chinese woman with four children stood on the far side of the cart, her head bowed. She looked up at Cheney, who was staring around, desperately attempting to get her bearings.

Her face streaked with tears, the woman looked at Cheney with such anguish that Cheney's heart went out to her.

Then she saw that it was Tang Lu.

16

A Day Without Sun, A Night Without Moon

Dr. Walker Baird was lying on his left side. His eyes were closed, and he wasn't moving. Cheney's heart quavered as she ran to him. Shiloh reached him first and knelt down beside him, placing two fingers to his neck, just below his ear.

Walker's eyes fluttered, then opened. "I'm . . . alive."

"I'm glad," Shiloh told him sincerely.

"I'm . . . not . . . so sure . . . I am," Walker gasped. "Hurts. Really hurts."

Cheney slid to her knees beside Shiloh. Neither of them touched Walker; they exchanged grave looks. "I'll check his spine," Shiloh said.

"Can feel my legs," Walker reported, teeth grinding. "And my right arm—and right side. Wish I couldn't feel my left arm. Ouch, Shiloh! I can . . . sure . . . feel that vertebra. . . ."

"Sorry."

Cheney narrowed her eyes and looked Walker up and down for a few seconds. She could tell by the way his left shoulder was crumpled—his head lay almost flat on the ground—that both his scapula and his clavicle were broken. He had a head wound just above his right ear. It didn't appear to be serious, but head wounds were so difficult to assess, even under the best of conditions.

"Oh no! Walker! Walker! Are you—" Brynn threw herself down by the little group, reached for him, then jerked back. "What . . . what happened?"

"He got whacked and flew out of the cart," Shiloh told her.

"Did you see me?" Walker asked anxiously, rolling his eyes uncomfortably to peer up at her.

"No! No—I—oh, Walker! What's—do something! You're a doctor, do something!" Brynn cried, turning on Cheney.

"Miss Winslow, he's going to be fine," Cheney asserted. "But I need your help. Will you help me?"

"Wh-why, yes! You mean there's—I can do something?"

"Yes, certainly you can. First of all, you can remain calm. That will help all of us. Then you can go into the house and get me a sheet. Two, in fact. The best, finest ones you have. Also bring me clean water. And do you have any laudanum? Good. Bring that and some of your mother's expensive brandy."

Brynn turned and ran into the house.

Cheney looked around anxiously at the people milling around the grounds of the villa. Nia was hurrying to her, holding out her medical bag. "Here, Miss Cheney. I knew you'd be needing this, with all these heathens around here bashin' folks."

In spite of herself, Cheney grinned. Her teeth shone very white in her grimy face. "Thank you, Nia. I saw that you defended it with great honor."

Nia made a terrible face. "That woman was trying to take it!" She turned and pointed accusingly to the woman that Nia herself had bashed. The Chinese woman was sitting on the ground, her face hidden in her hands, her shoulders shaking. "And there was already Mr. Shiloh's bag in the cart!" Nia finished with disgust.

Cheney sat up alertly. "What about Walker's bag, Nia? Was it in the cart?"

"I'm injured. I'm not . . . deafened," Walker put in with weak indignation. "It's on the verandah. I took it and went to sit down and straighten it up—shouldn't have left the cart—"

"You couldn't have stopped them. There were too many of them," Shiloh growled, still pinching and prodding his back and the back of his legs. "We still have two medical bags. That's good. That's real good."

Brynn came running back out, her hair loose and flying. She held a jumble of things in her arms—flapping sheets, two fingers precariously grasping a heavy crystal decanter, scissors, a canteen hung by the straps and banging against her legs. "Here, I got all this. And—Dr. Duvall, here's some absinthe. Are you familiar with it?"

"Oh yes, and thank the Lord," Cheney replied fervently, taking the small bottle of thick emerald-green liquid. "Very, very good, Miss Winslow."

"What else can I do?"

"Take Nia into the house. Find a bag, any bag that can be comfortably carried. Help her stock it with medical supplies. She knows what to do."

"Nia? Is this your maid?" Brynn asked, looking the young Negro girl up and down with disbelief.

"Yes, and I don't really have time to offer you her excellent references right now, Miss Winslow," Cheney said sharply. "Please do as I say."

"Yes—all right . . . Walker?" she asked, leaning close to his face.

"Yes, Miss Winslow?" Even in his great pain, his indigo eyes lit up.

"You may call me Brynn," she murmured. "I just wanted to tell you that I think I'm very fond of you, and I should like it ever so much if you would not . . . not . . ."

Walker's eyes opened as wide as a toddler's on Christmas. "Not d-die?" he finally stammered.

"Yes," she breathed. "Don't die."

"I know I probably shouldn't . . . tell you this, considering . . . how well things are going," he muttered with difficulty, "but all . . . that's wrong with me . . . is a broken clavicle and scapula, and a slight head abrasion."

"What . . . what's broken?" Brynn stammered, looking up beseechingly at Shiloh.

"His shoulder blade and collarbone," he told her. "He'll live."

"Oh, thank the Lord," she whispered. Rising to her feet, she declared, "I'll do as you say, Dr. Duvall. Miss—what did you say your name was?"

"Nia is fine, ma'am."

"Then come with me, Nia." The two women hurried back into the villa. Brynn brushed by her mother, standing on the verandah. Denise appeared to have recovered her senses, for instead of the blank, unfocused stare that made her face like a corpse's, she was looking around the chaotic scene with an expression of livid anger.

"Tang Sun! Chen Guifei! Come attend to me this instant!" she roared. "Do you hear me? This instant!"

The elderly couple were with Tang Lu's children—their grandchildren. Cheney saw Tang Lu attending to the man that Walker had struck and knocked out. After a hurried conference, Chen Guifei hurried to Mrs. Winslow, while Tang Sun stayed with the children.

Cheney turned her attention back to Walker. She took out a clean bandage and began washing out his head wound. "Don't move, Walker."

"Don't worry. I'm dreading it."

Cheney and Shiloh glanced at each other. Shiloh was busily ripping up the sheets that Brynn had brought. But as he worked, his eyes darted around, scanning the knots of people and the dramas unfolding.

"There are so many people here," Cheney murmured.

Grimly Shiloh nodded. "Servants. Not all of the Chinese were trying to steal the cart. Pat and Will and George Han were trying to stop them."

Cheney glanced at the three Chinese men. One of them was the young man who had been sitting on the ground, stunned, when she and Shiloh came outside. "I've seen those two young men. They're the stableboys, aren't they?"

"Yeah. Wu Pat and Wu Yijun, they're brothers. Orphans. Everyone calls them Pat and Will. The oldest—Pat—he's the one that got hurt."

"He did the same thing I did," Walker said weakly. "And he got the same treatment I did. Is he all right?" The three men, now joined by Fang Jinglan and Lela Han with their baby, were behind Walker.

"He looks fine," Cheney said reassuringly. "Nia checked on him a few minutes ago. He must not have been hit as hard as you, Walker."

"Hope not," Walker grunted. "Hurts."

"Did you know that the guy who decked you—the one driving the cart—is Fang Shao's oldest son?" Shiloh asked in a hostile tone. "The other jolly fellow with the whip is his second son. That maid, Fang Jinglan, is his other daughter."

"Fang Shao?" Cheney asked, following Shiloh's dark gaze. "You mean that he—that man who tried to steal the cart—is Tang Lu's husband?"

"That's right," Shiloh grunted with disdain. "His sons—you know, by the first wife or second wife or whatever he's got going on with them—didn't show their sainted father much respect, did they?"

"So many . . . and children . . ." Cheney whispered.

"Yeah. So far I make it over twenty people wanderin' around here."

Wordlessly Shiloh looked up at the sky. Even the pallid light was turning a helpless gray, the color of twilight shadows. The cloud, still black and threatening, loomed above, ridden with lightning, constantly muttering thunder threats.

Ignoring the dread and fear she felt, Cheney turned her full attention back to Walker. After washing out the wound, she saw the abrasion was shallow, but Walker did have a long swelling above his ear. She washed his face and neck and checked for Battle's sign and telltale bruising around the eyes, but saw no indication that he had any serious blood pools or brain swelling. "How many fingers?" she demanded.

"Two," he sighed.

"What's your name?"

"Dr. Matthew Walker Baird."

"Where are you?"

"Winslow Villa, the island of Maui, Hawaii."

"What's the date?"

"Don't have a clue," Walker said with faint cheerfulness.

"Neither do I," Cheney admitted. "I thought perhaps you might tell without my having to admit it."

"It's the twenty-third," Shiloh said with an air of superiority. "And it's October. In 1867."

"Ah." Cheney nodded. "And what day is it, Mr. Almanac Man?"

"Dunno," he said. Then he lifted his chin. "But I do know that tonight's the new moon."

Cheney sighed and sat back on her heels. "A day without sun, a night without moon. Not good omens, Shiloh."

"How about shoulders busted all to pieces?" Walker added querulously. "There's an omen for you."

"I'm sorry, Walker," Cheney said quickly. "I'm going to give you something for the pain in just a minute. But first I have to confer with Shiloh. All right?"

"Dr. Duvall, I beg you to remember whom you're talking to," Walker said with a trace of his father's imperiousness. "I am a doctor, you know. You don't need to coddle me, and I certainly intend to be a party to any conversations about my condition."

Keeping her amusement in check, Cheney replied, "Sir, I beg you to remember whom you're talking to. I'm your physician, duly appointed. Remember?"

"Oh," Walker mumbled, his boyishness returning. Then he brightened somewhat. "Then you're fired. I'll be my own physician."

"Not possible, I'm afraid," Cheney said firmly. "It's battlefield conditions, and I'm the field surgeon. Shiloh? Would you step over here for a moment so that we may confer about this difficult and fussy patient?"

"Fussy!" Walker grunted. "I am not fussy! Dr. Duvall! Shiloh! Come back over here—"

Ignoring him, Cheney said in a low voice, "You know what the problem is, don't you?"

"Think so," Shiloh replied. He rubbed his forehead, leaving muddy black streaks. "If we dope him up enough to deaden the pain, he's not going to stay conscious. He won't be able to walk."

Cheney nodded. "But if we don't, he won't be able to walk, anyway. He'll keep passing out from the pain."

"I know. I vote for the dope."

"Me too," Cheney said with relief. She trusted Shiloh, and she relied upon his judgment, particularly in difficult situations such as this. With his experience in the war, he was an expert in coping with crisis conditions. "I think both the clavicle and scapula are clean breaks," she went on. "I think we should set them now. We're going to have to make a litter, and he's going to be jostled a lot. Don't you think so?"

Shiloh nodded thoughtfully. "Have you ever set both at once, Doc?"

"No, I haven't. Have you?"

"Yeah, and it's hard. Best way I've found to do it is to sit facing the arm, use your right hand for the collarbone, the left hand for the scapula."

"But, Shiloh, I don't think I'm strong enough to pull his arm out far enough to get the bones back in position to reset them," Cheney worried, glancing at Walker lying in a misshapen heap on the ground.

Shiloh put two fingers under her chin and tilted her face up to his. "No, you can't do that, Doc, but I can. You can set those bones, no problem. You know what you're doing."

They stared into each other's eyes, and finally Cheney nodded. "You're right, I do. Okay, let's go ahead and get him medicated. You have the slings ready?"

"Sure do."

Returning to kneel by Walker, Cheney said in a no-nonsense voice, "I want you to drink about half of this, Walker. I'm going to pour it in your mouth, but since you're in such an awkward position, you're going to have to kind of lap it up."

"I don't want absinthe," he muttered darkly. "It makes you so silly."

"It'll take away the pain. And you're going to have lots of pain," Cheney said bluntly.

"I know that," he said quietly. "But I also know that absinthe will likely put me out. And I have to walk, Dr. Duvall. Lying here this way, my ear's been flat on the ground, and what I've heard isn't good. I think this mountain's just about to explode."

"Then stop wasting time and drink this, Walker." Cheney stuck the bottle, which had a small neck, into his mouth and tilted it upright. Walker grunted, protesting, a couple of times, but Cheney saw with satisfaction that he did drink the rich green liquid. Immediately his eyelids got heavier, and his stare grew warm and unfocused.

"Thank you," he said fuzzily.

"Yes, well, you might not later," Cheney retorted briskly. She and Shiloh stood up, and Cheney checked the sheets that Shiloh had torn for slings. Mostly, however, they were just giving Walker a few moments for the drug to take full effect. "Walker was exaggerating, I think," Cheney whispered. "I don't think this whole mountain is going to explode, but I do think that it's getting worse. Except for the ashfall. That's still sporadic and not as heavy as this morning."

"These tremors, they're getting worse," Shiloh said, his jaw clenching. "Have you noticed? They make my teeth hurt. Like biting down on tinfoil. And they are pretty continuous now."

Cheney concentrated and did become aware of a very slight vibration, mostly sensed in her feet. The day was still dark, sullen, the air still. It was much like a summer day in New Orleans, just before a big storm. The vast darkness above them, still flogged by zigzagged lightning, seemed to be dropping, falling, settling down farther on the mountain. *Or perhaps it's just that we're closer to it,* Cheney thought with uneasiness. *After all, the villa is about four thousand feet above sea level, isn't it?*

"We're just closer to it, Doc," Shiloh said reassuringly as he followed her worried gaze. "The villa's about four thousand feet higher than the village, you know."

Cheney stared at him, startled. She started to say something, but from the ground at their feet came Walker's syrupy voice.

"Is someone there?" he inquired pleasantly. "Oh, hello. Would you help me up, please? Just realized it's awfully uncomfortable lying on the ground like this. . . ."

Instantly Cheney and Shiloh knelt by him. "All right, Walker, let's get you sitting up," Shiloh said. "You ready, Doc?"

She settled close by Walker's head. "Yes."

"Okay. I'm gonna push him up in a sitting position. Then I'm going to lock his arm around my left one, and with my right arm I'm going to push against his side, while I'm pulling with my left. That ought to separate the breaks enough for you to set them. Got it?"

"Got it," Walker mumbled.

"Yes, I understand," Cheney said steadily.

Fortunately, Walker gave one small groan and then passed out cold as they were sitting him up. Cheney and Shiloh set the bones easily, then quickly and efficiently put his left arm in a sling, up high against his chest and tied securely to his torso. When finished, they laid him down flat on his back and then sat down in the fine gray dust on either side of him.

"Bet he was glad he missed that," Shiloh said. "That absinthe is good stuff."

"Yes, but you know what happens when they wake," Cheney said wearily. "They talk a lot. The most absurd nonsense you've ever heard."

"Yeah," Shiloh agreed. "I was thinking about putting a sling over his mouth—"

"Keakea! My brudder!"

Keloki came running up, followed by his entire family. This was the first glimpse Cheney had gotten of Malani, the eighteen-year-old girl who was Keloki's daughter but wasn't, and who had evidently fallen in love with Shiloh. She was lovely, of course, as young Hawaiian women seemed to always be, with long glossy raven hair and warm skin and flashing white teeth. She caught sight of Cheney sitting on the ground and smiled brightly at her, with no hint of self-consciousness. Taken aback—Cheney was more accustomed to cattiness from Shiloh's many admirers—Cheney did still manage to return the girl's courteous greeting with a nod. She glanced at Shiloh, but he was rising to his feet to greet Keloki.

The big man, with no sign of tiring from his dead run, barked, "Keakea! We gotta go, brudder! Gotta go!"

Shiloh searched wildly around. "What is it, Keloki? Besides"—he waved around disdainfully—"the usual?"

Ignoring his dark humor, Keloki looked grave, even frightened. His family gathered in a knot around him. "We gotta go now, Keakea," he said again. "Pele is coming."

"You sure?" Shiloh asked alertly.

"Yeah."

"You know where she is?"

Keloki shook his head.

Cheney stood up and said impatiently, "What nonsense is this, Shiloh? Pele, the goddess?"

"Yeah, Doc. She's the fire goddess, the creator of volcanoes," Shiloh answered with a hint of impatience. "And it's not all nonsense, Doc. You just have to understand what Keloki means." He turned back to the Hawaiian, who was staring at Walker's prone body with the bulky white sling around his neck and swathing his left arm. "Keloki, you have any idea how long?"

Keloki shook his head, then pointed to Walker. "He dead?"

"No, he's just passed out."

"Kimo, go back to the hale, get Ilima *he'e nalu. Holo! Wikiwiki!*" Keloki thundered, and a slender, handsome teenaged boy turned and ran, his bare feet barely skimming the ground, back toward the servants' cottages.

Keloki turned back to Shiloh and laid his enormous brown hands on his shoulders. "Keakea, you tell them. Tell all to get water to carry, and we go. *Now.*"

Shiloh's eyes went down to Walker. He was coming out of his faint, for he stirred, his right hand twitching a bit. He moaned almost inaudibly. Cheney knelt back by him and grabbed his wrist to try to take his pulse. It was very difficult in the tumult, as the vibrations of the earth were increasing in intensity. Muttering, she took her stethoscope out of her bag and pressed it against his chest. Keloki's children squatted down to watch Cheney with avidly curious expressions. "I'm listening to his heart," she told them. "Or trying to."

Malani, ten-year-old Ilima, and even the grandchild, two-year-old Anika, put their hands over their left breasts. *This would be amusing,* Cheney thought, *if we weren't living a nightmare....*

" . . . should tell them, Keloki, these people don't know me," Shiloh was protesting.

"You Keakea-keiki. You haole *kahuna,*" Keloki said stubbornly. His son, Kimo, came skimming back up, carrying a long oval wooden board made of the fine, light koa wood. It was his little sister Ilima's he'e nalu, or wave slider. It would make a fine litter. Ignoring Shiloh, Keloki turned to his son, took the board, and squatted down by Cheney, talking to her in a low voice.

"No, Keloki, they're not going to listen to me. I'm not the boss. I'm just—oh, forget it," Shiloh complained, then muttered, "They put people in Bedlam that talk to themselves." Jumping up on the verandah he shouted loudly, "Listen, people! All of us haoles are going down to the lagoon. All of you should get all the water you can carry and come with us. We're leaving in just a few minutes, but I think all of you with children should get some water and go ahead. Mr. Tang Sun, will you see to it that everyone gets a jar or canteen or whatever you have that water can be carried in? Good."

Several things, several ghastly things, took place in the next few minutes. To an outsider stepping in, the scene would have been meaningless, pure and utter chaos.

But to Cheney, each and every moment was forever etched in stark colors of black and dead gray and crimson, burning into her brain. The pictures, vivid and clear, were unforgettable.

Tang Lu turned to her husband and began talking in fast, high Chinese. She laid her hand on his arm and pointed down toward the lagoon. Fang Shao snarled, then cuffed her. She flew backward, twisted, and landed facedown on the filthy earth.

Denise Winslow, standing on the verandah near Shiloh in her exquisite turquoise carriage costume, stepped up to him and screeched, "How dare you incite this rabble to steal from me?" Then she slapped him, so viciously the sound was like a whip's crack.

Brynn was coming out of the open door and saw her mother slap Shiloh. Brynn leaped between them, brandishing a white piece of paper like a knife, close to her mother's face. "No! How dare *you*, Mother? How dare *you*!"

Behind them, above them, and finally surrounding them, came the mountain's voice. It started out as a roar, then grew to deafening thunder, like thousands of great artillery guns that kept firing and firing and firing. Everyone turned, and everyone's face, frozen with fear, looked upward.

High up on Mount Haleakala, a tower of flame shot into the black cloud, blood-red against night-black. Hundreds of feet of liquid crimson spewed triumphantly up to set fire to the sky, and perhaps to the whole world.

★　★　★　★

Denise Winslow was screaming, that much was obvious. She ran wildly, her eyes huge and bulging, her mouth gaping. But her scream was lost in the mountain's bombardment. Denise kept running, weaving from one side of the road to the other, falling, scrambling, rising,

202

running around the house to the east road that led down to the lagoon.

Fang Shao ran to his children, grabbed up his son, and took off. Zhu Ki grabbed her four-year-old daughter in one arm, took her son's hand, and ran close behind him. Tang Lu ran to her mother and the children; Chen Guifei stood frozen, staring after Fang Shao and her only grandson. Tang Lu screamed at her, picked up Liu, and screaming orders in Chinese, she and the children ran. Chen Guifei shook herself, then hobbled as quickly as she could to where her husband still stood on the verandah, staring up at the nightmare fountain of lava. She said something to him, and the two hurried into the house. Brynn, staring after her mother with mingled fury and disgust, lingered only a moment, then turned and followed the servants into the house.

George and Lela Han looked around desperately, their fear and indecision clear. The stableboys, Pat and Will, and Fang Jinglan, looked stunned, their eyes wide and vacant. Shiloh dashed to them. "Take Lela and the baby! Go! Help the others, Pat!" George grabbed the baby and his wife's arm, and they disappeared down the road. Pat, his brother, and the girl roused and ran.

Cheney and Nia were trying to arouse Walker. He wasn't precisely unconscious, but neither was he fully aware. He was groggy, limp, unresponsive. Keloki's family kept pulling at Cheney's arm and shouting something at her, but brusquely she shoved at them and kept trying to get Walker to his feet. Shiloh, with one worried glance at the door to the villa, turned and hurried back to them. "Don't, Doc! We've got the litter!"

"But you can't carry him alone!" Cheney yelled. "We'd do better to try to help him walk!"

Shiloh shook his head furiously, then turned to Keloki. "Keloki, I hate to ask you this, but I have to, because this man is my friend," he said. He had to shout over the fearful din. "Will you help me carry him?"

Keloki actually smiled. It was a tense smile, not nearly as wide and joyous as usual. But still, it was a glad smile, a reassuring smile. "Sure, brudder. I, Keloki, am *nui*! Big! Like *alii*! I will help carry the Walker."

"Thank you, friend," Shiloh said, then hugged him hard. "Now, send your family on down the mountain."

Keloki nodded and waved nonchalantly to his son, Ulu Nui. As one, the entire family turned and started running.

Shiloh turned to Cheney and Nia. "Go now, Doc! I can take care of Walker!"

Cheney ignored him. She struggled to get long strips of the sheets underneath the smooth board. "Help me! We've got to tie him to it, or he'll just melt off of it!" She turned and ordered, "Nia, go on! Right now! You can't do anything here, but you can help the others!"

Nia looked rebellious for a moment, but then she nodded and dashed toward the house. But at that moment, Brynn, Tang Sun, and Chen Guifei all ran out of the villa, each of them loaded down with canteens and sizable leather bags of water. Nia ran to them, took two skins from the older couple, and started down the hill with them. Brynn ran over to Walker, but Shiloh said, "We're coming, right now! Go on with Sunny and Fay and Nia!"

With a last longing glance at Walker, she followed Nia and the old servants.

Cheney and Shiloh tied Walker to the board. He was mumbling the entire time, his eyes opening and closing, as if he were blinking in impossibly slow motion. Cheney was shifting him, trying to make certain his broken left shoulder was in the best position, when she heard him say, "Hey, Dr. Duvall, would you go ask that nice Miss Winslow to come talk to me?"

Cheney replied in his ear, "Later, Walker."

"All right," he said agreeably. "Huh? Did that hurt, didn't it?"

"Sorry!"

" 'S'okay . . ." He kept on talking in a polite monotone, but Cheney lost the rest of it.

Finally they had him strapped onto the board. Keloki took his feet, Shiloh his head. They squatted, grabbed the board, and stood easily. Cheney walked beside the litter.

They had just reached the end of the villa grounds and started down the red dirt road when the ashfall started again. But this time the ashes were live. And then, like diabolical hail, small pebbles, some of them flaming blue, rained on them, mixed with the hissing ashes. She felt one, then two, sting her hand. She felt heat rising, her hand burning, searing . . .

"Stop!" she screamed. Shiloh and Keloki immediately halted and lowered the board to the ground.

Cheney's skirt was on fire. She threw herself to the ground.

She rolled. Shiloh leaped to her and smothered the flames with his hands.

"Are you all right?" he shouted, grabbing her by the shoulders and yanking her so hard her teeth rattled.

"I'm f-fine," she replied, as calmly as she could manage. "It didn't t-touch my skin, Shiloh. I'm fine."

He sagged with relief, then hunched over her, trying to shield her. "Listen, Doc! We've got to soak down! Keloki's got some water. We've got to wet ourselves down!"

They stood up together, Cheney huddling close to Shiloh. She smelled fire and smoke and burning. She was more frightened than she'd ever been in her life. But she forgot her terror when she caught a glimpse of Walker on the stretcher.

"Oh, horrors! He's—Shiloh, help me!"

Walker was lying on his back, facing up to the sky. Weakly he was moving his head back and forth and spitting, trying to combat the burning grit as best he could. But Shiloh and Cheney had unthinkingly tied down his good right arm, so he couldn't shield his eyes or brush the hot ashes from his face. Keloki, who had run to Cheney, now turned and saw Walker. He took one step, popped the cork of an enormous waterskin he had hung across his chest, and poured water all over Walker's face and singed hair.

"Well," Walker spluttered. "This is something new."

Shiloh, Cheney, and Keloki all stared at one another for a second, helpless amusement widening their eyes.

But as they again looked behind them, the sight sobered them. Quickly the three poured water over their heads, their hats, and Shiloh knelt and soaked Cheney's skirt all the way down to the hem. Then they lifted Walker, and Shiloh shouted out a double-time cadence that Keloki immediately understood. They ran.

Behind them lava spewed up about three hundred feet. Below it curled black smoke and flickers of flames in the darkness.

The jungle was on fire.

17

You Know You're in Trouble . . .

They're all still here! What in the world—now what's happened?

Shiloh and Keloki, carrying Walker's litter, ran straight to the ridge above Bain's Stream and set the litter down. Cheney collapsed to the ground beside Walker. All around them people ran, children cried, women called in high, frantic Chinese, men shouted in hoarse baritones.

Why haven't they gone on down to the lagoon? she wondered. But she was too exhausted to care much just yet. The run from the villa, even though downhill, had been exhausting. The problem was not so much the physical exertion as it was the heat. Every breath burned, seared their nostrils, scalded their throats. Though they'd gotten out of the range of the fountain's burning rockfall and live ash, smoke from the fires grew thick, enveloping them, blinding and choking them.

Shiloh sat down close to Cheney, holding out a canteen. Just as she shakily reached for it, the now familiar swell of the earth's fury sounded, and the ground began to tremble. Cheney was so exhausted she just braced herself, her palms flat on the shifting ground, and dully waited for it to be over.

It lasted only a few seconds. An eerie silence fell, and for the first time Cheney could hear the pounding of the surf. Everyone had fallen to the ground, and even the children had been shocked into silence. But that, too, only lasted a few moments before the cries of panic began again.

"Here, Doc, take a drink," Shiloh said. "I'll go see what's holding up this bunch."

Gratefully Cheney drank the lukewarm water, then leaned close over Walker to see if he was awake. His eyes were wide, his mouth strained into a tense line, his jaw clenched. His shoulder felt as if a thousand burning knives were sticking in it, front and back. The pain was like a live thing, a gnawing animal, that ran from his shoulder to his neck, down his back, in his head. "Sure . . . sure is n-noisy around here," he wretchedly joked.

Hurriedly she wet a clean bandage and sponged off his face, which became the only glimmer of white in the leaden landscape. "The medication's wearing off, isn't it? All right, time for another dose."

This time Walker didn't protest. He was, in fact, using every ounce of the pitiful energy he had left to keep from crying out. The frantic run down the mountain had continuously jarred his shattered shoulder. Over and over he'd tried to hold his breath, hoping he'd pass out. Unfortunately, he hadn't. Fear had kept him conscious. But now he knew that he was so drained and weak that if he tried to walk he would certainly faint.

"Here," Cheney said, sliding her hand underneath his head and propping him up to drink. "Finish it."

Obediently he drained the rest of the absinthe.

"Now water. Just a little, Walker."

"Yes, ma'am," he said faintly, then lay back, exhausted.

Cheney continued to sponge his face with the now filthy bandage—everything exposed to the air immediately received a covering of dirty ash—and tried to assess the situation.

It was full night, the air dyed a murky gray. The infernal crimson glare from above them made the scene visible, but it was no comforting light. Ghostly gray figures, featureless and insubstantial, aimless and panicked, ran in and out of the writhing smoke.

A woman's voice—Cheney knew it was Denise Winslow's—shrieked piercingly above the other cries, screaming for Brynn. Scathingly Cheney thought, *That's just wonderful. The horrible earthquake sounds and thunder and volcano noise is muted down here, so we can all hear Denise Winslow clearly. . . .*

Dusty boots stamped in front of her, and Shiloh came down on one knee to talk to her at eye level, but then his gaze wandered off beyond her left shoulder. "You know you're in trouble," he drawled, "when the earthquakes are the least of your worries."

"The least of your worries," Walker solemnly echoed.

Shiloh looked down at his pale face, flashed a quick grin, and touched his hand. "Hey, Walker. Good to see you're doped to the eyeballs again."

"Eyeballs," Walker intoned.

Cheney sighed deeply, her throat making a harsh rasp. "All right, I'm ready. What's the most of our worries?"

"The first-most one, you mean?"

"Rank them from largest to smallest," Cheney suggested wanly.

"Okay, you're the Doc." Shiloh settled his hat more firmly on his head. "The stream's about thirty feet wide, it's about knee-high, and it's rushing like Noah's flood."

"And?"

"And it's boiling," he finally said bluntly. "There's boulders still big enough to cross on, but it's going to take some big steps, or jumps. None of the kids will be able to do it, and I've got my doubts about the Chinese ladies."

"What? Well, we . . . we have to do something! Build a bridge, or . . . or . . . maybe go farther upstream, find an easier crossing—"

Shiloh shook his head. "Keloki says there is no easier crossing. And, Doc . . ." Warily he looked over his shoulder up at the menacing cinnabar glow that was increasing in heat and intensity as it neared the thickly wooded ridge. With his face turned away, Cheney could barely hear him finish. ". . . not sure . . . enough time." He turned back around so Cheney could hear him. "Uh, by the way, *Locke's Day Dream* isn't here. Big surprise there. Anyway, now I'm not too sure what we're going to do when we get to the lagoon."

With a grim nod behind them, Cheney said tightly, "We've still got to get to the lagoon."

Shiloh nodded. "Me and Keloki and Ulu Nui carry everyone who can't get across by themselves."

Cheney's eyes flew down to Walker, and Shiloh went on in a low voice, "Don't worry, Doc. I can carry him."

"I'll carry him," Walker volunteered.

"That's okay, Walker," Shiloh said with a hint of amusement. "I'll carry him. You can watch."

"Watch for what?"

Keloki and his eldest son, Ulu Nui, materialized out of the grizzled dark. Ulu Nui was twenty-three, solid and handsome, but not nearly the Titan that Keloki was. Neither was he as easygoing. Ulu Nui's wife, Kiko, and their two-year-old daughter, Anika, were with them, and he seemed much more tense than his father.

"Keakea, we gotta get over the little water," Keloki asserted. "Pele's fire—who knows? Might come running down the *auwai*, we can't get over it."

"He means—" Shiloh began.

"I understand," Cheney said firmly. "The lava flow may come down the stream bed, and we couldn't cross that. All right, let's figure out how to—oh, good, there's Nia." Her maid was wandering around, staring hard at the anonymous gray figures. "Nia! I'm here!"

"These folks is crazy," she announced when she swished up to the group. "You better do something, Miss Cheney, Mr. Irons."

"Stay here with Walker, please," Cheney ordered. "Give him a couple of small sips of water and try to sponge his face. And drink some yourself, Nia."

"Yes, ma'am." With open relief, Nia sank down to sit beside Walker's litter.

Walker said, "Hello, Mia. Mia? Meow?"

Nia took a drink, then rasped to Cheney, "Absinthe, huh?"

Cheney almost smiled as she nodded.

Cheney, Shiloh, Keloki, and Ulu Nui all went to look over the edge of the ravine. The path downward wasn't steep, although the rocks had been loosened by the earthquakes, making the footing tricky. At the bottom of the path, by the raging stream, was a six-foot bank. When Cheney faced directly down, the heat blasted her face. The stream gurgled greedily, and occasional air pockets in the shallow bed and porous rocks split, venting steam like hissing vipers. Narrowing her stinging eyes to bare slits, Cheney tried to take deep breaths, breathing in through her mouth and out through her nose. It hurt abominably in her nostrils, her throat, her chest.

Turning back, she looked around the crowd of frightened people and said grimly, "This is going to be difficult."

"The three of us can carry everyone," Shiloh asserted.

"I know you're all strong enough," Cheney countered, "but the problem is the wet heat. It's very difficult to breathe. It's going to make you all short of breath, and that's going to make you light-headed."

The three men looked at one another, then as one looked back at Cheney. They didn't even need to say it; she knew they were determined. There was, after all, nothing else to do.

"I think that the three of you ought to go in turn. Each take the children in a family, and then take the mother," she said steadily. "Rest on the other side for a few moments. Some of us can come across ourselves, and I'll send those after you one at a time."

"My wife can cross by herself, and she can carry Anika," Ulu Nui said instantly.

Cheney nodded thoughtfully. "Yes . . . yes, that's a good idea. In fact, let's send Leilana across, then Kiko with Anika. They'll be over on the other side to keep everyone from panicking and jumping into the lagoon." She gave Shiloh a wry look. "You know you're in trouble when lava is the least of your worries."

"Yeah," he fervently agreed. "I'd rather try to outrun lava than wade through rockfish and man-o'-war."

"And *lua*," Keloki put in with feeling.

"Lua? Would that be sharks? Of course," Cheney said wearily. "Anyway, while Kiko and Leilana are crossing, we'll be organizing everyone else. And, Shiloh, don't even start trying to boss me. I'm going to stay here, on this side, and try to keep everyone orderly and ready to go when it's their turn."

"I guess I gotta go along with you on this one," he said to her surprise. "They're going to come closer to listening to you than anyone else, Doc. Okay, I'm ready."

"I'm ready," Keloki declared, and Ulu Nui just nodded. Then they went to talk to Leilana and Kiko.

Cheney shouted as loudly as she could, "Everyone listen to me, please! We're going across the stream now! Gather round, please, right here, that's it . . ."

They formed a ragged circle around her, though Denise Winslow was fussing loudly and Fang Shao was shouting at Tang Lu, who stood, head bowed. The four children cowered behind her, and Fang Jinglan stood mutely behind her father, unmoving. Cheney frowned and signaled Shiloh. He hurried to the Chinaman and clapped his hand heavily on the smaller man's shoulder. Fang Shao jerked and whirled, frightened. Shiloh said something to him, then pointed. Sulkily the man moved off about three feet from his family.

Cheney continued, "We're taking the children first, and then their mothers—"

"Taking?" Denise shrieked in a high voice. "How? This rabble stole my horses and my cart! We can't cross that stream, we can't even—"

"Be silent, Mother!" Brynn cried. "Let Dr. Duvall speak!"

"Well, if anyone is going to be taken anywhere, it's going to be me and you!" Denise clamored. "Why should we do what that woman, that . . . that . . ." She was accusingly pointing at Cheney.

"Excuse me, Mrs. Winslow," Shiloh growled, suddenly looming very close over her. "I don't think you want to finish that sentence. Not in my presence."

An awkward silence ensued, so Cheney began to instruct the mothers with children where to stand and who was to go first. But uppermost in her thoughts was Shiloh Irons, and the tears that stung her eyes had nothing to do with smoke and fire.

★ ★ ★ ★

Leilana was barefooted, so Keloki gave her his boots. He and Ulu Nui were wearing boots so heavy and crude they looked as if they'd been hobnailed in the eighteenth century and stowed in some sea dog's chest since then. Cheney said, "But, Keloki, now you're barefooted and you can't possibly go across that way!"

He shrugged carelessly. "My feet like lua skin—tough. I run fast first time, and then get my boots."

Next Ulu Nui's wife, Kiko, went—wearing Ulu Nui's boots—carrying Anika. Kiko leaped lightly and gracefully, without effort, over the turgid river.

"Now, Shiloh, take Walker," Cheney directed. "Keloki, you take Vanda Han, all right? And Ulu Nui can take Lela. But both of you must tie rags on your feet, at least. It'll help some."

"Ready, Walker?" Shiloh said lightly, going down on one knee beside him. Cheney had untied him from the he'e nalu board, and he'd lain quietly, humming and looking around with drowsy curiosity from his insect's viewpoint.

"No, Keakea, no, Doctor," Keloki objected. "I'm bigger. I carry the Walker."

Slowly Shiloh stood. "I can't ask you to do that, Keloki. He's my friend." Walker wasn't a large man; he was about five ten and had a lithe frame. But he was solid, of lean muscle, and weighed about one hundred eighty pounds. He would almost certainly be dead weight. It was going to take superhuman effort to carry him across the treacherous hot stream.

Keloki shrugged. "I'm nui, like alii. You skinny haole. I carry the Walker." In a manner that forbade further discussion, Keloki knelt by the litter.

"Hullo, Keloki," Walker hummed. "I've been thinking 'bout you.

212

Really, I've been thinking 'bout your feet."

Keloki grinned widely, his teeth glowing like lanterns in the gloom.

Walker nattered on, "I think you should take my boots. I want you to have them. My boots."

Gravely Keloki said, "Mahalo, Walker. You honor me with this gift. I will take your boots, not for me, for my feet are hard and tough from walking this mauna all of my life. But for my keiki, my Malani. Her feet are still like haole's little pink paws. She will wear the boots of the Walker."

"Good," Walker said vaguely. "At least now I don't feel totally useless. . . ."

In a quick motion, before Walker could have time to dread the awful shock to his system, Keloki slid his arms under Walker's back and knees and stood up. Walker gave an odd little moan, almost a sigh, and passed out cold. Keloki looked down at him. The lurid crimson glare on Walker's face didn't distort its boyish lines, its youthful fullness.

"Keakea, you tell me?" Keloki asked, puzzled. "Why you call him the Walker—when he the only one who don't walk?"

Shiloh laughed and startled everyone. But Cheney, who smiled tentatively herself, saw weak smiles touch several faces, especially the children's. Shiloh's laugh was infectious; it was hard not to smile.

"I'll explain that later, Keloki," he promised. "For now, let's get this wagon train on the move."

"Okay," Keloki agreed. Taking sure, sturdy steps, he carried the unconscious Walker down the incline and started across the stream while everyone watched anxiously. Keloki seemed not to be affected by the suffocating steam coiling around his massive figure. With care he stepped, always pausing to steady his footing on each boulder. Cheney noticed as she watched nervously that the steam rising from the hot river dissolved the smoke so that they could see all the way across to the beach on the other side. A hot wind blew in across the lagoon. Blown sand so fine it was like ground glass stung them. Though Cheney dreaded to, she turned to look at the fire glow on the heights above. Such a wind would feed the fires, fanning them to speeding walls of flame.

"Let's go. Let's hurry," she insisted. "Shiloh, take Vanda Han first. Ulu Nui, you take Mrs. Han. Unless, Mr. Han, you'd like to take the baby across yourself."

His face was troubled, his voice low. "No, no, Dr. Duvall. I . . . wish . . . I could, but I'm afraid I'm not strong enough. If . . . Mr. Irons and Ulu Nui will help us, then I must humbly accept."

Cheney patted his shoulder. "Sir, none of us is ever strong enough all the time. This time, however, Shiloh and Ulu Nui and Keloki are. Next time it may be you. It takes great courage to ask for help when we need it."

Shiloh said, "Mr. Han, I'm honored to be entrusted with your baby. I swear no harm will come to her." He took the ten-month-old baby, securely wrapping her under his canvas coat. He started confidently across the stream, and when he'd gotten to the fourth stepping-stone, Ulu Nui started across with Vanda's mother, Lela Han. But when Shiloh took another step, his boot slipped down the side of the boulder almost into the water. Cheney stifled the scream, and the effort made her choke slightly. Patiently, unhurriedly, Shiloh shifted his weight, then pulled his foot up until he stood solidly. Behind him Ulu Nui stood waiting, and the two men called back and forth. Finally Shiloh moved ahead and got to the other side without incident. Ulu Nui was close behind.

Cheney turned back to the crowd, and Nia stepped forward. "I'm going across right now, Miss Cheney," she said firmly. "I need to go look after Dr. Baird."

Denise stamped up to Cheney. "Who do you think you are? Sending your friends across, that silly little man, of all things! And now your colored maid goes across first? I'm not going to allow—"

"Fine, Mrs. Winslow," Cheney interrupted mildly. "You may go on across now."

"What? Oh no, I'm not going to cross that stream myself! One of my servants—did you hear me, Dr. Duvall? They are *my servants*—is going to carry me!" Turning around, she screeched across the ravine, "Keloki! Get back over here this instant!" Triumphantly she whirled back to Cheney. "Now, you just keep all of your little ants off the path until Keloki comes back to get me!"

"No, ma'am, I'm afraid that's not possible," Cheney said as politely as she could manage. "Nia, go on."

Giving Denise Winslow, who looked murderous, a wide berth, Nia scooted around, ran down the path, and jumped lightly from boulder to boulder, never pausing, as if she were playing a complex game of hopscotch. Cheney held her breath, watching her, but Nia was quick and didn't falter. When she reached the sand on the other side, however, she ran a few steps, then sat down hurriedly. Cheney could see her shoulders heave as she took gulping breaths. Shiloh, Keloki, and Ulu Nui had moved away from the cauldron for a few moments and stood, hands on knees, just breathing.

Denise did not cease to complain at the top of her lungs, and Brynn tried, ineffectually, to soothe her. Finally Brynn put her arms around her mother's shoulders and led her away, but Denise's strident clamor grated on Cheney's ears and nerves so badly she thought she could cheerfully strangle the woman.

"Mr. Han, you may cross so that you can be with your wife and baby," Cheney said in a low voice.

"I think," George Han said thoughtfully, eyeing Denise Winslow and the uneasy crowd, "that I'll stay here and help you, Dr. Duvall."

"Thank you," she said gratefully. "All right, everyone, next we'll send Liu and Wen and Kwan—"

Zhu Ki burst into a hysterical tirade, shoving her two children forward so hard that her little girl Atu Ki fell to the ground. But Zhu Ki didn't notice as she stumbled to the edge of the ravine where Cheney stood.

"Zhu Ki, all of the children—everyone is going to get across—" Cheney tried to tell her.

But she was hysterical, screaming and flailing her arms, her eyes wide with panic. George Han stepped forward and spoke sharply to her, but Zhu Ki kept shrieking. George bent and picked up Atu Ki, who was sobbing. Finally Zhu Ki's tirade petered out, though her eyes were still darting, panicked. George thrust the baby into her arms and gave her a curt command in Chinese. She stood uncertainly, holding the baby. At least she remained quiet.

Shiloh, Keloki, and Ulu Nui crossed back over. When they moved to the top of the ravine, they were bent double, gasping for breath. Cheney sent Malani—proudly wearing Walker's boots—across, and then Kimo. The agile young man sprinted carelessly across, carrying the he'e nalu board, and without stopping to catch his breath ran on down the beach. Little Ilima, ten years old, was the only one of Keloki's family that remained.

"Ilima goes next," Cheney decided. "Then Tang Lu's children, and Tang Lu."

"Good, Doc," Shiloh nodded, catching his breath.

Seeing his cracked lips and the swelling of the tender skin of his eyelids, she suggested, "Maybe we should try wetting some kerchiefs and putting them across your face."

He shook his head. "The main problem is just pulling enough air into your lungs. It's so hot, and the steam stings—you don't really take the deep breaths you need to. I don't think we need to put anything over our noses and mouths." He turned to Keloki. "I'm ready now. Keloki, I'd be honored if you'd allow me to carry your daughter."

"Mahalo, Keakea brudder," Keloki nodded. "Mahalo."

Shiloh carried Ilima; Keloki carried little Liu; Ulu Nui carried Wen. When the three men were on the other side, recovering, Fang Shao suddenly scooped up his son, Kwan, and elbowed his way to the head of the path. "I go now, take son," he said curtly.

George Han stepped forward and said something in Chinese, grabbing Fang Shao's arm. Fang Shao sharply twisted away and dropped the eight-year-old boy. It was obvious he couldn't carry the boy securely; Fang Shao was wiry and strong for his build, but he was a small man, with short legs and arms. Cheney stepped up and sharply ordered, "Fang Shao! Stay where you are! The men are coming back over now, and you aren't to block their way!"

He snarled something up at Cheney and looked down at the stream, considering; but facing the advancing army of Shiloh, Keloki, and Ulu Nui was too much to contemplate. He slunk to the back of the line, back in the gloom, leaving Kwan sprawled in the dirt.

When the three men reached the top of the ravine, they were swarmed by Denise Winslow, Zhu Ki, and Fang Jinglan. Cheney tried, in a dignified manner, to keep the shrieking women from pawing the three exhausted men, but they were like a cloud of harpies. Towering above them, Shiloh shouted, "Who next, Doc?"

"Kwan, Tang Lu, and Zhu Ki's youngest," Cheney helplessly shouted back. She and Brynn were trying to untangle Denise Winslow's death grip on Keloki's arm, but it was like trying to pry off a barnacle. Confusion reigned. Denise wouldn't let go of Keloki, screaming for him to pick her up; Zhu Ki had so lost her senses that she was trying to make Ulu Nui take her instead of her daughter; Fang Shao picked up his son, ran down the incline, dumped him on the stream bank, and started across the stream by himself.

Keloki stood unmoving, a confused giant, more afraid of the crazy haole wahine than he was of Pele's fire. Shiloh moved up to Denise but looked uncertain. Never in his life had he laid angry hands on a woman, and he was loath to start now, even on this woman.

But Ulu Nui was another story. His wife and child were already at the lagoon, and he was in a hurry to rejoin them. He shook off Zhu Ki as if she were an unwanted cloak, then came up behind Denise, grabbed her by the shoulders, lifted her up, and set her down about two feet behind him. Denise started beating on his strong back, but she might have been no more than a butterfly poofing around the muscular Hawaiian. Calmly—over Denise's turmoil—he said to his father, "Take Kwan, Keloki. We need to wikiwiki."

With relief Keloki nodded, then looked around in bewilderment. "Where is Kwan?"

"He's down there," Wu Pat said in alarm. No one had noticed Fang Shao and his son in the confusion. Now they saw the boy sitting by the side of the hissing stream, crying, and Fang Shao about halfway across the stream. He took long moments each time, standing uncertainly on each boulder and taking one or two false starts before moving to the next.

"Hey, Fang Shao!" Shiloh called out in a ringing voice. "I'm coming! I'll be there in a minute, and if you're in my way, I'll stomp you like the little bug you are!" He ran down the slope, scooped Kwan up, and almost ran from boulder to boulder. Cheney could tell by the way he moved that he was truly halfway hoping to catch up to the faltering Chinaman.

But Shiloh's warning proved to be a powerful incentive for Fang Shao. He scooted across the stream in record time and took off running in a direct line toward the pier.

"Hey, Fang Shao!" Shiloh called after him. "Why don't you take a swim when you get to the lagoon!"

"Shiloh!" Cheney called out sternly.

"Sorry!" he answered, but he didn't sound a bit apologetic.

Denise pushed everyone aside, including Cheney, to get to the edge of the ravine. Cheney considered for a moment just pushing her on over—*she'd just roll like a child's ball full of hot air*, she thought with malicious pleasure—but to Cheney's credit, she only considered it for a moment. Perhaps two.

"Look! Look out there!" Denise's hand, shaking and trembling, pointed out toward the sea. "That's a lantern! That's a ship! Bain! Bain! Bain!" Wildly she ran down the ravine, stepped on the first boulder, stopped, threw back her head in terror, and screamed. "Help me!"

No one moved. They were searching desperately in the direction Denise had pointed, eyes narrowed, looking for a lantern. Cheney thought that the woman's mind had finally snapped, and she'd seen a ghost ship, as people see mirages in the desert.

But then Cheney saw it. Beyond the reef floated a round, weak orange-yellow globe of light. "It is!" she cried. "Look—see it! It's a lantern, no—two! More! It's a ship!"

Denise stopped her screaming, picked up her skirts, and fled over the torrent of scalding heat as lightly as a roe.

18

BEACONS OF HOPE

Denise Winslow passed Shiloh like a stampeding mustang. With disgust he returned to the stream to cross back, then saw that up on the ridge everyone was shouting and pointing. He looked back, puzzled, then whirled and crossed over, stepping lightly and confidently now. Urgently he shouted, "Signal! We have to signal!"

"Oh no! I hadn't thought of that! What if they don't see us?" Cheney cried. Desperately she looked around, already knowing that the two lanterns they had brought when they left the guest house were still in the cart—wherever that was. "How can we signal? What can we do?" she demanded, grabbing Keloki.

He looked puzzled for a moment, then his face lit up and he turned to his son. "Papala? Up there?" He pointed up the road from the villa.

Ulu Nui frowned, then his face cleared. "Yes, I remember. I'll go."

"Wait!" Cheney ordered. "The fire's getting too close! I don't think you'd better go up there, Ulu Nui. And besides, we still have people here who have to be carried over."

Shiloh appeared beside her, gasping for breath but talking fast. "No, go on, Ulu Nui. Doc, we've got to signal them. I don't think they can see us. They're at least a mile past the barrier reef. Keloki and I will just have to double up, go across and back each ... uh ... four times? Yeah. Eight to go who can't cross by themselves."

Cheney looked up at the ominous red glow in the sky, out to the beacons of hope at sea, and finally nodded. Immediately Ulu Nui turned and sprinted up the road, his muscular figure garishly outlined in the firelight. "All right, everyone!" she called. "No more nonsense. Everyone is going to stay calm! Shiloh, take Ming. Keloki, get Tang Lu. Hurry."

The two men snatched up the girl and her mother and ran. Zhu Ki started howling and dropped Atu Ki, and Fang Jinglan started wailing and running back and forth, waving her arms as if she were fighting off hordes of hornets. Wu Pat, the stableman, went to her and tried to calm her, while Cheney went up to Zhu Ki, grabbed her shoulders, and shook her hard enough to rattle her teeth. "Listen to me! They're coming back, and they're going to take your children, then you, Zhu Ki! You must calm down, or I swear I'll tell them to take you last, because the way you're behaving is making it harder for them!"

For good measure Cheney gave her one last shake, and that seemed to be the final straw for Zhu Ki. Her cries were cut off cleanly, and she stood staring at Cheney with wide, unseeing eyes. Hiding her exasperation, Cheney knelt and put her arms around Zhu Ki's daughter and son, four-year-old Atu Ki and seven-year-old Atu Bao. "Keloki and Shiloh are taking you across next. Don't be frightened—"

"Dr. Duvall," Brynn said from behind her. "I think you'd better go back over there, because Nia's with Mr. Irons and Keloki and she's obviously upset. I'll take care of the children and Zhu Ki."

Cheney ran to the edge of the ravine and saw that Nia was talking to Shiloh and Keloki, making frantic gestures, pointing toward the lagoon. Shiloh nodded, and Cheney could see the bone-deep weariness in him, and a wave of pity swept over her so poignant that she almost wept. But there was no time for weeping right now. She thought she already knew the problem down at the lagoon.

As Shiloh and Keloki crossed over the stream again, Cheney looked out in the direction of the sea. At first she didn't see the ship's lanterns, and for the first time that terrible day and night she felt the first flutterings of an overwhelming panic. Then she did catch sight of a single light, but it was close to the southern headland of the lagoon. Were they going to just circle the island, never seeing the thirty-one stricken souls from the villa?

A flaming papala spear, a thin stream of clean white flame, arced high over Cheney's head, cleaving the smoke and shadows, a beacon of hope. Another one whistled after it, and another. Ulu Nui's skill was such that the sharp thin reeds speared straight up in the sand, far down the beach. Each of them burned brightly right down to the ground.

Shiloh and Keloki joined Cheney, scrambling up the side of the ravine. Both of them now had to use their hands to drag themselves up the slope. They stood beside her, gulping and panting. Suddenly Shiloh turned and sprinted off to their left toward the treeline. Cheney knew he was vomiting; she was only surprised that he had gone this long, overheated, overexerted, and breathing the foul stench of smoke and sulphur, without getting sick.

Wiping his mouth, his face grim, he returned to them. Cheney handed him her canteen and said evenly, "Small sips only."

He nodded, drank, washed out his mouth, spit, and drank again. Keloki thirstily drank, too, and took his canteen to Ulu Nui, who was methodically lighting papala spears and throwing them.

Shiloh turned, his eyes searching the darkness beyond the stream. "Nia said there's big trouble down on the beach."

Cheney nodded sadly. "I thought so. All of the . . . um . . . troublemakers are there."

"Yeah, and more bad news. There's a real high tide, and there's live jellyfish and man-o'-war, and Nia said there's even a stingray beached," Shiloh said with disgust. "The pier's awash, and people are fighting, trying to get on it. But it's not safe right now, not at all. So everyone's running nuts, and Leilana's having a hard time trying to keep everyone from getting hurt—and from hurting each other."

"You've got to go down there, Shiloh," Cheney said firmly. "Get them in some order."

"No," he said flatly. "You have to go, Doc. Here." He opened his coat and pulled out his Colt revolver. "I used one round at the villa. When you get down to the lagoon, fire one round as a warning shot. You'll have four rounds left."

"But . . . but . . . I'm not going to shoot anyone!" Cheney protested.

"I know that, but they don't know that. You won't have to shoot anyone, Doc. But you will need to have the gun."

"All . . . all right," she said shakily. "But I-I'm . . ."

He listened, scrutinizing her face, noting her restless hands. "You really are all right, aren't you, Doc? I mean, if you don't think you can cope anymore, that's okay. You've already done more than anyone could expect. You can't bear the burden of taking care of all these people."

Cheney rubbed her hand across her forehead, pressed her eyes tightly shut, and then looked back up at Shiloh with determination. "Oh, but I can, Shiloh, because I have to. Just as you do. I'll go. I can do this."

"I'll carry you," Shiloh offered quietly.

Cheney considered it, envisioned it, dreamed of it a little. It was a most attractive offer, and she admitted to herself that it wasn't just because she was afraid of crossing the treacherous stream. Resting in Shiloh Iron's arms for a little while would be heavenly in the midst of the terror and darkness.

"No, Shiloh," she finally said, tracing the V scar underneath his eye and then caressing his face. "You must carry the ones who can't save themselves. I'm strong."

"I know," he said and softly kissed her lips.

She turned and ran down the slope to the boiling river.

Brynn Winslow followed right behind her. Shiloh and Keloki were preparing to bring across Zhu Ki's two children. Slim fiery beacons rained down from above them. Cheney marveled that even with the strong wind blowing inland, Ulu Nui's thin reeds were falling to the beach well past the far stream bank.

"Atu Bao, Atu Ki, Zhu Ki, Fang Jinglan, Sunny, and Fay," Cheney muttered to herself. "That's all they'll have to carry. . . ."

"Yes," Brynn agreed from close behind her. "That will just leave George Han, Pat, and Will, and they can cross by themselves."

Cheney hesitated, recoiling from the scalding steam rising off the superheated river rushing by her. Branches of trees and smaller rocks hurtled by, crashing haplessly against the large boulders they'd been using as a footpath. The rocks were lava cobbles, ancient chunks of black lava that had been rounded and smoothed by aeons of tumbling water. They looked shiny and slick. Cheney swallowed hard, thinking of what would happen if she slipped . . . one leg down in that water . . . her foot, ankle, calf, knee, all covered in oozing blisters, scalded red skin peeling off for days . . .

"Doc? You sure you're okay?"

From the ridge above, Shiloh was watching her. *He knows*, she thought suddenly. *He knows that I'm so afraid . . . of burning . . .*

She waved jauntily, though she could barely stand to open her eyes and her heart was batting along erratically, skipping beats and then thumping fast in a crazy response. Turning around, Cheney Duvall, M.D. took over, and she set her mind on accomplishing the task at hand. That's all she saw, that's all she knew, that's all she concentrated on: *This boulder. The next step. Wait! Wait! Now, a little bit of a jump to this one. (Hot, hot. No, don't think about that.) Small rock right by your right foot. Next . . . next . . .*

Triumphantly Cheney jumped onto the fine sand of the beach. She held out her arms for Brynn, for the gap from the last stone to the sandy bank was about four feet. Cheney was five-ten, with long legs, and made the jump easily. But for Brynn it was quite a leap, and Cheney privately thought that it was only because Brynn was agile and athletic that she could make it. Cheney gave the group up on the ridge a reassuring wave. Shiloh and Keloki started down the slope with Atu Bao and Atu Ki.

Cheney and Brynn stopped to catch their breath for a few moments. Gratefully they gulped in great lungfuls of air that, even though it was torrid, was like sweet mead to their throats. No choking ashes, no parching smoke, no stink of sulphur was carried on the sea wind.

"Do you really know how to use that thing?" Brynn asked as they hurried down to the beach. Cheney was carrying Shiloh's gun, elbow bent close to her side, barrel upright.

"Yes."

"Are you planning to use it?"

"No."

Brynn looked at her curiously but said nothing else.

A sorry sight met their eyes when they neared the lagoon.

A few feet to their right, Keloki's youngest daughter, ten-year-old Ilima, was cleaning a ragged little circle of beach, sweeping lustily with a sharp-spiked branch of palmetto. Around them was a litter of coral rocks, jellyfish, sticks, and lumps of sodden coconut leaves and seaweed. Cheney saw something that looked like a medieval mace and realized it was the poisonous crown-of-thorns starfish; Ilima poked and prodded it gingerly with the end of the branch. Walker lay on his he'e nalu board. Koki, holding little Anika, sat close to him.

Everyone else was staggering around in the three-foot waves, shouting about the boat and begging to go to the end of the pier. Denise stood, hands knotted into fists straight down at her sides, her head thrown back as she shrieked imprecations at Leilana. Tang Lu, holding Liu, ran back and forth in the seething surf, her children stumbling, falling along behind her. Nia chased the children, calling for Tang Lu to go back up on the beach. Even Lela Han, holding the baby Vanda, stood at the foot of the pier, begging and sobbing, dashing frantically back and forth up the beach, dodging the crashing waves.

The worst was Fang Shao. Directly at the foot of the pier, he ran about, threatening, shouting, waving a large stick, darting back and forth as nimbly as a spider.

At the very end of the wooden dock, Leilana appeared majestic and unmoved. Waves sucked at her ankles, yet she stood as solid as a Corinthian column. Arrayed in front of her were her son, Kimo, and her daughter, Malani, both of them weaving in counterpoint to the Chinaman who was trying to rush them. Fang Shao ran this way, then that, trying to get past them. Kimo and Malani stayed in a half-crouch, hands out, ready to move. Leilana stood with her arms crossed, her massive bulk unmoved and unmoveable. She looked down at the screaming little Chinaman, her full rich lips curved with disdain, as if he were a noisome insect.

Cheney fired the Colt into the air.

Fang Shao whirled around, his face distorted with terror. Denise's maddening outcry stilled. Tang Lu and the children stopped, bewildered.

"That's enough!" she shouted. "Everyone get up there, past the high tide mark! Move! Fang Shao, drop that stick and pick up your children!"

He stayed motionless for a moment, baring his teeth, the thick club held high. Then warily he stepped sideways, keeping his eyes on Cheney, moving crablike up the beach. Cheney turned slowly, following him with her gaze, though she still had the gun propped upright. Tang Lu and the children darted past Cheney, and Denise, walking heavily as if she were unbearably burdened, started stumbling inland. Brynn hurried to help her.

When Fang Shao got past the high tide mark, without turning Cheney shouted, "Leilana, Malani, Kimo! Come up here now!"

They walked, tall and unhurried. "I'm stung," Kimo announced proudly as soon as they reached Cheney and Brynn.

"What? By what?" Cheney demanded.

"Little sneak jellyfish," he scoffed. "Not blue death jellyfish, not rockfish."

Cheney, somewhat relieved, glanced down at his feet; one ankle had a telltale rash of red marks just above the ankle bone. "Does it still hurt terribly?" she asked. "I've always heard jellyfish stings do."

"Yeah, it does, haole doctor wahine," he declared. "Every time I get stung I swear never to again. But always do."

Cheney looked at Leilana and Malani. Kimo's mother was shaking her head and rolling her eyes, and Malani looked coolly amused.

"Neither of you got stung?" she managed to ask.

"No, Doctor," Leilana answered. "Hawaiian ladies too smart. Silly little boys stomp them, think it's funny."

"Kimo, you didn't!" Cheney gasped.

He grinned. "No, Doctor. Not this time. This smart jellyfish, he sneaks, hides, boom! Got me quick. Like your gun." He looked wistfully at the enormous pistol Cheney held.

"This is Shiloh's gun," Cheney said briskly. "If you ask him nicely, someday he'll probably give you lessons." The boy's dark eyes gleamed like polished onyx. "But for now, Kimo," she added sternly, "you go over there with everyone else, and Nia will put some ointment on those stings."

They joined the rest of the group. Cheney made Kimo sit down by Walker and announced, "Now, everyone, I know you're all scared. But Ulu Nui is signaling the boat, and I'm certain they'll be coming to pick us up soon. Meanwhile, the lagoon and the pier are unsafe. There's apparently some kind of . . . plague . . . of jellyfish. Look around, you can see dozens of them washing in with each wave. And there are poison rockfish all over the reefs in the shallows. So everyone just stay up here on the beach until we get organized!"

She waited, searching the faces around her. Denise looked furious. Fang Shao looked murderous. Cheney stared at him, unafraid, and then called out, "Is anyone else stung? Come over here if you've stepped on anything on the beach. And listen, everyone—especially stay away from the blue jellyfish! Those are Portugese man-o'-war, and their sting is deadly!" Cheney could see several of them littering the beach. They looked deceptively mild with their sky-blue color and their shape something like a child's toy ball.

Lela Han came forward, shamefaced. "Dr. Duvall, I wasn't stung, but I scraped my leg against one of those rocks. It was like rubbing against ground glass."

Cheney saw her leg, which was deeply abraded. Blood was running down, covering her foot and making small pools in the sand. "Yes, the rocks are coral rocks, and they're very rough," she said, speaking more quietly, since everyone had gathered close around. Everyone except Fang Shao. He had called sharply to Tang Lu and the children, and they'd joined him in a forlorn little group about six feet away from everyone else. His eyes kept cutting toward the jetty, and he still held the club.

Cheney held the pistol, butt-first, out to Brynn. "Here, Miss Winslow. Take this and watch him." She pointed—a clear message sent—

directly at Fang Shao. His face took on an ugly cast, and his fists tightened on the club he held.

Brynn looked at the gun, licked her lips, and said quietly, "Dr. Duvall, I've never held a gun in my life. And I don't think I'm the right person to . . . to . . . that is, I just can't command the authority that a person such as you—"

Denise hurried up and made a swipe at the gun. "Here! I'll take charge of it!"

Cheney yanked it up out of her reach. She was at least six inches taller than Denise, and ludicrously, Denise actually jumped for it twice. "Stop it!" Cheney ordered. Whirling, she turned her back on Denise to step close to Leilana.

"Have you ever shot a gun, Leilana?"

"No, Doctor."

"Would you?"

"Yes, Doctor." She grinned broadly.

"Here. Point this end at—whatever's coming—and pull this little lever here. It'll stop."

Deliberately Cheney turned her back on Denise Winslow and hurried to Walker, with Brynn following her.

Denise blustered, "Brynn! Come back here this instant! Where are you going?"

"Oh, Mother, sit down and shut up!" Brynn shouted.

Several people chuckled weakly. Little Liu, two years old, giggled and jumped up and down and beat her stubby little hands together.

But when Denise Winslow glowered at them, they grew sullenly quiet again.

Cheney first knelt by Walker, but Brynn was right alongside of her and asked, "Dr. Duvall? If you'll tell me what to do, I'll be happy to take care of Dr. Baird."

"Oh, I'm glad," Walker said, making a hazy attempt to focus on Brynn's face. "Miss Winslow? Is that Miss Winslow?"

"No, no. Call me Brynn, remember?"

"Oh yes, I need to talk to her too . . . something I need to tell her . . ."

Cheney said, "Well, Miss Winslow, I believe I will allow you to straighten out this little misunderstanding. In the meantime, all we can do for him is make sure he gets very small sips of water, and try to make him as comfortable as we can. Call me if he starts feeling pain again."

"I don't think he's feeling much pain," Brynn murmured, brushing a lock of Walker's thick ash-blond hair from his forehead. Walker smiled up at her with groggy delight.

Cheney wondered how many Brynns he was seeing. "I think not, not now," Cheney agreed. "I hope the last dose of absinthe I gave him will last—"

"Absinthe? Oh, gracious! I forgot!" Brynn jerked up, then started frantically rummaging in a canvas bag she had strapped across her chest.

"You have more?" Cheney asked hopefully.

"Yes, another bottle . . . but . . . that's not what I . . ." She stopped her frantic mining and looked at Cheney with a peculiar expression. "I found something while I was looking for my mother's little cache. Absinthe—she keeps it hidden, supposedly for medicinal purposes. But I found something that belongs to Mr. Irons." Brynn swallowed hard and stared at Cheney.

Cheney could clearly see what Brynn was feeling: great guilt and great fear. Comfortingly Cheney laid her hand on Brynn's arm and gave it a gentle squeeze. "That's fine, Miss Winslow. I'm certain he'll want to see whatever it is when we have more time and leisure. But for now, all I care to know about is what's best for my patient."

"That's me," Walker told them with satisfaction. "She's my patient. I'm her doctor."

Cheney rolled her eyes. "He's fine right now, Miss Winslow. Just call me if you see that the drug's wearing off."

Cheney went to Kimo, and Nia was already slapping a paste of bicarbonate of soda and water on his ankle. She was steadily fussing, too, and he looked thoroughly chastised. "Prancin' about in that water without any boots on," she muttered. "Serve you right if you'd stepped on one of those spiky devilfish, now, wouldn't it? Then I guess that Mr. Fang Man could bash you with that stick all night long, and all you could do about it is sit there and cry and pick devilfish stickers out of your foot. . . ."

Cheney could see Nia had this thoroughly under control, so she sat Lela Han down and began to wash out her scraped leg with clean water.

"Look! Everyone else is coming!" Malani called, pointing.

The group that had been left on the other side of the stream was trooping across the beach. Cheney, exultant but silent, continued working on Lela's leg. The scrape was long but not deep. "This is going to sting," she told the woman.

Lela nodded absently; she was searching the approaching group for her husband. Presently George Han broke into a run and reached them first, sliding to Lela's side. "Are you all right? Is Vanda all right?" he asked anxiously.

"Oh yes, it's nothing!" she replied. "Just a scrape. It's nothing. Are you all right?"

Lela didn't even notice as Cheney poured carbolic acid over the scrape. Efficiently she wound a clean strip of linen around it, tying the ends firmly but not tightly. "Keep that as clean as you can, Lela," she admonished her, but Lela was talking to her husband.

Cheney hurried to Shiloh. He stood at the head of the group, scanning each one, watching Fang Shao with narrowed eyes. His lips were cracked and bleeding, his eyelids blistered. His shoulders, usually so ruler-straight, were rounded with weariness. But he looked triumphant. "We got 'em all," he murmured. "All thirty-one of them. We got them across safely."

"What you and Keloki and Ulu Nui did is miraculous," Cheney murmured. "You have great courage and great strength, Shiloh."

He looked down at her, and a smile lit his eyes for a moment, but then he grew somber. "We got a signal from the ship. They're sending a boat into the lagoon to pick us up."

"Thank the Lord!" Cheney said fervently.

"Well, we still have problems, Doc," he said wearily. "Big ones. A ship's lifeboat . . ." He looked around at the thirty-one people on the beach doubtfully.

"I . . . I don't suppose a lifeboat could carry this many people," Cheney said slowly.

Shiloh shrugged. "Won't know how big it is till it gets here."

Denise Winslow had been pacing, rounding and rounding the group in obsessive circles, kicking up little mounds of sand with her heeled boots. Passing by Cheney and Shiloh, she overheard the last exchange. "Lifeboat! *Locke's Day Dream* only has two little dinghies!" she shouted. "And you, Mr. Irons, and all of your friends are not going to be the first ones in them!"

Shiloh shrugged wearily and said to Cheney, "See what I mean? It's going to be the same as at the stream. Only worse." He turned and headed for the pier.

"Shiloh, wait!" she called.

He did wait for her to join him, but when she reached him he said lightly, "Doc, I don't wanta pick jellyfish and rockfish out of your forty yards of skirts again."

"Don't worry, I really hope I won't have to learn to swim tonight," she said, eyeing the turbulent surf warily. "But please, let me come with you."

He studied the waves, which were wild and frenetic. They weren't rhythmic, as incoming tide normally was. They capped this way, then that; some had long running ridges with fat spume tops; some were triangular splashes with sharp white flashes. The water beat, slapped, pushed and pulled at the beach. About once every minute or so a wild wave broadsided the jetty and put it awash ankle deep. Shiloh looked doubtful, but Cheney stared at him with such hope and longing that he relented. "Okay, Doc. But—'scuse me—I think you'd better hitch up those skirts a little so no nasty critters get tangled up in 'em."

On the left side, her overskirt had been burned up to her knees, and both her overskirt and petticoat were a sandy, filthy, stinking mess. Hastily Cheney drew up what was left of her skirts into a wad in front and pulled them up about midcalf, showing only her sassy Wellington boots. "I'll be careful," she promised.

They walked out onto the jetty, and before they'd taken too many steps, a wave washed over their feet. It left behind two jellyfish several feet in front of them, and Shiloh carelessly kicked them over the side. "Hate stompin' those things," he muttered. "They're squishy. Besides, the stingers still work even when they're dead."

Cheney gulped but didn't say anything.

The night was so complete they couldn't see even to the barrier reef at the mouth of the lagoon, much less the sea beyond. But Cheney did see the lantern coming toward them. Cheney chewed nervously on her lower lip as she watched the glob of light bouncing across the lagoon. The lantern was swinging wildly, jerking from one side to the other, sometimes heading diagonally away and then hastily righting its course. Occasionally it jumped up, then plummeted down, like a clown tossing a yellow ball.

"Shiloh . . ." she murmured.

"Yeah, I see. Looks like they're having a hard time. I can't believe this lagoon, enclosed like it is, is so wild. It looks like a storm in the North Atantic."

"Maybe it's—"

But Cheney never finished her sentence; indeed, she didn't have to.

Without the roar of warning they'd come to expect, the earth convulsed, an enormous heave that threw Cheney facedown, hard, to the pier. Shiloh stumbled and went down on one knee, then leaned over her, pinning her beneath his chest, securing her with both arms down at her sides. Another staggering shock wave ran over them, making the wooden jetty scream like a wounded animal. Two pilings, with a deafening groan, seemed to bend backward, and then flew up into the air. That side of the six-foot floor section waved up and down as if it were in a strong breeze, then one end dipped downward and crashed into the surf. A tremendous explosion from the south pounded their ears. Cheney and Shiloh lifted their heads, and in seconds a strong heat blast scoured their faces.

When they could open their eyes again, they saw the second eruption. It was low on the flank of Mount Haleakala, about a mile away. Lava spewed three hundred feet into the air, then splashed back down to the black earth and ran downhill in a flood. Dumbfounded, Cheney and Shiloh watched the fire flee all the way to the foothills of the mountain, and the crimson flood spill over into the sea.

The road south was cut off.

THE ENDS

OF THE EARTH

Hast thou not known?
Hast thou not heard,
That the everlasting God, the Lord,
The Creator of the ends of the earth,
Fainteth not, neither is weary?
He giveth power to the faint,
And to them that have no might
He increaseth strength.

Isaiah 40:28, 29

19

BEDLAM

When the world once again stood still, Shiloh Irons slowly rose to his feet. He helped Cheney to stand, and she fiercely clung to him. They stood together, their arms around each other, staring at the deadly blazing display that set their road south afire.

A spectacular river of lava flowed from the new fissure on the flanks of Haleakala. It streamed, fast and hot, down the slope to the buttresses that formed the mountain's giant feet, and then poured into the sea. Even from a mile away they could see the great clouds of steam rising from the waters below the black ramparts.

"Oh no . . ." Cheney whispered, close to Shiloh's chest.

"Oh no is right," he sighed. "You know you're in trouble when the *second* volcano is the least of your worries."

"What?" Cheney pulled away from him, bewildered, and saw the direction of his gaze. With dread she followed it up to the closest ridges of Mount Haleakala—the cliffs directly above the lagoon.

The lava fountain that had erupted to the north and east of Winslow Villa had disappeared. The last earthquake, the strongest yet, had widened the fissure horizontally. A long red gash, shaped like the jagged streaks of lightning that had ripped at the summit, tore horizontally across the northern slope of Mount Haleakala. Spilling from it was a river of molten lava. Cheney could actually perceive the progression of the wide river as it poured down the steep slope, so hot it was the consistency of tomato soup.

Soon it would cover the beach.

As one, Cheney and Shiloh whipped around to search for the lifeboat struggling across the lagoon. They saw nothing except raging two- and three-foot waves, topped by angry whitecaps. They ran down to the very end of the pier and searched anxiously.

"There, over there," Shiloh said, pointing to his left. "The boat had been thrown far off course, but at least it was afloat, and the lantern had somehow stayed lit.

Bedlam erupted behind them.

Shiloh wheeled, growled something under his breath, and pounded back down the length of the pier. Cheney ran behind him, suddenly conscious of how shaky the long wooden structure had become. Each step shook the entire length of the dock, and it wheezed and groaned in protest. Several of the pilings were leaning at crazy angles, and the floor was no longer even.

Leilana fired the gun into the air; they saw the spume of fire from the barrel, far up on the beach. A woman screamed, long and loud. Men shouted and children shrieked. As Cheney ran on the pier, she felt it shake so hard that for a moment she thought it was another earthquake. But then she realized that several people had jumped onto it and were fighting at the beach end. At about the middle of the structure, the section that had lost the pilings was tilted downward, with the unsupported ends of the wooden slats in the sea. Shiloh easily leaped across the five-foot damaged part, then skidded to a stop to look back at Cheney.

"Go on!" she cried. "I can make it!"

He turned, about to run on, but several figures pounded down the pier right toward him. Instead he stood still, drew himself up tall, and roared, "Stop right there!"

They didn't stop. They kept running, screaming, crying. . . .

Denise Winslow was in the lead. At her heels ran Brynn, desperately trying to stop her. Behind Brynn, George Han was dashing in pursuit so he could help Brynn. Fang Shao came fast behind, carrying the club in one hand, with his son Kwan clinging to his back. Fang Jinglan followed her father, crying and pleading, while Pat trailed at the rear.

The pier swayed and the wooden protests grew to the volume of shrill shrieks. Terrified shouts filled the air. The sea roared. Cheney, clinging to a piling and standing tiptoe at the secured end of the damaged section of the pier, shouted too. She simply couldn't think of anything else to do.

Denise reached Shiloh, and like a madwoman, she barreled straight into him. He stood like a rock, unmoving, his hands down at his sides.

Denise bounced backward, her feet actually leaving the pier. It would have been comical under other circumstances.

"Mrs. Winslow, it's very dangerous for you to be out on this pier right now," Shiloh said calmly. "Everyone must go back to the beach until it's time to get into the lifeboat."

"You! You! As if you would let me get into a lifeboat!" she screamed. Her hair was filthy and wild. Her hands, usually so elegant and refined, were twisted into ugly claws. Her face was so distorted with hate and fear that she barely looked human. "If you don't get out of my way, I'm going to push you over into the sea and let the sharks eat you! If they'll have you!" she screeched.

Shiloh folded his arms and looked down at her with sudden pity. "You don't have to be so scared, ma'am. All of the women and children will be rescued first. I think you know that."

Enraged and maddened, Denise couldn't speak. She tried, but only a hissing sound came from her mouth. Brynn, silently slipping up behind her, slid her arm around her mother's waist and started to say something.

Denise jerked spasmodically, her eyes bulging, and lashed out. She half turned and struck out with her right hand, hitting Brynn across the neck. Brynn staggered, stumbled, fell against her mother. Denise insanely shoved at Brynn; the two seemed to grapple for a moment. Then, their arms still entwined, they toppled over into the raging sea.

Before anyone could move, Shiloh dove in after them.

He has his hat on, Cheney thought numbly. *He would hate to lose that hat . . . General Forrest gave it to him. . . .*

The three of them surfaced. Denise and Brynn had already been pulled by the current about ten feet away from the pier. Denise, choking and screaming, flailed about in the water. Brynn, calm, tried to speak reasonably to her mother, but to Cheney's horror she saw Denise put her hands on Brynn's shoulder and push her under. In her mindless panic Denise was trying to climb up on Brynn's shoulders.

Shiloh surfaced about six feet from them.

Behind them, Cheney saw the first dark triangular fin swathing through the water. She screamed.

Brynn came up, choking, and Denise pushed her under again.

Shiloh, in two strokes, reached the women. He seemed, somehow, to rise up in the water. Drawing back his fist, he hit Denise Winslow squarely across the jaw, abruptly cutting off her hysterical screams. She lay limp in his arms.

Crooking his right elbow under her chin, he reached out with his left hand into the water, then pulled. Brynn Winslow surfaced, spitting out water and gagging. "Are you all right?" he shouted.

"Y-yes," she managed. "I . . . I . . . can . . . swim."

"Shiloh, swim! Hurry!" Cheney screamed. "Hurry!"

Brynn cast a fearful look behind her. There were two fins now, crisscrossing a speeding figure eight about ten feet behind them. She struck out, moving slowly because of her constricting clothing, which probably weighed around thirty pounds. Shiloh, by contrast, swam easily, a sidestroke, pulling Denise's lax body along as if she were a leaf.

"Hurry up, Brynn! Swim! Hurry up, girl!" he encouraged her.

Brynn reached the pier. George Han reached down, put his hands under her arms, and bodily lifted her up. Shiloh, his legs kicking like iron pistons, held up Denise Winslow. George couldn't manage her by himself. Finally coming to her senses, Cheney hurried across the slanted boards in an odd running tiptoe and helped him lift Denise up and lay her down on the pier. Shiloh jumped up behind them, then reached down and swiped at the water. He came up with his hat.

Standing before them, his canvas coat dripping like a summer storm, water sloshing out of the tops of his boots, he flipped a jellyfish off his hat and grumbled, "You know you're in trouble when you've just knocked a woman out cold, and it's the least of your worries."

Cheney, kneeling beside Denise, said, "She'll be all right, Shiloh."

His head was down, and he fiddled with his hat. "Couldn't tell how hard I hit her. Tried not to hit her that hard . . . didn't think I'd knock her out. . . ."

"She's fine," Cheney repeated firmly. "She might have a shiner, but she's all right."

"Her jaw's not broken, is it?" he asked anxiously, still not looking up.

"No. I promise you she'll be just fine." Cheney jumped up and stood in front of Shiloh. Gently she placed her hands on his cheeks and tilted his head up so he'd meet her eyes. "You did the right thing, Shiloh. You saved their lives, both of them. We all saw; we all know. You need to know it too."

Because of the unfolding drama, no one had noticed that the lifeboat had at last struggled to the end of the pier, where it bobbed frantically up and down in the unruly surf. A man slowly and carefully stepped onto the pier's ladder and pulled himself up. He walked toward them, holding a lantern. Stepping cautiously, he made his way, clinging to the shivering uprights as the sea sloshed up onto the pier. When he reached the damaged section, Shiloh suddenly became aware of his approach and turned to grasp the man's arm and help him across.

Shiloh's body blocked the view of everyone else, so Cheney stepped to his side in order to see around him.

An older man stood directly in front of Shiloh. With shaking hands, he lifted the lantern high so that the uncertain glow fell full on Shiloh's face. The man was tall, but because his shoulders were stooped and he slumped with weariness, he wasn't quite eye level with Shiloh. Still, he was over six feet. His gray hair gleamed in the lurid glare, and his glasses glinted weirdly with reflected red light.

In a choking whisper he croaked, "Rory? Rory? Is . . . it . . . you?"

Shiloh simply replied, "No, sir."

Behind them, Brynn struggled to her feet. She slipped past Cheney and took Shiloh's arm. "Father, no, it's not Uncle Roderick. He's Locke, Father. Locke Winslow. Uncle Roderick's son."

The old man's mouth trembled. He stared first at Shiloh, then at his daughter, almost pleadingly. His blue eyes were drawn inexorably back to Shiloh's face. "Rory . . . Rory . . ." he whispered pitifully. His face suddenly contorted with pain, the blood draining from it and leaving it a sickly white mask. He clutched his chest, coughed wrackingly, and collapsed.

20

BEFORE THEM DEATH, BEHIND THEM FIRE

"Help him."

Shiloh gave the curt order to Cheney, vaulted over both the man and the broken section of pier, and sprinted toward the lifeboat.

Cheney knelt by Logan Winslow, who was conscious but gasping and deathly pale. She looked up at the group of people standing just beyond Denise's prone figure. "If all of you don't get off this pier right now," she said harshly, "I'm going to tell Shiloh when he gets back to push you in the drink. And no one can save you but him."

Fang Shao muttered something under his breath, then wrenched his son around toward the beach. Pat pulled Fang Jinglan along, protesting.

"Mr. Han, please stay with us, if you will," Cheney asked. He was holding the still unconscious Denise by the shoulders, propping her up so that the waves didn't slosh over her face.

Brynn, kneeling by her father, looked up at Cheney pleadingly. "He has heart palpitations. Help me—most of the time he carries digitalis—" She was trying to hold him up and search through his pockets at the same time.

Cheney found a small bottle of pills in his vest pocket and gratefully Logan opened his mouth to put it under his tongue. "Hurts—"

"I know, Mr. Winslow," Cheney said calmly. "You must stay very still. We're going to take care of you, but you must remain calm. Try to take deep, even breaths. Close your eyes, please. It will help you concentrate."

Obediently he closed his eyes, and Brynn took his hand. "Father, I'm so glad to see you. Everyone is all right. We're all perfectly fine. Don't worry about anything."

"But . . . Rory . . ." he whispered.

"Don't worry about anything," Brynn said more firmly, giving Cheney an agonized look.

"You're going to be fine, Mr. Winslow, and your entire family is just fine," Cheney added. "Now, you relax. I'm a doctor, and Shi—I mean, there are two highly trained nurses here. Everyone is going to be all right."

She rose and went to Denise. Denise's eyelids were fluttering, and she moved her hands. The left side of her face was red and swelling, and Cheney could clearly see now that she would have a black eye. "Mrs. Winslow, be still, please. You're all right. Just stay still and calm." Denise opened her eyes, but they were flat, unseeing. Cheney took her hand and patted it. "Just stay calm. Your husband is here, and the lifeboat is here."

Denise jerked upright and started to say something, but a wet wracking cough convulsed her. Then she threw up water. George Han tried to hold her head, but Denise was so agitated she knocked him away.

Shiloh came running back to the group. He glanced cursorily at Logan and Denise, then said curtly, "It's a five-man dinghy. Takes two stout men to row it in this sea. Walker's going, Mr. Winslow's going, Brynn, you're going, and you, Doc. I'm going to carry Mrs. Winslow back to the beach, and I'll bring Walker back. Doc, can Mr. Winslow walk?"

Cheney stared wide-eyed, first at Shiloh, then at Mr. Winslow.

"I . . . can . . . walk," he said, slowly sitting up. "If—" Clutching his chest, his face distorted with pain, he collapsed back.

"It's all right, sir," Shiloh said. Then without any wasted movements, he picked up Logan Winslow as if he were one of Tang Lu's smallest children and started down the pier. Over his shoulder he ordered, "Doc, come on. Right now. You're wasting time."

Cheney, still stunned, looked blankly at Brynn, who was now trying to help her mother stand. Brynn looked back at her, and her face was a pale glimmer, a fearful wraith-face in the volcanic darkness.

"You . . . you go on," Brynn said in a choked voice. "Walker and my father need a doctor. You have to go."

"But . . . I—"

Brynn shook her head, a frantic and desperate denial. "You know, and Mr. Irons—I . . . I mean, my cousin Locke knows that I . . . I can't go instead of my mother."

Cheney stared at her. Suddenly, in a jerky half-run without her usual fluid grace, Brynn turned and hurried down to the end of the pier. Her mind was numb, plodding along so slowly that she was, for all practical purposes, moving along by instinct alone, blind, deaf, speechless.

But Cheney's instincts were not merely those of a panicked woman. The part of her that was the core of her being—her soul—was something else altogether, something higher, nobler. It was her heart, and her heart belonged to God. Now her heart took over her mind and said the One Name that would save her, now and forever.

Jesus . . .

Cheney stopped, her head lifted alertly, her eyes focused faraway.

Jesus . . . my Savior . . . walk with me . . . talk to me. . . .

Deliberately Cheney turned and stared up at the fury of Mount Haleakala.

One dinghy . . . three people. Four, if they push it, and the smallest children could count as one adult. Keloki and Leilana and Ulu Nui . . . have to go one at a time. Half an hour to the ship, half an hour back. Anywhere from eleven trips back and forth. . . ?

The fiery red river was inexorably running down the mountain. Cheney could see it, judge it, all too clearly from far out on the long pier.

We can't all make it to the ship. Some people may have to die. . . .

Like a startled flock of screaming ravens, panic flew up from Cheney's chest, choking her, bulging her eyes, drying her mouth, screeching wild warnings of doom in her ears. She staggered, her knees betraying her, giving way. Horrified, she grasped the wooden pier support, sliding helplessly, her hands razed by splinters.

"Oh . . . oh no . . ." she groaned.

But still Cheney's heart, which was not under her control, but under God's control, was strong.

Fear not: for I have redeemed thee, I have called thee by thy name. . . . Thou art Mine.

"That's right . . . I remember. . . ." Cheney breathed. Closing her eyes, she sighed gratefully, "Oh, thank You, my Lord. I hear You. I know You're right here . . . I know You'll help me."

Straightening, her shoulders thrown back, her face set and her step determined, Cheney went to Shiloh. He was kneeling at the end of the pier, talking to the two sailors who were in the lifeboat. Logan Winslow was slumped in the middle bench seat, but he was sitting up of his own accord.

The two sailors were at either end of the small boat. It was moored to the pier by a bowline, but they were standing, or staggering, in the boat, using their oars to fend off the bow or stern from crashing into the pier as the little craft pitched dangerously. They were both strong men, swarthy from the sun and hardened by the sea. One was about thirty, dark, with a heavy mustache and beard, and a tattoo of an anchor on his arm. The other was younger, maybe twenty-five, clean shaven and baby faced. Both were muscular and brawny; both looked frightened.

Shiloh turned as Cheney grew near. "Come here," he ordered. "I'll get you in the boat."

Cheney shook her head defiantly. "I'm not going this time, Shiloh."

He crossed his arms and stepped so close to her that he brushed her heavy, sodden skirts. "Yes, Doc, you are," he said with soft warning.

Cheney's first impulse—as always—was to stand up to him, to try to overrule him. She was like that. But suddenly she softened, her confrontational stance melted. She laid her hands on his crossed forearms. They were wet, and the muscles were knotted with tension. For a single moment she caressed them and smiled up at him. His expression changed from hard anger to surprise. "Shiloh, I don't have time to explain, but I'm not—supposed—to go. Not right now. So please, let's not quarrel. It's time for you to go get Walker."

He looked rebellious for a moment, and they stood close, facing a watery sea of death, behind them a sea of fire. Abruptly Shiloh pushed by Cheney, muttering, "Blasted know-it-all, fix-it-all doctors! Think they can save the world!"

Cheney actually managed a weak giggle at this, then saw the two sailors watching her with incredulity, and she nodded as if they were being introduced at a soireé. She called to them, "Take care of Mr. Winslow, he's ill. We'll be back with the other passengers very soon."

As she hurried after Shiloh, the older man, Coston, stared after her in disbelief. "Who is she?" he muttered.

Weakly Logan Winslow answered, "I don't know. She's a doctor."

"Her? That fine lady?" The younger baby-faced man was called Dare, because he was always doing dangerous stunts to prove he wasn't as cherubic as he looked. His seraphic face, however, made him a hit with the ladies in every port.

"Fine lady or no," Coston said, his black eyes cutting to the rivers of fire streaming down toward the beach, "she's gonna die if she don't change her mind and her ways."

Logan Winslow, grimacing, pulled himself up straight. "Listen to me, Coston. That man, the one they call Shiloh—he's my nephew. My brother Rory's son. You . . . you . . . have to save him. Next trip . . . make him come in the next trip. . . ."

Coston and Dare stared at him with disbelief. "Beggin' your pardon, sir, but ain't no two of us is gonna make that Irons do nothin' he don't want to do. Even if we could get outta this little dinghy, you think us two could wrestle him down and toss him in?" Coston shrugged eloquently.

Logan's face, already ravaged by pain and fear, fell hopelessly. "No. I don't suppose you could do that. But perhaps . . . he will decide to come . . . after the women and children?"

The two sailors looked up at Haleakala's fire above, and the fury of the lava spewing to the south. Coston's coarse features grew hard, but Dare, who did have a soft spot in his heart, said comfortingly, "Mebbe so, sir. Mebbe so." But over Logan's head, the two sailors exchanged hopeless glances, for they knew that some of the thirty-one people on that island weren't going to leave it.

Perhaps ever.

★　★　★　★

Cheney hurried as quickly as she could, but the pier was so damaged that each step was treacherous. It was empty. Shiloh was already up on the beach, and evidently everyone had finally seen that they couldn't wait on the wooden pier. With each wave it shuddered, with each burst of wind it trembled, with each step it shook. Narrowing her eyes, Cheney searched around the shallows by the beach. *Wonder if there's any place, any little hole at all in the coral reefs for the dinghy to come up closer to the beach? We could wade . . . we might get stung or step on those accursed fish, but it would be better than . . .*

Leaving the thought unfinished as she looked at the fire surrounding them and the molten river approaching them, she set her mind and her face toward the group of people on the beach. They needed her. Especially Shiloh needed her.

And I need You, Lord . . . and I thank You.

She was calm.

Ulu Nui was stationed at the foot of the pier with the gun. He heard

Cheney approach and stepped aside to let her pass. She patted his arm reassuringly, but he still looked tense and grim.

Denise was howling, of course. Other people were shouting, too, but Denise Winslow had that sort of piercing cry that rose above everything, above the roar of the waves, above the raw hot winds, above the cries of children. Cheney wearily thought that she would have nightmares of that horrible banshee wail. She marched directly up to Shiloh, touching his arm lightly to let him know she was there. He was facing Denise Winslow's wrath—again.

"I *own* this beach; I *own* that pier; I *own* that boat, and I *own* that ship! You will not dictate to me who is going! I'm leaving, and Brynn is leaving, and the rest of you can just go hang!"

An ugly outcry came from the people surrounding Denise and Brynn, but Denise, in her madness, could see nor hear nothing. Tears rolled down Brynn's face, making odd white streaks in the grime covering her gentle features. "Mother, you are hysterical. Please, please calm down. . . ."

"Calm down? This . . . this . . . ruffian tried to murder me! He assaulted me! And you're going to obey his orders! No! No!" Denise was so overwrought, her mind and voice so strained, that spittle flew from her mouth as she shouted. She was shaking so hard she could barely stand.

Shiloh drew himself erect and roared, "You, woman, are not going this time. You can go in the next boat! That's it—and if I have to hit you again, I will!"

With a wild shriek Denise ran, stumbling and weaving, to the pier. Ulu Nui stepped in front of her, but he was holding the gun up toward the sky. He looked at Shiloh helplessly as she reached him, for Denise threw herself down on her knees, clasping his legs and crying and sobbing.

"Let her go!" Cheney shouted. "Ulu Nui, let her go!"

Still the big Hawaiian looked uncertainly at Shiloh.

"Please, Ulu Nui, let her go!" Cheney called. "We'll all be much better off!"

Shiloh stared down at her. "She doesn't deserve to live, Cheney. You do. It's that simple."

Cheney said with somber intensity, "Listen to me, Shiloh. I'm a Christian, and if I die, I will walk in heaven with my Lord Jesus forever. That woman"—she pointed to the pitiful figure of Denise Winslow, groveling and screaming on the ground—"will go to hell. I must give her a chance to live. I must."

He stood very still, staring down at her. His eyes seemed an unearthly blue fire in the darkness of his face. "You mean to tell me that you're going to let everyone who's not a Christian go before you."

"Yes." She stood up and threw her head back defiantly to stare directly in his eyes.

"Even that animal?" Shiloh, with a savage nod, indicated Fang Shao.

"I have to. Shiloh, I have to do this."

They stared at each other, and to both of them the world, the fire, the people, the death and destruction faded away. It was quiet, a grave and heavy silence between them. Oddly, Cheney thought she could hear Shiloh's heart beating, fast but strong, a reassuring measure of life. He seemed to have no face, no body, only those eyes that burned with an inner fire so hot that Cheney almost flinched from the feeling of heat.

Without turning Shiloh shouted, "Ulu Nui! Let her pass." Still staring down at Cheney he said, "I'm taking Walker now. But, Cheney, you have to understand something. You say you must do this. I'm telling you that there are certain decisions that I, as a man, must make, and there are things that I must do, or I won't be able to live with myself. Do you understand?"

"Yes," Cheney sighed. "I do. But for now, for this moment, Shiloh, you have to take Walker. All right?" She turned and said to Brynn, who was kneeling by Walker's litter. "Go on, Miss Winslow. You need to be with your family."

Brynn slowly rose to her feet. But instead of answering Cheney she turned to Shiloh. "There are two dinghies on the *Brynn Annalea*, Mr. . . . Mr.—"

"Just call me Shiloh," he said shortly. "I know that. They just brought the one because they didn't know how many people were here. They thought, when they saw the papala spears, that maybe a fisherman or two had gotten caught down here on the beach."

"But surely, when we go back to the ship, we can bring back both dinghies," Brynn insisted.

"Yes. Coston said maybe . . . maybe they could get a couple more sailors. . . . But the sea is rough, and the water's full of sharks and rays. But Coston said he'll try to explain the situation to the captain. They're scared. Coston and Dare were the only two who volunteered to try to bring in that little boat."

Brynn glanced fearfully behind her shoulder at the fire descending. "You could do it, couldn't you? You could bring in the other dinghy by yourself, couldn't you, Locke?"

In her desperate plea she didn't notice that she had called him by the name given to him by his father. But Shiloh noticed, and for a moment intense gratitude and warmth flooded his tired face. Then, concentrating, he turned and looked at the lagoon, the Styx of this place, the crossing of death. "I could," he murmured. "I could bring it in—there's a strong surge washing inland, Coston said. It's not just brute strength, it's control. Yeah, I could do it." He turned back to her, frowning. "But that means—"

"Yes. Go." Brynn neared him, pulled him down, and kissed his cheek. His surprise and pleasure were childlike and innocent. "Go, cousin. With two boats, maybe we can get everyone before—" She waved jerkily behind.

"If you will promise to go in the next boat," he said steadily.

She nodded.

Shiloh turned to Cheney. "Last chance."

"No, it's not. Hurry and go, and hurry back, Shiloh."

He grimaced, then knelt and lifted Walker in his arms.

"Oh—ugh—sorry, Shiloh, but something hurts—can't quite figure out where . . ." Walker faltered. "Miss Winslow—"

Brynn stepped close to him, then with a delicate air of embarrassment, she bent down and kissed his lips lightly. He was so surprised he was speechless. "I'll join you soon, Walker."

"Yes . . . yes . . . Brynn . . ." he whispered, groaned, and passed out.

Shiloh whirled, carrying Walker easily. "I'm not through with you yet, Doc. I'll be back."

"I'll be waiting," she promised. "God go with you."

He turned and disappeared into the swirling blackness.

21

OF COURAGE AND SACRIFICE

Cheney watched Shiloh disappear into the swirling darkness. With a sudden heaviness she sank to the sand. The desolation that swept over her, bitter and powerful, at the realization that they were separated, threatened to defeat her.

As soon as she knew it, she stopped it.

You are my Savior, she vowed to God. *You only are my Savior. Only in You will I put my trust.*

Brynn sat by her, watching her curiously.

Cheney smoothed back her hair—it felt like an impossibly long tangle of dirty sheep's wool—and rubbed her face. "I must look like . . . like—I can't imagine what I look like," she said with exasperation.

"You look like the rest of us," Brynn said dryly.

"Ah . . ." Cheney studied her. "Wretched, hmm?"

"Wretched, yes."

Nia appeared, throwing herself down beside Cheney, sitting cross-legged in the sand. "Here, Miss Cheney, you drink some water. I've been watching you, and you haven't had a drink or a rest for hours."

"How much water do we have left?" Cheney asked anxiously.

Nia rolled her eyes. "You never mind that. If we need to, Mr. Shiloh can bring some back from the ship. Right, Miss Winslow?"

"Yes, of course. I hadn't thought of that, but he certainly could take the empty canteens and skins we have and fill them from the ship's stores."

Cheney sat up, took a drink, then poured a little into her hand and rubbed it over her face. "I've got to . . . wake up, think. . . ." She started to get up, but Nia yanked on her arm, pulling her back to the ground.

"You can think sitting down," Nia asserted. "We've got time before the boats get back."

"Yes . . . you're right. As usual." Absently Cheney opened Shiloh's watch and listened to the sad tune. He had given it to her just before he'd left in the lifeboat. "It says it's eleven-fifteen. Or eleven-thirteen, as Shiloh would say. But I don't—is it day? Or night?" Bewildered, she looked around.

"Why, I . . . don't know," Brynn said in confusion. "It just seems as if it's neither . . . and never-ending."

It was dark, an inky blackness that was lightened only by the lava and flame behind them. Errant puffs of wind blew this way and that, but the clean ocean wind had died. There was no color. People were only shadows of lifeless gray and charcoal. There was only the crimson fire backlighting the scene, flickering and hellish. The heat pressed them, smothering them, burning their noses and lips and eyes; but sweat dried on them before forming, so they felt dry and tight and chafed, the way a bad sunburn feels.

"It's night, Miss Cheney," Nia whispered. "This is darkest night."

"All right," she said with an attempt at briskness. "We have to get organized. The boats will be back in about half an hour, I think; that would be quarter to midnight. We have to decide who's going next and get them out on the pier."

"You do, Miss Cheney," Nia said in a low voice.

"Yes, I'm afraid it's fallen on you," Brynn agreed quietly. "I'll help you all I can, Dr. Duvall, but I'm afraid everyone is depending upon you."

Cheney's heart pounded at her words, and she looked around at the people who seemed to have come under her care. And a heavy, burdensome care it was . . . deciding their fates. Deciding their lives. Or their deaths?

Far to their left, Fang Shao had his family grouped together in the sand. Tang Lu and the four small children huddled together in a mass, staring up at him. Stalking back and forth, he talked incessantly in a high-pitched whine. A little behind Tang Lu and the children stood Fang Jinglan, watching her father with hopelessness making her young, full face sag. Pat stood close by her, talking to her, but she seemed not to hear. Will hovered close to his older brother, pacing restlessly behind him and Fang Jinglan.

Most everyone else was sitting on the sand close to where Cheney sat. The elderly Chinese couple, Sunny and Fay, sat holding hands, their heads close together as they talked. Lela and George Han took turns holding the baby, soothing her. She cried incessantly. Zhu Ki sat a little apart, her head down, her shoulders bowed. Her two children sat close to her, crying and pulling on her clothes, but she was lifeless, like a huddle of rags someone had tossed carelessly aside. As Cheney watched, Koki, who was sitting close to Zhu Ki, called the two children softly. They looked up, their little round faces lit with hope, and she motioned for them to come to her. They crept close, and she enveloped them in her arms. Her daughter, Anika, sat on her lap quietly.

Down by the pier, Ulu Nui stood talking with his mother and father. Cheney sighed deeply as she studied them. They were magnificent people, all three of them tall and strong, built as solid as the mountain itself. And they were big. Too big for the dinghies—at least, maybe with only one other person, someone small, a woman or one of the young Chinese boys.

"Why me?" Cheney finally burst out despairingly. "I . . . I'm . . . having enough trouble with just my own decisions! I can't . . . I can't! I shouldn't!"

"Then who will?" Brynn said softly.

Cheney was silent. Both Nia and Brynn looked at her with pity, but it also showed on each of their faces that, somehow, Cheney was the only one who could take this awesome responsibility. If she couldn't, or didn't, they were lost.

"All right," Cheney finally said wearily. Pulling herself to her feet, she turned in a little circle, searching for—something, she herself wasn't sure what. She stared up at the lava that steadily crept toward them. "Don't fuss, Nia. If I'm going to do this, I have to stand up."

"I knew it," Nia sighed. Cheney didn't hear her.

"Miss Winslow, there are only the two dinghies, right? On the *Brynn Annalea*?"

"No, there are two other lifeboats—longboats. But they're twenty-man boats, and they couldn't come through the barrier reef. They'd have to come around to the northern entrance by the cliffs. That's why they didn't try to bring them, I think. It would probably take twenty strong men to maneuver them in. Then, of course, they couldn't carry anyone back." Brynn got to her feet and joined Cheney in staring up at the burning cliffs of Haleakala above them.

"How much time do you think before the lava covers the beach?" she whispered.

Cheney shook her head. "I have no idea. Isn't it odd that women don't seem to be able to judge spatial and temporal relationships as well as men do? I can't guess how far it is. I can't judge how fast it's moving. It just looks—close. Every time I look I can see that it's closer."

"I'll bet Locke knows," Brynn said.

"Locke . . . I'll never get used to calling him that. . . ."

"He's wonderful," Brynn asserted. "He's strong and courageous, and he has a generous heart."

"Yes."

Brynn turned to stare directly into Cheney's eyes. "You love him."

Cheney swallowed hard. "Everyone loves him. Especially women. But right now is not the time to have girl talk about Shiloh." Firmly Cheney turned and pointed to the south. "What about those barrier rocks that go out into the sea entrance? Could a person walk along them all the way out to the end?"

"No, I'm afraid not," Brynn answered. "They're big enough, even in this unearthly tide, but there are huge gaps between them."

"We have to think of a way," Cheney said fiercely. "There must be some . . . escape, someplace safe."

Steadily Brynn said, "There won't be enough time to get everyone to the ship, will there?"

Cheney stepped close to her, searching her face. Brynn looked frightened, but she was in firm control of herself. No sign of panic or hysteria marred her pretty, gentle features; no restlessness or weakness showed in her stance. "No, Miss Winslow," Cheney finally answered her. "But you will be going in the next boat."

Brynn dropped her eyes. "I . . . I heard what you told Locke. I have to tell you . . . I have to tell someone. I became a Christian. The other night, during the plague of centipedes."

"That's wonderful," Cheney said warmly, clasping her hands. "Now I can see why you're so steady. Now I know why you're strong. You haven't even fainted!"

"And you haven't been rude," Brynn replied with a hint of a smile. "It . . . just has to be the Lord. Otherwise I'd be behaving just like my mother, I think." She looked ashamed and anxious at the same time.

Cheney squeezed her hands lightly. "You should be with your family. Just because I know that the Lord has directed me to stay here doesn't mean that you must, you know. He has a path for each of us. He has a plan that He formed before the foundation of the world for each of us. He means for me to stay. You must ask Him—not me, or your mother, or even yourself—what He wants you to do."

Brynn looked startled. "But . . . how does one go about doing that? I mean, it's not as if He speaks to you like you're speaking to me!"

Cheney smiled. "You may be surprised. Right now I'm going to go get the others whom I've decided to take out on the pier to wait on the boats. You pray and ask Him what to do. He'll tell you."

She walked away, but then hesitated and turned back to Brynn. "For my part, Miss Winslow, I felt that the Lord was directing me to pick the ones to go . . . just now, as I was praying. And I was fairly certain that you should be one. Also, I must tell you that if you think Shiloh—Locke—is protective of me, you must be prepared to be . . . er . . . treated even worse, or better, depending on your point of view. I truly don't think that he would force me to go . . . but I do think he would you. He's been searching for you for a long time, you know. He's not going to let anything happen to his family now."

Tears welled up in Brynn's eyes, and then she nodded with sudden certainty. "Dr. Duvall, I'm going on the next boat. But now I'll come help you get everyone else together."

"Good," Cheney said. "All right, I think we're going to have to send Tang Lu and the children right now before Fang Shao does something awful. They can go with Shiloh. In the other boat, with Coston and Dare and you . . . I think we can risk sending three. . . ."

Cheney's eyes fell on Nia, who put on a face so stubborn only the Clarkson women could project it with such force. "No, ma'am. I'll go when you go."

"No, Nia," Cheney said ominously.

"Yes, Miss Dr. Cheney Duvall," Nia said, mimicking her voice of doom. "You'd best remember, ma'am, that I'm a child of God too. I can make decisions about it just like you. And my Blessed Lord Jesus told me to stay with you. So I'm staying."

Cheney put her hands on her hips with exasperation, and Nia, facing her, mimicked her gesture and expression. Then Cheney sighed and nodded. "You're right, Nia. You have the same right to make your own decision as I do. And . . . I'm glad you're staying with me."

Nia sniffed. "I should think so. Now, I'm going to go start herding Tang Lu's babies together, and that Mr. Fang Man just better keep his hands and his sticks to hisself."

"I'll come with you," Brynn said. "He wouldn't dare assault me. He knows if he does they'll just toss him overboard when he gets to the ship."

"That's true," Cheney agreed. "All right, you two go on and start the fight. I'll take a few minutes and try to decide who else can go."

Brynn and Nia hurried off, and Cheney was amused to see that they reached out and held hands for a few moments. "Imminent death," she speculated to herself, "certainly brings people closer together."

"Doctor," a deep voice boomed. Cheney turned and hurried over to Keloki, Leilana, and Ulu Nui.

"Oh yes, Keloki. I . . . I—there's something I need to—I have to—"

Keloki grinned, and his teeth were very big and very white in the dimness. "We already know it, Doctor." He glanced first at his wife, then at his son. "We're nui, like alii," he repeated the mantra. "Too big for falling pier. Too big for little haole boats."

"I'm . . . so sorry," Cheney faltered. "If we just had time—"

"No time for us to go out to ship one, one, one," Keloki grunted. "We know. We stay. Me and Leilana and Ulu Nui."

Cheney stared at them helplessly.

Keloki grinned again. "Don't worry, haole wahine. We're Pele's people. We run fast."

"I hope so," Cheney murmured. "I hope I can run fast, too, Keloki, because I don't think we'll have time to get everyone off the island. So my question is, where could we run to?"

"Me and Ulu Nui go look," Keloki replied, pointing south. "Pele's fire, she's bad down there. But this side? Maybe up, maybe we find someplace?"

Cheney turned to look. The second fissure was still steadily firing spews of lava into the air. Above the fountain the jungle was already blazing. But it was true that the fissure directly above them and the fires to the south didn't meet—yet. There was a narrow long ribbon of jungle this side and above the second volcano that was still dark and inviting. "All right," she relented. "Perhaps it would be best if you could go see about crossing Brynn's Stream and if there's somewhere we could find shelter. The Seven Sacred Pools, perhaps?" Cheney asked hopefully.

Keloki frowned. The redness reflected angrily on his worried face. "Think Pele's fire this side of it, Doctor. But Ulu Nui and me, we find a place. We find a way."

"Yes," Cheney said. "Good. And maybe it might be best to go ahead and take—some people—soon." Anxiously she stared at the fires coming closer to the beach.

Keloki nodded. Then Leilana spoke, quietly and anxiously. "Doctor? I'm not sorry I stay with Keloki. But my children, my keiki. Can they go in haole boat?"

"Why of course!" Cheney cried. "Your wife and baby, Ulu Nui—they should go first. Miss Winslow must go this trip. I think . . . yes, Anika and Malani. But Kimo . . ."

"He strong. He's not afraid," Leilana said stoutly. "He will wait."

"Good. But I promise, Keloki, Leilana, Ulu Nui, because of your courage and your sacrifice, we will send your children first."

Ulu Nui looked more relieved than he had the entire horrible day and night. "I'll tell Koki good-bye. Then we go, Father. Yes?"

"Yes." Keloki and Ulu Nui went to where Koki sat in the sand playing with Anika and tending Zhu Ki's children. Zhu Ki still was a defeated huddle on the sand, alone.

Leilana clasped Cheney's hands and kissed them.

"No, no, Leilana, I—it's not really my place—to make these decisions," Cheney stammered.

Leilana looked up at her and smiled. "But it is, Doctor. The gods, they say it is. We all know. We all understand. The *Pake*, they don't. But we do."

Numbly Cheney nodded. "Well . . . anyway, we need to get everyone, in a calm and orderly fashion, out on the pier. Come and help me, Leilana. Tell your children to stay in single file, on the left. The right hand side of the pier is collapsing. Do you understand?"

"Yes, Doctor," she said quietly. "I understand. And I'm not afraid. Not now." And she slipped away.

"I wish I wasn't," Cheney muttered. Because she was afraid, of course. But it didn't rule her. Underlying the sudden wrenches of fear, the horrible uncertainties, the agonies of making wrong decisions, she was at peace. Like a rock standing strong in a killing wind, she knew that her soul was in the hands of the Almighty God.

Thinking again, Cheney smiled a little.

Perhaps she wasn't so afraid after all.

To her left, Fang Shao started shouting, a high cry of menace. Keloki and Ulu Nui looked up, frowning. Leilana took a step toward the group that included Nia, Brynn, Tang Lu, the children, and Fang Jinglan.

"No, Leilana!" Cheney cried sternly, already sprinting toward Fang Shao. "Get your children onto the pier! Keloki, you and Ulu Nui go on! Leilana, take the gun and stand guard at the foot of the pier! If Fang Shao tries to get on the pier or tries to stop anyone else from getting on the pier—shoot him!"

Leilana looked as grim and determined as an avenging angel.

But Cheney, as she passed them, suddenly skidded to a stop.

Lord, how can I keep making these horrible, awful decisions? This is . . . unthinkable! I can't keep on . . . I can't!

But she could, and she knew it.

"No, wait," she said with finality. "Give *me* the gun, Ulu Nui."

"I'm not afraid," Leilana said stoutly.

"I know," Cheney said resignedly. "But the truth is, Leilana, I'm a good shot. A very good shot. You probably would have to kill him. I can probably wing him."

Leilana grimaced. "You hurt him, he goes."

"I know," Cheney said helplessly. "But if he dies, he goes to hell. I have to try to keep that . . . from happening. Do you understand?"

"No," she said stubbornly. "Why you care? I don't. No one else does."

"My God does," Cheney said. "Now, give me the gun, Ulu Nui. Leilana, you still might have a chance to toss him in the sea. If he just runs by me . . . I'm still not too sure I could shoot him. Or hit him in the leg or arm."

"Hope you miss," she sneered. "Hope I get him."

Cheney grabbed the gun that Ulu Nui was reluctantly holding out to her and ran toward the little group. Fang Shao was swinging the club in vicious wide arcs around him, though no one was approaching him. His eyes were wide, unseeing, and his face was distorted with mindless anger. Flecks of spittle were on his cheeks, and the cords in his neck stood out.

"Fang Shao," Cheney called as softly as she could. "Calm down. Listen to me."

He kept swinging the club, screaming in Chinese.

Tang Lu got up and made a wide circle around her husband, her eyes cutting fearfully toward him. She hurried to Cheney and bowed low. "He doesn't speak good English, Dr. Duvall," she said in a low voice. "He's frightened, and no one will listen to him."

Cheney sighed. "Tang Lu, I'm sorry for him. I truly am. But I'm also sorry for us all, and I don't think he deserves any special treatment. Women and children first. That's the way it must be."

"He can't understand that," Tang Lu insisted, though her demeanor was riddled with shame. "The Chinese are not like that. We are different."

"I don't care!" Cheney snapped. "Surely you don't think that he should go instead of your children, Tang Lu! Or do you?"

Her face, round and usually so expressionless, was distorted with uncertainty and shame. "I know . . . you can't understand our ways, Dr. Duvall. But he is my husband, and I must obey him. Only men and . . . and . . . boys are important."

"Get your children, Tang Lu," Cheney said harshly. "You and the four smallest are going on the next boat. As soon as all of the women and children are safe on board the *Brynn Annalea*, the men will come. That's the way it's going to be, no matter what you say or what your husband does. Tell him that."

Defeated, Tang Lu turned and shouted sharply to Fang Shao. He stopped his tirade long enough to listen.

Cheney said quietly, "You tell him that I will use this gun if I have to, to protect the women and children. Make him understand that too."

Stifling a sob, Tang Lu stepped closer to her husband, her head bowed submissively, speaking quickly. As he listened, his rage grew, and he stared at Cheney with such hatred that she almost flinched. Still, she stood strong and faced him—she hoped, with dignity and without anger.

"I'm sorry," she said to him.

He stepped close to Tang Lu, and Cheney jerked. She had no intention of letting him hit her again, but what could she do? She couldn't fight him, and she wouldn't shoot him for that. Would she?

Should she?

Oh, Lord, give me wisdom—

"Now what!"

Cheney had never in her life heard such a welcome sound as his voice. Shiloh's voice. Dry, half-amused, thoroughly angry. She turned and practically fell into his arms.

"Hi, Doc. Got some trouble here?"

"Hi," she said tremulously. "Uh . . . a little. But I think Mr. Fang is coming around."

"Yeah? Well, I'm tired of that little whelp wasting everybody's time and money," Shiloh growled, stepping up close to them. Fang Shao bared his teeth and half raised the club. With exquisite disdain and blinding speed, Shiloh reached out and plucked the thick stick out of his hand. Then he threw it far down the beach, toward the lagoon, as easily as if it were a balsa sliver. "Get back," he ordered, and Fang Shao stumbled back a step. Turning to Tang Lu, Shiloh said, "Ma'am, no more foolishness. Get those children and go get in the boat. Right now."

With a last furtive glance at Fang Shao, Tang Lu gathered up the four children and hurried them in the direction of the pier. Fang Jing-lan, with a terrified look at Shiloh, scuttled off, followed by Pat and Will.

Shiloh, Cheney, and Brynn still stood in a loose circle around Fang Shao.

He burst into tears. He wailed, long loud cries of agony that made Cheney feel ill. Brynn started weeping. Shiloh looked thoroughly disgusted. "Get your chin up, you little girly muffin!" he blustered. "Blue blazes, your two-year-old daughter's got ten times the guts you do!"

He howled, then crept closer to Shiloh in a lurching, shambling half-bow, half-step. "You—haoles! You say women, children! But you send your friend, your cripple! Oh yes, he go! White people go, always go. Chinese last! I die, I die, but you won't!"

"Stop that mewling," Shiloh said with disdain. "My friend, and my . . . uncle went because they were ill and injured."

"Huh? What you say?" Fang Shao said alertly, his tears abruptly drying up.

"They were hurt! Sick! Hurt!" Shiloh shouted. "Now, listen to me, you—"

With a half-mad, half-crafty look, Fang Shao turned and sped down the beach. He ran straight and fast, and Shiloh was stunned for a moment. Then he realized what the man was doing and sprinted after him.

But Shiloh's moment of hesitation was too long, and the Chinaman too quick. Fang Shao ran straight into the pounding surf and stamped back and forth. Cheney, running behind Shiloh, could already see blood, black and watery, running down both of Fang Shao's legs as he lifted them high, then stamped gleefully down. He was shrieking in pain and insane triumph.

Shiloh ran into the surf, and Cheney screamed, "No, Shiloh, just let him—"

But he paid no attention. He took two leaping steps, reached the man, scooped him up, and ran back to the beach. Then he threw him down to the sand and stood over him, glowering murderously.

"You fool," he gritted, his eyes flashing cobalt flame.

Cheney fell to her knees beside Fang Shao, and he cowered. "Be still," Cheney said, not ungently.

He had jellyfish stings already swelling both ankles. There was no way to know if they were from man-o'-wars or the other less lethal kind.

Shiloh, reluctantly going down on one knee to look at his feet, grimaced. "He stepped on a rockfish, Doc. See there? Two spikes, still stuck in him. No, don't touch it! If it cuts you or even gets into a little scrape on your hand, it'll poison you too."

"But what are we going to do?" Cheney asked.

"Have to get some pliers," Shiloh answered, his voice defeated and weary. "Take 'em out on board the ship."

Fang Shao, whimpering and groaning, still managed to cry out in triumph, "Now I go, you! Now I go! Now who is fool?"

Rising, Shiloh grunted, "You are, my friend. You're going to the ship, all right. But you're going to lose that foot too. Maybe your leg."

Fang Shao cried out, a shrill scream sounding like that of a dying animal.

"Oh no," Cheney murmured, agonized.

"You going now?" Shiloh demanded. "You going to take care of him?"

"I . . . I can't," Cheney said, anguished. "Shiloh, I can't explain it to you—there's no time—"

He smiled down at her, touched her face. "Doesn't matter."

"It doesn't?" Cheney gulped.

"Naw," he drawled softly. " 'Cause I already know."

Her eyes alight, she whispered, "You always have."

He nodded. "And, Cheney, my love, I always will."

22

ANGELS OF LIFE

Shiloh bent, picked up Fang Shao, and threw him over his shoulder like a sack of coal. The Chinaman whimpered in pain and fear.

"What can be done for him?" Cheney worried.

"Not much, from what I hear," Shiloh answered. "Get the spikes out. Pour carbolic acid over the entry wounds."

"His foot's already swollen to twice its size."

"Pretty soon he'll have a high fever and vomiting," Shiloh said evenly. "Then he'll have convulsions. The poison will rot his foot, and it may make his whole leg gangrenous. He may die. But it was his choice, Doc. Don't forget that."

"I know . . . I was just wondering who might take care of him on the ship."

He gave her a sidelong glance. "They don't have a ship's surgeon, if that's what you mean. Captain Sloane keeps the medicine chest and tends to injured or sick men. He'll take out the spikes and clean out the wound."

"That's good, I guess," Cheney murmured, staring at the man's foot anxiously. It was already turning a menacing bluish-purple.

In a low voice Shiloh said, "Doc, the ship's going to have to leave soon. You know that. It's only a few hours to the hospital in Lahaina, and then this worm will be in better shape than you if you won't come this time."

Cheney glanced at the fire wall anxiously. "You made the trip really fast, Shiloh. I was figuring forty minutes. But it was quicker than that, wasn't it?"

"Yeah," he grunted. "But coming inland, empty, was too easy. There's a strong incoming tide, and that light little boat just kind of skimmed along like a he'e nalu board. But there's a strong riptide pulling north, and it's not going to be so easy going seaward with five people in the boat."

Cheney frowned. "This time, you're going to have the four children and him, right?"

"Right. I sure wish it was Tang Lu instead." Angrily Shiloh jostled the Chinaman's legs, ostensibly getting a better grip.

"Shiloh," Cheney said reproachfully.

"I don't care, Doc. He's no better than a criminal, as far as I'm concerned. This muck of taking men instead of women and children just eats at me," he growled. "Goes against everything a man stands for, believes in, fights for."

Cheney said mildly, "But, Shiloh, you didn't feel that way about taking Walker, did you?"

"No. But he didn't bust his own shoulder to little jagged pieces to get to go first either."

"But what you're saying is so important," Cheney persisted, "is not just a mindless rule about women and children. It's about the strong being generous enough to take care of the weak. The weakest ones, the ones who can't help themselves."

"I get the feeling," Shiloh rasped, "that you're making a point."

"I am."

"Okay, I get it, Miss Super Doctor. I get it."

They reached the foot of the pier, where Leilana faithfully stood guard. Nia was waiting with her, holding the empty canteens and water skins she had collected from everyone.

"What happened to him?" Nia asked with disgust. "Lightning strike, mebbe?"

"Suicide," Shiloh said gruffly. "Close to, anyway. Now I get to go tell Tang Lu that she's gotta get outta the boat and leave her kids with this toad."

"Shiloh, couldn't you maybe take her?" Cheney asked hopefully. "I was just thinking that you'll have the four children, they're small, and Fang Shao is a small man."

Uneasily Shiloh shifted the man on his shoulder; Fang Shao now moaned piteously with each breath. "Shut up, you," Shiloh muttered. "I . . . can't do it, Doc. She couldn't help . . . but I think I could take someone who could help me row."

"Kimo!" Cheney said gladly. "I promised Keloki and Leilana. But where is he?"

"He's already in the dinghy, keeping it from breaking up against the pier," Shiloh answered. "I told him to stay in it while I went to see

260

what was holding up my passengers."

"Kimo's going, Leilana," Cheney said, patting the woman's massive arm.

"Thank you, Doctor," she said. "Thank you, Keakea."

"I wish everyone would stop thanking me," Shiloh grunted with a trace of embarrassment. "Seems like I'm not doing anyone any favors."

"I know what you mean, only too well," Cheney sighed. "But anyway, let's go. I'll come with you. Bring these water skins and canteens. And I'll get Tang Lu."

They hurried down the pier. To Cheney it seemed that the entire thing would crash down into the sea, board by board, like falling dominoes, any minute. It was so shaky it was like walking on a child's seesaw. The lagoon was as wild and tossed as the North Atlantic in a winter storm, and the waves now bashed against their knees instead of their ankles. It was frightening. There were so many jellyfish, starfish, and even small live fish washed up onto it in the highest waves that they simply tried to step over and around them instead of kicking them back into the sea. Cheney literally pulled herself from piling to piling, hanging on with both arms whenever one of the big waves washed over her. But Shiloh walked as tall and steadily as if he were carrying a sack of grain down a quiet street.

As they approached the end of the pier, Tang Lu looked up and saw them, and without a word got out of the boat, climbing up the ladder quickly. Behind her, the children let out a wail, crying "Ah-ma! Ah-ma!"

Tang Lu turned, shook her head sternly, and the children quieted down. Shiloh set Fang Shao down on the pier. "Kimo, you're going this trip, so just stay there. Yes, your mama said for you to go." Propping his hands on his hips, he looked down at Fang Shao. "Get in the boat. Betcha can manage that by yourself."

Sure enough, though he whimpered and didn't put any weight on his injured foot, Fang Shao managed to get into the lifeboat and collapse onto the stern seat, where Min and Kwan sat. He pushed his children away.

"You lay a hand on one of those kids, I'm going to dump you overboard," Shiloh warned him. "Now that I mention it, I wish you would backhand one of 'em. Go on, just touch one of 'em, gimme a chance."

Fang Shao ignored him, slumping down almost prone and hanging his head over the side. He wasn't vomiting yet, but he was beginning to shiver with fever.

Shiloh turned back to Tang Lu and took her hand. "I'm so sorry, Miss Tang Lu. All I can say is I'll take good care of the children, and I'll get Miss Winslow to watch them until you get there. You'll be in the next boat, I promise."

Tang Lu, whose only expression this entire horrible time had been one of sternly controlled fear, suddenly started crying. Her face did not lose its closed expression; tears just welled up in her dark almond-shaped eyes and flowed down her cheeks. "Thank you, sir," she managed. "Thank you for everything."

"Don't thank me yet," Shiloh said, half turning to Cheney. Tang Lu took the hint and crept along the pier by herself, clinging to the uprights as Cheney had done.

"Okay, I'm gone again," he said grimly. Without looking up at the mountain, as they struggled not to do any more than necessary, he said, "You know we don't have much time left."

"I know," Cheney whispered. "Do . . . do you think one more trip?"

"Maybe. Gonna try."

Cheney nodded.

"Doc, I'm only going to make round trips. You understand what I mean?"

She started. "No! Next trip, you stay on the ship! Keloki and Ulu Nui are finding us a place to go, and I'm going to leave with them and take whoever's left after the next trip!"

"No," he said blithely, then hopped onto the middle ladder step, and then down into the boat. "Be back in about thirty minutes, Doc. Have 'em ready."

"You're the stubbornest creature on this earth!" Cheney shouted.

"Naw," he bawled out. "That title belongs to you, ma'am!"

By the time Cheney had taken two steps down the pier, the lightness she felt when she was with Shiloh had dissipated.

Eighteen people left, counting me and Nia and the children . . . For a moment she clung to one of the uprights of the pier, pressing her hot cheek against the roughness of the wood. *Lord, I am so tired, so dead tired and sick of trying to make these decisions. . . .*

Well, why should I? I've decided my own fate according to the Lord's will. I've tried to do the best I could . . . but there's ten-month-old Vanda Han still on that beach. That was a wonderful decision you made there,

Cheney girl. The littlest baby . . . she should have gone in the first boat! What have I done? What am I doing?

As if she were an old, crippled woman, she staggered down the pier, clinging helplessly to the supports as the sea raged. Bitterly she made herself look up at the volcano, the mountain, the fire.

The jungle close behind the beach was blazing. Soon the last line of coconut palms would be burning. The wall of descending lava wasn't far behind the fire. So fatigued she felt stupid and slow, Cheney thought, *Don't even know if we'll have time to wait for Shiloh to get back . . . might have to take everyone and run. Wish Keloki and Ulu Nui would return with good news. . . .*

She did see that the fire on the crests of the mountain hadn't extended far over to her left, to the south. It didn't look like it had passed Brynn's Stream, and there was still a dark and untouched ribbon of jungle that reached all the way up to the summit of Mount Haleakala that wasn't burning. It gave Cheney hope and a little more strength.

But as she neared the end of the pier and all of the people waiting for her, her resolve waned again. Suddenly frustrated, sick, and impatient with the world, she pushed by Leilana without a word and sank to the sand, her head bowed. Everyone was gathered in a group close to the surf now. The fire behind them was much more frightening than even the deadly rockfish and man-o'-wars.

"The boat's coming," she called out dully. "The one with Coston and Dare. Three adults, maybe four if one can row. Two children can count as one adult."

No one spoke, and then everyone spoke at once. Some of them were entreating Cheney, and some of them were arguing. Cheney tried hard to block out the strident voices and the cries of the children who were left. Surely they would have the common sense and decency to send Lela Han and the baby? And Zhu Ki and her two toddlers?

And there's Sunny and Fay, and they're both over sixty years old. Tang Lu, their daughter, with four children already aboard the ship, with only her husband, who is probably dying. Those two Chinese stableboys from the villa . . . the oldest is Pat . . . take such good care of that awful little Fang Jinglan. She's just like her father . . . but the younger brother—what do they call him?—is just as courageous and unselfish . . . and then, of course, there's little Nia . . . they'll never let her go . . . and Leilana, whose courage certainly has earned her a place, but she has none . . . I won't! I won't tell these selfish, silly little sheep what to do anymore! I can't!

Her litany of misery was so successful that for a while she was able to block out everything and everyone—except herself. But gradually the arguments close by, in Chinese that sounded more and more hysterical, filtered in. Cheney, drawing her knees up and burying her face in her filthy, wet, stinking, gritty skirt, tried to lose herself in her own anguish.

But Cheney Duvall was not by nature a selfish or self-centered woman, and she was also highly attuned to her God. He allowed her to wallow in self-pity for a few moments, but even as she did, she knew, deep in the quiet and peace of her mind where the Lord dwelled, that she would tire of it soon. And she did, much sooner than she thought. Her head still down, she made a face at herself. She knew that Nia was sitting by her, unspeaking.

"Go away," Cheney said, her voice muffled in her skirt. "I'm not through sulking."

"Oh yes, you are, Miss Ma'am," Nia said sharply. "If you don't get up and take somebody out there to meet that boat, they'll stand here 'til Judgment Day arguing about it."

Cheney jerked upright, the slightest trace of bitterness still reflected in her green eyes. "Why me?" she demanded. "I mean, I'm going to go do something about it, but I still don't understand why in the world I've been elected the Angel of Death here!"

To Cheney's shock, Nia laughed. "Angel of Death! Why, Miss Cheney, what's the matter with you? You're smarter than that, I know you are. You better get your head back on straight. Angel of Life is more like it. You and Mr. Shiloh."

"Oh yes, we've done marvelously, sentencing this one to life and granting this one death," Cheney said ungraciously.

Nia shook her head. "Miss Cheney, you're a doctor. No, you're a healer. So is Mr. Shiloh. This is no different from what you do every day. People depend on you, sometimes for their very lives. What's the matter with you? You don't get all het up whenever you're doctoring someone who's dying! You don't get all sniffy and snuffly when you have to decide whether or not you can save someone's life! You just do it! Plain and simple, you just go on and get it done. Because that's what the Lord's meant for you to do in this life. Your ministry to people, for His glory, is to be a healer. You hold life and death in your hands. You always will."

Cheney stared at Nia, thunderstruck.

Nia stared back at her with a mixture of pity and sympathy.

Cheney scrambled to her feet. "You're dawdling, as usual, Nia," she said in a snooty voice. "Come help me get these people sorted out right now!"

"Yes, ma'am."

They barged right into the tight circle of the Chinese people left on the beach. Immediately everyone fell silent and looked at Cheney expectantly.

"The other boat, the one with the two sailors, will be here any minute now, and Shiloh won't be far behind," she said calmly. "Lela Han and Vanda, Zhu Ki and your two children, and Tang Lu will go in the first boat."

Lela Han began weeping, and George Han looked ill. He looked at Cheney, pleading, but said nothing.

Cheney took a deep breath, hardened her heart, and said, "Shiloh can take five people, provided that at least one of them can row. Sunny, Fay, you two will go for sure. Fang Jinglan in that boat. And I believe that Nia should go now. That leaves one place; Pat and Will, I'm very sorry, but one of you must go."

"Excuse me," Tang Lu said, stepping forward. Cheney was startled; she had never yet seen the woman speak without being addressed. She stood so quietly and still that it was easy to forget that she was there. "I think that Mr. Han should go with his wife and baby."

"No," Cheney said firmly. "Your children are already on the ship. Your husband is gravely ill. I think you know, Tang Lu, that he may even die. I don't think it is God's will that four orphans result from this tragedy we're in. I won't allow it."

Patiently Tang Lu listened to Cheney, then said, "Doctor, I think you will see, if you look and listen, that the sea has risen even more. I think you will find out that the two sailors will not want three weak women on board that little boat. I think they, too, will want at least one person who can help row."

Cheney hesitated, and her eyes fell on Zhu Ki. The young girl flinched away, grabbing her two children, and cried, "No, no—please!"

Cheney did feel like the Angel of Death at that moment, and Nia took her hand and squeezed it. Cheney swallowed hard, then said, "But, Tang Lu, I mean what I say about your children. It's not . . . personal, not for any of you. It's just the only way I can think of to be truly just and . . . godly. To try to make certain that families are not completely ruined."

Tang Lu smiled. It was just a slight twitch of the corners of her straight mouth, and it was without humor or joy; but it was still a smile, the first one Cheney had ever seen on the reserved Chinese woman's face. "I am honored," she said softly, "that my mother and father have offered to care for my children. I would wish this for my children. My mother and father would be better parents than my husband or I will ever be. Give my place to Mr. Han."

Cheney still hesitated.

"That is my decision, Dr. Duvall," Tang Lu said. "You have made yours. I have made mine."

Finally Cheney said, "Very well. Mr. and Mrs. Han, come with me. Zhu Ki, I'll carry Atu Bao, and you must carry Atu Ki. The pier is very dangerous and hard to walk on, and the children are too small to do it themselves. Can you do this?"

"Oh yes, Doctor," the young girl said with more animation than she'd shown for a day and night. "Thank you, thank you, Doctor!"

Grabbing Zhu Ki's seven-year-old son, Cheney muttered blackly, "If one more person says 'Thank you, Doctor,' I'm going to scream!"

The little boy in her arms regarded her gravely.

"Thank you, Doctor," he said.

Cheney melted. Hugging him, she whispered, "Thank the Lord, little Atu Ki. Say thank you to the Lord."

★ ★ ★ ★

"We were attacked by a school of minnows," Coston told Cheney caustically as he lifted Atu Ki into the dinghy. "Dare was scared out of his scarce wits, but he fought 'em like a cornered badger."

"It's not funny," Dare, the cherubic sailor, grunted. "Miss, this lagoon is just about to get impassable."

"It does seem the waves, or tide, or whatever it is, is worse," Cheney agreed anxiously.

"Whatever it is," Dare intoned. "Cap'n says it's like a storm surge before a hurricane. He's thinking there might be one behind it. But I dunno . . . I've never seen fish act so curious. Could be it's just the volcano."

"Or the earthquakes," Cheney said wearily. "Or maybe we are in for a tsunami. If our luck holds, we certainly will have one. Maybe two."

"Anyway, the fish and sharks and things are maddened," Dare went on, ignoring Coston's muttered jeers. "They're not . . . acting right. We saw sharks, about twenty or thirty of 'em, in a feeding frenzy. It ain't right."

"What do you mean?" Cheney asked with dread.

"They swim fast, careless like, and they're real aggressive," Dare replied, his smooth baby features wrinkling. "One of 'em bumped the boat. And what Coston said was true, and it weren't no joke. It was a school of thousands of rainbow fish, and they just clouded around my oar like a swarm of mosquitoes. Just sat there, and I kept bashin' em, and they didn't spook. It don't make no sense."

"Are you telling me," Cheney asked evenly, "that this is the last trip you'll make?"

Coston and Dare looked at each other, and Coston asked dryly, "Ma'am, you gonna be here in another half hour or so? 'Cause if'n you are, I'm guessin' you'll be a pillar of fire. That lava's close. Whoever's left better be gettin' off this beach."

Cheney nodded, knowing they were right.

"Here, ma'am, we brung you two lanterns, and the captain sent his spyglass," Coston said, handing her a heavy canvas sack. "He said to tell you that we're gonna take these people to Lahaina and come back at daylight. We'll patrol up and down this end of the island. You people go find a wet cliff to cling to, and we'll be back at dawn to pick you up."

Cheney swallowed hard and then said clearly, "You are both brave and honorable men, and I thank you for your courage."

Dare said quietly, "Won't you come, ma'am? Looks to me like you should come instead of this here Chinaman."

George Han blanched and shot a shamefaced look at Cheney, who kindly replied, "No, that's not possible. He's that little baby's father, you see. And Mr. Han has acted with great bravery and sacrifice himself, so I know he will be treated with the utmost respect. Now go! And if you pass Shiloh—Mr. Irons—tell him to row with all his might!"

Coston nodded, and they shoved off. Before they disappeared, he lifted his hand in a salute and called, "I'll see you at dawn, ma'am! Me and Dare, we'll find you!"

Cheney held up both her arms in farewell.

23

AIR, FIRE, WATER, OR BLOOD

Cheney started to return to her charges, but as she struggled with the heavy bag she recalled what Coston had said.

Captain Sloane's spyglass . . .

She found the telescoping glass with fine brass fittings, set it, and pressed it to her eye.

At first she saw nothing except whirling blackness. Until now, she hadn't really noticed how thick the smoke from the fires had grown. Raggedy gray ashes floated thick on the heavy hot air. The listless puffs of wind from the sea barely stirred them. She finally became fully aware of the stench of wood smoke, of sulphur and other noxious gases from the bowels of the earth, of the deafening cracks and shrieks of ageless trees burning, of the deep-chested roar of the thunderous sea. She was in a maelstrom.

And so was Shiloh Irons. She caught a moment's glimpse of him as the heavy smoke curled wrathfully this way and that. The lantern, a bleak circle of amber jerking on the front mount of the little dinghy, lit his face and chest and arms. His sculptured features were distorted with agony as he strained, fighting the sea, the smoke, the heat, the world itself. He had been fighting, struggling, ignoring pain and fear and defeat for an eternal night and day and yet another endless night. His muscular arms, in sharp relief in the smoky light, were lumped and bulged, the muscles strained and wracked, as he pumped the oars up and down, up and down, against inhuman odds. His chest, even in the semidarkness, glistened with spray and sweat.

He must be . . . almost . . . dead. His body must be agonized, wracked and screaming in pain. He must be so weary, so fatigued that he can't think. But he just fights on, and on, and on. . . .

And so must I.

She turned and ran down the pier, carelessly now, leaping over missing boards, barely stopping as monstrously strong waves hit her knees so hard she was almost knocked down.

She reached them, the lost ones, the last ones.

"He's coming," she gasped. "Five, if one can row."

They all stared at her, then at each other. They all looked frightened, they all looked ashamed, and they all looked guilty. All of them wanted to live.

None of them wanted to die, especially in Pele's fire.

In the moment of their silence, the lava came rushing down Bain's Stream, a glowing scarlet ribbon that screamed as it flowed, then hissed like a million snakes as it roiled into the sea.

Fang Jinglan screamed, and kept on screaming and screaming.

Leilana kept looking, searching to their left for a sign of her husband and son. She was straining, almost quivering, to go, to run.

Tang Sun and Chen Guifei, the dignified older couple, clasped each other. Fay began to cry against her husband's shoulder.

Pat and Will hugged each other close. Pat was rubbing Will's back as if he were an infant.

Tang Lu turned her back on them. Her hands, as always, were hidden in her tunic. She watched the river of lava coming, so close now, with a blank expression.

Nia screamed but abruptly cut off the involuntary cry. She stepped close to Cheney but did not touch her or speak. She simply stood by her.

"Sunny, Fay, Fang Jinglan," Cheney yelled, "Come on! Two more, but one has to be able to row! Tang Lu! You can go, but you have to try to help row."

Without a word, Tang Lu looked pointedly at the insane waves, looked back at Cheney, shook her head, and turned her back on them.

Will and Pat looked at Cheney, clasped each other around the neck, and shook their heads. "You and Miss Nia must go, Doctor! You're strong. You can row as good as one of us! Me and my brother, we stay together," Will insisted. Tears were rolling down his cheeks.

Cheney stepped up to them, clasped Pat's face, and leaned down to speak to him in as normal a tone as possible. "Are you a Christian?" she asked with intensity.

He stared at her, his Oriental eyes unreadable. Very slightly he shook his head. "I—we don't even know what that means," he said so quietly Cheney could barely hear him.

Cheney drew in a shuddering breath. "Then one of you must go for me!" She turned to Nia with a pity so wrenching that she almost wept. "You have to decide, Nia. This judgment I cannot make."

Nia's hope died in her dark innocent eyes. They filled with tears, she sobbed, then clasping Cheney's hand she cried, "I have to know something. If the lava comes, if we get trapped, we will try swimming, right? You and me, Miss Cheney? We can try to swim, can't we?"

Cheney knew what she meant, exactly, and the fear was almost a physical agony. In the corners of her mind, the little rats, the little dark things, had been gnawing away at the strongholds of faith and reason and wisdom and understanding. . . .

Please, God, I just can't burn . . . and I can't just let sharks . . . sharks . . . kill me . . . if I try to swim but can't, and I go under, and the water gets in my nose and mouth . . . that last moment, that one single moment, if I just breathe in, if I just breathe, just breathe—

Every breath is Mine. Even as I first breathed into My son Adam, so every breath of yours is Mine. Would you turn away from that gift? Would you look at a gift, directly from My hand, and call it evil?

Cheney was crying, though she hadn't known when she started. Nia was waiting.

With a strangled sob Cheney answered, "Every breath we take is from Him, Nia. He will give us breath. Even the last breath we have on this earth, whether it is air, fire, water, or blood, it is from Him."

Nia comprehended only too well the portent of this answer. She sobbed once, then impatiently swiped at her face and said loudly and defiantly, "I stay, Miss Cheney. I don't want to, I'm scared, and I don't know why I have to, but I know that's the truth."

Cheney turned to Will and Pat and said, "Let's go. You two help Sunny and Fay, and I'll help Fang Jinglan. In this sea, both of you will have to half kill yourselves trying to row. And just so you'll be at ease, I don't think Shiloh would have tried it without you."

Both boys, so young, so frightened, still looked dismayed. Pat went first to Tang Lu, who still had her back to the group. He got down on his knees and kissed her hand. "Thank you, Tang Lu. I'll come back for you. But for right now, I promise I will, from this day on, take your children as my own. I'll never leave them. I'll take care of them until I die. I swear."

She looked down at him, touched the top of his head so he would look up at her. She nodded.

Pat hurried to Nia, again threw himself down on his knees and kissed her brown hand. "Forgive me," he said gutterally.

Nia started crying again, but after a moment the old stubborn look came over her face. She fell to her knees and took the thin young man by the shoulders. "You get up right now, Mr. Pat. Take off, and hurry up. You don't need my forgiveness. All you need is Jesus. But since you feel like you owe me, I charge you to go find a Christian and find out all about Him. That's all you owe me."

He looked mystified but nodded, then he and his brother took the old couple by the hands and led them down the pier.

Fang Jinglan started after them, still wailing and weeping. Cheney was going with her, but Leilana called out, "Doctor! Keloki and Ulu Nui—there—coming!"

Cheney turned and saw the two men running across the sand. "Go on, Fang Jinglan, and be careful! Tell Shiloh that I'll be there in just a minute!"

Ulu Nui reached them first. He was barely breathing hard. "Big stream okay! Hot, but okay! Up there—Na'maka's Mirror, Mama! Remember? Na'maka's Mirror!"

Leilana looked mystified. "Na'maka's Mirror?" She shook her head.

"But you've found a place?" Cheney cried urgently, grasping his arm. It was like grabbing an oak log.

He nodded but looked uncertain at the same time. "Too far, we don't go all the way up to it. But we remember it, Doctor. We take you! Everyone go now, yes?" Keloki joined the group.

Cheney said, "I've got to go tell Shiloh not to come back. But you take everyone now, Keloki! Just tell me which way to come to find you!"

Keloki had a mulish look on his face. "You go on, Doctor. I wait for you here. Ulu Nui can take these."

"But—" Cheney decided that arguing would waste more time than doing, so she turned and ran down the pier. Two more pilings on the right-hand side had fallen over, and six of them were leaning, jostling loosely in the surf. Cheney had learned to run from piling to piling on the left-hand side, grabbing them as she ran, and sort of slingshotting herself from one to the other. Every so often a wave washing over the decrepit structure would oblige her to stop and anchor herself on an upright, but generally she was getting pretty fast at making her way up and down this dangerous obstacle course.

The last five lifeboat passengers had made fairly good time. They had just reached the end of the pier when Cheney came running up. Shiloh stayed in the boat, and he was breathing so hard each intake was a groan, each exhale a thrust of his chest.

"Hi, Doc," he wheezed.

In spite of it all, Cheney managed a smile at his usual drawling greeting. "Hi, you. Not tired, are we?"

"Naw," he grunted. "Good evening, Miss Fay. Glad to have you aboard. Watch your step there, Mr. Sunny. Why don't you two sit right back there? Good, good. Who's left, Doc?"

Cheney realized with a start that he didn't know—couldn't know—how many and who the other lifeboat had rescued. The two boats' trips had been staggered. "Just Nia and Tang Lu, of the civilians," she tried to say jauntily.

"And you," he said darkly. Miraculously, he was actually gaining his breath. Even as he pulled and lifted everyone into the lifeboat, he had started taking deep breaths in and blowing them out in measured exhales. Cheney marveled at his strength and stamina.

"Uh . . . yes, me. But Keloki and Ulu Nui and Leilana are taking care of us dumb city folk—they've found a safe place for us, up on the mountain, over there," she said, waving vaguely.

"Oh yeah?" he said with unnatural brightness. "Where?"

"Uh . . . something . . . somebody's mirror," Cheney stammered.

"Say that again?"

"Na'maka's Mirror," Pat put in. "She's Pele's sister."

"Oh, that's real good news," Shiloh said dryly.

Everyone was loaded, so Cheney stood up and took a step backward. Shiloh started to climb the ladder, then looking around at the darkness, the smoke, and the sea, he stayed in the dinghy. He looked up at Cheney with an intensity she'd never seen on any man's face. But his voice was deliberately light. "You leaving now?"

"Yes, I'm going," she said, firmly and without fear, she hoped. "So you don't come back, right? No one's going to be here. You just go on back to the *Brynn Annalea* and stay on board. They're coming back in the morning, Coston and Dare said. I'll see you then."

"Yeah, okay," he said carelessly. "Bye, Doc." He sat down and grabbed the oar.

She gulped. "Um . . . good-bye, Shiloh. God go with you."

After a careless wave of the paddle in farewell, he skillfully turned the dinghy and started yelling at Pat and Will. "Row, you two! Will, you watch me and do exactly what I do. Pat, you watch me and do exactly the opposite of what I do. Me and Will row on this side, you row on the other . . . got it? That's it. . . ."

Cheney stood at the end of the pier, alone.

Her heart felt like a lump of cold dead stone in her chest. Her eyes sprang with bitter, searing tears that burned her more than even the hellish fires she was so close to.

He . . . he left me! He's gone, he . . . didn't even . . . say good-bye!

Wait a minute, stop acting like a hysterical woman! Good grief, so he didn't have a big parting scene . . . after all, you are going to live (aren't I, Lord?) and you will see him tomorrow. He probably doesn't realize how . . . how close to (death?)—the lava and everything—you are. After all, you're not in any more danger than he is!

When Cheney realized she was standing on the end of a pier that was in the direct path of burning lava, and that this same pier was going to collapse any minute right into some shark's lap, and that salvation was back on the beach for the next few minutes anyway, and she was standing there moping and frittering because Shiloh hadn't had a dramatic death scene with her . . .

"Lord, please let this be the last stupid thing I do for a while," she yelled to the heavens. Then she turned and ran.

The faithful Keloki was waiting for her, a pillar standing at the end of the pier, arms crossed, frowning at the sea. "I carry you, Doctor?" he asked politely.

"Good heavens, no," she blustered. "If there's one thing I've been practicing the last night and day, it's running. You just go, Keloki, and don't worry about me. I'll keep up."

They ran down the beach, skimming along at the very edge of the waves. The coconut trees had all burned down to fiery stumps. Even as Cheney watched, the first fingers of lava ran onto the sands of the beach. She was morbidly fascinated to see that it wasn't running evenly, like water; lumpy fingers ran ahead, then seemed to slow as the rest between the fingers caught up. It wasn't moving very fast, as she had imagined with dread as she watched it come down the mountain. It was lethargic and chunky, sometimes folding over itself as it moved forward.

But it was definitely coming.

They ran and ran, then Cheney had to stop. She half hoped that

Keloki wouldn't notice. The air, with the nearness of the lava, had become the temperature of the inside of a furnace. She tried hard to breathe it in, but her mind—and nose and chest and throat—rejected it. She slid to a stop, put her hands on her knees, and leaned over, gasping and retching.

The problem, she thought clinically, *is that it burns your nose. It hurts, really bad . . . so you quit breathing it in. Come on, Cheney. You're a woman of some intellect. You can convince your nose to stop sending those imbecilic "stop breathing" signals to your brain!*

So she lectured herself as she gasped.

Looking up, she saw no sign of Keloki.

She was half relieved, half terrified.

Then he appeared out of the blackness, frowning. "Miss Doctor! I carry you!"

Cheney shook her head mutely, then took off running again.

Resigned, Keloki moved in front to lead.

Finally they made it across the expanse of beach to the cliff above Brynn's Stream. In the firestorm's fury Cheney couldn't hear the water, and in the suffocating smoke she couldn't see it.

"It's hot, Doctor! But can wade it," Keloki bawled in her ear. He looked down with disapproval and shook his head. "Too many clothes, Doctor. Other lady, Nia, she take off all white stuff under." He pointed to a shabby pile of lace and linen lying by the side of the stream.

"Nia took off her petticoats?" Cheney gasped. This shocked her, perhaps more than anything that had happened so far. But sternly she gathered her wits and ordered, "All right. So will I. You go on, Keloki. I'm right behind you. We're following the stream uphill, right?"

He grinned knowledgeably, and Cheney could feel herself blush. She knew it was silly, a sort of nasty-nice delicacy, to be modest about removing an underskirt right now, under these life-and-death circumstances. But on the other hand there was no sense in throwing out all modesty and convention just because—

You're going to die? the nasty little rat in Cheney's mind supplied.

Keloki was saying, "Okay, I go on. Follow stream. I'll be up there."

Cheney nodded, and he slid down the side of the ravine.

Hurriedly Cheney yanked up her overskirt, found the tie of her single petticoat, and fumbled to untie it. The problem was that Nia always tied them so securely, it generally took a second person to see how to untie the knots. Impatiently Cheney fumbled and pulled, then finally yanked it, breaking the satin ribbon ties. She shimmied a little and the underskirt fell to the ground in a sodden, filthy heap.

"Goodness! I feel about ten pounds lighter!" Cheney said to no one in particular.

She sat down, groping below with her feet for a secure step.

Suddenly a thunderstruck look made her eyes widen, but they were unfocused, blank. Her mouth opened a little, and her lips quivered.

She saw Shiloh.

Before her, with clarity, she saw Shiloh. She saw the raging sea, the black side of the *Brynn Annalea* soaring above him, the little dinghy tossed fitfully against it. She saw him sit down, grimace, and lift the oar.

She saw him paddling like a madman for the barrier reefs.

Still blind, still unseeing, she scrambled to her feet. "O God, no, don't let him! He's coming back! Oh no!"

The vision broke into a million wisps, insubstantial as the tendrils of smoke she now saw.

But Cheney knew he was coming back.

She turned and ran back onto the beach.

As she ran she saw that the first fingers of lava, the longest grasping claws, were only about ten feet from the tide mark.

She ran into the surf, taking hard grinding steps, her teeth gritted, hoping against hope that she would stomp anything deadly.

She ran, her mouth and nose on fire, burning, pain piled on top of pain. Her chest felt as if she were being stabbed.

The pier appeared, wreathed by the devilish smoke. More pilings were down, more boards were lost in the sea.

Cheney flew over them. She was ankle-deep in water now, and the biggest, cruelest waves smashed against her thighs. She stumbled, clinging desperately to this piling, the next . . .

She fell to her knees, got up again, took two more steps, fighting the hateful sucking of the water at her legs.

The end of the pier was still standing, but it shook as if from mortal fear.

She stood at the end, straining on tiptoe at the last board, and shrieked, "Shiloh! Shiloh!"

A wicked gust of wind tossed her screams back in her face, mocking her.

"Shiloh! I'm here! Hurry, hurry!"

She saw nothing, only blackness.

"Fool!"

The spyglass, which she had tucked securely in her waistband before following Keloki, had been cutting into her for the last half hour. Yanking it out, sobbing, groaning, she set it, then pressed it to her eye so hard her eyes watered in protest at the pain.

Pulling it down, bowing her head, Cheney took a deep breath and ordered herself to calm down. Then, with deliberate movements, she lifted the glass to her eye.

She found him. He was rowing so fast and hard she could barely see the oar. But he seemed to be standing still; she watched, holding her breath so she could be motionless.

A wave tossed him, the stern of the dinghy lifted high above his head. He wasn't making headway, she saw with horror, because the boat was sloshing with water.

And he couldn't stop rowing to bail.

Behind Cheney, she heard a horrible screeching sound, and without turning to look, she knew that the far end of the pier was collapsing.

"Row! Row!" she groaned between teeth so gritted that shooting pains gripped her jaws.

Shiloh rowed and fought valiantly.

Cheney saw one—three—a dozen—more, she couldn't count them because they were swimming, darting, jerking, all around the little boat. Black triangular fins, appearing and disappearing as quick as blinks, here, then there, turning, swirling . . .

"Sharks! Oh, Shiloh! Shiloh, hurry! Hurry!" she screamed.

Wrenching the eyeglass away from her face, she strained her eyes to see, to try to judge . . .

Just a glimmer, just a smudge of light, only a little way out. . . .

How far? Cheney's mind screamed impotently. *A mile? Two miles? You don't know! Can he make it? How long? HOW LONG!*

Pressing the glass to her eye again, she set her jaw and focused on the lonely figure in the pitiful little boat. He still fought, but Cheney could see that each swell, every few moments, swamped the boat. It was doomed. Shiloh was doomed. She screamed again, and he looked up, startled.

He had heard her.

Grimly he set to paddling again.

Then, impossibly, something black, something malevolent, came up, crawling on the dipping oar, writhing, oily, flailing tentacles—

Shiloh stood up, lifted the oar with the oily blackness fouling it, shook it, and shouted out with a fierceness rarely seen in men except in deadly battle.

And so it was. A manta ray, about six feet in diameter, had thrown itself up onto the paddle.

Shiloh shook the oar—the manta flailed as if it were made of thick oil—Shiloh threw the oar, far out into the maelstrom.

Then, with no panic, with a curious grace, he dove into the boiling water.

Cheney tried to scream again, but her voice was gone.

She heard nothing.

She saw nothing, except the little round circle of vision surrounded by black, twelve inches in front of her.

There was nothing.

After an eternity of deafness, muteness, mindless terror, she saw his blond head surface.

"Shiloh, sharks! Shiloh, swim, oh, Shiloh, swim! Sharks!"

He cut the water cleanly, never wavering, never faltering.

A black triangular fin cut right in front of him.

He struck it, stopped, went under.

Cheney dropped the glass, her fingers bloodless and dead. She dropped to her knees and closed her eyes. "God," she said softly. "Let him live, please. I ask this mercy, please, Lord. In Jesus' blessed name, let him live. . . ."

Yes, Lord. If it must be, so be it. I will die for him. Take me instead. Please.

Something hit her, hard. In the pit of her stomach. She bent, then tumbled, dizzy, lost.

She was in the water, and something was pulling at her.

Was it a shark?

Fuzzily she thought, *Doesn't hurt. Yet.*

Water in my nose . . . Lord . . . can I . . . please?

She grabbed her nose with her thumb and forefinger, holding it. She held her breath and squeezed her eyes tightly shut against the hot salt water. She was going around, up, then in circles, backward, tumbling . . . where was the surface?

Where is my breath, Lord?

She felt . . . something.

It was hot, stinging air. On her face.

Very slowly, as if she were in a slow-motion dream, she let go of her nostrils and cautiously took a breath. She choked, gagged, but then sucked in great lungfuls of air. Then she opened her eyes.

Shiloh Irons looked down at her. She was floating, lying in his arms like a limp little sock doll.

He grinned. "Hi, Doc."

24

AND SHILOH, WHO BREATHED

"You're alive."

"Yeah. You are too."

Cheney marveled at this for a while, staring blankly into Shiloh's face. *Thank you, Lord, for his life . . . for my life . . . for Your mercy.*

She roused a little, reality seeping back in. Shiloh was carrying her in his arms . . . but she was floating . . . wasn't she? "We're in the water!"

"Be still, Doc. Just relax for a second, can't you?"

"But . . . the rockfish . . . and . . . and . . . sharks!" She flailed wildly, and he pulled her close, pinning down her arms.

"Listen! Listen to me!" he ordered sharply. "We're okay!"

"We're okay? What does that mean! We're not okay! I saw a shark— I saw you—I thought you—"

"Oh, that," he scoffed. "Yeah, well, that ol' lua was in just as much of a hurry to get out of this accursed lagoon as I was. The worst problem we had was tryin' to get out of each other's way."

"Stop joking about it! I thought you were . . . were—and you're joking about it!"

"Sorry, sorry," he said repentantly. "But it is the truth. All of the fish and sharks and even the jellyfish are trying to get out of this death-trap, out to sea now."

"But why?"

He glanced at her with a trace of pity. " 'Cause the lava's reached the water, Doc. You really didn't realize it, did you?"

"No. No, not really."

"Did you know that the pier was collapsing? That's why I had to jerk you into the sea?"

"What!" Cheney struggled in his arms, turning to look back behind her.

All that was left of the pier were the last four uprights. Even as she looked, one of them leaned over in a sickly way and then disappeared.

"So, at least sharks and jellyfish are the least of our worries right now," he said, narrowing his eyes to mischievous slits.

"What . . . what. . . ?" Cheney suddenly perceived how shrill she sounded. She shut up, cleared her throat, and became still and passive. Immediately she could tell that Shiloh was moving faster, with more ease. "Then what is the most of our worries?" She sounded a little less hysterical.

"Just the same tired ol' lava," he drawled.

"Oh. Where . . . is it? Where are we?" Cheney could see nothing except his form, the tatters of the white shirt he wore, and a faint glimmer of his face. With odd fascination she thought how nice it was to see a real face, instead of the filthy gray wraith-faces they'd all had for the last so many hours. It occurred to her that she felt clean, and it was wonderful, even though the water was sandy and rough and much too warm. Still, she was grateful, for she felt she'd been filthy for ages and ages.

" . . . wading to Brynn's Stream," Shiloh was saying. "The lava's coming down at an angle, with the lowest point over at Bain's Stream. So it's reaching the water at different times. We're . . . uh . . . outrunning it, I guess you'd say."

Now Cheney paid full attention to her surroundings. She twisted so she could look behind them. Too close, it seemed, back where there had once been beach was now a glowing crimson river. She heard the sea boiling like a thousand feral cats hissing, their teeth bared. "Oh, dear, maybe I should—could I . . . um . . . run, or wade? Surely we could move faster if you weren't having to drag me along!"

He shook his head and bent close down to her face. "I don't mind. Seems like most of the time it's you who's dragging me along. Kinda nice for a change."

"Shiloh! This is not funny!"

"I know. Sorry. Anyway, the answer is still no. With all those wet clothes you're wearing, you couldn't move, much less run. So the one thing that'll make it easier is if you'll just relax, go limp. Less resistance that way."

"Less resistance," Cheney repeated between gritted teeth, "is not exactly my way."

"I noticed."

She tried to relax, but of all things this was just about as difficult as any task she'd set for herself. She was as tense, as highly strung, as a piano wire. When she got her shoulders lax, her legs stiffened. When she got her stomach unknotted, her shoulders stiffened back up. Her neck felt like an iron bolt.

"It's no use," she muttered. "I just can't do it."

"Never mind. We're almost there. No, Doc, don't look back there. It won't do any good. I promise you, we're going to be okay."

She took a deep breath, squeezed her eyes shut, and murmured, "All right. I trust you."

He looked down at her, startled. But her eyes were closed, and she said nothing more. He fought on. Behind them, creeping closer, was the lava spill, boiling the water close to the beach on contact. Though every fiber of Shiloh's being fought against it, he went farther out, deeper, away from the superheated currents of water in the shallows. It made the going harder, and slower. But still, it wouldn't do them any good to get there quicker if they were parboiled.

Ahead was the most welcome light he'd ever seen. It was a lantern, far up on the ridge above Brynn's Stream. "Hey!" he yelled, raising one arm and waving. Cheney was startled and jerked, and he pulled her closer, unthinking. For a few moments she just clasped him around the waist, holding on to him, savoring his strength and comforting presence.

"Hey, we're here!" he shouted.

He heard a return shout and was fairly sure it was Keloki.

Shiloh grabbed Cheney, striding through the water with new strength, actually creating a wake behind them. Now she clung to him with desperation. He had to go out seaward, around the lowering escarpments that ridged the stream. He knew that they didn't have time to climb up on the beach and run up to the ascending path. He'd have to come into the stream from the sea and work his way up.

"Listen to me, Doc," he said urgently. "For a little while—not long—we're going to be in deep water. I'm going to swim around this ridge, okay? On the other side is the mouth of Brynn's Stream."

"Yes, I understand," Cheney said calmly. "What do I do?"

"I'll pull you, just like I did Mrs. Winslow. I'll crook my arm under your chin, and if you'll relax, you'll just come right along. You take a deep breath and hold it. That inflates your lungs and makes you float. When you get uncomfortable, take another. Got it?"

"Yes. I'm ready." She took a deep breath, held it, and was a little surprised to feel her body lighten and float upward. Shiloh gently crooked his arm under her neck, and she felt them gliding along. He didn't try to fight the waves crashing around them. Cheney could feel him knifing, making his body long and stiff, his one arm extended, so that he cut through the middle of the waves instead of them tossing him. Of course, that meant that they spent a great deal of time underwater, and Cheney felt panicky. But with a great effort of will, she made herself concentrate on how best to deal with it. After the third try she realized that if she did as Shiloh had first told her—let her body be completely relaxed and loose—when she went underwater she just sort of rippled with the force of the water.

She was concentrating so hard on doing her part that she barely noticed the terrible effort Shiloh was expending. He swam steadily, never slowing or weakening. But finally he went limp, let go of Cheney, and stumbled a little. She realized they had reached the mouth of the stream, which was waist-deep. They staggered up the narrow gorge a little ways, until the water was just above their knees. But Shiloh was too spent to say anything. He was groaning again, each breath an agony. Helplessly Cheney laid her hand on his back. There was nothing else she could do.

Only God gives us our breath, a faint little voice in her mind said. *God give him breath. . . .*

Keloki stood with them, solid and real and welcoming, before they had even seen the lantern light approaching.

"Keakea! You!"

Shiloh grunted something unintelligible.

"He's out of breath," Cheney explained anxiously. "He just swam for about fifty miles, pulling me like a dead weight."

"F-fifty miles?" Shiloh rasped.

"Don't try to talk now, you fool," Cheney scolded.

Even in his extremity, Shiloh half grinned.

Keloki looked from one to the other, clearly puzzled by the haoles' odd sense of humor. Shrugging, he said, "Breathe good, Keakea, and breathe fast. We gotta go. We gotta hurry."

"What a surprise," Shiloh growled. "Just . . . gimme a minute."

"Go ahead. I'll wait," Cheney declared.

"We'll wait," Keloki said.

Shiloh nodded gratefully, bent over, put his hands on his knees, and convulsively gulped for air. Cheney, her hand still lightly placed on his straining back, turned to Keloki.

"The others?" she asked anxiously.

"Up there. Waiting for us. You didn't come," Keloki said reproachfully. "I come back for you."

"Thank you, Keloki," Cheney said. "But I had to come back for Shiloh, you see."

Keloki nodded, though it couldn't have made sense to him.

Right now, it only made sense to Cheney. And to Shiloh, who breathed.

★　★　★　★

They worked their way upstream.

The water varied from knee-deep to waist-deep and flowed swiftly. The stream bed was rocky and treacherous. To their right, on the other side of the ridge, the glow from the lava lake was a baleful crimson, and the heat rolling down into the gorge from it was stifling. A dense dark jungle lay to their left.

But Brynn's Stream wasn't hot. It was warm, yes, and must have been swollen somewhat, for small rocks and sticks and debris were tumbling along, hitting the three waders' feet. Still, it obviously hadn't been corrupted by the volcano—yet.

"You okay, Doc?" Shiloh called for the dozenth time. Keloki led, Cheney was in the middle, and Shiloh stayed close behind her. He always grabbed her arm when she stumbled.

"Yes, I'm just fine. Don't worry."

Ahead of them rose the dark colossus of Mount Haleakala. They could see it, sometimes, when the smoke writhed away. The dull orange of fire wreathed the heights, though it did seem to be far up, near the summit.

They saw another lantern ahead.

Nia ran to Cheney and almost knocked her down as she climbed up onto the small left-hand bank. "Miss Cheney, what in the world were you thinking? You scared us to death!"

"I—"

"She rescued me," Shiloh said.

"Hardly!" Cheney scoffed.

"You did, Doc," he said, suddenly grave. "I know it. You know it."

They stared at each other, forgetting everyone else.

Keloki reluctantly interrupted this emotional interlude. "We have to keep going, Keakea. Can't stay here."

With a weary glance at the menacing glow on the other side of the stream bank, Shiloh nodded. "Keloki, you lead. I'll bring up the rear. Everyone all right? Can everyone walk? How about you, Miss Tang Lu? How's that leg?"

Cheney, to her shame, had completely forgotten Tang Lu's centipede bites.

Tang Lu, a dusky shadow, answered, "Miss Nia has doctored me. I feel very well, thank you. I can walk."

"You sure?"

She nodded confidently. "Thank you, yes."

"Okay, let's march."

They crashed through the jungle, bearing directly left. Keloki, leading, carried a long sharp machete. Alongside him, Ulu Nui carried one of the lanterns from the *Brynn Annalea*. Behind them Leilana confidently stamped through the thick undergrowth. Then came Tang Lu, Nia, and Cheney. Shiloh trailed them, carrying the other lantern.

Cheney looked neither to the right nor the left. She walked, fought, blindly following the rough path that Keloki was literally cutting out of the thick jungle. She was filthy again, and so hot she felt fevered. She saw curious movements, little frightening dartings in her peripheral vision, but ignored them, knowing that such worrisome little hallucinations were a sign of fatigue. She hurt. Everything hurt. Every muscle was sore, her clothes felt like hundred-weights, her face felt burned. Her mouth was parched, her throat raw. But she walked on.

She looked downward, doggedly watching her feet, ordering them to take this step, then that. Nia trudged along in front of Cheney, and Cheney literally barreled into her. Keloki had ordered a stop.

They were in impenetrable jungle, but they were facing another stream. This one hurtled over great knobby black rocks, whitewater spume spraying high into the air. It steamed.

"Another one," Cheney grumbled.

"It is said there are a thousand and one streams on Mount Haleakala," Leilana declared.

"Wonderful," Cheney said. "But do we have to cross all of them tonight? We're away from the lava flow, aren't we? Couldn't we just stay here?"

Shiloh hurried up to talk to Keloki. The others gathered close, listening. "What do you think?" Shiloh asked.

Keloki turned to face up the mountain. The fires were closer. The smoke was beginning to trickle down. "I think Pele's fire will come down this water," he said quietly. "I think she started over there, close to haole hale. But I think she's coming this way."

Crossing his arms, Shiloh stared up at the live coals of the heights. Then he turned and said reluctantly, "I think he's right. From out at sea—I guess the *Brynn Annalea* was about a mile and a half away—you could see the fissure. It was wide at the north end, and the flow was a lot faster close by the villa. But the crack ran sideways, along the mountain, not down it. It was thinner over at this end, so the lava flow was definitely slower. But I do think the fissure extends over this far. I judged it to be past the stream that feeds the Seven Sacred Pools—this is it, isn't it, Keloki?"

He nodded and pointed. "Fourth pool is way up there."

"But . . . wouldn't one of the grottoes, with one of the big waterfalls, be the safest place?" Cheney asked wearily. "I mean, is this volcano really going to overcome this stream? Shiloh, you told me it's enormous, flowing downhill like a loose cannon, all the way from the summit! And that two of the pools are huge!"

Shiloh shrugged. "I just don't know, Doc. I guess no one really knows. But one thing I do know is that this jungle is all going to burn. It's bound to, sooner or later."

Cheney felt like throwing a tantrum. She wanted to sit down and refuse to move and never get up again. Mentally she railed at the volcano, at the fires, at the mountain, even at Keloki. But sullenly she admitted to herself that this would do no one any good, least of all herself.

I'm just so tired, so deathly, painfully tired. . . .

No more than anyone else, she scolded herself. *Imagine Nia and Tang Lu! They're so small, so delicate, like children. You big strong ox, you ought to be ashamed of yourself!*

"All right," she said as sturdily as she could. "Then let's go on. Now, where did you say we should go, Keloki? To someone's mirror?"

"Yeah, to Na'maka's Mirror," he said eagerly. "We can hide from Pele there."

★　★　★　★

"This is it?" Shiloh asked uncertainly. "That's Na'maka's Mirror?"

"No, no, Keakea," Keloki answered disdainfully. "This *goes* to Na'maka's Mirror."

Shiloh looked doubtful. "Uh . . . think I can fit?"

Keakea grinned. "I can. Ulu Nui can. Leilana can. You skinny haole, you fit."

Everyone stared at the round black hole in the side of the mountain. It was about three feet in diameter, an almost perfect circle.

"Miss Cheney . . ." Nia whispered uncertainly, moving close to her. "I don't know about this . . ."

Cheney sighed and looked around. The jungle on their right was on fire. It couldn't have been more than a hundred feet away, raging and crackling, the heat stifling. To their left, farther away and below them, the second lava fountain was still raging. "I think we have to do this, Nia," she said as confidently as she could. "I'll tell you what. I'll make a pact with you. As you go through, you pray for me. As I go, I'll pray for you."

"A-all right."

"Okay, guess we'll go in the same order we've been walking," Shiloh said with an air of decision. "Lead on, Keloki."

The big man dropped to his knees, wiggled through the opening, and pulled the lantern in. It lit the tunnel for about a one-foot diameter. "Gets better," he called, his voice echoing weirdly out of the hole. "I'm going on, make room for everyone."

Leilana went, then Ulu Nui. Tang Lu dropped to her knees and unconcernedly crawled in. Nia dropped in front of the hole and looked back at Cheney with anguish. "Miss Cheney, I don't like dark, closed-in places. I . . . can't help it. It . . . it . . . really, really scares me."

"I'm right behind you," Cheney said quietly. "And I'm starting to pray for you right now. Turn around and start praying for me. You promised."

Nia took a deep, shuddering breath, turned, and scooted into the tunnel like a scuttling spider. Cheney heard her whispering to herself, praying. Nia crawled fast, zigzagging a little, and Cheney realized that she must have her eyes closed. Quickly Cheney crawled in behind her, murmuring a prayer just loud enough so that Nia could hear.

They crawled for what seemed a long way and a long time, watching the blob of yellow light flickering ahead. The floor of the tunnel was like ground glass and cut their knees. Cheney saw lots of dark crawling things, just outside the lantern's light, and she deliberately looked away from them. In front of her, Nia kept skittering along, muttering. Then Cheney heard Tang Lu make an "oomph" sound.

"So sorry. Please excuse me, Miss Tang Lu," Nia twittered nervously. "I didn't see you."

"Didn't see her?" Behind Cheney, Shiloh's voice floated, full of mirth.

"For your information, Mr. Big Iron Man, I've got my eyes closed tight, and I aim to keep them shut!" Nia snapped. She even turned to "look" at him accusingly, which was even more comical, because she did indeed keep her eyes closed.

"Sorry, Miss Nia," Shiloh said, fighting to keep from chuckling.

"I should hope so," Nia muttered, then turned around and kept crawling.

But just a few feet beyond her, Tang Lu was standing. She knelt, though she carefully didn't touch Nia, as she was sure the girl would ricochet off the walls for hours if she felt something brush her. "Miss Nia," she said softly. "We can stand up now. Would you like me to lead you?"

"Hmm?" Nia opened one eye cautiously and saw that Tang Lu was standing. "No, no, this is much better, thank you. I just don't like something pressing in on me up, down, and all around. At least here is some room for us and air both."

Cheney and Shiloh reached them and stood, but both of them had to bend over, for the tunnel was only about five and a half feet tall. But still, it was better than crawling along on their scraped and raw hands and knees.

They hurried now, Keloki in front almost running.

The tunnel was hot and airless. Cheney noticed that the walls were solid black, a uniform roughhewn, sharp rock. "You know what? I think this is a lava tube," she speculated.

"A what?" Shiloh asked.

"A lava tube. Sometime a long time ago, hot lava was flowing down the mountain. But the outside of the flow cooled, and hotter lava kept on coming through, making this tunnel. I read about them somewhere. Sometime."

"Oh. So we're in an old lava tunnel. Is that good or bad?"

Wryly Cheney replied, "I don't know."

"I say it's good."

"All right," Cheney said generously. "Then so do I."

Like the mere touch of a silk swath, a wisp of cool air brushed Cheney's cheek. She stood alertly, banging her head on the ceiling of the tunnel.

"Doc, be careful," Shiloh rasped.

But Cheney ignored him, hurrying to join the others, who had stopped.

Keloki held the lantern out at arm's length. The tunnel ended abruptly, and only black space showed beyond. Cheney stopped and looked over the edge of the precipice.

Small, narrow stone steps, cut into the side of the cliff, led downward. Glimmering far below was a reflection, a still and quiet water reflection of a faint red glare. Startled, Cheney looked up. The walls of this canyon were hundreds of feet above them, and from here the red of fire and the heat of the inferno were faint and faraway.

They had reached Na'maka's Mirror.

25

THE ULTIMATE PRICE

It was an ancient secret place.

The steps carved into the cliff below the lava tube were man-made, but the men who had hewn them were long dead. Aeons ago, in some earth-shattering volcano when Maui was young, the terrific weight of the lava flowing through the lava tube had overcome this part of the earth. A great plug had fallen, crashing straight downward hundreds of feet to form an almost perfectly round sinkhole. The walls surrounding the sinkhole were undercut so that the cliffs rose above it at a sheltering angle. The circle of red sky above the seven refugees was much smaller in diameter than the glade where they rested, two hundred feet below the surface of the earth.

A perfectly round pool was at the exact center of the crater. It was still, unmoved by the infernal heat roiling so far above and unaffected by the fury of the earth below. The bank surrounding the tiny lake was small, only about eight feet at the widest part. Through the ages the rock had crumbled, seeds had settled, and tropical plants had taken hold. The entire bank was covered with a soft, fragrant moss and *uluhe* ferns. Ohia and olapa trees, those hardy survivors of all of Hawaii's temper tantrums, grew in one corner. Scraggly shrubs no more than three feet high, the ohia tree even had a few pink pompon blooms.

Directly across from the lava tube that the refugees had come through was an identical opening high up in the cliff, with stone steps leading up to it. But from that end of the lava tube, a small waterfall descended. It didn't fall into the pool, as the cliff was about eight feet away from it. But as the stream fell from the undercut cliff, it formed a lovely shower. The water was lukewarm, but sweet.

The eight exhausted travelers descended the steps without a word. As one, they moved to the blessed streams of water flowing down the mountainside. They stood still, faces upturned, eyes closed, and let the clean water wash away the grime, the weariness, and even some of the fear.

For the first time in many, many hours, they felt safe.

Cheney, her shoulders stooped with exhaustion, her face pale and drawn, walked slowly to the pool. She sank down on the bank, pulled her filthy, ragged skirt up to her knees, and struggled to take off her boots. Her feet felt like great lumps of hot dough.

"Here, Doc. I'll help you." Shiloh's voice was gentle.

Cheney nodded and maneuvered around so that Shiloh could remove her water-soaked boots. When he did she immediately turned and stuck her feet in the water. It felt cool, not cold. Cheney thought it was the most soothing, restful sensation she'd ever felt.

Shiloh stripped his own boots off with some difficulty, then sat beside her. He didn't even bother to roll up the legs of his breeches when he put his feet in the pool. Cheney glanced at him, and for the first time, he looked tired. His shoulders were bent, his hands listlessly down at his sides. She took his hand and held it. They sat without speaking.

Soon everyone else joined them, sitting around the pool, soaking their tired feet. It was like some long-ago, half-forgotten dream; they had all been brought together for a purpose, for a reason, by some forces that were not quite understood. They were here now . . . waiting.

"Na'maka-o-Kaha'i is Pele's older sister, the goddess of the sea," Keloki said dreamily. "This place used to be called Kipuka Na'maka. It means an opening, a doorway. Na'maka and Pele, they fight. Pele lives in the fire, and Na'maka quenches it. Kipuka Na'maka was kapu for as long as anyone remembers. We believe this pool goes all the way down to the sea, and then to the end of the world."

"Why do you call it Na'maka's Mirror now?" Shiloh asked curiously.

"My father's father," Keloki said proudly. "He didn't mean to come here. It was kapu, but he found the hallway in and was curious. When he came back, he told us he'd found Na'maka's Mirror. We've called it that ever since." He looked around restlessly, and he and Ulu Nui frowned. "I've never been here before. My father's father and my father told us it was bad mana to come here and disturb Na'maka's Mirror."

"But how did you know where it was?" Shiloh asked, astonished.

Keloki shrugged and looked down, idly making circles in the water with one foot. "Me and Ulu Nui, we find hallway. Think maybe

Na'maka let us come in, hide from Pele."

Cheney started and looked around as if a veil had been lifted from her eyes. "I believe," she said clearly, making everyone turn to stare at her, startled, "that the Lord Jesus Christ spared our lives this night. I believe that He brought us to this place of safety. I believe that He watches over us, each of us, and that we have nothing to fear anymore."

She waited. No one said a word. They all just looked at her with varying expressions. Tang Lu looked as politely distant as ever, sitting by herself on the other side of the pool. But she listened closely. Shiloh smiled a little, staring down into the dark depths of the water. Nia nodded, both with understanding and agreement. Keloki and Leilana, sitting close together, seemed a little confused, but not upset. Ulu Nui did look troubled but said nothing.

Cheney said quietly, "I am not criticizing you, Keloki, and I intend no disrespect. My Lord does not look kindly upon people who arrogantly scoff at those who don't believe in Him. So if you won't be offended, I would like to say a prayer of thanks to God for His mercy upon us all during this terrible time."

Keloki, Leilana, and Ulu Nui exchanged glances. Then Keloki nodded permission to Cheney.

She bowed her head and prayed a simple prayer:

"Lord of Heaven and Earth, God of Creation, You are also our loving Father, and we thank You for Your mercies and watch care this long night. We look to You, Father, for our path, for our knowledge, for our lives—for our very breath. Thank You for Your Son, who died for us all. Thank You for our safety. Thank You for this place. Thank You for our lives. Amen."

No one spoke for a long time.

Leilana roused and got to her feet. "We have coconuts," she announced. "We have water. We eat, then sleep, okay?"

"First," Cheney said firmly, "we doctor. Every cut, every scrape, every scratch, every sting, every bite. No one here is going to go septic on me. Not after all we've been through." She began to struggle to her feet, but Shiloh pulled her back down.

"I'll do it, Doc. You rest."

Nia jumped up, brushed off her filthy skirt briskly and uselessly, and said, "Finally, something I can do! Both of you sit still. I'll tend to everyone. And you just leave me alone, Miss Cheney. I haven't done anything yet. Everybody else has carried us, babied us, saved us, rescued us, kept us alive. I guess I can slap some iodine on scratches, thank you very much. Besides, you can't do it anyway."

"Why not?" Cheney asked, bewildered.

"Well, where's your medical bag?" Nia asked innocently.

"Why—I—it's—"

Nia sniffed. "You don't know, but I do. I've never in my life known you so tired and worn out that you forgot your medical bag. You'd prob'ly be putting laudanum on our cuts and giving us carbolic acid to drink."

Cheney giggled weakly. "You may be right. I'm having a hard time . . . gathering my thoughts right now."

Nia softened. "I know, Miss Cheney, I know. But I can tell you that you've done your part. You've done all that God required of you this night. Now rest."

Cheney nodded, so grateful she couldn't speak.

Leilana, Ulu Nui, and Keloki had salvaged a lot of things that had gotten loose and lost and forgotten in the last day and night. Leilana had carried Walker's medical bag since they'd left the villa. She had also picked up Shiloh's hat and canvas duster when he'd carelessly tossed them away on the pier after the lifeboat had come the first time and he'd decided to go back to pick up the other dinghy. Cheney's hat and jacket had been left on the beach like refuse, and Leilana had picked them up. She also kept track of the two lanterns the sailors had brought. All of this she had stowed in an enormous canvas bag she carried on her back. In addition, she had water skins, kukui nuts for candles, lucifer matches, and a bag of mangoes she'd grabbed from her kitchen as they'd left the villa.

Keloki and Ulu Nui had carried water, matches, machetes, axes, and rope. When they left the group on the beach to search out a place for them to go, they had prudently stopped and harvested several coconuts from the palms on the beach before they burned. They'd thoughtfully grabbed two green ones for the medicinal gel.

Nia had kept up with Cheney's medical bag until they'd left the beach. Then Leilana had offered to carry it for her. Gratefully Nia had let her. The bag full of surgical instruments and bottles was heavy and felt as if it gained a pound or so with each step she took as she ran.

Keloki and Ulu Nui cracked coconuts and shared a little of the milk with everyone. Then they peeled away the sweet white meat from the tough husk, and Leilana served everyone a mango and chunks of the juicy coconut meat. Cheney thought that manna from heaven could not have tasted so delicious.

Nia attended to everyone's scrapes and scratches, which were profuse. All had mild heat burns, like sunburns, on their faces and hands. Keloki, Shiloh, and Ulu Nui had blisters around their eyes, and their mouths were burned and cracked from prolonged exposure to the steam as they had crossed back and forth Bain's Stream. Nia doctored every single injury, no matter how small, that she could see in the indifferent lantern light. No one spoke except to thank her.

Cheney dragged herself over to the cliff wall, shifted until she found a comfortable way to lean up against it to support her back, and ate in silence. Shiloh sat close to her. She noticed that he only ate two bites of mango and three pieces of coconut but drank great quantities of water. Without speaking, with only a tired smile, he lay down and immediately fell asleep.

Cheney ate slowly, her body gradually loosening, coming to a rest.

Her thoughts were formless, just disconnected and vague impressions and sensations of vast relief and a sense of security. She smiled a little as she watched Shiloh sleep.

I love him. . . .

Cheney jerked up, scraping her back against the rough cliff wall, almost choking.

What? What was—did I . . . ?

Sudden desolation swept over her, defeating her utterly. Now bitter and powerful, her thoughts were loud, insistent, accusing. Unbidden, unwanted, tears stung her eyes.

I can't do this! I must not! I can't let myself love Shiloh! O God. What have I done, Lord? How could I have been so foolish, so blind? How could I have . . . deceived myself so utterly? Even worse . . . to pretend to ignore it, to pretend to You that I was guarded, that my heart was shielded, that I just wanted to be . . . his friend? And now . . . what do I do? What can I do?

In despair, she sank to the fragrant moss, closing her eyes, weeping silently. Her fingers dug into the soft moss, and the fragrance, refreshing and pure, filled her nostrils.

. . . for a sweet savor, a sacrifice made by fire unto the Lord . . .

Those were Cheney's last thoughts that terrible, endless night.

★ ★ ★ ★

"Do you feel feverish?" Nia asked Tang Lu anxiously.

"No. Your medicine—it's good. The bites are much better now."

"They feel better, but I sure can't see them too good," Nia complained. "Where's Keloki? Maybe we could put some of those kukui nuts in the lantern, get more light."

"I think I am fine, Miss Nia," Tang Lu said politely. "Perhaps we shouldn't waste the kukui nuts. And I must be honest; I would like to sleep."

"Me too," Nia admitted. "Okay, I'll just dab on a little carbolic acid and put on a clean bandage."

Tang Lu submitted to Nia's ministrations. She was closer to the little waterfall, leaning against a big boulder. Nearby on her left Cheney slept. Just beyond her was Shiloh, lying on his back with his hands on his chest. Leilana had folded up his overcoat and put it under his head. Nia worried because Cheney didn't have a pillow, but then Leilana made a makeshift pillow for her from her jacket. Cheney had stirred restlessly when Leilana arranged it under her head but hadn't awakened.

Tang Lu watched Nia gravely, then asked, "Your mistress, she is good to you, isn't she?"

"Yes, she is. My family works for her family. We've always been with the Duvalls. We're kind of like one family, really."

"That is very unusual."

"Yes, it is."

"You and your family, you are still the servants, though," Tang Lu carefully established.

"Yes, we are."

"You confide in your mistress? And she confides in you?"

Nia shrugged. "I know it's not how most people act toward their servants. But we've been blessed. Both my family and the Duvalls."

Tang Lu, always still, grew very intent. "Blessed," she repeated carefully. "Do you mean by Dr. Duvall's God she prays to?"

Nia gave Tang Lu a keen glance, but her face was unreadable. Her eyes, however, had an intense light. "God is not just Dr. Duvall's God," Nia said slowly. "He is the God of all creation. He made the earth. He made people. He made me and you."

Tang Lu asked hesitantly, "You say He made me? How can that be? We have many gods, but we don't have this God. We don't know Him."

Nia frowned with concentration. "Well, I don't know much about other gods, Miss Tang Lu, but I don't believe they really are gods. There is only one God, one Creator, one Lord. And you may not know Him, but He sure knows you. Personally, I mean. He made you, after all. He fashioned you before the foundations of the world. He even named you. And best of all, He loves you."

Tang Lu was quiet for a long time. Nia finished bandaging her leg and put the medical supplies back in Cheney's bag slowly. Then, pulling up her knees, she sat with Tang Lu, sensing that she needed to be quiet and wait.

Finally Tang Lu asked in a voice full of wonder, "But . . . how can this be? You tell me that the one true God, the only true God, who made the earth and the stars and the sky and time itself . . . loves me? Knows me?"

"Oh yes. You are one of His beloved children. God is infinite, and His love knows no end. The problem with you is the same problem with all of us. We choose evil. The first man and woman He created, perfect and without sin, chose evil instead. So has everyone else ever born. So have I, and so have you. It separates us from God."

"Yes," Tang Lu said in a low voice. "I know that I do evil. I don't want to, and I try not to, but still, I do."

"All of us do," Nia assured her. "But God made a way to bring us back to himself. He gave us a way to become perfect in His eyes so that we could be His children again. He is pure good, you see, and can't tolerate evil, so He had to make a way for us to be saved from sin."

"How did He do that?" Tang Lu asked eagerly.

"He became a man," Nia said sadly. "The God of all creation, because He loved us so much, humbled himself to become a man. He is God's beloved Son, and His name is Jesus. He came into this world, born of a woman. He lived a perfect life, without sin. But we killed Him. Of course He allowed it to happen. He invited it to happen, even. Because in that way, He died for all of us. He took on all of our sins—every human being's evil from the beginning of time until the end—and let himself be pronounced guilty for them. Then He paid the ultimate price: He gave His life."

"So this man is dead, and I didn't get to meet Him?" Tang Lu cried.

"No," Nia said with calm assurance, "God raised Him from the dead. He lives, now and forever. He is our Savior, our Lord, the Lamb that was slain. He is the Alpha and the Omega, the beginning and the end. And because of Him, of His sacrifice, we live too. We live forever. We will always live with Him."

"You will? How do you know? How do you get this wonderful gift?" Tang Lu demanded.

Nia smiled. "It's very simple. 'If thou shalt confess with thy mouth the Lord Jesus, and shalt believe in thine heart that God hath raised him from the dead, thou shalt be saved.' That's in the Bible. The Bible is God's Holy Word."

"Would you repeat that, please?" Tang Lu asked politely. "More slowly?"

Nia, amused, recited, " 'If thou shalt confess with thy mouth the Lord Jesus—' "

Tang Lu, staring at her intently, said, "I confess with my mouth the Lord Jesus."

Nia was surprised, but went on, " '—and shalt believe in thine heart that God hath raised him from the dead—' "

"I believe in my heart that God raised Him from the dead," Tang Lu solemnly declared.

" '—thou shalt be saved.' "

"Am I saved?"

"You are."

"Thank God. Now we must sleep."

Immediately the tiny Chinese woman lay down and curled up into a tiny ball.

Nia smiled and lay down close to her. She managed a short prayer of thanksgiving before she went to sleep, but her last thought was more prosaic.

At least now I know why You wanted me to stay.

26

QUICKENING BLOOD

A growl of thunder awakened them.

Shiloh jumped up and grabbed Cheney, sheltering her.

Keloki and Ulu Nui clasped Leilana.

Tang Lu and Nia cowered against the cliff walls.

Suddenly Shiloh scrambled up, his face turned to the colorless sky. "It's not an earthquake or a volcano!" he shouted.

"Well, what is it, then?" Cheney cried fearfully.

"It's rain. Just rain."

It was a summer storm, blustering and fitful. High above them, heavy torrents gushed from the swollen clouds. Because of the sheltering cliffs and the luxuriant undergrowth lining the opening of the crater, barely any rain fell all the way down. But still, welcome splashes occasionally blew downward, tinkling into the stillness of Na'maka's Mirror.

"I . . . I can't believe it," Cheney murmured, slowly and painfully getting to her feet. "You mean it's a natural and normal weather occurence? No typhoon? No poisonous beasts? No fountains of killing lava?"

"Just a sweet summer storm," Shiloh answered. " 'Bout the best one I've ever seen."

They all stood out in the open for a while, savoring the occasional fat drops that filtered far down into their hideaway.

Then Cheney moaned, "Oh, my goodness, what time is it?"

"Dunno, Doc. Last time I looked, you had my watch. Guess the lua have it now, huh?" Shiloh said lightly, but his brow wrinkled with worry.

"No, I have your watch, Keakea," Leilana said reassuringly. "I take good care of it too." She retrieved it from her little cache she'd stowed in a hollow by the waterfall.

"Thanks, Leilana," Shiloh said with relief. "The Doc gave me this watch. It's my most treasured possession." He smiled warmly at Cheney; her return smile was rather wan.

He opened it, and the tune faithfully played, the tiny little chimes sounding foreign and surreal in the dramatic surroundings. "It's eight minutes after eight," he announced.

"Oh dear, the *Brynn Annalea* was returning at dawn to search for us!" Cheney fretted. "They've probably been here for hours, patrolling, and we—"

Shiloh hurried to her and grasped her gently by the upper arms. "Doc, calm down," he said gently. "You don't really think that they're going to just sail on by here if we're not standing out there at the crack of dawn, do you? 'Course not."

"No . . . no. They wouldn't do that, would they?" Cheney said, still with a touch of anxiety.

"No. They wouldn't. So let's sit down, have our morning water and coconut, and then go down to the sea," Shiloh cajoled her. "I promise you the *Brynn Annalea* will be there."

They ate sparingly, as there was very little coconut and only two mangoes left. Each of them was groaning, their backs sore, their injuries more insistent, their feet swollen and painful. Shiloh advised them to get up and move around, stretching and swinging their arms. It did loosen their strained muscles and heat their blood.

"I feel better," Cheney said after their short exercise session, "but I still feel as if I'd been in a pugilistic match—and lost. I'll bet you know exactly what I mean, Mr. Iron Man."

Cheney was teasing him, but she was unusually listless and lethargic. Shiloh, although he hadn't awakened and witnessed it, knew that she'd been crying in the night. "Naw," he drawled, stretching, clasping his hands high over his head and arching his back. "I never lost."

"Oh yes, that's right," Cheney said absently. Her attention was already wandering.

Shiloh gave her a keen look, which she didn't notice. "Still, I gotta admit that sometimes the next morning I couldn't tell whether I'd won or lost. Didn't make much difference. Hurt like blazes anyway."

"Oh?" Cheney said vaguely. She didn't meet his eyes; she was staring vacantly into space. "I should think that losing makes an immense amount of difference. I should think that it would be very, very difficult to lose . . . to lose."

Shiloh knew very well that she wasn't talking about boxing.

But oddly for him, he had no idea what she *was* talking about.

They went back through the lava tube, and Nia still crawled through the last small bit with her eyes closed. She was cheerful and merry, however, and she and Tang Lu walked together, talking incessantly in low tones.

Cheney barely noticed. She was so distracted and so depressed that she hardly comprehended what she was doing or where she was. She couldn't bear to think of Shiloh, or look at him, or talk to him. Her mind was a barely functional drone, so she thought of only the most elementary things. *Don't step there . . . watch that branch . . . wonder how much farther it is . . . so much easier going downhill . . .*

Once, behind her, Shiloh said lightly, "At least in Panama we had a railroad track, huh, Doc?"

"Hmm? I beg your pardon?" She didn't look around.

His brow furrowed, he prompted her. "Panama. Seems like every couple of years we're destined to trek through some hostile jungle, huh?"

"Yes—I mean, no. I hope not."

She was obviously paying scant attention. Shiloh thought that she was just absolutely exhausted. Later he would talk to her.

The rain fell steadily, and no one minded. In fact, they enjoyed it. Even Cheney felt a little refreshed. To their left, they saw great clouds of steam rising.

"Rain's cooling off the lava flow, I guess," Shiloh ventured. "Looks like it's still real hot and fresh lava, though."

To their right, where the second lava fountain had erupted, they didn't see any evidence of a continuing flow until they were almost to the coast. Then they saw some steam but no lava fountain shooting hundreds of feet in the air. The steam rising wasn't nearly as spectacular as the wide fissure's flow to the north. They saw, here and there, burned and burning jungle. But the narrow section of jungle that hid Na'maka's Mirror remained unscathed.

That was why at dawn the rescue party had stopped precisely at the spot where the seven emerged from the jungle. It was the only place where the refugees might have found a place to hide—and live. When Captain Sloan saw the devastated five-mile stretch of coastline with the single green ribbon of jungle standing out among the black and scarlet burnings, he dropped anchor right in front of the only beach, right at the foot of the strip of untouched jungle. It was a little sandy tongue, huddled between soaring ramparts of black rock.

It took three hours for the refugees to work their way down the escarpment to that little beach. It only took ten minutes for the lifeboat to take them to the haven of the majestic clipper, the *Brynn Annalea*.

★　★　★　★

Shiloh stood at the rail, near the prow, watching the eastern shore of Maui wash out of sight by the rain. In spite of everything, he still thought this place was the loveliest, most peaceful place he'd ever seen. He hoped to come back someday.

Behind him, a man cleared his throat delicately. Logan Winslow stepped up to stand beside Shiloh at the railing. He was drawn, his features ragged and worn, his shoulders stooped. He wore a muffler and shivered a little in the fog-hung rain.

"Are you feeling better, sir?" Shiloh asked politely.

"Physically, yes," Logan answered in a hoarse voice. "In other ways, no, I can't say I am feeling well at all."

Shiloh nodded, understanding, and turned to watch the last glimpses of Maui fade behind them. Above them, the sails caught, snapping crisply in spite of the wetness of the breeze. Like the fine thoroughbred she was, the *Brynn Annalea* lifted her head and began to run. Shiloh sighed with pleasure. He loved sailing. He knew nothing about it; he had rarely been on a sailing vessel, but his affinity for it ran deep within him. Especially he loved clippers, the sleek and graceful queens of the seas.

"Would you accompany me to the officers' mess?" Logan asked abruptly. "We need to talk."

"Yes, sir."

Logan had given his quarters to Cheney and Nia. Captain Sloan and First Officer Gann had given theirs to Keloki and his family and Tang Lu. So Logan led Shiloh down a spiral stairwell to the small dining room where the officers and, of course, Logan, as the owner, dined. The paneling was sturdy English oak, the table and sideboard a fine polished mahogany. Brynn sat waiting for them. She smiled brilliantly at Shiloh as they came in, though she, too, looked as pale and delicate as a fading flower. Folded neatly on the table in front of her was Shiloh's tapestry. Resting upon it was his fish compass, a small square of gold with an ornate design, and a folded piece of cream-colored parchment.

Logan sat down, huddling in his chair, his head sunk on his chest. His hands, brown from the sea sun but finely manicured, rested lethargically on the table like small dead animals. Brynn reached over and patted his hand. "Father, I know this is hard," she said in a strained voice. "But I truly believe this is going to make a difference in our lives. This is going to change us. Finally, we are going to live in truth, with the truth. It will make us all better men and women."

His shoulders rose, then fell with a curious helplessness. "I know," he said in a muted voice, "but it is still very difficult."

Shiloh listened gravely, watching the two. After a moment's awkward silence, he said quietly, "I believe, Miss Winslow, you told me that I am your cousin, Locke Winslow. I am, you said, your uncle Rory's son. I hope you both know that right now that's all I'm interested in. I want to know about my father and my mother. The past is long dead, unchangeable. Whatever has happened, whatever has been done doesn't make any difference to me now. I'm just glad that I've found my family."

"You won't be," Logan said heavily. "Those fine and noble sentiments will change when you find out what my—what I've done."

"It wasn't you, Father," Brynn protested. "And you can't fool Locke by telling him it was. It was Mother. He knows that."

"Begging your pardon, ma'am, but I don't know that," Shiloh interposed. "And right now that's not the most important thing to me. I just want to know about my parents."

Logan sighed, a long pitiful sound. Then he began speaking, and his cultured British tones were dulled with sorrow.

"Your father's name was Roderick Jesse Winslow. I . . . I loved Rory. Everyone loved Rory. He was exactly what men wish to be, and exactly what women wish men to be. He was dashing and handsome, devil-may-care, restless, fearless."

"Like you, Locke," Brynn said, her dimples showing faintly.

"Thank you, ma'am," Shiloh said, a little embarrassed. "My father—he was your older brother, sir?"

Logan stared, unseeing, down at his limp hands. "We were only ten months apart. He was born in January of 1815, and I was born in November. The same year. We were very close, and Rory was always so loyal to me, more like a . . . twin, I suppose. But we were very different

. . . I always felt rather like he was the golden one. His was the birthright, and I was the dark child born out of due season." He wavered, his voice breaking, and fell silent.

Shiloh gave Brynn a sympathetic look, and she was profoundly grateful. They waited.

Finally Logan cleared his throat and began again. "He was first a midshipman in the Royal Navy at sixteen years old. Impossible to stop him from that time on. He loved the sea. He loved sailing all over the world. At the unheard-of age of twenty-two, he obtained the captaincy of a merchant clipper. Rory had had his eye on the Hawaiian Islands ever since he first visited them when he was eighteen."

A humorless smile twisted Logan's mouth. "He became friends—actually became friends!—with King Kamehameha III. Rory was nothing if not shrewd. He always brought the king gifts, unique and fine gifts, from wherever he'd been all over the world. They played poker . . . Rory taught him. That's how Rory got this land. He won little parcels, little meaningless squares, of Maui from the king. Only Rory . . .

"Within a year he owned the entire eighty thousand acres of Winslow Plantation. He started harvesting his sandalwood, and it, of course, was in very short supply. So he started farming it, along with taro and sugarcane. But Rory despised being tied down to the earth, and he asked me—or rather, granted me—the job of overseeing his holdings here in Hawaii.

"In 1840, my brother told me that he had everything, the world and more, and then he gained heaven. In that year he commisioned and bought the *Day Dream*. And in that year he met Kallan Torbjörn."

"My mother?" Shiloh exclaimed, his blue eyes as wide and innocent as a child's. "Her name was Kallan?"

"Yes . . . Kallan Torbjörn," Logan repeated. For the first time he looked up at Shiloh, and his blue eyes were soft and misty with long memories. "She was Swedish. Rory, for all his rowdiness and carousing, never looked at another woman after he met her."

"Kallan . . ." Shiloh repeated with pleasure. "Such a pretty name."

Numbly, Logan nodded. "And such a striking and vibrant woman. She and Rory were so happy. He met her in February of 1840, and they married at the end of that year, in December, at Christmas. In Sweden, at her home, with her family. After that, they traveled all over the world on the *Day Dream*. They only came here once for a very short visit. My wife and your mother . . ." Logan sighed heavily. "But that's for . . .

later. Anyway, Kallan loved that ship fully as much as Rory did. It was, in fact, their home. I didn't even know Kallan was expecting. I received this in the mail, from Sweden . . . at Christmas. In 1843."

His hands trembling, he handed the square of gold to Shiloh.

It was a folding double picture frame, with the left-hand side empty. The right-hand side held a portrait, clear and sharp, of a young couple. The woman was holding a newborn baby.

Shiloh stared hungrily at the woman—his mother. She was properly unsmiling for the somber occasion of having her portrait done. She had the angular and sharply refined features typical of Nordic women. Her eyes, in the black-and-white photograph, were a remarkably light hue. Shiloh knew they were an icy diamond blue, and even in the flat tones of the photograph, he could see the glint of life and the sparkle of humor. Her hair, pulled back and curled high on the crown, was a white-blond so unusual to adults. Her complexion was fine but was an unorthodox golden tan. It was a startling, but far from unpleasant, contrast to her cool Nordic features.

He studied the infant for only a moment. The child, tightly swathed in plain white linens, was asleep. Newborns, Shiloh thought, were all alike, anonymous, without the imprint of life on their features yet. He felt no empathy with this likeness of himself, barely born. He felt only a curiously displaced sympathy for this baby—himself—whom he knew would be orphaned so soon after this portrait was done.

Then Shiloh Irons looked at his father. It gave him a start, a physical feeling of quickening blood and thickening heartbeat. This, more than anything that had ever happened to him, gave him a sense of identity, a sense of belonging, of his rightful place in the earth, and a recognition of his soul. Locke Alan Winslow had grown to be his father. He was the mirror image of the man who had given him life.

Shiloh swallowed hard, his eyes riveted on the daguerrotype. He whispered so softly that Brynn and Logan barely heard him. "You got this . . . after we were already dead . . . by that Christmas there was only Shiloh Irons left. No Rory, no Kallan, no Locke. Only me, and I was lost."

Logan jerked as if Shiloh had struck him and buried his face in his hands. Brynn's face was wreathed with anguish; tears filled her eyes, and in the heavy silence a small sob escaped her.

Shiloh started, then looked up at her and smiled. "Please don't cry, cousin," he said gently. "I hate it when ladies are sad."

"I'll . . . try," Brynn shakily promised. "But I am so sorry, so utterly sorry, Locke. . . ."

"Don't be," he said quietly. "Because now I'm found."

Logan rubbed his face wearily, then took off his glasses. Looking down, he polished them with the tail of the muffler. "We didn't know about the . . . the . . . tragedy until March of 1844," he said in a dead voice. "We got a report from a Lloyd's of London agent. The *Day Dream* was assured, of course. I had to go to London to settle the claim. They said that the ship went down with all hands."

"I'm not surprised," Shiloh murmured. "I sorta got . . . lost in the shuffle, you might say. It was a bad storm and a terrible accident with two ships. A lot of confusion afterward."

Logan Winslow was weeping, still obsessively polishing his glasses. Shiloh felt clumsy, like a rude interloper, and didn't quite know what to say.

Brynn said calmly, "I believe I can pick up the story from here, Locke. Some months later—let me see—" She unfolded the fine piece of parchment. It was old and worn and creased. "Yes, in June of 1844 a letter was sent to my father in care of Winslow Villa, Maui, the Hawaiian Islands. It was from the harbor master of Charleston. A witness, who had left Charleston shortly after the wreck of the *Day Dream*, had returned and related to the harbor master that there had been a child, an infant whom he had taken to a local orphanage. The harbor master was inquiring if the child had been a passenger aboard the *Day Dream*." She handed the letter to Shiloh.

He barely glanced at it. "She kept this?"

Logan jerkily hunched his shoulders in a vague protest, but Brynn answered steadily. "Yes, she did. She didn't keep a copy of her reply, but of course we know now that she denied it—denied you. I found this in some of her personal things when I was trying to get ready to leave the villa. My father"—she cast a worried glance at him—"was gone at this time, Locke. He had nothing to do with it. My mother's never told anyone, you know. She . . . she still refuses to speak of it."

Dully Logan said, his eyes downcast, "Bain and Brynn never knew about you. In fact, they never knew anything about Rory. We never spoke of him again."

Shiloh shifted uneasily. He regarded his uncle with a new hardness in his eyes. Politely he asked, "Miss Winslow, I would like to talk to you later. But would you please excuse us now?"

Brynn glanced at her father uncertainly. Logan didn't look up at her or Shiloh. Finally, he made a dismissive gesture, a wave of his hand that signaled defeat.

Brynn rose and went to the door. Turning, she said quietly, "Locke, I can understand that you must be angry with us. But my father is not well. I would ask, as your cousin, that you . . . that you—"

Shiloh smiled at her, though it was perfunctory. "Don't worry, cousin. I don't want to hurt your father, or you, or even your mother. You're my family."

Brynn took note that Shiloh didn't include her brother in this declaration. But there was nothing she could do, no defense she could offer for Bain. Indeed, she didn't even want to try. She turned and left, closing the door quietly behind her.

Shiloh waited, watching his uncle, who still refused to meet his eyes. The whispers of the ship as she slipped through the sea were soothing to him. When he spoke, his voice was kinder. "Uncle, there are things that I believe are the responsibility of men. I also think there are things between married people, parents, that their children shouldn't have to know or deal with."

Logan nodded. "Yes." After another long silence, he finally lifted his head to face Shiloh. "When Rory married, Denise . . . changed. I couldn't understand it. She became bitter and . . . and . . . cold. When we finally received word that you were born, she went into a towering rage."

He hesitated, but Shiloh merely waited patiently.

"Then . . . when we received word . . . that Rory was dead . . ." His voice caught in his throat, and with difficulty he finished, "Denise almost went insane with grief."

To Logan's shock, Shiloh nodded. "She was in love with my father."

"How . . . how did you know this? How *could* you know this?" Logan murmured.

Shiloh replied casually, "I dunno. The thought just kind of occurred to me. You didn't realize it until my father died."

"N-no, I had no idea." His face showed such pain that Shiloh became concerned about his heart again, but Logan, as if it were a vast relief, went on with determination. "We became estranged after that. I'm a weak man. I couldn't bear the sight of my own wife, and I never even . . . tried to . . . make the situation better. Not for her, and not for my children, either. I just left. I ran."

In an edgy voice, Shiloh said, "I've met Alena Zeiss."

Logan flinched visibly. "Yes ... she, perhaps, has suffered more than anyone. Except you."

"No one," Shiloh said adamantly, "is going to suffer anymore. Not at the hands of your wife or your son. Not if I can do anything about it. I hope you understand that, sir."

Logan nodded, a gesture of final defeat. "So I started traveling extensively. I told myself that I was making a better life for them. And the business did grow and prosper. I commissioned a ship that year, in 1844. When I named her, Denise told me that she would never again allow any mention of Rory—or his wife and child—in her house."

Curiously Shiloh asked, "Why did you do that, sir? Was it to punish her?"

For the first time Logan showed some life. He shook his head vigorously and met Shiloh's gaze unflinchingly. "No. I dedicated that ship to your memory, Locke. Rory had left his imprint on this earth, and I'm certain that your mother had a full, rich life, and that—somewhere—people remembered her with love. But you—his son—never had a chance to live, to be remembered. I vowed that I would honor you and my brother in this way. It was a fitting memorial, for *Locke's Day Dream* is a sister ship to the *Day Dream*. They are just alike, in all ways, in beauty and speed and grace."

For the first time, Shiloh smiled at him. "I thank you, sir. That was an honorable and courageous thing to do."

Logan was startled, and a tiny light of hope crept into his weak blue eyes.

"There are a lot more things that we're going to have to deal with, sir," Shiloh continued firmly, "but they can wait. You're obviously tired, and I'm worried about your health. But I do have one more question."

"Of course."

Shiloh's face wrinkled with puzzlement. "I don't understand why your wife was so—is still so—filled with hate and bitterness toward me. It just doesn't make sense that she would go to so much trouble to ... to—well, right now I guess you don't need to deal with all that's happened in the last month. But anyway, I wondered why she still fights so hard, even though everyone, including me, finally knows the truth."

Logan's incredulity was evident. "It's obvious, isn't it?"

"Well . . . not really, no."

Logan smiled, a humorless, self-disgusted twist of his mouth. "You really don't understand yet, do you? You, Locke Alan Winslow, are your father's heir. Everything we own, all of the Winslow holdings and possessions, lawfully and rightfully belong to you."

27

THE EYES OF ETERNITY

" 'The Lord is merciful and gracious, slow to anger, and plenteous in mercy.' "

Cheney whispered this verse from her favorite psalm to herself and was at peace.

She was sitting in the stern window of Logan Winslow's cabin. It had a narrow cushioned window seat, and she curled up in it, pulling her knees up and clasping her arms tightly around her legs.

These last days have been earth-shattering—literally and figuratively—and life-changing, she reflected. *I simply must organize my thoughts. I must get back in control of myself. I must center myself, once again, in the Lord. If I don't, I'm lost. . . .*

She made herself be quiet, as quiet as a person can be muting the insistent little nag that talked incessantly in her head. Slowly she recognized the presence of the Lord, though not in any tangible way. She just knew, deep in her spirit, that He was there, He was with her, He was showing her the way.

"Funny," she murmured. She didn't mean it humorously, she meant it ironically. *One moment all I can think about—agonize over— is facing the dismal fact of how much I'm in love with Shiloh, a man whom I respect, a loyal and true friend, who . . . who . . . seems so right. But he can't be, and he isn't. He's not a Christian.*

That ends the argument, but it doesn't end the pain. . . .

She closed her eyes, swaying gracefully with the dreamy movements of the ship.

And all that I've gone through in the last days . . . so much fear! I was so afraid all the time. I was terrified! I still feel battered, bruised, full of apprehension. . . .

"But still, I'm at peace . . . I've found peace. How is that? I know, Lord, that it comes from You, but where—what part of me is so calm and serene, while the other part of me is so . . . torn and anguished?" Cheney spoke as if Jesus were in the room sitting next to her. And, in a manner of speaking, He was.

And so He answered her.

"For He knoweth our frame; He remembereth that we are dust. . . ."

Yes, that's it. My flesh, it is full of fear and doubt and longings. But my spirit, it dwells with the Lord, and there is peace. There, in that secret place with Him, there is nothing to fear—not death or pain or love lost. . . .

There, with Him, I know that this life, these problems, these fears, they will all pass away. I suppose that being so close to death, facing it time and time again, gives one a different perspective, another mind and heart . . . way of seeing . . . with the eyes of eternity. . . .

A discreet knock sounded at the door.

Calmly Cheney called, "Come in, Shiloh."

He came in, holding his long-lost tapestry. Looking around, he asked, "Where's Nia? She's supposed to be taking care of you."

"She's with Tang Lu," Cheney replied. "Captain Sloane told us that last night Fang Shao died soon after they reached Lahaina."

Shiloh nodded. "Yeah, I forgot. Poor Miss Tang Lu. She really seemed to care for him, even though he was worthless."

"She's doing very well under the circumstances," Cheney said carefully. "But she and Nia seem to have grown close, so I thought it best that Nia stay with her for the rest of the journey."

He gave her a semiprofessional once-over. She was pale, and her clothes were as filthy and ragged as a street urchin's. Her hair was wild, tangled, a mass of sodden mats hanging down to her waist. She had washed her face and hands—and her feet, Shiloh noticed, which were bare and peeping out from under her tattered skirt. Like everyone else, she looked haggard and exhausted. But she seemed tranquil, more at ease than she had since before their ordeal had begun.

She smiled at his sharp assessment. "I'm fine, you know. Really."

He nodded with relief, then handed her the tapestry. "Her name," he said quietly, "was An Mei."

Cheney caressed the glossy satin, the intricate needlework. Her head bent, she asked quietly, "And what is your name?"

"Locke Alan Winslow." He sounded distant, disconnected from his voice and especially the words.

Cheney breathed on the thick window, making a small fog circle, then wrote "Shiloh," smiling to herself. "I don't think that I'll ever get accustomed to calling you by your real name."

"I'm still not so sure that's my real name." He came to stand by her, staring out the thick wavy panes of glass. "I think ... I'd rather you call me Shiloh."

She nodded, understanding. They stared out, but there was nothing to see. The fog and rain was an impenetrable curtain.

"I'll always think of her as 'Pearl' too," he said in a low voice. "I'll never forget her."

"Was she the one we dreamed she was, Shiloh?"

He nodded, and one corner of his mouth turned up in a slow smile. "She was an orphan, a pearl diver. She worked for two men—Englishmen—who were cruel masters. My father and mother saw them, in the port of Macao, weighting her down and making her dive over and over again, beating her when she was too slow. My parents went over to their junk, and my father bought it. That's right—junk, pearls, oysters, diver, and all. Then he knocked down both the men and gave everything to An Mei."

"How wonderful," Cheney breathed. "And how like you."

"They left her on the junk and went into Macao. She followed them and found them the next day. She asked if she could be their servant."

"She did? Voluntarily?"

"That's right. My uncle didn't really understand it either. But she became my mother's maid and stayed with them. With me ... until she died."

Cheney murmured, "She must have had money. Probably a good sum of it. I wonder..."

Shiloh's eyes lit up. *The gold! The gold that poor Miss Linde took ... it didn't belong to my parents at all! It was Pearl's ... she gave it to me. How—what kind of love must that be? How can one person freely make such sacrifices?*

"Tell me about your family, Shiloh," Cheney said, bringing him out of his reverie.

"It's a long story, and we're almost to Lahaina," Shiloh said. He reached down and smoothed her hair. It was tangled, knotted, filthy. To him it felt like rich velvet.

"It's so ... strange, Doc," he murmured, and his face grew sober as he looked at her. "All my life I've been alone with not a single thought about a family. Sometimes I'd look at familes and a knot would form in my belly. Once I saw a big family reunion—it was when I was sixteen years old—on the beach at Charleston. There must have been over a hundred people—parents and kids, uncles and aunts, grandparents. They were all laughing and talking and hugging. I stood back and wondered what it would be like to know *who* I was. I mean—who was my father? What kind of man was he? And my mother, was she kind and beautiful? And where did I *come* from?" His eyes were somber and half-hooded as he stood there for what seemed a long time, then he shook his shoulders together and turned to face her. "Well, now I know. Logan talked to me a long time about my parents, and then he showed me a chart of the Winslow family. It was kind of like a tree turned upside down, Doc. At the very top of it was a man named Gilbert Winslow. He was born in 1600 in England—he was on the *Mayflower*. Think of that!"

"Why, you're one of the firstcomers, Shiloh!" Cheney exclaimed. A smile touched her lips, and she added, "You probably won't have anything to do with me. I'm just a common immigrant!"

"I doubt that!" Shiloh said and lifted his hand to stroke the smoothness of her cheek, then said, "He married a woman named Humility Cooper after they got to America, and the chart shows all their descendents. Doc, it was amazing! There have been Winslow ministers, generals, admirals, lawyers, judges—everything!"

"Were they all heroes?"

"Logan said not. He warned me that if I studied the family carefully, I'd find some horse thieves and such—but I don't care, Doc. I've got a *family*. I know who I am and where I came from!"

She looked up at him, her expression unreadable. He bent and kissed her. Cheney, in spite of the fact that it hurt her unbearably, kissed him, both her hands caressing his face. It was a long, slow, warm kiss, without urgency. To Cheney it was the first, and last, surrender. She couldn't guess what it was to Shiloh.

His face was still close to hers. "Everything is different now, Cheney. This has changed everything."

She nodded, then leaned back wearily and turned to stare out the window. "I know. I don't think it will ever be the same. You'll never be the same, no matter what I call you."

"But I will," he insisted, shrugging and moving to sit at the other end of the window seat. "Well, I'll be the same. But I guess my . . . uh . . . trappings will be a little different."

She smiled at him. "Ah yes. The cares of a moneyed man. The responsibilities of ownership. The woes of proprietorship. The constraints of wearing neckties."

"Huh? You mean I gotta wear a necktie? Maybe this deal of having wealth ain't all it's jimmied up to be. Maybe I'll let Auntie Denise keep it," he said slyly.

"Maybe you would," Cheney shrugged, "but I'll bet you won't let Bain keep it."

Shiloh's face turned hard, his jaw tensing into carved lines and his mouth thinning into a straight line. "You're right about that, Doc. My cousin is going to be relieved of all his burden of responsibilities of possessions. As soon as anybody finds him, that is."

"Mr. Winslow doesn't know where he is?"

"No one knows where he is. But I'll bet he's either in San Francisco setting up his new business, or in Shanghai, restocking his inventory," Shiloh said savagely. "When I find him, he is going to pay. I don't feel that anyone in this family owes me a thing. Not even my aunt Denise. I can kinda understand why she acted, and acts, the way she does. But Bain's a different story. He's a man with no honor, and he will pay for the shame he's brought on this family. He owes my father, my uncle, my cousin Brynn, and he owes me."

Cheney was silent, a little overwhelmed by Shiloh's ferocity. He gave her a repentant glance, then took a deep breath. He relaxed, so Cheney felt herself relaxing. "*Locke's Day Dream* . . . I assume that the ship must belong to you."

"She does. Mr. Winslow—Uncle Logan—named that ship in my memory," Shiloh asserted. "It cost him too. Mrs. Winslow never forgave him for it. She forbade him to ever mention my father's name, or my name, again."

"But why? Why was Denise so full of hatred and bitterness?"

Shiloh gave her a peculiar look, an oddly impassioned plea. "She wasn't full of hatred back then. Far from it. It was love. She was in love with my father."

Cheney gasped, then moaned, "Oh, how . . . dreadful . . . for everyone."

He nodded, his eyes focusing faraway. "Yes. To love when it's not fitting, not seemly, causes everyone a lot of pain."

Cheney smiled dryly. "Yes, I know."

He gave her a sharp, piercing glance, but Cheney asked lightly, "So,

Mr. Moneyed Winslow, what are you going to do now?"

"Got 'bout a million things," he grumbled.

"Let me put it this way," Cheney suggested. "What is the first-most of your worries?"

"I don't worry," he said gravely. "I gave it up."

"Excellent idea," Cheney agreed. "Especially after the last few days. It does seem now that so many things aren't worth worrying about, doesn't it?"

"Yeah. Funny. I used to feel this way after the war. Didn't really care, didn't really think about life—or death." A sly glance from sky-blue eyes slid Cheney's way. "But then I started worrying about you. I still do."

"Nonsense," Cheney scoffed. "You don't either. You just like to aggravate me."

"It is kinda fun."

She punched his arm lightly, and he mumbled, "Ouch. You got a mean right, Doc. Always did."

"To get back to my question," Cheney said firmly, "what are you going to do now?"

He shifted in the seat, turning so he could look out the window. "Well, I have a family now. Seems like I've kind of got some responsibilities there."

"Seems like," Cheney agreed.

"So first we have to find out how much damage has been done to the plantation," he said thoughtfully. "And to Hana. The villa's gone, we're pretty sure. But Captain Sloane said that it didn't look like the lava had gone anywhere near the village." He stirred restlessly, then said, "But that can all wait. I want to know what you want to do, Doc. I want to know what I can do to help you."

She sighed at the warmth and pleasure that washed over her at his care for her. Sadly she said, "I must return to San Francisco. You know that, don't you? I have obligations there, and I really must get back."

He nodded. "Thought so. What do you think about Walker?"

"I need to examine him thoroughly as soon as we get to the hospital. I can't be sure, of course, until then, but I suspect I'm going to have to recommend that he rest quietly for a couple of weeks. No sea voyages."

"I figured that." Shiloh grinned mischievously. "But I don't think Walker's gonna be too upset at having to stay in Hawaii. Not with my lovely cousin taking such good care of him. She asked me 'bout a million questions about him."

"Yes, I think she's quite taken with him," Cheney said with satisfaction. "And I don't think, I know, that he's a fool about her."

"He fell hard, didn't he?"

"Literally," Cheney quipped, and they both chuckled. Then Cheney grumbled, "I'm not looking forward to explaining all this to Dr. Baird. After all, I've been chasing around for a month now. His son—another of the hospital physicians—is injured and, poor thing, confined to his bed in Hawaii. And you, his golden boy nursing supervisor, are now a feckless youth with all kinds of money."

"I dunno about that," Shiloh said, averting his eyes. Idly he leaned back against the window frame, thrust out his long legs, and crossed them.

"You don't?" Cheney asked brightly. "But I simply must know something about your prospects, sir."

"Yeah? Like what?"

"I have to know if you have more money than I do," Cheney said impishly.

He couldn't keep from grinning at her. "I dunno. How much money you got?"

"I dunno," Cheney replied airily. "I would have to check with my financial advisor—that's Victoria, of course—and my investment banker and my solicitor and—"

"Never mind," he said hastily. "I'm sure not ready for all that yet. But I know one thing, ma'am. I own this ship."

Cheney's eyes shone. "You do? Both of them? *Locke's Day Dream* and the *Brynn Annalea*?"

"Yep. And I'm going to take you back to San Francisco in style."

"You are? Oh, how wonderful! Thank you, thank you, Shiloh!"

"I'm coming with you."

"That's even better."

"It is?" He suddenly grew somber and leaned up to grasp both of Cheney's hands. "Listen to me, Cheney. There's something—a lot of things—that I want to say. A lot of things that I need to tell you."

Her heart lurched, and Cheney's voice trembled slightly as she said, "Shiloh, I think I know . . . what you . . . mean. But I also think we both realize that now is not the time. It's not . . . fitting, right now. You've just found your family. You have obligations and . . . and . . .

responsibilities. Here, in Hawaii. I must return to San Francisco. We're about to have to say good-bye again." She was afraid, literally fearful, that he would argue with her, insist on opening this door, this dangerous door that Cheney was not yet ready to enter.

But to her surprise and almost overwhelming relief, he released her hands, leaned back, and nodded with understanding.

"You're right, and I'm really glad that you see it, Doc. I see it exactly the same way."

Cheney, unable to speak, turned away to stare unseeingly out the window.

"But you were wrong about one thing," he said.

"Wh-what is that?"

"We won't say good-bye, Cheney. I'll never say good-bye to you." It was spoken as a vow.

Through a soft mist of tears, she smiled at him. "Shiloh, you'll never have to say good-bye to me. That much I can promise you."

It would prove to be promises that they both, forever, would keep.

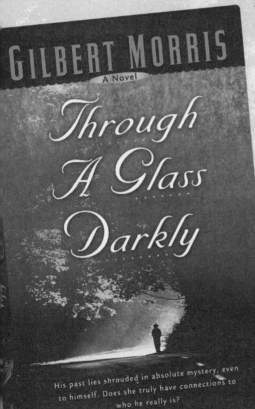